THE FOLLY BEACH CHRISTMAS MYSTERY COLLECTION

BILL NOEL

ISBN: 978-1-948374-39-2

Enigma House Press

Goshen, Kentucky

www.enigmahousepress.com

Also by Bill Noel

The Folly Beach Christmas Collection

Silent Night

Chapter One

S*ilent Night, Holy Night! All is calm, all is bright,* I sang as I took the early-morning, five-block walk from my house to the Lost Dog Cafe. Before you proclaim me certifiable because of my song selection, it's two weeks before Christmas and pitch dark. The cloudless, predawn sky was speckled with stars that went on forever, and for mid-December in South Carolina, the temperature was cool although not unbearable. Yes, all is calm, and I'm thankful.

The Lost Dog Cafe was a block off Center Street, the center of commerce and figurative center of the small, barrier island located in the shadows of Charleston. The Dog had been my favorite breakfast spot since I retired to the beach nearly a decade ago, and I was not alone in favoring the canine-centric, colorful restaurant. In season, the wait for tables could approach an hour, since it was not only the favorite breakfast locale for thousands of vacationers who arrived like swarms of locust, but also for locals who were hard-pressed to find a better alternative. The locusts, umm, vacationers, left as quickly as they had come and between Labor Day and spring, the island moved on laid-back, Folly time.

Two other things could be counted on during the winter months in the restaurant: extended, daily visits by Jim Sloan, better known as Dude, and city council members Marc Salmon and Houston Bass. Today, Dude was seated at his usual table along the wall, but neither of the people with him answered to Houston or Marc.

He saw me and waved his ever-present copy of *Astronomy Magazine* in the air and pointed to the vacant seat beside him. I took his less-than-subtle hint and headed over. Dude could have been mistaken for folk singer Arlo Guthrie with his long, stringy, graying, sun-bleached hair. Complimenting his nineteen sixties look was one of his many tie-dyed T-shirts with a psychedelic peace symbol adorning the front.

Dude said, "Yo, Chrisster, Ho, ho, ho."

Dude owned Folly's largest surf shop, had been a resident since I don't know when, and was famous for mangling the simplest sentence. People who didn't know him well had sworn it would take a cryptographer to understand what he was saying. Those who knew him better had gone through a steep learning curve, or had access to a translator, but I had gotten the drift of his "unique verbal styling."

"Ho, ho, ho, back at you," I said, in the spirit in which it was divvied out.

Dude, at sixty-three, was three years younger than me, and at least three decades older than his table mates.

"Chrisster, amigos be Finley and Teddye."

The *amigos* looked up from their eggs and gave me a bored grin.

I held out my hand to the female. "I'm Chris Landrum, and I assume you're Teddye."

It was a slight gamble on my part since their names could have been attached to either gender.

The attractive young woman nodded. Her long, blond hair contrasted with her black jeans, black turtleneck, and black boots. "Pleased," she said.

I paused waiting for more, but she must have learned verbal parsimony from Dude. I turned to the other stranger. "And you must be Finley."

He was also dressed in black, but his hair was bleached blond and as long as Teddye's. He shook my hand, shrugged, and said, "Duh."

"Chrisster, these be surfin' buds." He pointed to Teddye and Finley like I wouldn't know whom he was referring to. "We be jabbering about posers invadin', and skimpy, hot dog budget wallets they be haulin'."

Posers were non-surfers acting like they could surf and I guessed hot dog budgets translated as short on cash. Regardless, I had little to add to the conversation. I didn't have to when Dude said, "They be askin' Dude how to rid surf of posers."

I glanced at Dude's friends who stared at me like they would at a pile of pooch poop they'd stepped in. "What'd you suggest?" I asked to put the conversation back in Dude's court.

"Said be season of peace on Gaia—sharing, goody- good will, yada, yada, yada. Said to chill, let be."

"Gaia?"

Dude pointed to the floor. "Gaia, third planet from Sun."

Teddye leaned forward. "He means Peace on Earth."

She rolled her eyes like she had to explain what a tree was to a forest ranger.

My phone rang as I was wondering how I could step out of this alternative universe, skip breakfast, and get out of the restaurant as fast as my aging legs could carry me.

I moved the phone away from my ear when it was assaulted by the ear-piercing voice of Burl Costello. "Brother Chris, my God. I'm glad I got you. Sorry for calling so early. Could you come to our crèche?"

Burl, more-formally known as Preacher Burl Ives Costello, started First Light, Folly's fourth and newest church, a couple of years ago. In good weather, its services were held on the beach near the Folly Pier, but when the weather didn't cooperate, which Burl said was the Devil interceding, services were conducted in a small storefront building on Center Street.

"When?"

"Now!"

I started to ask why, when he yelled, "Somebody stole Jesus!"

FIRST LIGHT'S CRÈCHE, or Nativity scene, was located on a small grassy plot adjacent to Pewter Hardware and next to the Folly Beach Post Office. The slice of green space was owned by my friend Larry LaMond, a former cat burglar, current owner of the tiny hardware store, and for the last six years, husband to Cindy, Folly's police chief.

Preacher Burl referred to First Light's attendees as his flock instead of members, but either way, Larry and Cindy were neither. When the preacher realized it would be impractical for the crèche to be on the beach and there wasn't enough space on the sidewalk in front of the storefront location, Larry volunteered the plot of land. The spot wasn't perfect since it wasn't visible to most visitors to the island, but as Preacher Burl had pointed out, the setting for the event some two thousand years ago, which had inspired decades of Nativity scenes was far from visible or popular. He also had pointed out First Light's scene was within a short walk from Folly's three traditional churches, and using a little imagination, Mary, Joseph, Jesus, and the assorted bit players could see the houses of worship from the crèche.

The Nativity was fewer than two blocks from the restaurant, and I made the trip in a couple of minutes. I noticed what normally was festive Christmas red and blue colors flashing and reflecting off the Nativity's makeshift wooden barn and the hardware store. This morning, the colors weren't nearly as festive since they were coming from light bars on two Folly Beach patrol cars.

Preacher Burl was as easy to recognize as Dude. He was five-foot-five, shaped like a football, portly in polite terms, had a milk chocolate colored mustache, and a balding head inadequately covered by a sad-looking comb over. Today, his hair was even sadder. He appeared to have been awakened and had rushed to the scene without glancing in a mirror. The preacher was standing close to Chief LaMond and his arms flailed around like he was describing an attack by a flock of seagulls.

He saw me, stopped flailing, put his hand on Cindy's arm, and pointed in my direction. "Brother Chris, I am so pleased to see you. This is the darkest of morns for First Light. The Devil has reached up and with his evil talons, yanked our sacred symbol from yon manger. It's thrown our ministry into darkness." He pointed at the empty, rustic, wooden feeding trough.

Cindy turned and faced me. "He means someone stole the replica of Jesus."

Burl's conversations often slipped into preacher-speak.

I said, "Thanks, Chief LaMond."

Cindy nodded toward Burl. "I was telling the preacher it was most likely kids playing a prank and we'd find, umm, Jesus somewhere around town. I'll have my guys nose around for it."

Burl shook his head. "Who would steal Jesus?"

Cindy was a couple of inches shorter than the preacher, but better built. She pulled her shoulders back, ran a hand through her dark curly hair, and frowned. "Stealing the baby from nativities is so common, it has its own name: Baby Jesus Theft. Puts them at the top of Santa's naughty list, if you ask me."

Burl didn't appreciate the chief's humor. He mumbled, "A sad day indeed."

TWO OFFICERS HAD BEEN PHOTOGRAPHING the manger and the other parts of the set, but I couldn't imagine them finding anything helpful. One of them came over and told the chief they had done all they could at the "scene of the crime." Cindy told him to tell everyone else to "scour the city" for the figurine. The chief asked if I could walk her to her vehicle and said she had something to tell me. I told Burl I'd be back and followed her to her unmarked GMC Yukon. Cindy slipped behind the steering wheel and I leaned against the door. "Chris, for some reason the preacher is way too upset about someone absconding with a wooden statue. He tried to tell me why it was, in his words, priceless, but he was so upset I couldn't follow the story. He insisted on calling you—heck if I know why—I suppose he trusts you. He needs reassuring. This is not a big deal; happens everywhere manger scenes are. The youngin' will turn up."

"I'll do my best."

"Could you do me another favor?"

"Depends."

She put her hand on my arm. "I'm saying this as your good buddy. Could you for once, not get in the middle of police business; for once, keep your weird friends from nosing in our job?"

Since retiring to Folly after spending what seemed forever in a boring bureaucratic job with a huge healthcare company, I had been involved in several horrific events, including multiple murders. A few friends and I had stumbled, bumbled, and through tons of luck and a little skill, brought some bad guys to justice. Chief LaMond was more than familiar with the escapades and whether she would admit it or not had helped us with a few of them.

"I can't promise—"

She interrupted, "I know, I know, but please try. Remember, in the words of Haven Gillespie, *He knows when you are good or bad.*

"Who's Haven Gillespie?"

"Look it up."

My friend Charles Fowler had a habit of quoting U.S. Presidents and I had never looked any of them up to distinguish Charles's fact from fantasy, so I wasn't about to research Gillespie. "What brings you out this early anyway? Looks like your guys had things under control."

"Holy moly, Chris," Cindy said in her East Tennessee twang, "Somebody stole Jesus."

Chapter Two

C hief LaMond and her officers had departed—the officers to scour the city and Cindy to the office to wade through "Smoky Mountains-high piles of paperwork." I returned to Burl, who was pacing in front of the manger and shaking his head.

I put my arm around his shoulder. "Bad morning."

I was surprised to see him wipe a tear from the corner of his eye. What was so important about the replica of the Baby Jesus? I understood the importance of the Nativity, but Burl seemed more concerned than should be normal.

"Terrible." He shook his head. "Terrible."

I waited for him to elaborate. The temperature was mild, although the wind had increased and the wind chill made it feel colder. To get out of the breeze, I nudged him toward the open side of the three-sided, nine-foot wide, six- foot high, wooden barn.

He pointed to the figure of Mary. "Brother Chris, as you see, the figures are fiberglass. Through generous donations by those in our flock, we were able to buy them from a supply house I found on the Internet."

I wasn't a regular at First Light although I had attended several services. I motioned for him to continue.

"The structure was built from scrap wood donated by contractors and fashioned into a barn replica by me and others in the group. All this could easily be replaced."

Burl had been a carpenter before joining the ministry. "You did a great job."

For a moment, he didn't say anything and then he pointed to the crib. "Baby Jesus is another story. Do you know Brother Robert Daniel?"

"Don't believe so."

"You probably don't. Brother Robert had attended services a couple of times before falling ill to pancreatic cancer. After that, I took my ministry to his hospital bed. He is … was ninety-three years of age. He passed three weeks ago, two days after his birthday."

"I'm sorry."

Burl's shoulders slumped. "As am I. Brother Robert's son, Robert Jr. was in the military and sustained serious wounds in the Vietnam conflict. He was sent to a hospital in Germany to recuperate, and while there, was befriended by a local family, a family of quality woodworkers as only the Germans can be. Robert Jr.'s friend, whose name I can't remember, bequeathed upon him a hand-carved, painted replica of the Baby Jesus that had been handed down through three generations." Burl gave a slight smile. "Of course, it was not an exact replica since no one knows what the Christ Child looked like."

"Why did they give Robert Jr. something that had been in their family for so long?"

"I was never clear on the details of the political situation in their hamlet, but during World War II the family did not adhere to the radical views of Hitler, and when the Americans entered the community, our soldiers did not condemn the family and provided them with much-needed food and supplies. They told Robert Jr. they were forever indebted to the Americans, and the carved gift was a token of their appreciation."

"That's touching."

"Robert said his son tried to decline such a significant gift, but his German friend insisted."

"Was Robert Jr. with his father when he died?"

Burl stepped close to the manger and slowly rubbed his hands on the side of the wooden crib. "Robert Jr. had secured a position in finance when he returned from Germany. His dad said he was quite good at his trade and had earned a significant amount of money. He was to return to Germany to share additional thanks to his friend and his family for befriending him and honoring him with the statue. He planned to return the icon to its rightful owners."

"Planned to?"

"Robert Jr. was in a meeting on the forty-third floor of the South Tower of the World Trade Center on September 11, 2001." Burl bowed his head and whispered, "His remains have yet to be identified."

Once again, I put my arm around the preacher. Burl said, "May I offer a prayer?"

He did, and we stood in silence. The wind whistled through the gaps in the walls. Typical morning life was beginning on Folly and a few cars passed in front of us.

"What do you want me to do?"

"Brother Chris, I know Chief LaMond and her officers will do what they can to find the priceless statue. They are good at their jobs. I am also wise enough to know a missing piece of carved wood can't take as much priority as crimes against people. It will be natural for them to lose sight of their quest for Jesus."

"You want me to find it?"

He nodded. "I have faith you will be able to achieve doing what others may find impossible. Your track record is such that it gives me confidence."

During my sixty-six years, I had been told by preachers I needed to find Jesus, but until this morning, two weeks before Christmas, never a wooden one.

"I'll do my best."

Burl smiled. "I know you will. And Brother Chris, I wish this not to be an undue burden, but Baby Jesus must be found in time for our Christmas Eve service. It must."

Holy infant so tender and mild. And gone.

Chapter Three

Burl had moved to the heated confines of his car, and I continued to stare at the manger. Other than search the backstreets and alleys and root through trash containers, what could I do the police couldn't do to find the icon? There was a good chance the chief was right about it being taken as a prank and it would turn up. Burl had good intentions, something he was never short on, but why place the burden on me to find it?

I was wondering what to do next when I heard heavy breathing behind me and a cane tapping pavement. The familiar voice of my best friend Charles Fowler said, "Are you delivering gold, frankincense, and myrrh? Couldn't three wise men make the trip?"

Charles was a few years younger than me, had lived on Folly thirty years, and for reasons no rational person could explain, we had become friends. We were as similar as a penguin was to a banana split, but there was no explaining the mysteries of the universe. I had labored most of my life in a bureaucratic office environment while Charles treated work like it was a strain of malaria. I was shy and reticent; Charles would talk to and befriend everyone he came in contact with, along with their pets. He was a voracious reader; I liked books as much as I liked ingrown toenails. Regardless, he would do anything for me, including risk his life. I knew because he had done it. I would do the same for him.

Charles was staring at me. He had his hands on his hips. His heavy, red jacket was zipped to his neck with the logo of the University of Alaska on its front. I started to explain why I was there and ask what myrrh was when he turned and pointed his ever-present cane at the manger and shouted, "Where's Jesus?"

"Gone."

"I may be old, not as old as you, thank God, and my eyesight's not what it used to be, but that fact didn't escape me. Did someone take him to change his swaddling clothes?"

I must also point out that Charles's sense of humor and approach to life has been considered a tad off center. Because of his disheveled appearance, unshaven face, and thinning hair that flowed to the beat of a different eclectic style, combined with his never failing to befriend the most downtrodden individual, others often assumed he wasn't among the, how shall I say it, intellectually elite. In reality, he was a textbook example of you can't judge a book by its cover. And speaking of books, he owned and claimed to have read, more books than are shelved in many small-town libraries.

"It was stolen."

Charles stared at the manger. "Burl will be heartbroken."

"He already is."

I explained about the preacher and the police already being here and that Cindy's guys had started canvassing the city for the statue.

Charles moved closer to the manger. He removed his Tilley hat and held it over his heart. "The statue's priceless. He must be devastated."

"Do you know its history?"

"Sure," he said, like who didn't. "He told me when I was helping build this." He waved his cane around the barn. Charles had become a regular at the First Light services after Melinda Beale, his elderly aunt and last living relative, passed away. Before that, he had avoided churches for most of his life.

He appeared lost in thought, so I didn't say anything until he returned his hat to its rightful spot on his head. "He asked me to find it."

Charles grinned and waved his cane toward the center of town. "What are we waiting for?"

At some point in Charles's reality-challenged life, he'd decided he was a private detective. His total experience receiving a payroll check had consisted of landscaping and an assembly line job at a Ford plant in his native Michigan. Those jobs had ended during Ronald Reagan's presidency. Since then, he had picked up a few cash-only jobs helping restaurants clean during their busy season, provided a couple of extra hands for local contractors, and delivered on-island packages for the surf shop. He was also the unofficial executive sales manager for Landrum Gallery, a photo gallery I had opened, and after losing thousands of dollars a year, was closing. Regardless of plus or minus zero experience in the field of detecting, he had decided after watching countless whodunit television shows and reading more than countless detective novels, there was nothing he didn't know about his chosen field of work.

For the next five hours, Charles and I got a month's worth of exercise, walking each street within a mile of the manger. Most of our walk was east and west since we were limited on the south by the Atlantic Ocean and on the north by the Folly River and the marsh separating the island from the contiguous United States. The statue could have been taken off island, but there was little we could do about it. And, if Cindy was correct about it being a prank, Baby Jesus was probably on our seven-mile long, half-mile wide piece of land.

All that resulted from our efforts were four sore feet and two red faces from the increasingly brisk winter winds blowing off the ocean. We ended our search at Charles's small apartment, and I limped the remaining seven blocks to my cottage beside Bert's Market. I was exhausted, and it was only three-thirty. A nap was next on my agenda until I was interrupted by a knock on the door, and found two teenagers on the porch, hands in their pockets, their coat collars pulled up around their necks.

"Good afternoon, Mr. Landrum," said the taller of the two. He was my height at five-foot-ten, sixteen years old, trim but muscular, and answered to Samuel Perkins. I had met the long haired, young man my first week on Folly Beach. We had become reacquainted a year ago when he had come to me after he had seen a woman being abducted. Because he'd witnessed the crime, his life had been put in danger, but through luck and the help of friends, I was able to save him.

"Hi, Samuel. Hi, Jason." Even in their heavy James Island Charter High School jackets, they were shivering.

Jason Lewis was the other visitor. He was a couple of inches shorter than Samuel and wasn't as skinny and didn't appear as athletic. I had known Jason nearly as long as I had known Samuel, although for different reasons. I had dated Jason's mom, Amber, for a couple of years, until she broke off our dating after I had exposed Jason to a murder victim. Amber felt it was too dangerous for her son to be associated with me, but despite that, she and I had remained friends. Amber was also the best waitress the Lost Dog Café had ever had and was ground central when anyone wanted to know the latest rumors.

Jason said, "Hello, Mr. Landrum."

"Come in." I waved them toward the living room. "What brings you out?"

Jason looked at Samuel, who said, "Mr. Landrum, we heard stories in school today that somebody sort of took Jesus."

I nodded and wondered how the word was already around. "How did you hear it?"

Samuel turned to Jason, who looked at the floor, and said, "My friend Hector's mom texted him during lunch. He told us."

Samuel interrupted, "She told him some kids sort of took it."

I looked at Samuel and turned to Jason. "Do you know anything about it?"

"Us?" Jason inhaled. "No, Mr. Landrum. That's why we came to see you."

Jacob, Jason's father, had told me his son had a tendency to exaggerate. While it may have been true, during my talks with Jason a year ago, the young man had been honest and accurate in whatever he had said.

They kept looking down at the floor and failed to make eye contact with me. I offered them a drink to calm them down.

Each declined, and I said, "I'm confused, why did you come to see me?"

Samuel looked at me. "Mr. Landrum, we want to help find the kid, umm, the Jesus statue. If a teenager took it, he could sort of go to our school. Jason said maybe we should go to the police and offer to look around for them. I told him the cop'd say something like, 'Now son, we'll take care of it. You all go back to your studies.'" He rolled his eyes. "I knew how you caught the killer, you know, the one the cops didn't think was real. You were a stand-up adult, and are good at finding bad guys, so I told him we should come see you and sort of offer our help at school." He smiled. "Here we are."

I returned his smile and waved for them to follow me to the kitchen and pointed at the chairs. They sat, and I again offered them a drink. They unzipped their coats and were warming up; warming up enough to say a Pepsi would be nice. I was pleased with their decision since water, wine, beer, and Pepsi were the only choices.

"The first you learned about the missing statue was after Hector's mom texted?"

Samuel said, "That's sort of what we said." He turned to Jason for confirmation.

Jason nodded. "You don't think we did it?"

I shook my head. "Not for a second. I asked because if someone at school knew it before you said Hector did, that person might have known it before the police were called."

Samuel pointed a finger at me. "Oh, I get it. That person could've swiped it."

"Yes. What can you do to help?"

Jason and Samuel alternated telling me their plan which amounted to "sort of casually" talking to classmates and see if they knew anything, and to "snoop around" to see if anybody in the other grades had any information.

They were right about what the police would have told them, but I also didn't want them snooping. If one of their classmates took the statue or knows who did, Jason and Samuel could end up in danger.

"It's great you want to find the thief, and it could be helpful if you kept your eyes open. But guys, it could be more than a prank and if the person who took it finds out you're looking, you could get in trouble."

Jason leaned forward. "Oh no, Mr. Landrum, we'll be careful. All we'll do is keep our eyes open. Our history teacher says we need to be more, what's the word, Samuel?"

"Vigilant."

"Yeah, vigilant. He said good citizens need to do that in these dangerous times."

"Your teacher's wise. If that's all you do, it could help. The statue means a lot to many people, and it would be terrible if anything happened to it."

"I knew you'd know what we should do," Samuel said. "Vigilant, that'll be it."

I looked at each of them. "Promise me one thing. If you learn anything, call the police. If they don't take you seriously, call me. Think you can do it?"

Jason said. "Yes sir, Mr. Landrum." Samuel nodded.

"And you won't confront the person who took it or try to get the statue back?"

They nodded.

Chapter Four

I grew up in Middle America where Christmas was wrapped in traditions galore. Mistletoe was prevalent in nearby oak trees, and dad made the most of it by taping pieces to each doorway, and a double dose over the door to my parents' bedroom. Mom took advantage of his strategic placing of the kiss motivator. We lived where stockings were actually hung from the chimney with care, although we didn't have a chimney, so our stockings were hung on a knickknack shelf over the television—with care.

Unlike most families, a fact I learned years later, Santa not only left presents under our tree, but he decorated the large, live fir that sat unadorned in the living room until the jolly one made his overnight visit. He earned the chocolate-chip cookies mom had baked for him. Santa had enough time to decorate the tree because he didn't wrap my presents, but staged them in their ready-to-play state for when I first laid my sleepy eyes on them.

It wasn't as often as I would like to remember, but a glance outside a few Christmas mornings revealed the ground covered with the white stuff depicted in many popular Christmas songs. Sleds had an immediate playground to slide across. Bicycles came with promises to be ridden once the snow melted. And, although there weren't any in our small, three-person family, little girls could begin playing with their dolls and easy-bake ovens as soon as the lights came on.

The birth of Jesus was never far from my parents' thoughts, although to my young eyes, Christmas was the tree, the presents, candy that was seldom available the rest of the year, and smiles of joy on mom and dad's face. We had a tabletop, ceramic Nativity and on Christmas Eve, dad read the Christmas story and mom tried to lead dad and me in singing hymns. Between my thoughts drifting to what might appear under the tree the next morning, and thinking our singing sounded more like a harmonizing trio made up of a screech owl, an alley cat, and a toad, the true meaning of Christmas was lost on me.

In the following years, Christmas ebbed and flowed in my thoughts. When I was living at home, I attended church with my parents. Santa stopped coming in the back door of our chimneyless house. Mistletoe appeared in fewer and fewer places, although dad and mom didn't need the seasonal incentive to kiss. For that we were thankful. The live trees that had enveloped much of the living room were replaced by a slim, artificial one which didn't need to be large, since underwear and socks didn't take up as much room under it as had bicycles and an electric train.

During the twenty years I was married to my high school sweet-heart, Christmas was a time for a few days off work, a time for us to spend Christmas Eve with my parents and one cousin, and for visiting my wife's family Christmas day. We remained childless and never experienced the joy of helping Santa agonize over the *some assembly required* gifts that included instructions written in thirty-seven languages, none of which were English.

My wife and I attended Christmas Eve midnight service a few years but felt guilty because with the exception of funerals, those were the only times we stepped in a house of worship. After the divorce, I failed to see anything positive about church and organized religion. I was a spiritual person and believed in a higher power, but the trappings of the church did nothing for me. I expressed my need to help those who weren't as lucky as I by donating to organizations that helped feed, clothe, and bring hope to those without the means to survive. I spent several evenings each holiday season serving food to the needy, and being thankful I was fortunate enough to have a good job, and a safe, comfortable home.

Over the last year, I had spent numerous hours with Preacher Burl. Some of the time I thought he could be a killer and wondered how I would prove it. Thankfully—and in his words, thank God—he wasn't guilty. The rest of the time with him, I saw the hope, joy, and happiness he brought to his flock and most everyone else with whom he came in contact. He didn't smack people in the head with the Bible, but taught by example, combined with weekly lessons from the Good Book he translated into terms, which could be understood by all.

As he stood over the manger this morning, I had seen hurt in his eyes and defeat in his slumped shoulders. His hands had trembled as he caressed the side of the wooden crib, and his eyes watered for what was no longer there.

Was the theft of Baby Jesus simply the work of bored pranksters and the missing statue would turn up soon? And, if it was pranksters, they had little or no idea how the loss would affect others.

What if it was more? What if the statue not only had spiritual significance, but a significant amount of worldly worth, and was taken to be sold, or to go in the collection of someone who needed a valuable centerpiece for his or her Nativity? Or, was someone trying to make a negative statement about Christianity?

What could I do beyond what the police were doing to bring Baby Jesus home to be enjoyed as a symbol of all that is Christian?

I fell asleep wondering.

I AWOKE to a weather report indicating today's temperature would reach seventy, only four degrees shy of the record high set a century ago. It would be a good day to join the search for the statue, but before I headed out, I wondered if the police had already found it or if someone had turned it in. A call to the chief was in order.

She answered. "No, Chris. We haven't found it." I hated caller ID.

"Why do you think that's what I wanted? Couldn't I be calling a good friend to see how her day was going?"

"No. First it's seven thirty, so my day hasn't been going long enough for me to know how it's going. Second, you're the second nosiest person I know, and it'd give you an ulcer if you had to wait longer to find out if the swaddling- clothed youngin's turned up."

"Guilty."

Cindy chuckled. "Shame I can't throw you in the hoosegow for that confession."

"Well?"

"Okay, okay. I repeat we haven't found it. Sorry."

"Hate to hear it. I know how much it means to Burl."

"I do too," Cindy said. "He told me each time he called last night. I had to tell him if we found it, I would come to his door, regardless of the time, and let him know. Then my wonderful hubby got on my case. Said the manger was on his store's property, so he felt responsible, and if I knew what was good for me, I'd better find the kid."

I told her I was going to look for the statue and asked if there was anywhere her officers hadn't had time to search. She reminded me the island covered more than a few zillion square miles of water surrounded by three square miles of land, and that off-island the rest of the United States covered "more square miles than there were words to count them."

I thanked her for the geography lesson and with an overabundance of sarcasm she thanked me for pestering her.

"One question, Chris."

"Anything for you."

"If the little statue is so valuable, according to the preacher, price-less, why in "Blue Christmas" blazes did he leave it in the manger, in a deserted area, and guarded by a passel of plastic people and a herd of fake animals?"

"I wondered the same thing, Cindy, but seeing what condition Burl was in yesterday, I didn't ask."

Cindy said, "Hmm," and was gone.

The temperature may reach seventy, but it had a way to go, so I put on a light jacket and my Tilley to keep my balding head warm. I figured the police would have done a good job covering the downtown area, so I walked closer to the beach and headed away from town. I had made it a block when I saw Dude and his puppy skipping along the side of the road. Dude was skipping; his Australian terrier, Pluto, was running as fast as his little legs could carry him. Dude had told me a while back he had read that skipping had the health advantages of jogging, but at a slower pace. I didn't know where he had read it, although I doubted it was in *Astronomy Magazine*.

They pulled up beside me and I stooped to greet Pluto, named after the dwarf planet. He licked my hand, more in appreciation for me slowing his master rather than for being glad to see me.

Dude waited for me to finish my bonding moment with his dog, and said, "Surfer buds say you be cool for a geezer."

That surprised me since the number of words in my conversation with his young friends could be counted on two hands. "Really?"

"Yep, the Finleyster and Teddyetress be quick deciders about peeps. Say you be okeydokey."

I couldn't think of much to say, so I limited it to, "Good to know." I also realized Dude wasn't as nosy as some of my friends so he might not know about the missing statue. "Did you hear about the missing Baby Jesus?"

He said he hadn't, so I told him what I knew. "Terrible. Preacher man be devastated. Dude be riled."

He kicked the gravel, Pluto jumped, and I was surprised how angry my friend was. He had been involved in the problems with First Light earlier in the year, and had attended several services. He had told Burl he worshiped the sun god, but enjoyed Burl's services because they were outside and he could see the sun while hearing the words of wisdom from Burl. Of course Dude didn't use that many words, but I think it's what he'd meant.

I explained the police were looking and that was what I was heading out to do.

Dude continued to kick gravel. "Me tag along. Triple number of eyes lookin'. Me be pissed. Whoa. Is it okeydokey to say pissed about Baby Jesus?"

I said in this case it was and I'd be glad to have him along. Pluto wagged his tail in agreement.

I continued walking away from town, now with four additional eyes to help with the search. Dude didn't say anything—not much different from when he did say something—but I could tell he was troubled about the theft. Every other stride he kicked the sand along the side of the road.

Dude stopped, Pluto came to a more abrupt stop when Dude yanked the rhinestone-covered leash. Dude said, "Direction change 180."

I thought he meant to go back, so I turned.

Dude put up his hand, palm facing me. "Word direction."

"What?"

"Almost forgot. Boss crime wave on Folly." He looked at me.

"Meaning?"

He blinked a couple of times. "Vernon ordered two custom boards from *moi*. Shipped U Pee S to casa. Vernon excited and boogied to door for boards. Be gone. Boards gone, not door." He held out both arms. "Boss crime wave."

Charles wasn't around to translate. I guessed Dude had two surfboards shipped to a customer.

"Stolen?" I said.

"There minute." Dude snapped his fingers. "Gone next. Crime wave."

"Did the customer see who took them?"

"Negatory. Man in brown say dropped on porch.
Vernon find empty porch."

"When?"

"Now minus eighteen hours. Day youngin' swiped from crib."

I couldn't imagine a connection, but asked, "Do you think the thefts are related?"

He looked down at Pluto like he expected him to answer. Pluto was more interested in sniffing a discarded drink cup. "Me be surfer. Think in waves. Folly small. Two humongous crimes same day. Boss crime wave."

I didn't think the theft of two surfboards would qualify as a humongous crime, but nodded. "Could be."

"See."

I didn't, but smiled as the image of a surfing Baby Jesus crossed my mind.

Dude said, "You be needin' to figure it out. Dude be pained to see preacher man sufferin'. He be helping everyone else. Now he needs help. Figure it out."

I started to say it's what the police were for, but Dude knew that. Besides, I agreed with him. Burl was a Godsend to Folly. If there was anything I could do to lessen his pain, I would.

Chapter Five

Groundhog Day must have come late this year. I opened the door to the same sight I had witnessed the same time yester-day. Jason and Samuel were staring at me with their hands in their coat pockets

"We meet again," I said.

Samuel smiled, and Jason said, "Good afternoon, Mr. Landrum." He looked past me into the living room. "Got more Pepsis?"

I motioned them to the kitchen, and they took the same seats they had occupied yesterday. I handed each a Pepsi and grabbed one for myself.

"Mr. Landrum," Samuel said, "since you're sort of in charge of our espionage—"

"Don't think it's espionage," Jason interrupted. "We're looking to see if anyone knows about the missing kid, umm, Jesus."

Samuel rolled his eyes. "Whatever. We're reporting in."

"Reporting in," Jason added, "and to see if you heard about the surfboard heist?"

Samuel said, "We think the baby theft and the surfboard one are connected."

I told them I was aware of the missing surfboards but didn't think it had anything to do with the statue.

Samuel shook his head. "Mighty big ass, umm, I mean, mighty big coincidence. Everyone who watches TV mysteries knows cops say there ain't no such thing as coincidence."

Jason shoved Samuel's arm. "Sure there is. Otherwise *coincidence* wouldn't be in the dictionary. Isn't that right, Mr. Landrum?"

I was amazed how quickly the conversation had headed downhill. "Yes Jason, there are coincidences, but the police look for connections before they write off two or more events as unrelated."

Jason turned to Samuel. "See." Samuel repeated, "Whatever."

Time to get the train back on the track. "Anything to report?"

"Jason and I walked all over town after we left here yesterday. I know it wasn't right, but we sneaked through some yards." He tilted his head toward Jason. "He dug through those big dumpster things behind two restaurants." He paused and grinned. "He fell in one."

"I didn't fall in, Samuel. I caught myself."

"Didn't look like it. The point, Mr. Landrum, is we didn't find Jesus."

Jason said, "Tell him about school."

"Well, we sort of asked everyone we knew if they'd heard anything about the statue. We acted like we just heard about it and wanted to hear if they knew anything more than we did. Didn't want it to sound like we were interrogating them, if you know what I mean."

I cringed thinking about how the questioning may have sounded to their friends. "Don't suppose you learned anything?"

Jason looked at Samuel and then at me. "Not a thing, Mr. Landrum. Most of the students didn't know that the baby was gone."

It appeared the price of two Pepsis bought me nothing other than a discussion about coincidences.

Jason said, "Don't worry, we're not giving up. There are a few kids we didn't see today. We're still on the case."

I again cautioned them not to do anything that could put them in danger. Again, they said they wouldn't. I walked them to the door and wondered if they would know what danger was and how it could sneak up on them.

Samuel turned as they reached the porch. "One more thing, Mr. Landrum. About the coincidence stuff, I sort of feel like the boards being taken has something to do with the missing baby."

I smiled and told them to be careful. As they headed out, I wondered what the odds were on them following my advice.

I MOVED to the recliner in the living room and allowed my mind to wander back to some of my most memorable childhood Christmases, when another knock disturbed my sleigh ride down memory lane.

Charles was standing on the porch, sporting his Tilley, wearing a jacket he bought in Gatlinburg when we'd been there a few years back, and pointing his cane toward the kitchen.

"Cooking supper?"

I laughed. The last time I'd cooked supper in my kitchen was—well, I'd never cooked supper there. Charles knew that, and I wrote off his comment as a joke rather than a symptom of early-onset Alzheimer's.

"Sorry, I was heading to the grocery to pick up some fresh fruit, vegetables, and tilapia, but got sidetracked by a total lack of desire and ability to cook it."

"So, are you coming with me to Rita's?" I smiled and grabbed my jacket.

Rita's Seaside Grill was two blocks from the house and situated on a prime piece of real estate. The property had been the site of a bowling alley, and several restaurants before it morphed into Rita's a few years ago. It had one of Folly's nicest outdoor seating areas although that feature was seldom occupied in December. We chose a booth inside and along the window overlooking the Sand Dollar Social Club, Folly's iconic private bar, open to anyone with a dollar and who could wait a day to become a member.

Ashley, who had waited on me several times, was quick to the table. She pointed to me and said, "Cabernet," and to Charles and said, "Budweiser."

We nodded, and she headed to the bar. Charles threw his jacket on the seat beside him. He wore a long-sleeve, green University of North Dakota Hockey sweatshirt. I glanced at the shirt and looked out the window at two customized Harleys parked in front of the Sand Dollar. Charles had three more sweatshirts than a Dick's Sporting Goods store, and I had been trying for years not to ask about them. I had more to do with my time than to hear protracted stories about the schools represented, their mascots, student population, number of faculty members holding PhDs in Pan American Studies, and other trivia. Ignoring him didn't always prevent him from sharing.

He pointed to his chest. "Get it? Winter, hockey." I stifled a whoop-de-doo. "Nice."

Ashley had returned with drinks before I heard more about the University of North Dakota than anyone outside Grand Forks would want to know. We ordered burgers.

Charles sipped his beer and glanced at me. "Has the APB on Baby Jesus captured him?"

An all-points bulletin was a slight exaggeration but said I didn't know.

"What did Cindy say?"

I shrugged. "Haven't talked to her lately."

Charles reached across the table, grabbed my phone, punched in a number, and handed it to me.

"What did I tell you I'd do if I found Jesus?" Chief LaMond shouted.

I said, "Fall on your knees and pray for forgiveness."

"Not funny, you sacrilegious senior citizen."

"Couldn't resist."

"Ha, ha. Now back to what I told you. Didn't I say the first thing I'd do was call you if I found the statue? Even if the person who absconded with it was shooting at me or trying to hurl me off the end of the pier, I'll say, hang on a sec. I've got to call Chris."

"You did, chief." I sighed. "I'm here with Charles and—"

"No need to say more. Two nosies don't make a right."

"I suppose it means two concerned citizens asking the finest law enforcement official on the island for an update on a criminal investigation."

Cindy giggled. "More like camel crap."

"You said it, not me. So, have you found it?"

She cleared her throat, Ashley set our burgers in front of us, the comforting smell filled the air, and Cindy said, "No, and it's not from lack of trying. Don't tell the mayor, but I added another patrol officer to the ones already on duty. They've checked everywhere. No Jesus." She sighed. "I know how much it means. Wish I could do more."

Despite a smart ass gene she and I had in common, and her irreverent take on most things, Cindy was sensitive, sentimental, and concerned about how others were treated. She hid most of it, but the more I got to know her, the more I admired her.

"I know you do, Cindy."

"I wish we had more time to look, but things are heating up around here."

Charles leaned across the table to try to hear her side of the conversation. The nearby tables were vacant, so I tapped the speaker icon. No need for Charles to dip his hockey sweatshirt in his burger while bending over to hear.

I asked. "Heating up, how?"

"Damned porch pirates. Two more deliveries have been stolen."

Charles said, "Surfboards?"

There was a hesitation before the chief said, "Chris, your voice has changed."

Charles said, "It's not Chris, chief. It's the smart one."

"Oh, hi, William."

William Hansel was one of our friends who was a professor at the College of Charleston. "Funny," Charles said. "Surfboards?"

"Nope. A woman's best friend." Charles said, "Dogs?"

"No wonder you're both single. Diamonds, dummies. Yellow and white diamond pendant from Tiffany. Cost more than I take home in months. Snatched off the porch at one of the McMansions out West Ashley."

Charles said, "Wow."

Cindy said, "You can say that again—but don't. The other one was a bracelet from Saks Fifth Avenue. Cheap, only cost a thousand bucks. Grabbed off the porch of a house on East Arctic."

"Leads?" I asked.

"Nope. The homeowners looked for the packages within an hour after they were delivered. The thief must've been following the delivery truck. Big-ole brown trucks ain't hard to follow."

"A crime spree," I said, channeling Dude.

"Wouldn't go that far," the chief said. "It's part of the dark side of Christmas in the Internet world."

Charles tapped on the side of the phone. "From Jesus, to surf-boards, to jewelry. Seems strange."

Cindy said, "The surfboards and the jewelry thefts were the same MO. I don't see a connection to the statue snatch."

I looked at Charles staring at the phone and said, "The surfboards could be pawned along the coast, and the jewelry anywhere. Unless the thief already has a buyer, the statue would be harder to unload."

Cindy said, "That's why I don't think they're connected."

"It doesn't mean they ain't," Charles added.

"No, it doesn't. I wish we could do more, especially about the statue. A couple of my guys have volunteered to spend off-duty hours driving around in their own cars following UPS and FedEx trucks. They're also looking for the Baby Jesus. The folks who could afford the jewelry will have a decent holiday even without the baubles although I suspect they will spend a bunch of it arguing with insurance companies. Preacher Burl won't have a decent Christmas. I feel like crap about it."

I thanked her for the update and asked her to let us know if she learned anything.

"Not a second will pass." She hung up.

Charles stared at the silent phone, took a large drag on his Bud, and looked at me. "Okay, what's our plan?"

I was afraid I knew what he meant, "Plan for what?"

"You heard the chief. She said she wished she could do more to catch the spirit of Christmas thief. She was begging for our help. So what's our plan beyond walking around like we already did?"

"Begging?"

"Begging," Charles said. "Plan?"

"I've got to sleep on it. Let's talk tomorrow."

"It'll have to do. See you at the Dog. Is seven too late?"

I shook my head and headed home. I didn't think I'd sleep in heavenly peace.

Chapter Six

I was wrong. I got a good night's sleep and slipped out of bed at five-thirty, an hour earlier than usual. Rather than visions of sugarplums, Charles's question danced in my head. What could we do that the police weren't doing to find the statue? It was worrisome that it hadn't turned up. The longer it was missing, the greater the chance it wasn't a prank, and if it was taken for more sinister reasons, I thought about Jason and Samuel nosing around and about how slim the odds were that they would stumble across the thief. Slim still left the door open.

Was it possible the grab-and-go thefts were related to the missing statue? Cindy didn't think so. Other than stealing something, there were no similarities in the crimes. Again, a slim possibility beat no possibility. Regardless, I couldn't think of anything to do.

Charles had said seven o'clock, which meant he'd be at the Dog when the door opened at six-thirty. In his parallel universe, on time meant thirty minutes early, and he wouldn't let anyone forget he or she was late when arriving at the designated hour. I was not disappointed; I stepped in the near-empty restaurant at six thirty-five and spotted my friend at my favorite booth. He pulled up the sleeve of his burnt-orange, long-sleeve Virginia Tech sweatshirt and glanced at his wrist where normal people wore a watch. He didn't own one, but the meaning wasn't lost on me.

Before I had time to take off my jacket, he asked, "Got it figured out?"

I started to say no when Amber appeared at the table with my mug of coffee. She had worked at the Dog since I had arrived on Folly. The waitress was approaching her fiftieth birthday and was attractive with her long auburn hair tied in a ponytail, but her usual welcoming smile seemed strained as she set the coffee down.

She leaned close. "I need a word when you're alone."

I was confused. Not only did she appear angry, but also in the past she'd never hesitated to say whatever was on her mind in front of Charles.

I smiled. "Sure."

She gave a quick nod. "Want breakfast?"

In the hundreds of times she'd waited on me, she had never been this abrupt.

I said, "French toast."

She headed to the kitchen.

For years, she had been on a one-person crusade to get me to eat better, and would chide me for ordering my favorite artery-clogging breakfast.

Charles watched her go. "What've you done now?"

"I don't know."

Marc Salmon was the next person to enter and distracted Charles from questioning me further.

Charles said, "Yo, Marc, join us?"

Charles was not prone to ask anyone to join us unless he had an ulterior motive.

Marc looked around the near-empty room and sat next to Charles. "Suppose I can spare a moment until Houston gets here. City business never ceases, you know."

I didn't know that, but did know Marc's daily meeting with Houston centered more around gossip and sharing stories, some true, with his fellow council member than with city business.

Amber was quick with Marc's coffee but didn't make eye contact with me. He took a sip, looked at me, turned to Charles, and smiled. "Anything this elected official needs to know this morning? Always looking for ways to make your city better."

Anyone who knew Marc would have known it was his way of asking for gossip. Charles wasn't going to let Marc's agenda get in the way of his. "Marc, I know you have your finger on the pulse of the community," Charles said in his best suck-up voice, "Any word on the crime spree?"

Marc jerked his head toward Charles. "Crime spree?" Charles seemed to forget about his quest for information and grinned knowing he may know something the inquisitive councilmember didn't. "You know, the theft of Baby Jesus, and the surfboards and jewelry heist."

Marc leaned back and sighed. "Oh, that." He sounded disappointed. "I wouldn't call it a spree. It's terrible about the things being taken off porches, and the theft of the infant was horrible."

I wouldn't call thousands of dollars' worth of jewelry *things being taken off porches*, but he wanted to minimize the impact. I did agree Baby Jesus being stolen was horrible.

Charles repeated, "Any word?" Nothing will keep him from his quest.

"I'm certain our Department of Public Safety is leaving no stone unturned."

"So, nothing?"

"Not yet." He shook his head. "I'm appalled anyone would desecrate the Nativity scene." He surprised me when he grinned. "I'm Jewish, but my kids love Christmas. After they were born, Mrs. B. insisted we put up a small tree. We have it to celebrate the season, but each year more and more presents appear under it."

Charles patted him on the shoulder, "Calvin Coolidge said, 'Christmas is not a time nor a season, but a state of mind.'"

Add a worthless fount of presidential quotes to Charles's long-sleeve T-shirt and sweatshirt assemblage, his library-sized collection of books, and the handmade wooden cane he carried for no visible reason. If *Jeopardy!* limited questions to presidents' quotes, Charles would be a TV star. It doesn't, and he isn't, but he still managed to impress those around him.

Amber clunked my breakfast plate down on the table and left without speaking. Houston rushed in before Charles could share more words of wisdom from Calvin Coolidge.

Houston moved to the table where he and Marc often sat and waved to Marc, and said, "Sorry I'm late."

Marc told us he'd better join his friend and said to Houston. "That's okay."

Marc didn't share Charles's obsession with promptness.

Charles watched him go and said, "That was worthless."

"Not completely, now you know you can give him a Christmas present."

Charles watched me take my first bite and said, "Did you know Saint Francis of Assisi created the first Nativity scene in Greccio, Italy, in 1223. It was a live one."

I stared at him. "Should have told Marc, although he prefers more recent gossip."

"Going to, but he left. In a cave, if you can believe that."

"Marc?"

Charles gave an exasperated sigh. "The first Nativity."

"Interesting," I said, although I'd already forgotten where it had been.

"So what's our plan?" he asked, making a sharp turn in the conversation.

"Don't have one. Remember, the Department of Public Safety is leaving no stone unturned."

"Good, we won't have to look under rocks."

Charles said he had to make a delivery for the surf shop. Dude had Charles make local deliveries rather than using the more traditional shippers. Charles's deliveries were nearby and limited to small packages since his only moving vehicle was a Schwinn bicycle. I told him not to leave whatever he was delivering on the front porch. He said no way and excused himself.

Amber must have been watching because she was at the table before Charles was out of sight. She glared down at me. "Meet me outside in ten. I'll be on break." She moved across the room to clear a table.

She didn't seem interested in wishing me an early Merry Christmas. I'd better enjoy the rest of my coffee and the next nine minutes.

THE DOG HAD two outdoor seating areas; one in front of the building and the other on the side closest to the city's combination library and community center. Amber was sitting at a table at the back of the side patio and out of view of customers entering the restaurant. The penetrating glare she'd used on me inside hadn't softened. She motioned for me to sit and made no effort to stand to greet me. It was cold in the corner. I pulled my jacket tight and waited.

"Chris, what in the hell are you thinking?"

I didn't suppose she meant what I was thinking about what she wanted me out here for, so I waited.

"Have you forgotten why we stopped dating?"

I will never forget. It was because she felt my amateurish attempt to catch a killer had put Jason in danger. He had told me about loud television sounds coming from the apartment of someone I had wanted to talk to about a murder. The television was loud, but its owner didn't care. She was dead. Jason had sneaked in the room while I was checking on the noise and saw the gruesome sight. Right or wrong,

Amber felt the need to protect her son from the events surrounding the body and put an end to our dating.

I looked at her and frowned. "I remember."

Her hands were balled into fists; her glare hardened. "Then what in all that's holy were you thinking by asking him to try to find the missing Baby Jesus? My God, the boy's sixteen."

Her level of anger shocked me. I reached out to put my hand over her fist. She yanked it back and stomped her foot on the wooden deck. "What?" she repeated.

I pulled my hand back and leaned closer. "Amber, I'm sorry, but I didn't ask Jason to do anything," I explained how Jason and Samuel had come to the house wanting to help find the statue; how they said they wanted to snoop around the school.

She flexed her hand. "Why did they go to you?"

"Samuel said it was because I had helped catch the guy he had seen abducting that woman. Said he could trust me."

"Did you insist they stop? To not get involved? To leave it to the cops?"

"I told them what they wanted to do could be dangerous; but to be honest, I doubt there was anything I could have said that would've stopped them. They're two headstrong, smart kids."

"You could've tried."

"Amber, I told them if they learned anything to tell the police and not to try anything to get the statue back. It's the best I could do seeing how determined they were."

She closed her eyes, shook her head, and whispered, "They respect you. They trust you. You could've stopped them."

She pushed up from the table and rushed inside. I remained seated and stared at her empty chair.

I thought about going inside and saying...saying what? I was sorry. But, sorry for what? Opening the door to the two teens, listening to their concerns. I knew they were determined to keep their eyes open and see if they learned anything about the statue and if they did, they said they'd contact the police. What was there to apologize for? Could I tell her I would have them stop whatever they were doing? I knew it wouldn't work. So what could I say? Nothing.

My phone rang as I continued running lose-lose options in my head.

"Dude here."

I sighed and grinned. "Chris here."

"Be having meeting at surf shop, sun duck behind marsh plus thirty."

I went out on a limb and decided since sunset was around five o'clock, he was having a meeting at thirty minutes past that time.

"Five thirty?"

"That's what me said."

Not exactly. "Meeting about what?"

"Surfer buds. Chrisster and Chuckster not be surfers, but invited— my place, my invite list."

Did I miss the purpose of the meeting somewhere in that? "What's it about?"

"Spirit of Christmas stealer. Be here?"

I figured all I would get from continuing this conversation would be a headache. "Yep," I said and hit end call.

Chapter Seven

As anyone who knew Charles could have predicted, we arrived at the surf shop thirty minutes before the time Dude had almost said. We would have been earlier if Charles hadn't stopped me three times to ask what the meeting was about. I had thought the *spirit of Christmas stealer* had summed it up, but it wasn't detailed enough for my friend. He would have to wait.

The surf shop, written without upper-case letters for reasons known only to Dude, faced Center Street and was in the heart of Folly's six-block retail district. He had owned the shop for a quarter of a century and had stocked it with everything an aspiring or a lifelong surfer would need except for the ocean. To say it was cluttered would be like saying a few revelers gathered in Times Square on New Year's Eve. I was surprised after Charles and I had made it up the steps to see the space inside the front door void of its usual racks packed with wetsuits, enough surfboards to outfit half the island, and colorful swimwear.

Stephon, one of Dude's two full-time employees who were listed in Wikipedia under *Horrid Customer Service*, was shoving the last rack of wetsuits toward the back of the room while cussing the entire way. Dude was waving his arm and yelling, "There be go." I assumed he was telling Stephon where to park the display.

The shop owner saw us and turned from his employee and pointed to the space vacated by the displays. "Surf shop official meeting room."

I had never seen this much open space in the shop and it could hold a dozen people. Charles offered to help do whatever needed to be done.

Dude said words that meant everything was taken care of. He added, "No be servin' munchies and champagne."

He had finished sharing the un-menu when three men and a woman arrived. They were less than half Dude's age and looked like a white rap group. Each wore black pants and dark gray hoodies.

The tallest member of the quartet looked around the open area. "Cool."

"I'm stoked, Dude," the second man said as he pushed the hood off his shaven head.

The woman pointed to the floor that had held a selection of surfboards. "Sick."

Charles leaned close and said, "Means good." I nodded thanks.

The fourth person didn't say anything.

Dude waved them in. "Welcome to el meeting."

Charles, whose goal in life was to meet every human on earth, walked to the group and held out his hand. "I'm Charles, the boring looking guy over there is my bud Chris." The newcomers looked at Charles's hand and glanced at me. The tall one who had spoken first shook the outstretched hand, and said, "Roscoe." He looked at the guy standing next to him who said, "Todd." The female stepped in front of Roscoe, shook Charles's hand and said, "Deb."

The fourth person remained in the back of the group, and muttered, "Ryan." He didn't shake anyone's hand.

The door opened before I could say something like it was nice to meet them, and I had already forgotten their names. Two more people entered and gawked at the empty space. I recognized them from when they were having breakfast with Dude. Charles and I hadn't gotten the memo about tonight's dress code. The newest arrivals, like their predecessors, wore black jeans and gray hoodies. I thought their names were Teddye and Finley but waited until they introduced themselves to Charles in case I was wrong— something I often was when it came to names. They seemed to know the first group and nodded in their direction. Stephon had finished doing whatever he had been doing and joined the expanding assemblage.

"When're we starting?" Stephon groused. "I want to get out of here."

Dude shook his head. "Be waitin' on two more. Cool it. You be getting paid."

Stephon mumbled something I couldn't understand, and the door swung open.

Dude looked at the two men who were entering. "Me be psychic. Here they be."

The two looked at him like "What's he talking about?" A common response to much of what Dude says.

Dude didn't explain and pointed to the latest arrivers. "Mustache face be Truman. Skinny, youngin' be Slick Surfin' Sal."

I assumed it wasn't the name on his birth certificate, but the *youngin'* nodded, and one from the first group to arrive, mumbled, "We know."

Dude moved to the corner of the empty space and waved his arms toward the center of the room. "Gather."

The *official meeting room's* furniture must not have arrived, so we stood facing our host. The space was near capacity, and we stood closer than I was comfortable with.

Dude shook his head. "Surfin' buds Teddye and Finley wanted gatherin'. Said wanted to—never mind, Finley, be your meetin'."

Finley had been behind us. I turned and saw him look at Teddye, shrug, and knifed his way through the group and moved beside Dude.

He held his arms to his side and then moved them behind his back. He clasped them in front of him like he was saying a prayer. Speaking to a group wasn't one of his regular activities.

Dude nudged him. "Words."

"Okay, umm, we all know some sorry ass thefted the statue of Jesus from the manger by the hardware store." He paused and most of us nodded. "We're surfers." He paused again and looked toward Charles and me. "Most of us. Where I grew up, Baby Jesus in the manger was sacred. Most times it was plastic, but to my folks and others in the town, it was the, what's the word, symbol, yeah, symbol, of Christ coming down here and saving our sorry-ass souls from evil." Not quite how Preacher Burl would have put it, although accurate.

One of the first arrivers said, "Me too."

"Anyway," Finley continued, "we're surfers and often get a bad rap. Folks think we're bad and scuzzy. Me and Teddye decided we needed to do something. We can't have someone stealin' the spirit of Christmas from our island."

Teddye was standing behind me, and said, "Tell them the rest, Fin."

"Oh yeah, we heard someone had the nerve to steal two boards right off the front porch up the street. Now I'm not saying the boards are as important as little Jesus, but it takes a lowlife to steal them."

I wondered if Finley knew about the jewelry, but this wasn't the time to ask. There was mumbling from the group. I assumed they agreed with Finley.

Finley nodded. "Anyway, me and Teddye decided to organize a group and call it Surfers Against Spirit of Christmas Thieves." He turned and patted Dude on the arm. "We told Dude, and he thought it was a boss idea and offered this space for us to get together and invited the rest of you to come out tonight. That's it."

Slick Surfin' Sal, a name I could remember said, "It's horrible someone took the baby and the boards. What are we supposed to do about it?"

"Don't know," Finley said. "That's what we're here to talk about." He pointed at the group. "Ideas?"

The person who entered with Sal, the one with the mustache whose name I didn't remember said, "Other people may think it was, but do any of you know it was a surfer who stole the stuff?"

Finley looked at Dude and at mustache man. "No, Truman, we don't, but I was thinking since he," Finley glanced at Teddye, one of the two females in the room, "or she, stole two boards, it could be. Who else would want a surfboard?"

Stephon had been standing outside the group and leaning against a rack of T-shirts, said, "Someone wanting to hock them. Could've been one of the bums who hang around, or one of those hoity-toity guys who look down their designer-sunglasses-holding noses at us."

"Stephon's right," Finley said. "Could be anyone. What can we do?"

One of the first folks to arrive said, "Catch them and cut off their hands. Stealing Jesus. Cripes, it's as bad as it gets."

Dude stepped in front of Finley. "No to cuttin' off hands. Season of peace. Other ideas?"

"Hand for a hand," one of the others said. Dude said, "Not be hand for a board." Teddye said, "How about a reward?"

Dude gave an exaggerated nod. "Boss idea. Me be donatin' five C notes."

"Five hundred dollars," Charles whispered. I told him I knew what C notes were.

Finley looked at Dude and said, "Let's pass a hat?"

Truman said, "Doubt many of us are carrying cash." Dude smiled. "Me be puttin' hat on counter *manana*.

Drop dough in."

Deb raised her hand, and Dude pointed at her. "I thought there are a lot of homeless people around here and others who don't have food. Dude, do you think we could take some of the money and give it to somebody who helps those people?"

Truman raised his hand. "That's a good idea. Lots of people slip through the cracks even with the organizations out there. Anything we can do would help."

Dude smiled. "Boss idea two. Bring big bucks and I'll figure where they can do good."

I was touched. I could be wrong, but it didn't appear there would have been many spare dollars among the group. I would contribute, although not five C notes.

Multiple discussions broke out, and Finley shrugged at Dude who raised his hands over his head and clapped. The talking stopped, and all eyes turned to Dude. "More ideas?"

The other female, Deb, I believe, said, "We could take turns and watch the Nativity scene from in the park across the street. Maybe the thief will come back to steal more of the stuff."

Finley said, "Good idea, Deb." He paused and pointed to each person in the room, except for Dude, Charles and me. "We could take, umm, let's see, three-hour shifts that'd cover all the time."

I thought it was a nice, generous offer, although from what Preacher Burl had said, only the Baby Jesus had significant value. I doubted the thief would return.

Dude said, "Cool. Sign up with Stephon for your shift."

Stephon rolled his eyes and muttered a profanity. Finley said, "More suggestions?"

No one said anything and Finley thanked everyone for coming and suggested since the group was called Surfers

Against Spirit of Christmas Thieves the meeting should end with a prayer, and asked if anyone would like to offer one. No one did, and Dude said, "Lip-sealed prayer, be boss." The room remained silent until Stephon said to hurry and sign up because he was going home.

Charles and I stayed after the group had left and Stephon handed Dude the sign-up sheet that had the next forty-eight hours covered before mumbling another profanity and slamming the door on the way out.

Dude watched him go. "He not be playing wise man in Christmas pageant."

Charles and I agreed.

Dude shook his head. "Think meetin' be good?"

I told him I was impressed by how compassionate the group was and how seriously they had taken the thefts.

"Be good peeps," Dude said. "But they—thanks for comin'."

Charles said, "But they what?"

Dude looked at the floor. "They be fearin' surfer be guilty."

"What do you think?" I asked.

Dude looked up from the floor and at the door. "Want not to be."

Chapter Eight

Like most kids, my early years were spent listening to my parents' music. Most of it was from a 1950s Magnavox record player where the sounds of Bing Crosby, Perry Como, and Frank Sinatra filled our modest home along with the smells of homemade spaghetti and chili. Being an only child, I had plenty of time to play by myself or listen to the music and my parents arguing who was the better singer: Frank or Perry. The rock-and-roll tsunami hit about the same time I was stretching my musical wings, and I fell hard for the rough, brash sounds that blared from seven-inch wide, thin, black, 45 rpm records; sounds dominated by Elvis Presley and Jerry Lee Lewis.

Then something happened. My friends were rocking along with Elvis, and I started enjoying the more mellow sounds of artists like Patsy Cline, Jim Reeves, and the piano of Floyd Cramer. Their songs were played on the rock-and- roll stations, so I didn't realize they were country. A year or two later, I would rather listen to Bill Anderson than to Dion; Roger Miller than to the Rolling Stones. I didn't want to be completely ostracized, so I did enjoy the Beach Boys and the Four Seasons, but country music either touched my feelings, my outlook, or simply sounded better.

When I learned someone on Folly was a country music singer and had charted a hit record, I made a point of getting to know him. True, his hit was pressed when I was fourteen, and the most fame he'd experienced since then was from several appearances on the Grand Ole Opry, all long before I was old enough to drive. Regardless, getting acquainted

41

with Calvin Ballew, better known as Country Cal, had been a trip, and not only down memory lane.

Four years ago, through a chain of events that would be fodder for a country song, and a story that's way too long to tell here, Cal became the owner of a run-down, rock-and- roll bar a block off Center Street and renamed it Cal's Country Bar and Burgers. Little positive could be said about the burgers, but as a country music bar, Cal's had it all: an old Wurlitzer jukebox stocked with traditional country songs, an open-mic night catering to area-wide wannabees, and the "country legend," Cal Ballew, performing on weekends. To quench his patrons' thirst, Cal featured a wide-ranging selection of beers as long as they wanted Bud or Miller, and a wine selection that included everything from red to white, with vintages dating back twelve months.

Crowds, using the term loosely, were thin in the middle of the week in December. Tonight, they were anorexic. Of the six people there, I recognized all but one, a woman who appeared to be in her late fifties who was sitting at the bar. What Cal's lacked in customer count, it made up for in Christmas decorations. Three—yes three—artificial Christmas trees were situated around the room. Their multiple strands of colorful lights matched the strands Cal had placed on each non-moving vertical surface. More were hanging from the ceiling.

The six-foot-three, seventy-year-old owner stepped out from behind the bar and greeted me with "Merry Christmas." He looked like a living version of Hank Williams Sr. Cal's long, gray hair inched out from around a Stetson that had traveled with him for forty plus years and

hundreds of thousands of miles around the South as he went from venue to venue singing his extensive list of traditional country tunes. In the spirit of Folly and the season, a strand of battery-operated LED lights was strung around the crown of his hat; he wore the rhinestone covered coat which had traveled as many miles as the Stetson; but, he had on bright red slacks and red tennis shoes. "Ho, ho, ho," came to mind as I gave him a holiday hug.

"I was getting us more drinks," Cal said and nodded to a table with one occupant. "Go on over. Wine?"

I succumbed to his high-pressure sales pitch and walked to the table occupied by Preacher Burl Ives Costello. Burl stood and pointed to an empty chair.

"Welcome."

Burl was the only person at the table so I pulled out the chair and now the *us* became Burl, Cal, and me. The preacher had told me before he'd moved to Folly he'd tended bar to make ends meet, so I wasn't surprised to see him in Cal's. Instead of beer, he had a can of Diet Coke in front of him. Cal returned and handed me red wine, my choice during the winter months, set another Coke in front of Burl, and flopped down in the chair. A slight mumbling from the other occupied table could be heard over the jukebox playing Skeeter Davis's "The End of the World."

I recognized the people at the table as employees of one of the town's small retail stores. From their colorful paper hats, I guessed it was their Christmas party.

I turned to Burl. "Heard anything about the missing statue?"

Burl shook his head. "No, Brother Chris. My heart is heavy and I feel such a tragic loss."

"The police are doing what they can. If it was taken as a cruel prank, it'll be found," I said.

Burl took a sip and set the can on the table. "Brother Chris, we are not going to be deterred. A kind, compassionate soul from the Methodist Church has offered the use of the Baby Jesus statue from his life-sized Nativity he displays in front of his home on Shadow Race Lane. He said it would be more visible in our setting and would tell whoever was overtaken by the Devil and absconded with our Jesus that good shall prevail."

Cal said, "Cool."

Burl looked at his drink. "Of course, his plastic statue is not as meaningful as the one taken, but I accepted his kind offer."

Eddy Arnold's version of "White Christmas" replaced "The End of the World."

Cal pointed to the jukebox. "My favorite Christmas song."

Burl said, "A pleasant one, to be sure."

"I have three versions on there: Eddy, Bing Crosby, and Loretta Lynn."

Each December, he added several Christmas songs to his musical selections. Believe it or not, he'd even added some recorded in the last two decades.

Burl was more interested in the statue than Cal's jukebox. "My heart is heavy about the theft, but my spirits have been bolstered. Several people who attend First Light have banded together and will be taking turns watching over the Nativity. And, in our common spiritual quest, members from the Baptist, Methodist, and the Catholic Church have volunteered to stand hand-in-hand with our flock overseeing the security of the Nativity." Burl smiled. "They will not be literally standing hand-in-hand, but will join our flock in watching over the manger and covering all hours of day and night. Praise the Lord."

"Burl," I said, "let me ask you something and I hope you don't take offense."

The preacher set his drink down. "You have my full attention and curiosity."

"I know how much the carved statue means to you, and was wondering why you left it unattended at the Nativity."

Burl looked at the jukebox, down in his drink, and at me. "Brother Chris, faith is the short answer. I had faith our fine residents would have cherished the icon as much as I did. I trusted the good in all of us would protect from anything untowardly from happening."

"Preacher," I interrupted, "you know——"

Burl raised his hand and stopped me. "No need to say it, Brother Chris, I once again misjudged the good in people."

"Preacher, it took only one misguided soul to take the statue. Your faith is admirable, and has served as an example for many of us."

I chose not to say it was naïve to believe the statue would have been safe where he had left it. I changed the subject and told Burl about the surfers and how they are keeping watch. If I hadn't, I could picture church members calling the police on the surfers, or the surfers trying to capture members of the Methodist Church, or combinations thereof. I also thought that while the plastic Baby Jesus would be safe, the hand-carved replica was still missing.

Cal leaned back and pushed his Stetson to the back of his head. I finished telling Burl about the surfers, and Cal said, "All will be well. I have faith." He turned to me. "Christmas, as Chris knows," he turned to Burl, "is my favorite time of year. All those years on the road, I spent most Christmas days in my car, eating the meager offerings from vending machines at the few service stations that were open, and looking around realizing there was no one to celebrate the holy day with. I heard stories from other men and women who were in the same sad fix—not only singers going from town to town, but homeless, or truck drivers, or folk between meaningful relationships."

"Sad, Brother Cal."

Cal shrugged. "It's what this is about." He pointed at each of the Christmas trees. "When the bar fell into my possession, the first thing I told myself, and all who would listen, was when the calendar page flipped to December 25, I was going to throw a—excuse my salty language Preacher—big-ass Christmas party and invite everyone who didn't have anywhere to spend the day."

"And he did," I added. "Country Cal's Christmas Celebration was a hit and it was packed."

Cal pulled his shoulders back and said, "Free food, free drinks, and free friendship. Nearly broke me. But it was damn—danged well worth it."

"That's wonderful, Brother Cal." Burl smiled. "I'm sure God was smiling over it."

Cal held up his beer. "Know what else I'm sure of, Preacher?"

Burl held up his Coke to toast Cal. "No sir, can't say I do."

"I'm sure this Christmas Day, if it's not too sacrilegious, you'll carry your priceless replica of the Baby Jesus in here, and I'll lead the group in singing whatever Christmas songs you request that'd best celebrate his birth. I promise."

I toasted the two, and prayed Cal's prophecy would come true.

The woman who had been seated at the bar had left, and the employees' Christmas party had broken up, and Cal twisted around in his chair and wished them a Merry Christmas as they left. Ned Miller was singing "From a Jack to a King," and we were the only three people left in Cal's when the door opened.

A man looked in the door and put one foot in like he was testing the water. He finally came in and closed the door. He was my height, had stringy, dark brown hair, a week-old beard, wore a faded army jacket, and gray dress slacks that were too large.

"Come in, Bernard," Cal said. "Come in."

"Where's everybody?" the man asked in a Southern drawl.

"Slow night," Cal said, stating the obvious. "Get you a beer?"

"Much obliged, sir," Bernard said, as Cal headed to the cooler.

Bernard stood in the middle of the room and looked around like he didn't know where to go when there were so many choices. Cal handed him a Budweiser and said, "Join us."

Bernard glanced at our table, over at the bar stools, and started to say something when Cal put his arm around him and ushered him our way.

Burl stood and reached out his hand to the stranger who looked like he would rather wrestle an alligator than join us. Burl introduced himself and pointed to me and told him who I was. I stood and shook Bernard's calloused hand.

"I'm Bernard M. Prine. Pleased to meet you, sir." Cal pushed him in the vacant chair. Bernard sat, wiggled, and took a long draw of beer.

Cal gave Bernard a brief bio on Burl and me. He told us Bernard "lived around town" and stopped in occasionally for a drink.

Bernard waited for Cal to finish, and offered a weak smile, "It's warmer in here than out there." He pointed at the door.

It seemed clear Bernard was one of the growing legions of home-less in the Charleston area.

"Can be pretty cold," Burl said.

Bernard ran his fingers through his beard stubble, looked at Burl, and snapped his fingers. "Your church's manger had Jesus stole, didn't it?"

"I'm afraid so, Brother Bernard."

"Do the police know who took it?"

"I don't believe so."

Bernard was peeling the label off his beer bottle. "Have you heard anything about it?" I asked.

Bernard's eyes darted from Burl to me. "Rumors."

"Rumors?" I said.

"Not that I believe them," Bernard said and glanced at Burl. "Heard it was a Devil worshipping cult, and one old drunk said it was a surfer." He shrugged. "That's it."

"Hear anything about someone stealing surfboards and packages off porches?" I asked.

Bernard gulped the last of his beer, and Cal asked if he wanted another before he could answer. Bernard nodded toward the bar, and Cal went to get another beer. The newcomer turned back to me. "No sir."

It seemed strange he knew about the statue theft but not the others. I told him what I knew, and Cal handed him his drink.

"News to me."

Cal waited to see if I was going to ask anything else, before he said, "Whatcha doing Christmas Day, Bernard."

Bernard coughed and laughed. "Let's see. Thought about flying to New York City and checking out the big Christmas tree, or maybe headin' to the Holy Land and seein' where the first manger was." He hesitated and held out his hands, palms up. "Instead, think I'll hang out around here and peek in windows at colorful trees and smiling kids. Why?"

Cal invited him to his Christmas celebration, Bernard gulped down his second beer, and Loretta Lynn sang "White Christmas."

"Might do that. I'll check my social calendar and see if I can work it in. Gotta be going."

"Beers are on me," Cal said.

Bernard reached in his pocket and pulled out a twenty-dollar bill and handed it to Cal. "Not this time, my friend. Got it covered."

Cal started to hand the money back, but Bernard waved his hand away and followed Cal to the cash register. I heard Cal say, "Win the lottery?" I couldn't hear Bernard's answer as Cal gave him change.

Bernard waved our direction, and said "Merry Christmas" as he headed out.

Cal returned to the table, and Burl asked, "What's Brother Bernard's story?"

Cal stared at the door as it closed behind Bernard. "Funny, it's the first time he's had money. Sorry, Preacher. What's the question again?"

"What's his story?"

"A sad one. Bernard's been in this area going on a year. I don't know about before, but he's been in and out of homeless shelters. The boy's got a quick temper and manages to get in fights in the shelters. Gets kicked out and after so many fisticuffs, not let back in." Cal lowered his voice and shook his head. "He's one I call ghost homeless. I hear there's more than a hundred of them in the area. There're a handful over here. They can't stay in shelters; they, honest to God, have nowhere to go. They bum food, sleep in the parks or behind vacation rentals when no one's renting them. Damned sad—excuse me, preacher."

"No excuse needed, Brother Cal. I know of a few of the people to whom you refer. One's a regular at First Light. I'm taking up a collection in Sunday's service to give to them. I won't give the money to the well-known shelters or organizations that care for the homeless, but to a man in my flock who knows places where it can do the best for the unknowns." Burl shook his head. "I'm not naive enough to fail to understand some of the money will go straight to alcohol or things worse. I only pray some of it will touch these folks in a good way."

Cal touched Burl's arm. "It will, Preacher. It will." Johnny Cash sang "Sunday Mornin' Comin' Down." And Cal's front door flew open.

Chapter Nine

S amuel took three steps in and slammed on the brakes like he was about to step on a rattlesnake. His hair stuck out from under a South Carolina Gamecocks ball cap. He glanced around the room and headed to our table.

"Mr. Landrum, Mr. Landrum, knew I'd find you here," he said and stopped and looked at Burl and Cal.

"How'd you know?"

He removed his cap and held it to his side. Static electricity wreaked havoc with his hair. "Everybody sort of knows this is where you hang out."

I needed to work on my image. I was here with a preacher, so that should count for something.

Cal said, "Getcha a Coke or bottle of water?"

"Umm, no, thank you, Mr. Cal. I'm okay."

"What can I do for you?" I asked. I watched as Samuel squeezed his cap and pushed his hair out of his face with the other hand.

"Could we talk to you?"

"We?"

"Jason and I."

"Where's Jason?"

Samuel looked down at the foot-worn thin, beer-stained carpet. "He's outside. He said his mom would sort of kill him if she found out he was in a bar. Could you come out and talk to us?"

I was in enough trouble with Amber and didn't want to incur more grief if she learned I was meeting with her son in Cal's sin-den. "Sure."

I grabbed my coat and followed the teen.

"Merry Christmas, Brother Samuel," Burl hollered as we walked away.

Samuel turned and smiled. "Thank you, Preacher Burl, sir."

Samuel led me a half-block up the street to the boys' bikes. Jason was sitting on his, and his eyes darted around like he was selling dope and hoped the police wouldn't see him. It was windy and cold, and he had his dark green, quilted jacket zipped to his neck. He wore gloves and a navy and gold Charleston RiverDogs cap.

"Thank goodness Samuel found you. We went to your house, and your car was there, but you didn't answer."

"What's going on?"

Samuel moved beside Jason and looked at him. "You tell him."

"I thought you," Jason said. "Never mind. Mr. Landrum, Samuel and I were riding by the Nativity a half hour ago and—"

Samuel interrupted. "Sort of like an hour ago."

"Okay," Jason said. "We were riding by, and Samuel saw a person—"

Samuel interrupted—again. "Suspicious character."

Jason jerked his head toward Samuel. "You going to tell it?"

"Sorry, go on."

Jason continued, "Anyway, the person, the suspicious character, was in the barn-like thing, and Samuel said he looked like he was going to steal something. We rode on by like we didn't see anything and parked our bikes and sneaked back to the barn."

"We weren't going to try to catch him, Mr. Landrum," Samuel added. "Honest. All we wanted to do was take his picture with the camera on my phone and tell the police."

"Humph," Jason interrupted. "Right when we were beside the barn, the person must have seen us. He took out running that way on Indian Avenue." He waved his hand toward the east. "We didn't get the picture so we started running after him."

Samuel said, "He had a big head start, Mr. Landrum. Our bikes were the other direction so we didn't have time to get them and ride after him. He was pretty swift but we were catching up."

"Until Samuel fell in a hole."

I glanced down and saw mud caked on Samuel's knee. "You okay?"

"Sure, nothing bad." Samuel looked at Jason. "Don't forget to tell him about what the stop sign did."

Jason gave Samuel a dirty look. "Bigmouth. Well, Mr. Landrum, after Samuel got up we started running again. It's mighty dark out there. I, umm, ran into a stop sign. Didn't see it."

Samuel laughed. "It honest to God meant stop."

"Are you okay?" I was beginning to sound like their mother.

Jason took off his cap, and I saw the red mark on his forehead. "Just a bruise. Mom'll kill me if she finds out."

"Then what happened?"

Samuel looked at Jason and said, "Sort of nothing."

"By the time we stopped and started twice, the thief was gone. It was dark."

"Did you get a good look at him?"

Samuel shrugged. "No. Don't even know if it was a guy."

"If it was a lady," Jason said, "she was tall, maybe as tall as Samuel. He, or she, had on an overcoat kind of coat."

"And one of those stretchy hats that pulls over the ears," Samuel said.

"Anything else?" I asked. "Fast," Jason said.

Samuel looked off into space like he was trying to picture the person. "And old, maybe even forty."

I considered giving Samuel another bruise. Jason said, "That's about it, Mr. Landrum."

"What made you think the person was going to steal something rather than looking at the Nativity? Could he have come from looking at the city's Christmas light display in the park across the street?"

Samuel looked at Jason, and at me. "He sort of looked sneaky. Didn't look like he was admiring the stuff, he wanted to steal it."

"But you only got a glance when you rode by?" Samuel said, "Yeah."

"Could you have thought he looked suspicious because someone had taken the statue and you thought the person would return to steal something else?"

"Umm, maybe," Jason said.

"And you were just riding by the Nativity?"

"Sort of," Samuel said.

Jason nodded.

And they expect me to believe that, I thought. I remembered what the surfers had said during their meeting. "Did you see anyone else?"

"Yeah," Samuel said. "The first, or maybe it was the second, time we rode by there was one of those surfer dudes sleeping in the park across the street. He was curled up in a sleeping bag on the side of the path with the bright Christmas displays, so we didn't figure he was going to steal anything." So much for the surfers' twenty-four-seven security.

"And that's it?"

"Yeah," Samuel said.

Jason said, "Yes sir."

Other than learning someone was looking at the Nativity, and he, or she, ran when two teenagers started chasing, a reaction that didn't seem abnormal considering the circumstances; and, learning the surfer patrol appeared less than effective; and, learning my two young friends were more clumsy than I would have thought; I hadn't heard anything to tie what happened to the theft of the statue, the surfboards, or the jewelry. Oh yeah, I was reminded Jason and Samuel had overactive imaginations.

Jason rubbed his shoe in the sand beside the sidewalk. "Mr. Landrum, you're not going to tell mom about this are you?"

I gave him a stern look. "Not this time. But listen, you said you were just riding by the Nativity, yet you told me you rode by two or maybe three times. Looks like you were riding by and hoping to catch the thief. Is that close?"

Samuel mumbled, "Sort of." Jason didn't say anything.

"That's what I thought. Now, what if the person you saw was the thief. He could have pulled a gun instead of running. Then what would have happened?"

Samuel took a step back. "Didn't think of that." A typical teenager's response: *I'm indestructible.*

"I want both of you to go home and spend time thinking about what might have happened. I know you want the thief caught. I admire you for that. I want it too, and so do the police. They're doing everything possible to find the statue." I stared at Jason and at Samuel. "Leave it to them." Jason hung his head, and Samuel stared at my feet.

Jason whispered, "Yes sir."

"Good," I said and pulled them close and gave them a hug. "Thanks for coming to tell me. Now get home."

Chapter Ten

I woke up hungry and started to go to the Dog for a hearty
breakfast, but the more I thought about last night and the potential danger Amber's son and his friend could have gotten into, I
wasn't ready to face her. If Jason had told his mom what he had done
yesterday and let it slip he came to talk to me, she'd meet me at the
door with a rolling pin, if those things still existed, rather than with her
warm smile. I wasn't ready for that fate this cold, crisp December
morning.

I searched my kitchen, a task that couldn't have taken more than
thirty seconds, since my food supply would be hard-pressed to feed a
family of four—mice. Hidden behind an empty cereal box I had saved
for unknown reasons, I found a muffin I had bought at Bert's a week
ago. It wasn't quite hard enough to pound a nail through hardwood, so
I stuck it in the microwave and softened it enough so it wouldn't shatter
my teeth.

It tasted better than eating the cereal box and gave me enough
energy to sit and worry about what Jason and Samuel were doing. They
were well intended, although had no idea what they were dealing with.
None of us did. Was the statue taken as a prank by someone harmless
who will abandon it and get a laugh out of it? Did someone who made
a habit of stealing take it; someone, if confronted, might resort to
violence rather than being caught? Considering how valuable Burl had
said the icon was, could it have been taken by someone who realized its
value and planned to sell it to a collector; someone who if confronted

would stop at nothing to get away with it? Was the person Jason and Samuel chased running because he, or she, planned to steal something or simply was startled by two teens wearing dark clothes?

I took the last bite, stared at the empty paper plate, and wondered if there was a connection between the theft of the icon, the surfboards, and the jewelry. All I realized after finishing the muffin and asking myself several questions was that I didn't have answers, but had a kitchen devoid of anything edible.

Most of my grocery shopping was restricted to Bert's Market, my iconic next-door neighbor, but I made at least one trip to the nearest big-box grocery every six months, whether I needed to or not. I spent the next hour driving off- island, stumbling dazed-and-confused through the aisles of Harris Teeter while pretending like I knew what I was doing. Christmas was around the corner, so I felt obligated to buy two boxes of Christmas cookies; holiday fruitcakes had a shelf life of three hundred years, so I grabbed one, and I selected a colorful box of Cheez-It crackers. I was more at home when I reached the wine department, and selected three bottles of the finest, screw top Cabernets. I headed to the checkout line feeling like a true grocery shopper.

On the drive home, I swung by the Nativity. Everything looked like it should and the borrowed Baby Jesus fit with the rest of the pieces. I didn't notice surfers or church members guarding the display but didn't stop to check. I was sure someone was nearby, and maybe awake. I pulled in the drive and was unloading grocery bags when I saw Jason and Samuel peddling up the street. My cottage faced one of Folly's busiest roads, and I hoped the teens realized bikes versus cars wouldn't be a fair match. I noticed a UPS truck a block ahead of my young friends. The truck turned left two blocks up, and Jason and Samuel did the same.

Oh great. I may as well have been lecturing to their bikes last night. I threw the bags back in the car and followed the mini-parade. The brown delivery truck had stopped in the street ahead of me, but I lost sight of Jason and Samuel. I was wondering where they were when Jason's head peeked over a shrub row a half block behind the truck.

The driver returned to his truck and moved on. I pulled off the side of the road ten feet behind the bicycles. Samuel was getting back on his when he heard me opening the car door. He jumped, and his bike clanked to the driveway where it had been hidden.

He grabbed his chest. "Geez, Mr. Landrum, you scared the shi— umm, crap out of me."

Jason was beside Samuel and chuckled at Samuel's reaction. "Didn't scare me. I knew it was you."

Samuel righted his bike and glared at Jason.

I slammed the door and stared at the boys. "What do you think you're doing?"

Samuel leaned against his handlebars and glanced at Jason. "Mr. Landrum, we're just out for a ride. The weather's not cold, and we're out of school. Peddling's good exercise, you know."

I pointed my thumb over my shoulder in the direction the UPS truck had gone. "And your ride had nothing to do with that truck?"

Samuel looked toward where I had been pointing. "Well—"

Jason interrupted, "It did."

Samuel said, "We were sort of following it."

"To catch the person who's stealing packages," I added and shook my head. "And what were you going to do if you saw him?"

Each boy reached for his phone.

Jason said, "We were going to take his picture and call the cops."

"That's all?"

Jason said, "Yes sir."

"When I pulled up, did you know who it was?" Jason nodded; Samuel shook his head.

"What if it was the thief? You might think you were sneaky, but you were about as conspicuous as two Hershey Kisses in a pile of M&Ms." They both looked at their feet. "I'm serious fellas. Leave it to the police."

They mumbled, groused, stood with slumped shoulders, and said they understood. I'm sure they meant it—for the moment.

CHARLES STOPPED by the house mid-afternoon. He threw his jacket on the table by the door and his Tilley on top of it. He wore heavy corduroy slacks and a blue, long-sleeve Widener University sweatshirt with a gold lion's head on the front.

"I've been thinking," he said.

Always dangerous, I thought. I motioned for him to continue.

"Surfboards, diamonds and gold, all things that could be sold."

I hoped that wasn't the result of his thinking. "So?"

"Cindy tells us every year thefts increase around

Christmas. Munchkin mouths to feed, gifts to buy, other stuff. Stealing the boards and the jewelry makes sense." He stared at me like I was supposed to say something profound. I didn't, so he continued, "But what's with stealing Jesus? I know it's valuable, but isn't most of the value sentimental? The other things could easily be pawned, except what pawn shop would give more than a few dollars for a wooden statue, even if it's Jesus?"

"Charles, we don't know the thefts are related."

"So true, oh wise one. Let's say they aren't, although I think they are. And, let's say whoever stole Jesus isn't building a hand-carved Nativity and needed a baby to stick in it and instead wants to turn the Christ Child into cash. Where would he be able to sell it for near what it's worth?" Since Charles had been thinking about it, I figured

I'd better give him the first crack at an answer. "Where?" He shrugged. "Heck if I know."

I wondered how much thought he'd given to come up with that.

"There's still a chance it was a prank," I said. "Don't that seem less likely every day that goes by?"

"True."

"Yep, it's what Cindy said this morning in the Dog. Said she's about given up on finding Jesus hanging around on the streets or lounging by the pool at the Tides Hotel. Dude was there and said if it was still around, his surfer group would find it. To tell the truth, he didn't seem more hopeful than the chief." Charles looked at the ceiling and out the window. "So back to my first question, where could the spirit of Christmas thief sell it?"

"Not a pawn shop," I said. Charles nodded.

"This was the first year for Burl's Nativity scene so no one knew about the statue from other years and planned to take it this season. If it wasn't spontaneous, it couldn't have been planned long. The thief probably wouldn't have taken it unless he knew there was a good chance he had a buyer."

"What's that tell us?" Charles asked. "Not much, just trying to talk it through."

"John Kennedy said, 'You know nothing for sure except the fact that you know nothing for sure.'"

I rolled my eyes.

Charles shrugged, "Thought it fit." He rubbed his five-day-old beard. "Anyway, the statue was old."

"According to Burl, a hundred years old and could have been more."

"From Germany," Charles added. "Antique dealer?"

Charles said, "Could be."

"A crooked one."

"Why crooked?" Charles asked. "Don't antique dealers buy old stuff?"

"Yes, but there's been one newspaper story about the theft, and it was on television and radio. No reputable dealer'd touch it."

"So all we have to do is find the crooked antique dealer, beat him in the head with thy rod and thy staff until he coughs up Baby Jesus."

"And how do you plan to do that?"

"Don't suppose any of the antique dealers' yellow page ads say anything about specializing in stolen Baby Jesus statues?"

It didn't deserve a response, and I was ready to suggest we talk to Chief LaMond, when the phone rang.

A high-pitched voice said, "Is this Chris Landrum?"

"Yes."

"This is Finley. You may not remember, but I met you in the Dog when I was with Dude. I also saw you at the surfers' meeting at the surf shop."

In fact, I did remember, mainly from the Dog. "Sure, I remember."

"Oh." He seemed surprised. "Well, I got your number from Dude. We're having a meeting tonight and wanted you to come."

"Who's meeting?"

"The group from the surf shop."

"Meeting where?"

"My house."

I said, "Why me?"

"Dude told me how good you were at catching bad guys and told me to invite you. We want to catch whoever's giving us a bad rap by stealing boards, and we're bummed about the statue. Could you come?"

I told him yes. He gave me directions and time, and I asked if Charles could come. He said, "Whatever."

I told Charles about the meeting. "Now we're getting somewhere." We were?

Chapter Eleven

Finley's house was on East Erie Avenue near 3rd Street, and four blocks from the ocean. The large, two-story, elevated structure's wood siding was black from weather and age with a second-floor balcony that spanned the front. A wide set of stairs led to the front door, and there was a newer set of stairs on the side of the house that led to the top floor. A tarp-covered vehicle and two motorcycles were parked under the house along with two sawhorses supporting sheets of plywood, and a Datsun pick-up truck missing its front two wheels was beside the house. Two cars were parked in the front yard, and another vehicle was off the side of the road with a newer model Ford pickup parked behind it with *Landscaping R Us* stenciled on the door. Two of the cars had surfboard racks. The house on each side of Finley's had fading *For Rent* signs in the front yards, while the houses across the street were newer and one was well landscaped and maintained, and probably occupied by permanent residents.

Rock music blared from the house, and the faint smell of marijuana greeted us at the door. Finley, wearing season-inappropriate cut-off jeans, and a sleeveless, Surfin' U.S.A. shirt that could have been as old as the Beach Boys song, also greeted us. He was more formal than during our previous meeting as he shook our hands and introduced himself as Finley Livers, which explained the mildew- covered sign over the door that said *Livers*. Under it was a newer wooden sign that read: *LIVErs TO SURF.*

Finley waved us in. "Welcome to my humble abode." Charles looked around. "Nice house."

Finley grinned. "Thanks, my granny left it to me. She owned it since the beginning of time. My parents are in California and didn't want it and my sister got a bunch of money from granny and lives in Houston."

Nosy Charles asked, "Live by yourself?"

"First floor," he said and nodded toward the ceiling. "Rent the upstairs to Ryan and Truman. We're all surfers." He yelled for us to hear him over the rock music blasting from deep in the house.

Charles looked toward the direction of the music and put his hands over his ears. "Neighbors ever comment on how much they like the music?"

Finley laughed. "Nah. Rentals on each side and in back. Seldom anyone's there." He lowered his voice. "Squatters sneak in, but they're in no position to complain. You the noise police?"

Charles made a faux gasp. "No way."

"Good," Finley said. "I didn't ask you here to talk about loud music. Come on back with the rest of the gang."

We followed Finley to a large sunroom that looked like a back porch that had been enclosed. There were ten mismatched chairs with seven of them occupied. Finley moved to the corner of the room and yanked the plug on a large, industrial-strength sound system. The smell of marijuana was stronger than it had been in the entry, but I didn't see the source.

The room turned silent, and most of the heads turned toward Charles and me. Someone mumbled, "The geezers have arrived." A couple of the others chuckled, and Finley moved to the center of the room.

"Folks, some of you know Chris, umm—"

"Landrum," I prompted.

Finley nodded. "And his friend Charles Fowler. They were at the meeting at the surf shop. Yell out who you are."

Two or three of them started talking, and Finley waved his arm. "One at a time."

"Teddye," said the young lady seated closest to me. I remembered her from the Dog and from the previous meeting.

Then the names flowed as smoothly as a choppy sea: Roscoe, Deb, Truman, Ryan, Todd, and the one face I was more familiar with, but still surprised to see, Dude's employee, Stephon.

After the introductions and my once again forgetting most of the names, Finley said, "Chris and Charles are here because of Dude. He said these two have caught more bad guys than all the police departments put together. Dude said if there's a crime, they'll solve it. He said, and I quote, 'They be best dee-tectives in galaxy.'"

Teddye giggled, and Stephon said, "Yep, it's what boss man said."

"Guys," Finley continued, "we're good surfers; we're good people. I've talked to each of you enough in the last few days to know you're bummed by the missing Baby Jesus. Some folks over here may not like us, heck, some think we're the scum of the earth. We love Folly and most of the time we love everyone's, well, most everyone's, tolerance and understanding. But, we don't know a pisspot full of, well, piss, about catching crooks. Stealing Jesus and the surfboards is a call to arms. It's why Chris and Charles are here."

He turned to the two of us. "We want to ask you what we can do to catch the scoundrel."

I wanted to duck behind one of the chairs. What did we have to offer? I glanced at Charles and waited for him to say something helpful. It was not to be.

"Gentlemen, and ladies," I said to fill the void. "We appreciate your concern and the invitation." Now, what do I say? "I don't have all the answers." I should have said I didn't have any of them. "I know a couple of things. You're taking turns watching the Nativity scene. That's great and will deter the thief from taking anything else."

"It don't get Jesus back," said the surfer to my right.

I believe it was Todd.

"True, but it helps protect the Nativity. That's important."

One of the others said, "Do you have any idea who it was? Are there witnesses to any of it?"

"No, umm ..."

"Truman," the questioner offered.

"No, Truman, as far as I know there were no witnesses."

Finley said, "Dude told me you'd catch him." I smiled. "I wish I had his confidence."

"What else can we do?" Finley asked.

Charles stepped in front of me. "Abe Lincoln said, 'It's not me who can't keep a secret, it's the people I tell that can't.'"

A couple of them chuckled. Truman said, "Funny." I resisted rolling my eyes, and said, "What Charles means is people, even the worst crooks, tend to run their mouths. They get satisfaction from what they did and feel the need to tell someone." Jason and Samuel came to mind. "The main thing you can do is remain vigilant. You can keep your ears open. Somebody may be bragging about stealing the statue or the other things. Don't do anything stupid. If you hear something, call the police. It's their job; let them do it."

Finley repeated, "Anything else?"

I knew it was a stretch but figured I didn't have anything to lose by asking. "Do any of you know any less than honorable people who might buy the statue, possibly an antique dealer?"

Roscoe said, "Because we're surfers you assume we know crooks —thanks."

Finley leaned forward. "I don't think it's what he meant."

"Absolutely not, Roscoe," I said. "If we're going to find out what's going on, we have to look at everything. We figured the thief wants money, and if so, he would have to find someone to pay top dollar for the Baby Jesus. A pawnshop or your average low life may buy the surfboards and jewelry, but not the statue. I figured you're smart people and might know or have heard about shady antique dealers. I'm sorry if I offended you."

Roscoe sighed. "Yeah, right."

Deb waved her hand in the air like she had a question or had to go to the restroom. Finley nodded her direction, and she said, "My uncle owns Winslow's Antiques on King Street in Charleston. If you want, I'll call him and see if he knows anyone who might buy stolen stuff."

Charles said, "That'd be great, Deb. I'll give you Chris's number. You can also tell your Uncle Chris, and I may come a callin'."

"Anything else?" Finley said for the third time. I shook my head, and Charles said, "Nope."

"That's all, Charles and Chris."

We were dismissed. Charles gave Deb my number, and he told her to call, day or night. Thanks, Charles.

Finley escorted us to the door and thanked us for coming. Inside, the sound system had been jacked up to the volume of a runaway freight train. On the way to the car, I noticed a light in the house next door. I hoped whoever it was had earplugs, but if it was a squatter, he probably couldn't afford them.

Chapter Twelve

The gods of winter had blessed Folly with a mild Friday so I walked to Cal's for a heart-unhealthy cheeseburger and to enjoy a few hours of country music. The temperature was mild, although I still needed a heavy jacket and winter Tilley. Two of the houses along the way were wrapped in Christmas lights. The sight reminded me of my dad driving mom and me around nearby subdivisions the week before Christmas and looking for the most colorful displays. A few of the years there was snow on the yards and roofs, and the colorful lights and wooden Santas and snowmen waved to us from the white lawns. I realized how old-fashioned I was since I preferred the low-tech displays with their large, colorful light bulbs rather than the LED displays that are common today. And, don't get me started on the ubiquitous blow-up decorations that may be attractive at night but during the day, when their inflating fans are off, look like Santa got run over by a steamroller.

I approached Cal's, smiled, and admitted most of my problems with today's decorations were because I was getting old and stuck in my ways. I smiled because I refused to get depressed over my rapid journey to Geezerland.

Friday nights in Cal's were festive. Locals and many vacationers stopped by to enjoy the retro atmosphere, the retro country hits, and the retro owner who entertained. No one would count the weekend before Christmas as crowded, but most of the tables were full, and Cal was on stage in his retro-rhinestone coat, his Stetson, cowboy boots, and strumming his Martin acoustic guitar.

Cal was on the last notes of "Oh, Lonesome Me" as I moved to the only vacant seat at the bar. His spine curved toward the antique microphone. "Ladies and Gents, I'm a goin' to finish the set with one of my favorite songs from my dear friend, God rest his soul, Hank Williams Sr. Hope you like my version of "Hey, Good Lookin'." He winked at two white-haired ladies sitting at the table closest to the stage and began the song he had sung three thousand times. Kristin, who typically waited tables, was behind the bar while Cal put a glass of Cabernet in front of me before I could take off my coat and decide what I wanted. She, of course, got the drink right, and I told her I'd take a cheeseburger and fries. She said she could probably find them somewhere in the kitchen.

Cal finished the song. "Now, before I take a pause for the cause, I've got a request." He waved his hand at the crowd. "All of us are lucky. We have somewhere to hang our hats." He hesitated and touched the brim of his Stetson. "We have food, and many of us have our health and someone to share life with." He paused and shook his head. "But not everyone on Folly is that fortunate. Sad as it might be, we have our share of homeless. Yes, people who have to depend on the kindness of others to make it through these cold nights and keep food in their bellies. With Christmas rolling around next week, I'm taking up a special collection with the donated dough going to the homeless."

I looked around and with the exception of one table where a couple was more interested in texting, or whatever they were doing with their phones, everyone focused on Cal. "Now open your wallets. Open them wide. When I'm on my way to take a pis—umm, to powder my nose, I'm going to walk by your table and hold out my hat. Folks less fortunate than you'll appreciate your kindness. And I'm aging a bit and coins are heavy, so make sure you drop in lightweight paper money. Appreciate it."

Cal removed his Stetson, smoothed down his hair, and headed to the table where the white-haired ladies were rooting in their purses searching for lightweight paper money.

I sipped wine and looked to see who was here. I didn't notice them when I came in, but Charles and Preacher Burl were huddled at the table in the back corner. I told Kristin where I would be and maneuvered around two tables to visit my friends.

I tapped the preacher on the shoulder, and Charles said, "Wondering when you were going to stop ignoring us."

"Didn't see you. Hi, Preacher."

"Join us, Brother Chris," Burl said and pulled out the chair beside him.

I said, "Working on your sermon?"

Burl laughed. "Yes, Brother Chris. I'm thinking about adding some of Cal's tunes to my hymn selections."

"May attract more sinners," I said. "No shortage already, Brother Chris."

Charles ignored us and had turned to the table behind ours and was talking to Finley, the surfer whose house we'd been to last night. The man with Finley was also at the meeting, but I didn't remember his name. The third person at the table was someone I didn't recognize. Charles held up his hand for Finley to stop whatever he was saying. Charles waved toward me. "Chris, you remember Finley and Truman don't you?"

I was getting older, but not senile, and said, "Hi, guys."

Finley waved at me. "Hey, Chris, meet Mary Ewing, a friend of ours."

Mary was in her early twenties, anorexic thin, with dirty blond hair, and a sad smile. She avoided my eyes and mumbled, "Pleased to meet you."

I said hi to Mary, and Finley and Truman resumed their conversation.

Charles leaned closer to their table. "Pull up a chair."

Finley looked at his friends and shrugged. "Sure." He slid their table close to ours. Burl moved his chair so the tables could touch. Mary scooted her chair closer but looked like she would rather not move.

Kristin arrived with my food, and Charles asked if the three newcomers wanted anything and said I was buying. Each said another drink would be nice.

Kristen headed to the bar at the same time Cal waved his Stetson in our faces. Burl, Truman, and I reached for our wallets. Charles didn't carry a driver's license and didn't have credit cards, so he had no use for a wallet, but pulled a twenty out of his pocket and dropped it in the hat. Burl and I did the same, and Finley started to add a five to the mix, hesitated, and said, "Where did you say the money was going?"

Cal hesitated, and said, "The needy." Finley said, "Who decides?"

"That's a good question, my friend. I'm turning it over to Preacher Burl."

Burl put his arm on Finley's shoulder. "Brother, umm—"

The surfer said, "Finley Livers."

"Brother Finley, I'm Burl Ives Costello and preach at First Light

Church. In good weather, we meet on the beach. In winter, our services are on Center Street."

Finley interrupted, "I've been a couple times. You're doing a fine job."

Burl looked closer at him like he was trying to remember. "Sorry, didn't recognize you. Anyway, at Sunday's service I'll be taking up a collection to provide food and warm clothing to needy families identified by my flock. Brother Cal has agreed to donate tonight's offering—collection—to what we get."

I interrupted and told the preacher that Finley and Truman were part of a group of surfers who're trying to find out who stole the Baby Jesus.

"Ah," Burl said. "So I've heard. God bless you. Please tell me if there is anything I can do to aid in your quest. I will be praying of course, but it may take more than that."

"Heard who did it?" Truman asked.

"Afraid not," Burl said. "I'm still hopeful it was a malicious prank, and the Baby Jesus will turn up."

Finley leaned closer to Burl. "I heard a rumor someone knew and told someone else a coven of witches took it. Wanted to ruin Christmas."

Burl looked at him. "I'm sure there are people with those inclinations, Brother Finley, but I don't put much credence in a rumor about someone telling someone who told someone—think I have it right."

Mary kept glancing around the room but smiled at Burl. "Reverend Costello, what time does church start?"

Burl returned her smile. "Sister Mary, call me Preacher Burl. We gather a few minutes before eleven and have fellowship around a container of lemonade, and as a concession to winter, coffee. The service begins at eleven. Shall you be joining us?"

She lowered her head again. "Are youngsters welcome?"

"Sister Mary, all are welcome. Do you have a child?" She smiled. "Two, Preacher Burl. Jewel's six and

Joanie just turned two."

"I'd love to see the three of you there."

Cal stood and leaned close to Burl. "My fans are getting antsy. Gotta start another set. Got something you can put this in?" He pulled the paper money out of his hat, turned each bill going the same direction, and handed it to Burl.

"Think it'll fit in my pocket. Thank you, Brother Cal." Burl looked down at the money. "This'll make some people mighty happy."

Finley leaned closer to Burl and pointed at the wad of cash.

"Preacher, I sure hope you don't give the money to the places that always get it. I drive a truck for Quality Auto Parts and deliver stuff to repair shops. I'm always driving in alleys and behind stores and see people, homeless, I suppose, who don't have anywhere to go and stay in the shadows. My dad worked for a welfare agency back home and was always telling us about those forgotten folks—he called them the invisible ones.

Burl nodded. "Brother Finley, throughout my years in the ministry, I have seen, and gotten to know some of those to whom you refer. A few had too much pride to ask for help; others are so socially inept that they can't adjust to being around others; and, there are other reasons I can't think of now."

"That's who I'm talking about, Preacher Burl."

Burl held the cash in front of him. "Brother Finley, I assure you these generous donations will go to those in dire need."

Cal opened the set with Freddie Hart's "Trip to Heaven," and the noise in the bar increased as customers talked over the music. Kristin returned with the drinks, and Mary looked at her watch.

"The Lord Knows I'm Drinking," was next on Cal's play list and we ran out of things to talk about. The surfers and Mary sipped their beers, and Charles tapped his bottle on the table in time with the music. Mary leaned forward. "I've got to get back to my gals."

Finley said he'd drop her off on his way to take the next shift at the Nativity. Truman stood and said he'd go to the Nativity with Finley.

Burl said, "I look forward to seeing you at our service Sunday."

Only Mary had said anything about attending.

Mary smiled, Finley shrugged, and Truman reminded Burl to not forget the needy.

"Nice folks," Charles said as they headed to the door. And Cal, saying it was in the spirit of the Christmas season, started singing "Grandma Got Run Over By a Reindeer."

Chapter Thirteen

The temperature on the last Saturday before Christmas was expected to struggle to reach the mid-forties with a light drizzle darkening the already gray day. I would have preferred to stay home, but realized even though I had made my semi-annual trek to Harris Teeter, I had little food in the house, and as the old saying goes, or should go, man can't live on fruitcake alone. I called Charles and asked if he wanted to meet for lunch at the Grill and Island Bar, a large restaurant that overlooked Center Street and was close to my friend's apartment. He said he could work it in his busy schedule and would meet me there.

The manager met me at the door. "Charles told me to tell you you're late and as usual he's waiting for you out there." He pointed to the patio.

Charles waved his watch-less wrist as I approached the booth located near a portable heater.

I got his meaning. "What'd you do, jog?"

"Jog," Charles laughed. "You're quite a jokester—a tardy jokester."

Dillon, a waiter whom I'd met on several other visits, was quick to the table and put me out of the misery of having to listen to Charles complain. I ordered a Coke, and Charles said, "Beer, any kind as long as it starts with Bud."

Charles watched Dillon leave and said, "It was nice of Cal to take up a collection. It'll help folks have a Christmas."

I agreed and asked, "Are you going to First Light tomorrow?"

"You bet."

Until Preacher Burl started First Light, Charles and I had probably attended church services about as often as a sea otter recites the Pledge of Allegiance. In the last few months, he has attended almost every week. Preacher Burl has a knack for reaching a wide range of people and making everyone feel welcome, regardless of social status or level of religious commitment.

Charles waited for Dillon to leave our drinks and continued, "Probably'll be a full house being close to Christmas and Burl's been telling everyone about the special offering."

As he was talking, I looked across the street and saw Jason and Samuel peddle up the sidewalk and turn on Indian Avenue. I hadn't realized I'd said anything when Charles said, "What's with *huh*?"

I pointed across the street. "Samuel and Jason. They're on their way to stake out the Nativity. They're determined to catch the thief and I'm afraid they may get in trouble." I told him about them following the UPS truck.

Charles took a sip of beer and chuckled. "Sounds like something we'd do."

We hadn't ridden around on bikes, but we had staked out a few spots, and had stumbled on some things we shouldn't have.

"True, although we're a tad older than those two, and more mature."

"Does tad mean a half century?" I nodded.

"That's what I thought. Folks'd give you a powerful argument against us being more mature."

"Either way, I worry about them."

Charles looked in the direction of the crèche. "What do you think the odds are on the thief trying to take something else?"

I looked across the street. "Low to nonexistent." Charles nodded. "Church members, surfer group, and now Jason and Samuel. Mother and substitute child may be sleeping in heavenly peace, but they're being guarded more closely than Colonel Sanders' secret fried chicken recipe."

"It makes them feel like they're doing something to help."

Charles returned to his beer, took another sip, and looked at me. "So how're we going to catch him?"

I shrugged and looked up and saw Chief Cindy LaMond standing beside the booth and pointing at Charles's beer.

She wore a down jacket and jeans, so I figured she was off duty. "Want to join us?"

"If you'll scoot your lard ass over so I can fit in the booth."

Cindy had a way of making everyone around her feel good. I moved over, she sat, and Charles said, "Find Jesus?"

"Golly, Charles, I never knew you were interested in my salvation."

Charles huffed. "You know what I mean."

Cindy smiled. "Of course I do. The answer's no."

"Looking less like a prank," I said.

Cindy said, "You're right." She looked around to see if anyone was close enough to hear. No one was. "That's not the worst of it."

Charles leaned closer to the chief. "What?"

"At seventeen hundred hours, yesterday, a delivery truck left a package about the size of a shoebox on the porch at a house in the five hundred block of East Arctic, and—"

Charles interrupted—one of his better-honed talents, "What's with the seventeen hundred hours jabber? You forget how to talk English?"

"Practicing. Our mayor told me I needed to start speaking like a professional law enforcement official. Figured translating big and little hand time to military gobbledygook would confuse the citizenry enough to sound professional. You want to waste time talking about my vocabulary or listen to what I was saying?"

Brian Newman was the mayor and had been chief for many years before he was talked into running for his current position. He had appointed Cindy chief over a few officers with more seniority. He had said he wanted to shake things up in the force and Cindy was the person to do it. Brian was right. He also was a friend and father of Karen Lawson, the lady I had been dating.

Charles tilted his head to the left and to the right. "Continue."

"At eighteen hundred hours—six hours past noon to you citizen folk—the homeowner got home and went to the porch to get the package."

"And it was gone," Charles interrupted.

"Shut your pie hole. I'm telling the story."

He made a zipping his lips motion.

"Good," Cindy said. "And it was gone."

I stifled a chuckle. "What was it?"

"Don't suppose it was what the thief had hoped for. It was a box of printer ink cartridges, total retail value ninety- eight bucks. And it's worth that much only if you have a highfalutin color printer to stick them in. The point is, the thievin' continues."

Charles said, "No one saw the thief?"

"Sort of."

Charles rubbed his chin. "Sort of saw him, sort of didn't see him? Sort of what?"

Cindy gave an exaggerated nod. "Yep. Now where's my beer." She turned and watched Dillon head our way.

We ordered more drinks and after a brief discussion, decided that since it was almost Christmas, our lunch could consist of sharing slices of Southern Pecan Pie, and Chocolate Lava Cake. Cindy was right to call me lard ass.

"Chief, did someone see the thief?" I asked to follow up on her less than illuminating comment.

"See, no; record, yes—sort of. A paranoid couple two houses down have security cameras all over their property. When the husband saw the police lights at the house with a printer and no ink, he came strolling up the street and announced he may have caught, in his words, 'the perp on camera.' To answer your question Charles, he sort of did. His camera wasn't close enough to catch much. All we could tell from the digital file—that's professional talk for what in your day was called tape—was that the thief was a male because of his height. We judged him to be five nine or ten."

Charles said, "Could have been a tall woman."

"It's possible, sir, although he lumbered away from the scene of the crime like a guy rather than like a graceful lady." She glared at Charles. "Now, back to my description, he wore a dark hoodie with the hood pulled up over his head. He appeared to be on foot since he ran out of the yard and away from the camera instead of hopping in a car."

"That's it?" Charles said. "Affirmative, sir."

Dillon returned with our lunch and interrupted Cindy's professional cop-speak. Charles had a mouth-full of pecan pie, but it didn't stop him from asking, "Know any crooked antique dealers?"

Another of Charles's areas of expertise was changing verbal directions without giving a turn signal or concern for what others had been saying.

Cindy, being the lady in the group, swallowed a bite of lava cake, wiped a napkin across her lips, and squinted at Charles. "Why? You steal a Roman pissing pot and want to turn it into cash."

"Umm, no," Charles said. "Just—"

Cindy snapped her fingers. "Don't tell me. You think whoever stole Baby Jesus will try to sell it, and no pawn shop will give him much, and no reputable antique dealer will want to put his white glove-covered pinkie on it."

Cindy wasn't chief only because of her pretty face and uncanny ability to shake-up the establishment.

Charles said, "Yes."

Cindy took another bite and said, "And you think you're smarter than the police and figured that out all by yourself while the cops are sitting around counting our toes?"

"Never."

Cindy said, "Mongoose manure."

"Mongoose?" Charles said.

"Charles, for your personal edification—how's that for professional?"

Charles said, "Move on, Chief."

Cindy smiled. "For your edification, at thirteen hundred hours yesterday—hell, I'm confusing myself. One o'clock yesterday, one of my guys contacted the sheriff's office to see if they were aware of antique dealers who may lean toward the wrong side of the law." Cindy took another bite of cake.

I waited, knowing she would tell us what she had learned. Charles, who counted patience as one of the deadly sins, said, "And?"

"And this is good cake. Stuff your mouth with some, Charles, so I can finish talking."

Charles stared at the chief.

"And the detective who specializes in that sort of thing is on a Christmas vacation with his family somewhere where Christmas trees look like cactuses. The guy my officer spoke to, said he wasn't aware of any crooked dealers, but would call the cactus man and ask him to call us."

Once again, Charles looked at his wrist. "He hasn't called you yet?"

"Charles, I'm off today and don't know."

"You've got to find out, so—"

Cindy waved her hand in Charles's face, sighed, and grabbed her phone.

"Is Officer Spencer around?" she asked after a long delay before someone answered. There was another delay and she said, "Have him call me ASAP, stat, or whatever our cop code number is for *now*." She hit end call and rubbed her forehead. "This pro-cop crap is giving me a headache."

I said, "Cindy, if the thief's trying to sell the statue, crooked antique dealers would be only one source. There're collectors who'd have an interest. How would we find them?"

Cindy moved her hand from her head. "We?"

"Meaning you."

"Right. Anyway, I asked Spencer to ask the detective that when he calls from vacationland. It's a long shot. I'm afraid it'll take a heap of luck for us to find Baby Jesus. I hate it for Preacher Burl, and to be honest, everyone here. A lot of folks who don't know the preacher or who don't attend his, or any church, but they look at the stealing of the statue as a personal affront to all who love Folly." She shook her head. "Gotta run some errands for hubby. He hasn't managed to get out of the store since I don't know when. It's revolting how many toilet plungers he sells this time of year."

It was more than I wanted to know. Charles said, "But—"

Once again, Cindy stuck her hand in his face. "Charles, as soon as I learn anything from the vacationing detective, I will not take another breath without calling to give you the scoop. Of course, you won't be home and since you're too cheap to buy an answering machine or one of these new inventions called a cell phone, I'll call Chris."

"That'll do."

Cindy put on her coat. "Good, because that's all you'll get." She headed to the exit.

Charles and I accomplished two things. First, we gained seventy pounds from stuffing ourselves with the rest of the holiday season entrees. Second, Charles decided we should go to Charleston and stop at antique shops and see if we could learn if they knew of any crooked ones. I had learned years ago once Charles was on a mission, little, if anything, could stop him. Instead of asking how he had planned to get this information, or what he planned to do with it if he was able to learn anything, I said I'd pick him up Monday morning. We did know one antique dealer to talk to.

Chapter Fourteen

First Light's foul weather sanctuary was on Center Street in a storefront next to my gallery. Christmas was the prime selling season for most retailers, but with so few vacationers here, and the apparent shortage of residents who couldn't live without having my photographs adorning their walls, I hadn't bothered to open the last two weekends and had taped a note on the door saying: *Open by Appointment*, along with my phone number. I hadn't received any calls, so at least I wasn't stuck in the gallery waiting for desperate buyers. I would miss having the gallery, but was looking forward to not having to consistently write checks that far exceeded its revenue.

A generous benefactor had donated money for the church to rent the space and remodel and members of Burl's flock had spent hours converting the long-vacant retail shop into a place to hold services. Before they had the storefront, Burl was forced to cancel services during inclement weather. I arrived fifteen minutes before the service was scheduled to begin, and was surprised by the large number of people already there. The room only held fifty, and it was full. Preacher Burl was near the door and talking to Mel and Caldwell, two friends of mine. He saw me and patted Mel on the back and pointed him toward the coffee urn at the front of the sanctuary. Mel and Caldwell headed to the liquid refreshments, and Burl welcomed me.

"Great turnout," I said.

"God has been good to us this morning. I have spread the word all week about taking a special collection and," he hesitated and waved his hand around the room, "several have come for that reason." He grinned. "Of course, they also desire to hear the word of the Lord, and, to be honest, the last Sunday before the day celebrating the birth of Jesus Christ, brings out the twice a year church goers."

Lottie, who had attended since the beginning and who had put in hours of manual labor fixing up the building, tapped the preacher's arm. "Preacher Burl, the coffee pot needs your delicate touch. Sorry, Brother Chris, I must borrow our leader."

I told her it was fine and looked around. Charles was in front of the room talking to Dude, Finley, Truman, and Deb. Roscoe was off to the side looking uncomfortable. I hadn't seen any of them here before. I barely recognized Bernard, the homeless man to whom Cal had introduced me. He had slicked back his hair, and had on a clean dress shirt, but the same slacks he had worn when he was in Cal's. He was talking to the tall, lanky singer who attended as seldom as Finley and his crew. Stephon, from the surf shop, was by himself and seated in the back pew, and there were several couples I recognized from other services but didn't know their names. A few others I didn't know were milling around.

Preacher Burl fiddled with the coffee pot and looked at his watch. He walked to an old lectern that had spent its better years in a high school gymnasium and cleared his throat. He didn't get the results he'd wanted, so he cleared it again; this time much louder, and said, "Please repose thyselves." He pointed to the pews

Several of his flock moved toward the pews; a few, probably those here for the first time, looked at him like "Repose thyselves?" Everyone moved to a seat. By habit, I headed to the back pew, but before I was seated, the door opened, and Mary looked in. She spotted me and I waved for her to enter. She stepped outside and seconds later she tiptoed in followed by two children. I slid to the center of the pew so there was room for them. The children's clothes fit poorly and had been mended in multiple places.

Preacher Burl raised both hands over his head. "Please silence thy portable communication devices."

To say he religiously began each service with those words, would be sacrilegious, but regardless, he had. To make sure newcomers understood his meaning, he waved his cell phone over his head.

Burl led us in the first hymn, and because of a shortage of vocal talents, he stopped after two verses. William Hansel, a close friend and regular at First Light, was out of town and unable to lend his incredible singing voice to the congregation. Burl shared what led up to the birth of the baby Jesus that I suppose is a ministerial requirement this close to

Christmas. The children began to wiggle in their seats and look around but weren't talking. Each time one of them started to stand, Mary touched the child's arm and nodded at the seat. I was impressed how well behaved they were.

After another failed attempt for the group to carry a tune, Burl reached under the pulpit—lectern—and pulled out a wicker basket. "Brothers and sisters, as many of you know, we are privileged to be able to come out on such a chilly morn, healthy enough to get here on our own, and from the looks of some of us, have no shortage of nourishment." Burl patted his ample stomach and chuckled. "For many, some here on Folly, food and shelter are luxury items and outside their reach. Can we feed, clothe, and shelter all of God's creatures who are less fortunate? No, but what we can do is to identify the most needy and give them some light on their Christmas morning, a toy for the most innocent of children, and food to nourish their stomach and spirit."

Burl bowed his head and gave us a moment for his message to sink in. He raised the basket. "Now is time for us to do our share. Please reach deep in your pockets and help brighten someone's Christmas. While Sister Lottie walks among you so you can contribute, I will tell you how we have selected the recipients of this love offering." He handed Lottie the basket. "I've named a small group from our flock, headed by Brother Dennis Richardson, a social worker with ties to local charities, to determine where our contributions will go. He's identified two such charities and with agreement from the other members of the group, will be dividing your givings between the two."

I glanced at Mary and her two children and wondered if she would receive some of the money or the food it would buy. I also saw her open a small purse with a broken zipper and pull out a wadded dollar bill and three coins. She handed the dollar to the oldest child, and the change to the youngest and whispered something to each of them. Lottie reached our pew and each child smiled and dropped the money in the basket. I turned my head to keep from tearing up.

Lottie returned to the front of the room and handed the basket to Burl, and he looked in and smiled. "Praise the Lord. You have made Christmas a time to rejoice for those in need. I thank you." He led the flock in singing "Joy to the World."

Maybe the spirit of the Lord was present. Our singing sounded decent.

CHARLES, Lottie, and I stayed after the service to help Burl clean the sanctuary. Lottie was in her forties and had been beautiful in her younger days, but life's trials and tribulations had taken its toll. She was still attractive, but wore baggy clothes to disguise her trim figure, and her dark-brown hair had seldom met a brush. We'd met the first time I'd met Burl when she and a couple of other volunteers were renovating the space. Today she wore newer clothes than usual and had made an effort with her hair.

She was in good spirits as she cleaned up around the coffee pot. "How'd we do, Preacher?"

Burl rested the basket on his lectern and had counted the donations. "Sister Lottie, we have 275 reasons for which to be thankful."

"Wonderful, Preacher Burl," Lottie said and hugged him.

There had been speculation Lottie was "sweet on" Burl, but if it was true, no one had offered proof. She had credited him with turning her life around, and she never missed a service, but it was all anyone knew.

"Yes," Burl said. "Add the $150 donated Friday evening by the fine patrons of Cal's, and we can give $425 to Brother Dennis to distribute."

Charles had been folding chairs, which had been added to the room to accommodate the crowd. He finished and said, "Preacher Burl, Lottie, could Chris and I take you to lunch to celebrate?"

Translated, it meant could we take you and Chris will pick up the check.

Burl looked at Lottie and at Charles. "Brother Charles, have you known me to turn down a meal?"

Charles smiled.

"And where shall we break bread for our celebratory meal?"

"The Dog," Charles said. "Lottie, join us?"

She shook her head. "I need to finish, there's still cleaning to do."

Burl said, "You can do it later. Why don't you come?"

She grinned. "That sounds nice."

Burl put the money in a small lock box and put it in the bottom drawer of the old metal desk. Lottie and Burl walked side-by-side with Charles and me following. The Dog was packed; members of Folly's other churches occupied most of the tables. We took a table that had just been vacated, and Amber was there with menus as soon as we were seated. Burl said water when asked for our drink order; the rest of us followed suit. Amber didn't make eye contact with me the entire time.

"Preacher, that was a fine message this morning," Lottie said. "Christmas is such a wonderful time, especially for youngsters."

"Thank you, Sister Lottie. I hope the offering will bring smiles to some children and food to their stomachs."

She smiled and twisted her hair around a finger. I was beginning to think Charles and I should move to another table. Maybe she was sweet on the preacher.

Charles didn't take kindly to being left out. "Preacher, what was Christmas like for you as a child?"

Burl looked at Lottie and turned to Charles. "I once told you I grew up on a cattle farm in Illinois. I confess church wasn't big on my parents' agenda and we seldom attended." He stopped and smiled. "The Christian Church in town had a grand Nativity scene, one of those living ones where real people played characters from the Bible. There were animals in the scene, and one of the deacons came to dad and asked if he could furnish a couple of cows. There weren't a lot of donkeys around and finding a camel in our neighborhood was out of the question." He laughed. "Dad didn't want to. He grumbled and said his cows had more important things to do than be actors."

Lottie must have been taking lessons in impatience from Charles. "What happened?"

Burl smiled. "Mom wasn't having any of it, and she told dad Christmas only came once a year, and she figured we could do without the cows for five nights. Dad gave in but said someone had to be with his animals at the Nativity.

I remember him stomping his foot on the floor and saying he wasn't going to be the one so mom said I could do it and it'd be good for me. I wasn't certain how it would be good."

Lottie put her hand on Burl's arm. "That's sweet. Did you do it?"

"It wasn't how I would have chosen to spend those long, cold, pitch-black nights, but if mom said it was what I was doing, it was what I was doing. It turned out I was glad I did and continued the tradition the next two Christmas seasons. Each night, dad would truck us to the Nativity but wouldn't get out, so I had to get the animals over to the scene. Most of the time the cows seemed bored by it all, but I watched the people from all over town as they inched close to the Nativity. They treated it with so much reverence that I was amazed." He shook his head. "To me, it just seemed like a bunch of people dressed up like they did in the old days and stood around the manger. To see the kids holding their parents' hands and tiptoeing closer to see Baby Jesus was something else. Some adults fell to their knees in prayer. It was life altering."

Charles asked, "Was it a real baby?"

"No one thought it would be a good idea to place a live child in the manger, but the baby was the only thing that wasn't real. I was fifteen the first time and didn't understand the impact the dressed-up people and animals had on people who came to see it. Heck, I'd been around cows my entire life and didn't see anything special about them other than giving us milk and stepping on my foot when I wasn't careful."

I asked, "Is that why you wanted to have First Light's Nativity, and were so upset when the Baby Jesus was taken?"

"Brother Chris, watching those people left a lifelong impression on me. I almost cried long ago when Christmas Eve arrived, and we stopped doing the Nativity. When I found my way to God years later, I told myself if I was able to help facilitate such a symbolic representation of what happened all those hundreds of years ago, I would." He pointed to the door. "There aren't a lot of cows on Folly, and sheep are in short supply, so I bought the plastic ones so we could have the Nativity. When Brother Robert offered us the Baby Jesus and told me its story, I'm not ashamed to say, I was ecstatic."

Charles said, "You'd also be hard-pressed to find three wise men around here. Present company excluded."

Burl laughed, accomplishing Charles's intent. The preacher turned serious. "I suppose it answers why it is so important." He lowered his head. "And now I feel like someone stuck a dagger through my heart. I know a carved piece of wood is only wood, but it means much more."

Amber arrived with our drinks and took our food order. She only looked my way when she asked what I wanted. I couldn't understand how she could be so angry about whatever she thought I told Jason and encouraged him to do.

Amber left to put in our order, and Lottie said, "Preacher Burl, the Baby Jesus you were given may be missing, but there's the one the kind man from the Methodist Church lent us, and look at all the good you've done this Christmas. Look at today's collection and the money from Cal's. Look at all the people you've touched over the year. You've done good."

"Thank you, Lottie." He asked each of us what we were doing Christmas.

We shared our plans, as meager as they were. Amber arrived with lunch and all conversation stopped. Burl told us how much preaching increased his appetite and patted his stomach as if we wouldn't figure out where the food was headed. Lottie shared that before Burl and his ministry had come into her life, she had gone days wondering where her next meal was coming from. She said he had given her faith and miraculously a bounty of food had followed. Burl was quick to point out it wasn't he but was the Lord who had provided. Again, she gently touched his arm.

Burl reminded us about the Christmas Eve service. "I'd prefer to hold it at midnight, but am in touch with my flock enough to know if I waited that late, I'd be talking to myself, and maybe a couple of our loveable intoxicated citizens." He smiled. "It's why I told everyone seven would be a good time." From the pulpit—lectern—he had said seven and if the weather was decent, the service would be on the beach. He nodded and looked at Charles and at me. "You will be joining me in sharing the blessed word of the birth of our Savior, won't you?"

"Of course," I said as if there could have been any other answer. Charles nodded, and Lottie said, "You know I will, Preacher Burl."

We spent a few minutes trying to remember what the weather gurus had said would be the temperature Christmas Eve. None of us knew, and Burl said God would be in control and hoped he blessed us with warmth.

Lottie was the first to finish and said she wanted to get back and finish straightening up the church. We thanked her for taking time to share a meal with us and she said it was her pleasure. She hugged Preacher Burl, and said she would see us Christmas Eve.

People who had just met him often underestimated Charles. Some people laugh at his ever-changing college T- shirt and sweatshirt wardrobe. Some find it curious that he constantly carries a handmade cane, while no one had been able to get an explanation why—me included. Strangers who saw him walking around town often thought he was one of the area's homeless. And, many of his conversations drifted south of normal. I must admit, when I first met him, I would have agreed. Okay, I admit, he's still quirky, although he's one of the most perceptive and sensitive people I've ever met.

Charles watched Lottie leave and turned to Burl.

"You two an item?"

Burl looked at Charles like he had accused him of being a warlock. "Brother Charles." The preacher's eyes opened wide, and he leaned back in the chair. "Why would you say that?"

"Preacher, even one of your dad's cows could see Sister Lottie's hankering to become a preacher's wife."

"Brother Charles, don't you think Sister Lottie is being appreciative for all First Light has done for her? It's nothing more than that."

Charles shook his head. "Preacher, I believe I can sum up my answer in two letters: NO."

Burl started to interrupt, and Charles stopped him. "Preacher, there's no doubt she's appreciative." Charles glanced at Burl's arm where Lottie had placed her hand more than once. "Get your nose out of your Bible and look around. Those touches and the look in her eyes say a heap more than appreciation."

Burl looked at his arm and back at Charles. "Heavens, I'm her preacher."

Charles said, "Preacher, I haven't spent a lot of time researching the mating habits of clergy, but it seems unless you're a Catholic priest—which I'm fairly certain you ain't—and maybe some other religions I'm not aware of, courtin', kissin', and marryin' are fairly common."

Burl leaned closer to the table and glanced around to see if anyone else was listening. "I must confess, Brother Charles, I find Sister Lottie, Miss Lottie, attractive and I know we share similar beliefs on many things, but—"

Charles leaned closer to Burl. "Preacher, unless the *but* you're going to say is *but* you don't know what preacher you could get to perform your wedding, I don't want to hear it. I would advise you to give serious thought to talking to Lottie about your feelings." Charles nodded. "I think a June wedding would be nice."

And that was marriage advice from someone who had never been married; someone who had asked Heather to marry him; and from someone who had called it off.

Burl didn't get a chance to respond. Lottie charged in the restaurant, her face red, and tears in her eyes.

"It's gone!"

Chapter Fifteen

All eyes turned to Lottie, who stumbled and tripped over a table near the door. The room got quiet as she regained her balance and approached us. Burl stood and wrapped his arms around her and eased her in the chair she had vacated minutes earlier.

"What's gone?" Burl asked, although I suspected he knew.

Lottie's shoulders sagged, she rested her elbows on the table, and put her head between her hands. "Christmas is gone. Hope for the needy, gone. Oh, Preacher, it's all gone." Amber had returned and squatted down beside Lottie. "Can I get you water?"

Lottie mumbled, "Please." I said, "What happened?"

Burl put his arm around Lottie who looked up with tears in her eyes. "Back door's open. Drawer smashed. The money's gone—it's gone."

Amber was quick with the water, and Lottie took a sip. I asked Amber for the check, paid, and said we should go to the church. It was cold outside, but I felt colder inside as we rushed to First Light. We entered the sanctuary, and I suggested Lottie may be more comfortable waiting on the back pew while Burl, Charles, and I continued to the office. The lock box was on the floor, open, and empty. The back door looked like someone had used a crowbar on it. I told Charles and Burl not to touch anything and called Chief LaMond.

Five minutes later, the chief entered followed by Officer Allen Spencer, whom I'd known for several years. Cindy wore jeans, a paint-stained sweatshirt, and an old leather jacket. Spencer's six-foot frame was decked out in a crisp Folly Beach Department of Public Safety uniform with a matching coat.

"Thanks for coming," I said and pointed to the back room.

Cindy nodded and walked to the office door and looked around before turning to Spencer. "Start processing everything." He nodded and left the building.

"He'll get a print kit," Cindy said, and sat in the pew in front of us and turned to Burl. "What happened, Preacher?"

Burl told her about the special collection, how much was in it plus the money from Cal's, and about Lottie coming to the Dog to tell us. He said it was all he knew. Cindy turned to Lottie and in a softer voice asked what had happened. Lottie added little since all she had done was return to the sanctuary, saw the empty lock box, and ran to the restaurant. Spencer returned and headed to the office.

Burl had his arm around Lottie and was reassuring her it wasn't her fault, and everything would be okay. A few minutes later, the officer rejoined us and was shaking his head. "There're some prints, probably yours Preacher, but most of them are smudged over. Looks like he wore gloves." He looked around. "Security cameras?"

Burl shook his head.

"Lottie," Cindy said, "I know the thief came in the back door but did you see anyone when you were coming here or after you found the box? There could have been more than one of them."

Lottie blinked. "An older couple was walking on the sidewalk when I got here. When I ran to the restaurant, I was so shook that I was lucky not to get run down crossing the street. I didn't see anyone. Sorry."

Spencer took Burl and Lottie's prints to compare to the ones on the box and Cindy asked him if anyone had been acting suspicious or curious about the collection. He shook his head. Cindy asked who would have known the money was there.

Burl hesitated and said, "Lord help me for saying this, but I would think everyone who attended the service would have known. They wouldn't know how much other than it was a decent amount considering the size of the flock."

Cindy asked if he would make a list of everyone he remembered being at the service. Burl said he would and asked Lottie and me to help with the list. Cindy told him to take his time and to call when it was finished, and she'd send someone to pick it up. She also said there wasn't anything else she and Officer Spencer could do but did offer to send Larry to repair the door.

"Sorry about this, Preacher," Cindy said and headed out.

I asked Burl if there was anything Charles and I could do. He said no, he wanted to be alone. I told him to call if he thought of anything or needed help with the names. He said he would. Charles and I left; Lottie stayed. Burl didn't want to be completely alone.

I closed the sanctuary door and realized I was fuming. It wasn't a huge sum of money, but I could still picture Mary's girls smiling as they contributed. The money represented the generosity of many, and several had given more than they could afford. This was now personal, and I had to do something.

I wasn't the least surprised when Charles stopped in the middle of the sidewalk. "We've got to find the thief, got to get the money back, and got to find Baby Jesus."

Saying it was easier than doing it. We went in the gallery to get out of the cold and decided all we could do was to do what we'd already decided: talk to Deb's uncle, to see if he knew any crooked antique dealers.

I WAS BECOMING as impatient as Charles. I was sitting at my kitchen table, and it was only six thirty, Monday morning. I stared at the clock annoyed that it would be more than three hours before Winslow's Antiques opened. Charles had insisted I pick him up at nine so we could be at the store at ten. As usual, it was lost on him that with normal traffic, the trip would take twenty minutes.

Not able to make the time go quicker by staring at the clock, I walked to Bert's to grab a Danish and cup of complimentary coffee. Not only was the coffee free, so was a pleasant conversation with Eric, the store's well-known employee, conversationalist on topics both large and small, and wearer of one of the most distinct beards to be found in the Low country.

Eric waited for me to get coffee before he said, "Chris, hear about the theft at First Light?"

Eric wasn't as well-versed in the town's gossip as Amber or Charles, but since Bert's never closes, word of most everything that happens on the island walks through its doors. The affable employee never hesitated to listen to the ramblings of his customers.

"Afraid so, I was with Preacher Burl when he heard about it."

"Sorry," he said. "Lisa and I were talking about it last night. Stealing stuff off porches, absconding with the Baby Jesus, and now taking money for the homeless. It seems someone is trying to suck the spirit of Christmas out of our community."

Lisa was Eric's wife and another of Bert's employees.

"Hear rumors about who might be responsible?"

Eric ran his hand over his beard. "Bum, Satanist, surfer, drug addict, run of the mill thief, ghost of Christmas past, jealous preacher from another church—I've heard them all. Ask me if I believe any of them." Eric didn't wait for my answer. "Not a one. If you ask me, it's someone who's needing quick cash for the holidays. Someone with a mess of youngins wantin' to give them a decent Christmas." He hesitated and looked at the double doors leading outside. "Chris, I feel horrible for First Light and especially Preacher Burl. He's a wonderful man doing great things for folks who don't fit in at other churches. I'm not condoning the thieving, but I also feel bad for the person doing it. If I'm right about the children, I feel worse for them."

"I agree, and Eric, could you do me a favor?" He smiled. "As long as it doesn't get me killed."

"It won't. Could you give me a call if you hear anything that seems more credible than a ghost?"

Eric cocked his head to the side. "You meddling in police business again?"

I grinned. "Yes."

"Good. You're the most interesting neighbor this store's ever had. Good luck, and try not to get yourself dead."

I paid for the Danish, said I'd try not to get *dead*, and headed out as a man being dragged by two Dalmatians entered the store. And it was still before seven o'clock.

It was a mild morning, so instead of heading home and staring at the clock, I walked three blocks to the Folly Pier, sat on one of the wooden benches in front of Locklear's Restaurant, and ate breakfast. The pier was deserted, and the walkway was illuminated with amber lights set at intervals along the railings. The lights reminded me of Christmas and the deserted pier made me think of how empty the holiday would be for so many without the happiness the donated money could bring.

Three hardy surfers were trying to catch an early- morning wave, and two couples walking their dogs on the beach. The sun had peeked over the horizon and there wasn't a cloud to be seen. I saw a few stars before the light from the sun overpowered them. My mind wandered back to my childhood and the most memorable of all the church services I attended. And, although I had trouble remembering what I had for supper last night, the words to "Silent Night" were as clear as the breaking morning light.

SILENT NIGHT, holy night,
   Son of God, love's pure light; Radiant beams from Thy holy face. With the dawn of redeeming grace, Jesus, Lord at Thy birth.

"YES, ERIC", I said out loud. "I am butting in. I must."

Chapter Sixteen

Charles paced the crushed gravel and shell parking lot in front of his apartment. He glanced at his wrist and announced I was late. It was lost on him I was there when he told me to be. He hopped in the car and unzipped his jacket so I could see his long-sleeve sweatshirt. The green shirt had the head of a ram in the center with Colorado State above it.

He patted his chest and said, "Reminded me of the animals in the Nativity. Thought it'd round up enough psychic energy to find the slime bucket who bought Baby Jesus."

He'd said it with a straight face, so I suspected it was spoken with a kernel of sincerity. Charles had been spending too much time around his girlfriend Heather, who prided herself on being psychic and a country music singer. Her psychic powers exceeded her singing ability, but if you'd heard her sing, you would know that didn't mean squat.

"It looks as much like the sheep in the Nativity as you look like a porpoise."

"Symbolism, my literal friend, symbolism. Did you know the Magi, those three wise dudes who brought gifts, didn't show up until days, maybe months, after Jesus was in the manger?"

"Interesting," I said, which was often enough to get him to move to another topic.

"My point, ye of lesser biblical knowledge, is that the sheep could have been rams. You're old, although not old enough to have been hanging out at the stable, so you don't know what was there."

I rolled my eyes. "Yes, your shirt will help." Charles grinned like he'd won a major victory.

King Street was home to some of Charleston's finest shops, ranging from well-known clothiers, to gift shops, to high-end jewelry stores. It also had the city's highest concentration of antique stores, with the most well-known being George C. Birlant & Co. Deb's uncle's store, Winslow's Antiques, was across the street and a half block south of Birlant. As predicted, we were standing in front of the historic building with Winslow's Antiques painted in script on the window when a man unlocked the door. He was in his seventies, five foot six, and better dressed than his visitors. He wore a dark-brown, three-piece wool suit, a starched white shirt, and a green and blue rep tie. He recovered from the surprise of seeing two men standing at his door, and looked us over like he was trying to decide if we were there to rob him. I would have done the same if a stranger looking like Charles had appeared at my door.

I stepped in front of Charles and extended my hand to the leery shopkeeper. "I'm Chris Landrum, and this is my friend Charles Fowler. We're from Folly Beach and your niece, Deb." I paused, realizing I didn't know her last name and had also assumed the man standing in front of us was Mr. Winslow. "She said you may be able to help us."

"Ah," he said. "Yes, she's a sweet girl, albeit a bit misguided. She called the other night and said there was a chance you might be stopping by. I apologize for my rudeness. I'm Saul, please come in."

The smell of dust, wood polish, and antiques assailed me as we moved past a row of dressers and tables halfway through the store to a desk that served more than an item for sale. It was covered by invoices and handwritten notes. There was a laptop on the back corner, but its top was closed and covered with a layer of dust. On the laptop was a cordless phone and a coffee mug with *When Did I Become an Antique?* printed on it. Perhaps there was a sense of humor inside the starched shirt.

Saul pulled up two frail looking chairs from a dining room set behind us and motioned for us to sit.

He waited for us to be seated before saying, "Could I interest you gentlemen in a cup of hot tea?"

We said no.

"Misguided how?" Charles asked.

Charles wasn't about to let the comment about Saul's niece go unexplained.

"Her parents are not as traditional as the rest of our family. They live on a small farm outside Summerville and raise miniature horses—

86

sell some, show some. Their goal is to live, umm, how do they describe it, off the grid with few connections with the outside world. As is the case with most people in contemporary America, they are not always successful. I'll leave it as they march to the beat of a different drummer." He paused and fiddled with a sheet of paper on the desk. "Are either of you fond of antiques?"

"I'm fond of Chris. Does that count?"

Saul chuckled. "I reached that vaulted status years earlier than your friend."

"How again is Deb misguided?" Charles said, although I didn't recall Saul saying how the first time.

"She came along later in my brother's life. He had already raised a family, and poor Deb received much less attention than her three siblings. I suppose it contributed to her drifting."

"Drifting?"

"Shall I say a more nomadic life? She doesn't appear amenable to settling down and from what I've seen, her friends share her alternative lifestyle."

"Like what?" Charles persisted.

"Perhaps drugs, perhaps not following the more defined mores of marriage and family. Don't get me wrong, she's a sweet lass, and I haven't had enough contact with Deb to understand her motivations. How well do you know her?"

"Hardly at all," I said. "We've met her twice and only talked to her once. She does seem nice."

"She's generous to a fault, always for the underdog and every lost cause. She has little, but would give whatever she has to anyone in need, and if possible, she'd take in any stray animal and any stray person. I can't tell you how many times she's requested I donate to one cause or another. I love her for it, and have given to some of them. I think her friends share her sensitivity to underdogs." He hesitated and held up his hand, palm facing Charles. "I know it's not why you're here. Deb told me about the purloined antique, a hand-carved statue of the Christ Child. A terrible situation. She said your theory was the person who walked away with it may try to sell it to a dealer of questionable repute. Is that correct?"

"It is," I said and explained about its value and why we didn't think it could be sold to a pawnshop.

"Logical," Saul said. "And you are asking me if I'm aware of unethical dealers."

I nodded.

"It puts me in an awkward conundrum. As you can imagine, I don't want to get anyone in trouble, and anything I say is based on hearsay."

I glanced at Charles and said, "Anything you tell us will be kept in confidence. All we are interested in is getting the antique back."

Saul looked at the paper he had been fiddling with. "As you may, or may not know, this stretch of King Street is known as the Antique District of Charleston. There are ten or more established dealers within a few hundred yards of us. Of course, not all dealers are located on King Street. Some are on East Bay, Savannah Highway, and others dot the county. The premiere dealers are no further from here than you could mallet an antebellum croquet ball."

"Crooked dealers?" Charles said.

"Now I'm not saying they're crooked per se, although there are two individuals you might want to take a closer look at." He sighed. "Are you sure this will go no further?"

I couldn't make that promise, but hedged by saying, "Your information is safe with us."

"I gave the question some thought after Deb's call. If I were looking for an antique of questionable provenance— which of course I am not, nor will I ever—I would consider shopping at Harold Lee's Antiques or possibly Arnold's Antique Barn. Mind you, I have no proof. I hope that helps."

I thanked him and got directions to the two stores. "Be sure to tell Deb I asked about her. She's such a sweet young lady."

I told him I would as he walked us out.

HAROLD LEE'S Antiques was off Savannah Highway in a strip center that was in dramatic contrast from the historic structures along King Street. It was built in the 1970s and from the worn lettering on the side of the building, it had been home to multiple tenants. From the outside, Harold Lee's Antiques looked more like a flea market than a reputable antique store. What it did share with Winslow's Antiques was the smell of dust and furniture polish. Also like Winslow's, this Monday in December was not a busy time for antique shoppers. Charles and I were greeted by the only other person in the building, a man in his mid-forties with the smile of a used-car salesman. He wore jeans and a white dress shirt and said he was Harold Lee, owner, as if we wouldn't know Harold Lee owned Harold Lee's Antiques.

"Welcome. It's nice to see customers so bright and early. As the saying goes, the early bird may get the worm, but it's the second mouse that gets the cheese." He laughed like it was the funniest thing he'd ever said. It may have been, but I wasn't amused. Charles and I smiled.

"Anyway," he continued after the moment of hilarity, "What may I interest you in this morning?"

It wouldn't be wise to say we wondered if he bought a stolen Baby Jesus, so I began a story we had crafted on the way to the store. "My friend and I inherited a collection of wooden statues my grandmother had said were hand carved a century ago in Germany. We have fallen in love with their intricate details and were looking to expand our collection."

Charles added, "There are several life-size pieces in the collection. Amazing, simply amazing. Would you by chance have similar items we could consider procuring?"

I wondered if we sounded sincere, or just gay.

Harold gave another car-salesmen smile. "I might have the perfect piece for your collection. It came in late last week, and I haven't had time to inventory it and to put it in the showroom. Pardon me a moment and I'll get it."

"Yes," Charles said as soon as Harold was out of hearing range.

No, I thought moments later when Harold returned with a giant smile and an equally giant carved eagle. It was life size, and no doubt valuable, but by no stretch of the imagination could it be confused with Baby Jesus. Charles made an audible sigh and I faked a smile as Harold held the eagle up for us to admire.

Harold quoted a price and said, "I'm sure this one- of-a-kind replica of our nation's symbol, would make a perfect addition to your collection."

"Excellent," I Led. "It's lovely." I ran my hand over its outstretched wing. "Do you have any other pieces we could combine with the eagle to possibly get a better price?"

Larger dollar signs may move him along. "I wish I did," he said. "This is all I have."

"Too bad," Charles said. "Oh, by the way, the other day I ran into another collector. He said he had bought a statue of Jesus out of an antique Nativity scene. He had to leave before I got his name." Charles turned to me. "We wanted to see who he is so we could see his collection. Did you, by chance, sell him the piece?"

Excellent question, Charles.

"Sorry, no. I don't know who you were speaking to. But I'll tell you what, because it's Monday, a slow day in the store," he waved his hand around the empty store. "I'll give you a twenty-percent discount on this impeccable carving."

Charles said, "My friend and I will discuss it and get back with you."

Harold's smile seemed forced. "Of course, the discount will end at closing today."

Charles smiled. "We'll get back with you this afternoon."

Now, he'd lied.

We left Harold smiling at the possibility of selling the eagle as we crossed Wappoo Creek and turned on Maybank Highway on our way to the second store Saul had mentioned.

"Well, that was unproductive," Charles said.

"Unless you want to buy a hand-carved eagle," I said as I pulled in a small parking lot in front of a two-story building with plate-glass windows across the front. It could have been a furniture store in earlier times. Today the large sign over the door indicated it was the home of *Arnold's Antique Barn. Where the past will bring a smile to you today.*

Charles looked at the sign and mumbled, "The only thing that will bring a smile to me today is if Baby Jesus is in there."

I opened the oversized front door and was struck by the smell of mold and mildew rather than furniture polish.

As was the case in Harold Lee's store, we were the only customers and were greeted by a man who was ten years older than Charles and me. He wasn't as cheery as the last dealer and looked like he'd be more comfortable selling caskets. He wore a black suit that'd been worn so often the lining was visible at his elbows. It could be an antique. The man's smile was somber, but hard to focus on because of his distracting comb over.

"Gentlemen," he said by way of greeting and proof he didn't know us. "May I be of assistance?"

We introduced ourselves, and he said he was Arnold Tunny. We gave the same fictional account for our visit we had shared with Harold. Arnold listened and gave a somber nod like he was racking his brain to identify something we couldn't live without.

"Your collection sounds interesting," he said. "I admire anyone who appreciates the quality of inherited items and finds it in his or her heart to add to the collection. And, antique wooden items from Germany are held at a premium. Were there any particular items you were seeking?"

You bet there is, I thought, but said, "My grandmother had a fondness for religious icons, cherubs, angels, even animals. Anything along those lines would interest us."

"What price point were you looking for?"

It was a question I hadn't anticipated and off the top of my head said, "Four hundred tops."

"Oh."

It may have been my imagination, but it appeared his smile, as weak as it had been to start, had now weakened more.

"Where did you say you were from?" he added. I hadn't, but told him Folly Beach.

"I hear it's interesting, although I prefer Isle of Palms. Neither here nor there. To answer your question, I don't believe I have anything that would meet your criteria. If you could leave your contact information, I will be glad to notify you if I come across something in which you might have an interest."

We thanked him for his time, avoided his request for our contact information, and pulled out of the parking lot.

"Another wasted stop," Charles said. "Not even an eagle."

"I'm not sure."

"Huh?"

"A couple of things bothered me." I turned on Folly Road and slammed on the brakes to avoid hitting a pick-up truck that had pulled in front of us. We skidded to a stop and glared at the man in the truck.

Charles braced himself on the dash. "Do I get to hear them?"

"Soon as I keep us from getting killed."

"I'll wait."

No vehicle body parts were exchanged, and we continued.

"First," I said, "he lost interest as soon as I said we had only a limited amount to spend."

"So," Charles said. "Maybe he only sells high-end stuff."

"Don't think so. The price tags on a few of the items near the front door were less than three hundred dollars, a couple less than a hundred. Besides, if he knew he didn't have the kind of German items we were asking about, why didn't he say it at first, rather than asking how much we were willing to pay."

Charles tapped on the console. "So you think he had the Baby Jesus, and either has a buyer who would pay more than you said, or knew it was worth more and didn't want to sell it to us?"

"That was my first thought."

Charles held up two fingers. "You said two things."

"Didn't you think it strange he asked where we were from?"

"Didn't think about it."

"I can see him asking, but at the beginning of our conversation. Clerks ask if they don't know the customer and want to have something to get them talking, but he asked after we told our story and he told us he didn't have anything. It struck me as odd."

"It's the kind of thing he might ask if he had the statue and knew where it had come from and was suspicious of why we were there."

I nodded. "I could be paranoid, but yes."

"Should we stop at Pewter Hardware and buy a crowbar and go back tonight and break in Arnold's and grab the statue?"

I hoped he was teasing, but at this point, I didn't have a better idea. "Don't think so."

"How are we going to find out if he has it?"

I asked Charles to punch Chief LaMond's number in my phone and hand it to me.

Cindy said, "What are you pestering me about now?"

I continued to bemoan the fact the words *hi* and *hello* were dropped from the vocabulary. "A pleasant morning, chief."

"Yeah, yeah. What?"

"Have you heard from the detective who was on vacation?"

"No, why?"

"I wanted to ask him about a certain antique dealer who might not be on the up and up."

"Meddling again?"

"Asking questions."

"Chris, if it wasn't so close to Christmas, and I knew the big guy at the North Pole and the other one in Heaven weren't watching to see if I've been naughty or nice, I'd lay a string of profanities on you and tell you you're going to be the death of me yet. Instead, I'll tell you to butt out, and you'll say you will, and you won't. Crap, excuse me big guys, never mind. I'll call and see if they can track him down."

"You're an angel," I said.

"Of course, I am." The line went dead.

"No luck?" Charles said. "Why don't you call Karen? She could ask around to see if anyone knows anything about Arnold."

Karen worked major crimes and had been a detective with the Charleston County Sheriff's Office for several years. She was aware of my tendency to get involved in things I had no business getting involved with. When we had started dating she tolerated my involvement, but lately she had become increasingly irritated when she found out about my adventures. I didn't blame her.

"She's been tied up with a couple of murders and has been working around the clock. I don't want to bother her."

He looked at me like I had just fed him a crock, but un-Charles like, he let it go. I pulled in his parking lot. "I'll call you when I figure out how to get Jesus back," he said, and got out of the car.

"Short of crowbarring his door?"

"Maybe."

Chapter Seventeen

Samuel and Jason stared at me from my front step as I pulled in the drive. They were wrapped in their high school jackets, and shivering like they had spent the day on an iceberg.

"Mr. Landrum." Samuel hopped up and jogged to the car door. "We thought you were never coming home."

"How long have you been here?"

Samuel looked at Jason, who said, "Hour or so.

Figured you couldn't be gone too long."

"We were sort of wrong," Samuel said

"Let's get in where it's warm," I headed to the door and noticed a box on the step. It was the size of a shoebox and had the Amazon logo on the side. The top was ripped, and there were cyan-colored stains on the bottom.

I motioned them in, and Jason picked up the box and followed me. I asked if they wanted anything to drink, and Samuel asked if I had hot chocolate. I said no, and they settled for a Pepsi. They followed me into the kitchen and after I had handed them their drinks, Samuel held the box in front of him like he was holding a gold bar.

"Mr. Landrum, we found the stolen package. It's not the valuable stuff, it's ink. It was already torn open when we found it. We didn't do it, honest."

He handed me the container. "Where was it?"

Samuel rubbed his hands together to warm them. "Sort of in a big ole' trash dumpster behind Planet Follywood."

"Why were you looking in a dumpster?"

Samuel started to say something but hesitated and turned to Jason, who said, "We figured the cops were looking all over town and didn't think they'd want to get their hands dirty and stinky from looking in the trash. We've been looking where people throw stuff away. Thought the thief may get scared with all the cops running around trying to catch him and would dump the statue. We didn't find Jesus, but this was stolen too. It's evidence so maybe the police can dust it for prints, or get DNA, or something."

"Fellas, other than the large dumpsters, have you been rooting around in trash containers around houses again?"

Samuel glanced at Jason and turned back to me. "Sort of."

I frowned. "Did it enter your mind the person who stole it could live in one of those houses and could have seen you digging through the trash? Do you know the trouble you could have gotten in?"

"But Mr. Landrum, we—"

I glared at my young friends. "I'm not finished, Jason. You know your mother blames me for what happened a few years ago, and now she thinks I've encouraged you to get involved in this mess. And Samuel, remember what happened last year when you came close to getting killed? Both of you are wonderful, and I admire your enthusiasm and desire to help, but you must leave it to the police. How many times do I have to say it?"

Jason bowed his head. Samuel held out the mangled box. "What about this? It's a clue."

I didn't think it was much of one. "I'll get it to Chief LaMond. I'll tell her how great it was you found it and I'm sure she'll see if there are prints on it."

Jason looked up. "Thanks, Mr. Landrum."

Samuel said, "We heard a rumor a bunch of money was stolen from First Light. Is it true?"

I told them it was.

"Jason and I were talking before you got here. We want to help get money to replace what was taken."

"That's kind."

Samuel smiled. "Yeah, we thought we could ride our bikes up Folly Road and rob a bank and give the money to Preacher Burl."

"He's teasing, Mr. Landrum," Jason added. "We were saying instead of giving each other Christmas gifts we could take what we already got back to the store and give the money we got for them to the preacher. Think it'd be okay?"

I was touched. I smiled and said, "It's a wonderful idea."

Samuel said, "We'd get more from the bank." Jason smacked him on the arm.

A week ago, I'd told Charles I would take him Christmas shopping in Charleston. He hadn't gotten Heather anything and said he could use my help in selecting the "perfect" gift. I didn't know what I was getting Karen so I doubted I would be the person to find a perfect gift and told him so. He said it was true, but he needed someone to drive. It reminded me of why Rudolph was selected to lead Santa's sleigh. He had a shiny nose, and I had a car. With everything going on, I had forgotten Charles's request until the boys told me about getting gifts, or, not getting gifts.

I called and reminded Charles of our task, and he asked why I didn't think of it this morning when we were in downtown Charleston. I pleaded a senior moment, and he agreed—way too quickly. A half-hour later, I had dropped the torn box at the police station and Charles and I were back in the car. We took a slight detour and cruised past First Light's Nativity. Dude's employee Stephon was sitting on a bench in the Folly River Park across from the scene with his coat pulled tight around his trim body and a pea hat covering his ears. I waved at the sentinel and he gave a feeble half-wave in return.

Charles looked at Stephon and across the street at the display. "Closing the gate after the horse has skedaddled."

I headed to Charleston and listened to Bing Crosby singing "White Christmas" on satellite radio. The sun was shining, and the temperatures were mild, and for a moment, I thought about my childhood and how much fun it had been to see snow on the ground a few days before Christmas. I also recalled I was too young to drive, and the snow was more fun with dad behind the wheel.

"What are you getting Heather?"

"That's why you're along," Charles said.

"I thought it was to drive."

"The Christmas Song" played in the background. "That too."

"How about a carved eagle?"

"Too big," he said with a straight face.

"How about a car so I wouldn't have to drive you everywhere?"

"Wouldn't fit under the tree. I was thinking jewelry she could wear when she's performing."

"I like the car idea better, although jewelry would work."

Charles tilted his Tilley down over his eyes and said,

"To the Market, James."

We parked in a surface pay lot at the east end of the historic Charleston City Market, and Charles, the master trivia collector, reminded me it was one of the oldest public markets in the country. He said there were more than three hundred vendors, and products ranging from pralines to purses, so he was certain he could find something for Heather. Karen was harder to shop for, and I had put off thinking about it until the last minute—not many minutes away.

A volunteer bell ringer manning a Salvation Army red kettle greeted us with "Merry Christmas" and a hopeful look as we crossed the street to the market's entry. Charles returned the greeting, and we dropped money in the kettle. We entered the crowded market, and I began thinking about someone's comment in the last few days about the "forgotten folks," the homeless who, for whatever reason, hadn't taken advantage of the charitable organizations, which provide services for the needy year-round, but more this time of year. I wondered how many of those people that organizations like the Salvation Army either are unable to assist or don't know about. Who had been talking about the forgotten folks?

Charles interrupted my thoughts when he held up a silver chain with an onyx palmetto tree dangling from it. "The perfect gift?"

"Nice," I said, not thinking it would qualify for the perfect gift category.

He shrugged, "Not Heather, is it?"

"Let's keep looking," I nudged him further down the aisle.

We stopped twice to sample the benne wafers and once for Charles to drool over, and exchange kisses with, a black and white Newfie the size of a Mini Cooper. We were blocking foot traffic, and I managed to separate man from dog. We weren't halfway through the market when Charles reminded me we hadn't eaten. I suggested the benne wafers were lunch and he suggested I was wrong, and pointed across the street and said he thought he heard Bubba Gump calling. I doubted it, but took the hint, and we walked over to Bubba Gump Shrimp Company and were seated at a table near the front of the chain restaurant.

"Shopping makes me hungry," Charles said as he scanned the menu. A waitress was quick to the table, and we each ordered a fish sandwich, a Dixie Fishwish in Gumpspeak, and Charles told the waitress he needed a beer because this was his busiest shopping day of the year. He was serious. I told her I needed wine because I was putting up with Charles. She headed to the kitchen and mumbled something that sounded a lot like, "Old farts."

"What are you getting Karen?"

"I hope I'll figure it out by the time we reach the end of the Market."

Charles looked out the front window where strands of colorful

Christmas lights could be seen strung along the Market's roof line. "Did I ever tell you what Christmas meant when I was growing up?"

He had never told me much about his childhood except the basics about his parents dying when he was young and being raised by his grandmother. "Not much."

He continued to stare out the window. "I was eight or nine and all I wanted for Christmas was a bicycle. I was the only kid on the block who had to run beside my friends while they were riding bikes. All that running kept me in shape, but it was embarrassing. Each Christmas it seemed like one of my buddies got a shiny two-wheeler."

Our drinks arrived, and Charles took a long draw of beer.

"What happened?"

"To make sure granny got the message to Santa, I wrote her a note and printed *BICYCLE* in big red letters so if the jolly old man didn't have his glasses on, he could still read it. Even wrote a reminder note and gave it to her Christmas Eve."

"I'm thinking you didn't get a bike."

"I got up Christmas morning, put on my tennis shoes so I could ride the bike out the front door, scampered down the steps, and couldn't find anything with two wheels on it—not under the tree, not in the kitchen, even looked outside. Being a selfish little brat, I decided it was the worst Christmas ever."

"I'm sorry."

Charles smiled. "I'm not. Know what I got?"

"A Corvette?"

Charles rolled his eyes but continued to smile. "Granny gave me a first edition of Agatha Christie's *The Hollow*."

I figured it must have been something special. "Wow."

"I didn't know what to make of it. Never heard of it. Granny explained it was a popular mystery written five years after I was born. She, being a librarian, was an expert on things bookish. She said the story was a great example of a 'country house mystery,' and she didn't think I would be interested in Tolstoy, Joyce, Eliot, or a bunch of other writers I'd never heard of. She thought a mystery might pique my interest in reading." He chuckled. "She said she'd paid $2.50 for it, and I'd better treat it like it was priceless."

"Did you ever get the bike?"

Food came before he answered. The sound system was playing "The Chipmunk Song," and Charles stuffed a fry in his mouth.

"Not for a few more years," he mumbled. "Know what I did get?"

I shook my head.

"An appreciation for books. Something about *The Hollow* grabbed

97

me; hasn't let go yet. It was the first mystery I read. Didn't understand much of the British stuff in it, but something about it was exhilarating. Think it's why I tend to stick my nose in when someone gets killed over here. Anyway, for the next three years, she gave me a first edition of a popular novel. The next one was James A. Michener's *Tales of the South Pacific*. My favorites were mysteries. Reading grew on me."

"It explains the library in your apartment," I said, and thought the trauma of him not receiving a bike was why Charles's most prized possession to this day was his pristine 1961 Schwinn.

"Granny wasn't a barrel of laughs and seemed to always be wearing her scrunched up, librarian's face, but she taught me a lot about serious stuff. There was an old Bible in the house, and after I got hooked on reading, I read it from crinkly cover to cover. Like the British mysteries, I didn't understand a lot of it, although I got the strong feeling it wanted me to be a better person than I thought I could be. It made me not want to hurt anyone and be nice to everyone. I'm not always good at it, but I keep trying."

Charles was one of the nicest, although strangest, people I'd ever met. If it can be attributed to his stern grandmother or the Bible, I was thankful. Chuck Berry was rocking through the sound system with "Run Rudolph Run," and our plates were empty.

Charles pulled on his lightweight red jacket. "Let's get this shopping done."

The Market was more crowded than when we broke for lunch, so we spent more time avoiding running into people or being run over than we did shopping, but Charles found the perfect gift, a necklace with a silver guitar charm. He said it would complement her normal stage attire of a wide-brim hat and bright-colored blouse.

Finding a gift for Karen proved to be more difficult, but twenty minutes later, I settled on a sweet grass basket. Fifty artists weaving baskets were spread throughout the Market, and there were hundreds of baskets to choose from, so the problem wasn't finding the baskets; selecting the right one was the challenge. I took the lazy way out and purchased one from the vendor with the fewest people blocking my way. We made it back to the car without stopping—actually not true, Charles managed to find two more dogs to converse with before I had the heater blowing full blast and we were weaving through the narrow streets on our way out of downtown.

We were tired after shopping and didn't say much most of the way home. I was listening to Roy Orbison singing "Pretty Paper," when Charles turned down the volume, and said, "I was thinking. Instead of you and me getting presents for each other, we could donate whatever we would've spent to Preacher Burl to help make up for what was stolen?"

I had already decided to reach into my savings and give the preacher whatever he needed. I thought it was touching that Charles had the idea.

"That's a great idea," I said, and told him Samuel and Jason were doing the same thing.

"Wonderful, some other people told me they were going to do that too. Nobody is going to get away with stealing the spirit of Christmas from Folly." He glanced over at me and smiled. "I think Preacher Burl will be able to use the lump of coal I was getting you."

"Ho, Ho, Ho," I said.

On the radio, Ray Stevens was singing "Santa Claus is Watching You."

Chapter Eighteen

We had passed Harris Teeter when I spotted a familiar person walking along the road and struggling to carry three plastic grocery bags. I pulled over and waited for the man to get beside the car.

"Bernard," I said. "Hop in, we'll give you a ride."

He panted, and between labored breaths, said, "Don't mind if I do."

He put his groceries on the back seat and slipped in. He was more clean-shaven than the last time I'd seen him, but his hair looked like it hadn't made contact with a comb in days. He had on a heavy Carhartt jacket, a vast improvement over the tattered army coat he'd worn in Cal's.

Charles said, "Grocery shopping?"

He exhaled. "Yes, sir. Never been in there before. It sure is big."

"A long walk from Folly, too," Charles said, leaning on the obvious.

"Yep." Bernard chuckled. "My Rolls is in the shop."

Charles laughed. "Hate it when that happens. That a new coat? Looks good."

I couldn't see Bernard's reaction, but heard him wiggling around in the seat. "Thanks, sir. Hitched into town yesterday and got it. It's good and warm. Christmas season's been good to me."

"That's great," I said. New coat, first time to Harris Teeter, three bags of food. Curious.

"What made it so good? I could use some of that luck." Charles asked.

He had a knack for asking personal questions without raising the ire of the recipient.

"Umm, came into a bit of money. Got a question, any—"

Charles interrupted, "Where'd it come from?" Charles wouldn't let go. If I was Bernard, I'd be flinging a banana from the grocery bag at him.

Bernard ignored Charles. "Ya'll heard if they caught the guy who stole Baby Jesus?"

I remembered how interested he'd appeared in the theft the first time we'd met.

"Not yet," I said.

"Hear more rumors about who it might be?"

"One, sir. The early talk about witches seems to be bad intel. Surfers are still the word around town."

"Where'd you say the money came from?" Charles "Persistent" Fowler asked.

Bernard laughed. "Charles, I don't recall saying." I thought, *Good for you, Bernard.*

Charles said, "Oh."

Bernard surprised me. "Might as well tell you. It was pretty exciting. I woke up the other morning and stepped out of my sleeping bag. Stumbled over a big ole rock in front of it and reached down to throw it away. Know what I found under the rock?"

Charles said, "A worm."

My admiration for the stranger increased when once again Bernard ignored Charles, and said, "Under the rock were six fifty-dollar bills. Not a soul around. It was like the bills crawled under the rock and were waiting for me to find them."

"Incredible," Charles said, and again asked, "Where'd it come from?"

"Can't say I've believed in Santa since—well, I don't know when. Yesterday morning all those visions of sugarplums dancing in my head rushed back. Nearly peed in my jeans, I was so excited."

Charles again said, "Where did—"

"I'm getting there. The funny thing is I don't know her."

Charles said, "Who?"

"The person who left the money, some woman named Tabatha."

"How do you know?" I asked.

"She left a note with the money. It said, *Merry Christmas from Tabatha.*"

I asked, "Still have the note?"

"No, sir. I stuck it in my pocket but it must have fallen out. I'll tell you one thing. Whoever she is, she sure made my Christmas."

Charles repeated, "Incredible," and threw out another question from the *none of your business* file, "Where are you staying?"

"Charles, you sure are a nosy one. Ain't anyone ever told you curiosity killed the cat?"

Three zillion times, I thought.

Charles laughed. "A time or two." It was one of the few times Charles understated something. "So where are you staying?"

"Nowhere in particular. You ain't going to tell the cops?"

"My lips are sealed," Charles said.

That would be a Christmas miracle, but instead of saying it, I kept *my* lips sealed.

"I've been spending nights under some of those elevated houses out past the dentist's office. Don't stay in one place too long. The cops frown on it if they start getting calls from people complaining about me hanging around."

"Ever stayed in one of those shelters over there,"

Charles asked and pointed toward Charleston.

"Used to, except some of those do-gooders who run them said I was prone to get in fights with their other guests. Told me not to come back."

Charles said, "That's too bad."

"Nah," Bernard said, "Didn't fancy being there anyway. Crazy people everywhere. Smelly. Danged drunks. Besides, the people in charge got it right about me. I have what you call a quick temper. Better being alone."

We were crossing the new bridge to Folly and I said, "Where do you want us to take you?"

"You can let me out anywhere. Won't be far to my mansion."

"Sure we can't take you closer?"

"Yes. I'll be fine anywhere, sir."

Clearly, Bernard didn't want us to know the location of his sleeping-bag mansion.

I pulled to the curb in front of the library and Charles turned to the back seat. "Don't forget Cal's invitation to his Christmas party. He's got a big day planned."

"I'll check my calendar," Bernard said. "While we're talking about Christmas stuff, think preacher, umm whatever his name is—"

"Preacher Burl Costello."

"Yeah, that's it. Think Preacher Burl would mind me dropping in on his Christmas Eve preaching?"

"He'd be pleased if you did," I said.

Bernard stepped out of the car, set his grocery bags on the sidewalk, and rubbed his mustache. "I'll try to be there. Will it be in the store?"

"The preacher is hoping for good weather so he can hold it on the beach," Charles said. "The storefront church may be too small to hold everyone."

"Reckon I can find it, fellas. Thanks for the lift."

We watched him walk in the direction of what I assumed to be the house he'd been staying under, and I pulled back in the line of traffic.

Elvis was singing his version of "Blue Christmas," Charles sang along with the last verse, and turned the radio's volume down. "Believe his story?"

"That Elvis'll have a blue Christmas?" Teasing Charles was one of my true pleasures.

"Bernard?"

"I'd like to. It's heartwarming, a Hallmark moment. Money left for a homeless person a few days before Christmas. But, I have trouble with it. It sounds unrealistic, and remember the other night at Cal's?"

"I need more information."

"Cal was surprised when Bernard came in and had a couple of beers."

"No surprise there," Charles said. "Didn't he say Bernard had come in several times?"

"Yes, but the other times he never had money. Cal footed the bill."

"Yeah." Charles rubbed his chin. "He seemed interested if the cops had leads on the Baby Jesus thief."

"Like he did a few minutes ago."

"Think he stole everything?"

"I hate to say it, although I wouldn't be surprised. If he did, he'd have had to have access to a vehicle or someone helping him. I can't see him walking around lugging two surfboards or the statue."

We sat in his parking lot debating Bernard's guilt, and realized while we may think he was guilty, we couldn't prove it. Charles asked if I thought we should tell Chief LaMond. I said we didn't have anything concrete to tell her.

"Let me throw out another thought," I said.

"Throw away."

"Say he's telling the truth and he did get the money with a note. Who's Tabatha?"

Charles tilted his head my direction. "I don't know any Tabathas. Do you?"

"No."

"She pays better than the tooth fairy," Charles said as he got out of the car.

I pulled out of Charles's lot and realized that while I wasn't hungry, I knew I would have as good a chance finding something to eat at the house as I would finding a Tyrannosaurus Rex in my front yard. I parked and walked across Center Street to Planet Follywood. Food might help me think.

Planet Follywood was one of the town's most popular restaurants and hosted live entertainment weekend nights, karaoke every Thursday, and a wide selection of beach grub all the time. Tonight it also featured Mayor Brian Newman at a table near the jukebox. He was alone, had a serving of fried okra in front of him, and was sipping a Corona. Brian waved me over and asked if I wanted to join him. He was mayor, father of the woman I was dating, and an all-around good guy, so I couldn't see why not. Camille, one of the waitresses, was quick to the table and asked if I wanted Cabernet. I said yes, and wondered if it was bad that I was known at most restaurants in town by my drink preference.

The mayor was a handful of years older than me, but unlike me, he had spent thirty years in the military as an MP and in Special Services. Also unlike me, he was tall, trim, confident and though he had been out for years, oozed military. He had been Folly's police chief for twenty years before becoming mayor.

"What trouble have you been getting in today?" Brian asked.

"None."

"Not how I hear it."

I gave him my most innocent look. "What have you heard?"

"Rumor is you and your sidekick Charles have been asking around about our recent rash of thefts."

On Folly, rumors spread as quickly as norovirus on a cruise ship, so I wasn't surprised he'd heard. "We're worried about Preacher Burl and how the theft of Baby Jesus has affected him and First Light."

Camille returned with my wine and asked if I wanted anything to eat. I asked Brian if he was getting anything else; he said a chef salad with grilled chicken. I refrained from saying "yuck" to his healthy choices, and ordered a patty melt.

Brian said, "Chris, I'm not encouraging you to meddle in police business." He hesitated and chuckled. "History says I couldn't stop you if I tried, but I'm as frustrated over it as I've been about anything since I've been mayor. The theft of a little wooden carving has done more to suck the life of Christmas out of this tight-knit community than anything I can imagine. Do you know how many people have come to me asking if it's been found?" I figured it was rhetorical, shook my head, and waited for him to continue. "I tell them no and they, to a person, tell me how much seeing First Light's Nativity had meant to them, and how devastated they are by the theft. The Nativity scene at the Catholic Church has always meant a lot, but something about First Light having one touches so many, especially so many who wouldn't set foot in other churches."

"I'm sure Chief LaMond is doing everything possible."

A reggae song blared from the jukebox. Brian stared at the machine, at the Christmas tree sitting beside it, and at me. "I told her to do whatever she needed to do. Forget our overtime restrictions and find the statue." He nodded and smiled. "When I was a kid, my two brothers and I got to play the three wise men in a living Nativity our Sunday school had." Brian smiled. "We got dressed up like the wise men you see in most scenes. We set up in front of our church and the two Sundays before Christmas we stood out in the cold while people came to the morning worship service. We looked silly in our fake beards and all, but I was amazed how many people stood and looked at us like they were looking at the real thing. I can't explain it. It was wonderful—spiritual, you could say."

I nodded. "That's what I've heard people say about the Nativity at the Catholic Church and First Light's scene."

"It's why the mindless theft of that small statue has torn a hole out of the heart of so many people."

Our food arrived, Stevie Wonder's version of "What Christmas Means to Me" played on the jukebox, and Brian drifted into thought. I wondered if he was reliving those memorable Sundays.

Our conversation turned to more cheerful topics and he asked if I had seen Karen lately. He seemed surprised when I said it had been a couple of weeks, but understood considering her workload had increased during the holiday season. Good tidings and great joy, mixed with excessive amounts of liquid spirits, sometimes disintegrated into tension, anger, and murder. As Karen had often said, "When bad things happen, I go to work." She'd worked a lot this holiday season.

Our food was gone as were two bottles of beer and two glasses of wine. Brian thanked me for joining him and letting him share his wise man story and bemoan the effect the loss of the statue was having on his city. I told him it was always a pleasure to talk with him and headed home.

I had turned on the light when the phone rang. "Dude be here."

"Chris be here."

"Intros be done. Message. Be having meeting of surfer crime stoppers."

"Surfers Against Spirit of Christmas Thieves."

"That's what me say."

Don't think so, I thought. "When and where?"

"Here. *Manana*. Two hours past sun disappearing."

"At the surf shop?"

He repeated, "That's what me say."

"Seven o'clock tomorrow?"

"You got it."

The phone went dead.

I stared at the phone, smiled, and figured he was inviting me to the meeting. That's what me say.

Chapter Nineteen

I called Charles the next morning and extended an invitation to what I understood to be a meeting of the surfer group. He pouted and asked why I hadn't asked him last night. I said I waited until this morning to irritate him; he said I had succeeded. He then told me he'd meet me in front of the surf shop at six-thirty. I said I hoped he didn't freeze waiting for me that early.

True to his word, Charles was standing in front of the surf shop at six-thirty. Untrue to my word, I was there as well. He smiled and said he was glad I'd learned to tell time.

Dude, Finley, and Stephon were the only people in the shop. The rest of the surfer group didn't follow Charles Standard Time. Finley seemed surprised to see us, Stephon gave his normal reaction and snarled in our direction, and Dude said, "Aloha."

Dude picked up Pluto, who had been leaning against his leg, kissed the Australian Terrier on the mouth, and turned to Finley and Stephon. "They be special guests."

Finley seemed less than thrilled, but thanked us for coming while Stephon continued to snarl. The awkward moment was broken when three more members of the group arrived. I recognized Deb, and Truman, but didn't know the third person. Dude continued to hold Pluto and pointed at the newcomers with his free hand and said, "Be Deb, Truman, and Andy."

Charles and I nodded to the three. Deb smiled and said, "Uncle Saul told me you came to see him. He's a little stuffy, so I hope he was friendly. He told me he was uncomfortable talking about dealers, but did anyway since I had asked him to help. Did he help you figure out who stole Jesus?"

Truman, Andy, and Finley stopped talking and stared at Charles and me.

I said, "Afraid not."

"Boards and bling?" Dude asked.

Charles said, "Nope."

Dude tapped the floor with his florescent-green tennis shoe. "Bummer."

Four more surfers arrived, and Finley looked at his watch. "Let's start."

The newcomers ignored the rest of us and were in deep conversation about parking tickets. Finley raised his voice and repeated it was time to start. It took and everyone moved to the center of the room. The display racks hadn't been moved as much as they had been for the first meeting and we were crammed together.

Finley pushed his long, sun-bleached blond hair out of his eyes and pulled his shoulders back. "It's almost Christmas, so let's begin by singing a Christmas carol. I was thinking "Jingle Bell Rock.""

I wondered in what carol book he'd found "Jingle Bell Rock," but was impressed he was trying to honor the Christmas spirit. Finley raised his arms like a choir director, lowered them and we began singing. The group's effort was spirited, although it became clear the first seven words were the only words any of us knew in the "carol." After repeating them twice, Finley waved for us to stop. The phrase *it's the thought that counts* popped to mind.

Deb and Teddye laughed. Truman said, "Good job."

"Okay, enough," Finley said. "This is important. Christmas Day is around the corner and I wanted to get together and talk about anything new we know about the stealing. Has anybody called about the reward?" Finley looked around the room.

Dude set Pluto on the floor and said, "That be *grande* N-O."

Finley looked at Pluto who had run to Deb and whimpered for her to pick him up. She did and Finley said, "That's what I thought. We've been watching the Nativity ever since we met here. I haven't heard anything, but has anyone seen anybody suspicious, something you may not have thought important at the time?"

Andy, the surfer I hadn't seen before, said, "Don't know how important it is. Two kids keep riding by. Saw them three or four days."

"Yeah," Teddye said. "They never stopped while I was watching. I saw them ride past a few times."

"Finley," I said. "That's Jason and Samuel. They're a couple of high school kids who are concerned about the thefts. The other day, they found one of the stolen packages and turned it over to the police. They're okay."

Deb said, "The jewelry?"

"The ink cartridges."

Stephon said, "A big whoop."

Deb said, "May not have been Jesus, the boards, or the jewels, but it's better than we've done."

Finley waited for Deb to finish. "Good, it explains the kids. Anybody see anything else suspicious?"

"A bunch of old folks sitting across from the Nativity in geezer cars, Buicks and Mercurys." Truman said. "Half the time they were asleep. They couldn't catch a cold on a germ farm."

Finley shook his head. "Truman, you know they're from the churches doing the same thing we are by keeping watch over the Nativity. We should appreciate them." He turned away from Truman. "What about you guys?" He stared at Charles and me. "You're the bad guy catchers. Who did it?"

I looked at Finley and at the others. "I wish we knew. What I will tell you is we're not done."

Finley shook his head and looked at the group. "Anything else?"

Andy said, "Yeah, well maybe." He hesitated and looked around. "A man who lives in my building lost his job a couple of months ago. He has some strange disease and kept missing work. He didn't want anybody at work to know about his illness and didn't tell his boss what was wrong. They fired him. He's squeaking by and about to lose the apartment. I've seen him going through the trash along the street trying to find something to hock or to eat. Poor guy. He'd told me he didn't want to get any help from the groups, which help people like him. Too much pride, and—"

Stephon interrupted. "What's your point?"

Andy glared at Stephon and turned to Finley. "I ran into him yesterday. He was getting out of his rusted-out Chevy pick-up truck. He had on a new winter coat. The tag was still sewn on the sleeve, but I didn't want to embarrass him by saying anything. I said, 'Nice coat.' His face turned red, and he mumbled thanks. I noticed he had spanking new tires on his truck. They stood out like an army tank rollin' down Center Street. He saw me looking at them and said, 'You won't believe what happened.'" Andy paused.

Paused too long for Charles. "What?"

Andy said, "Now I'm reporting what he said, you understand? He went into this unbelievable story. Said he came out of his apartment the day before yesterday and there was an envelope taped to his door. Guess what he said was in it?" No one guessed, so Andy continued, "Ten, fifty-dollar bills—yep, five hundred bucks stuck on his door."

"Sure there were," Stephon said and rolled his eyes.

Finley asked, "Who were they from?"

"Claims he didn't know. Can you believe it?"

"Wow," said Truman. "It's great, since he wouldn't ask for help from anyone. It's nice somebody wanted to help. I wonder how many more people around here can't get help when they need it? I think I know who you're talking about. Isn't it—"

Andy waved his hand in Truman's face. "We shouldn't say his name."

Truman started to say something, but hesitated. "Okay."

"You think he's lying and he's the person who took the baby and the other stuff?" Deb asked.

Andy said, "I don't want to say that. I feel sorry for the man. He seems like a nice guy, but doesn't it sound fishy? Someone stuck money on his door and he doesn't know who."

Stephon said, "I think he's the thief."

I thought of Bernard's windfall and the note from Tabatha. "Was there a note with his money?"

Andy seemed surprised I had spoken. "He didn't mention one. He was all excited about the cash. Why?"

"Curious," I said. "If you would, ask him the next time you see him."

"Okay, I guess."

A couple of the other surfers started talking.

I stepped close to Finley and looked at the group. "I don't know if the man you're talking about stole the statue, or for that matter, stole anything." I pointed at Andy. "You need to tell the police, and if there was a note, please let me know." He wrote my number on his palm and said he would.

"What have the cops done so far?" Stephon grumbled. "Why do you think they'll do anything?" Charles, who had been silent, stepped beside me.

"Chris and I know Chief LaMond better than any of you know her. She's as concerned about finding the statue as you are. I'd trust her with my life and Chris is right. You need to talk to her."

Andy looked for support from his fellow surfers and turned to Charles. "Okay, but it won't do any good."

Dude took three steps and took Pluto from Deb's arms and pointed a finger at Andy. "You be seein' chieftress."

Andy nodded. "Soon," Dude said.

Andy nodded a second time.

Finley asked if there was anything else to be shared and when no one answered he asked if we wanted to end the meeting with another Christmas song.

Unlike the group's rendition of "Jingle Bell Rock,"

"No!" was shouted in perfect harmony.

Each of the surfers patted Pluto's head before heading out, most to local bars to get more in the holiday spirit. Charles and I stood on the sidewalk.

Charles looked up the steps to the door of Dude's shop. "The five hundred dollars stuck on the door sounds like another story we heard."

"Bernard's three hundred dollars under a rock."

"Yep. It's why you asked about a note."

"Both men down on their luck," I said. "Both, for whatever reason, unable or unwilling to get assistance."

"If they're telling the truth, it seems we have a secret Santa handing out big bucks."

"Secret Santa named Tabatha. I still see more questions than answers. Are Andy's neighbor and Bernard telling the truth? If they are, is there a connection between the thefts and the gifts? If so, why would someone commit crimes and give the money away?"

Charles said. "I think the person who stole the stuff is doing it. It's Robin Hood in our hood." He pulled his jacket closed. "Tell you what else I know. I'm freezing my keister off. Let's figure this out tomorrow."

Chapter Twenty

I had a hard time sleeping. I tossed, turned, and replayed the meeting in my head. Christmas Eve was two days away, and it didn't seem I was closer to honoring Burl's request to find Baby Jesus than I was the morning I had learned it was missing. What I did know was the theft of the statue wasn't a prank, and the surfer group, the church members, and the police were doing what they could to find it. Since the surfer meeting had ended, something was tickling the far reaches of my memory, something important. But what? It was tied to the surfer meeting, or something said at the meeting that reminded me of something else. The only thing that struck me as important was Andy's neighbor finding the money, if, in fact, he had. Did the neighbor have anything in common with Bernard, the alleged recipient of another gift? There was no doubt both were down on their luck, although so were many others. Is Tabatha the link?

What else did I know about the missing items? Chief LaMond assured me she was working with the police in Charleston to check the city's pawnshops to see if the jewelry showed up, but I wasn't optimistic. Years ago, Brian Newman had told me pawn shops were good about record keeping and identifying people who left items with them, but no shortage of other less-savory individuals would buy and fence items. The no-questions-asked crowd could have purchased the jewelry, and the police wouldn't have a way to trace it.

What about the statue? I thought about Charles and my conversation with Deb's uncle and the antique dealers he'd referred us to. What was it that bothered me about the last dealer we talked to? Oh yeah, Arnold at Arnold's Antique Barn, and how we'd told him we were looking for German antiques and he didn't say he didn't have any until we told him how much we wanted to spend, and how unusual it was when he asked us where we were from. When we said Folly, he rushed us out of the store. It was as if he knew what we were looking for. Granted, there was nothing in what he had said that could implicate him, but it felt off.

There was still something bothering me from the meeting in the surf shop.

Sleep must have come, because the next thing I remembered was waking up, glancing out the window, and seeing daylight. What I didn't see was an answer to what had bothered me.

I WAS HEADED to Bert's for coffee when I saw Mary Ewing leaving the store. She had a paper bag in one hand and held her two-year-old's hand with the other. Her older girl was on the other side of the young one and was holding her hand as they crossed the street and headed toward the beach. Three cars stopped for them to cross.

There were half dozen customers in the store. Three were standing at the coffee urn in back, two were fawning over a Lab near the beer coolers, and, Lisa, the clerk, was adjusting the volume on an old-fashioned boom box behind the counter. It was playing "Little Drummer Boy."

I waited for one of Bert's regulars to put sugar in his coffee, and I drew a cup. Lisa had finished with the boom box and waved at me. "Merry almost Christmas."

I smiled and thanked her. She asked if I was doing anything special for the holiday, and I said I was going to First Light's Christmas Eve service and planned to be at Cal's Christmas Day. She said she had to work Christmas Eve but was off Christmas and would try to "meander over to Cal's." She asked if Karen was coming and I said I didn't know.

"I know what you mean," Lisa said. "Seems killings are almost as common around Christmastime as sales at the mall."

I looked at the door. "Lisa, what do you know about the lady and the two kids who just left?"

"Mary, Jewel, and Joanie?"

I wasn't surprised Lisa knew their names. "Yes."

"Don't know a lot. They come in a couple of times a week. Jewel's six and Joanie's two. Mary usually buys milk and packaged food. She pays with a handful of change; counts it out like it's precious diamonds." Lisa hesitated and lowered her voice. "She doesn't always have enough. We kick in the difference. It's only a dollar or two. Figure most of the food's for the kids."

"Know where she lives?"

Lisa shook her head. "She doesn't say much, sort of shy, I think. I don't like to ask many questions. Ever once and a while, when she has a few extra dollars, she hires one of our young clerks to babysit for a few hours. Mary takes the kids to the sitter's apartment so the sitter doesn't know where they live. Why?"

"Curious. I met her with a couple of surfers at Cal's the other night."

Two more customers entered and Lisa said she'd better get to work. I thanked her, paid and grabbed my coffee. "Have a Merry Little Christmas" was playing in the background. From the way things were going, I began to doubt I would.

Instead of going home, I zipped my jacket, pulled my Tilley down low on my head, and headed in the direction Mary had gone. The temperature was mild although the breeze off the ocean was chilling, and the sky was clear and the bright sunshine tempered the chill, but only a little.

I crossed East Arctic Avenue, looked each way, but didn't see Mary. I reached the wooden walkway that crossed over the dunes line separating the small parking area from the beach, and saw Mary sitting on the other side. A child was on each side of her, huddled close to their mother, and eating powdered mini-donuts. Mary had coffee in one hand and a plastic orange juice container in the other. She also had on what appeared to be a new, mid-length cloth coat.

I pretended to be surprised to see them and Mary looked at me like she recognized me from somewhere but didn't know where. I told her we had met in Cal's and at church. She smiled and apologized for not recognizing me, and said she had been distracted. The kids looked over their shoulder at me and smiled. Each had on new clothes.

Mary pulled one of the children closer so I could pass. I did and pointed to the oldest child's fire engine red, mud boots. "Pretty boots."

She gave a wide smile and Mary turned to her. "Jewel, thank the nice man."

"Thank you," Jewel said, much more polite than most of my friends would have been. "They're new." She stood and pirouetted. "So's my coat and dress."

"They're lovely," I said and returned her smile.

Joanie looked at her mom and raised her hand. Mary put her arm around her and said, "Joanie's boots, coat, and dress are new too." Joanie tried to pirouette like Jewel had and tripped and landed on the ramp. Jewel giggled, and fortunately, so did Joanie.

Mary pulled the girls close. "We don't live far from here, but the girls don't get to see the ocean often."

I kneeled and looked at the little girls. Powdered sugar was sprinkled on the front of their coats. "The ocean's neat, isn't it?"

Jewel answered. "It sure is. Momma said she's going to bring us here every day until Christmas and even on Christmas Day. She got us these new clothes, but said seeing the ocean is our Christmas present. She said kids everywhere could get clothes, but only special ones could see the ocean for real and not just in books or on TV."

"Your mom's a smart lady." Jewel nodded. "Me, too."

I smiled. "You sure are."

Joanie raised her hand again, and I patted her on the knee. "You are, too."

Mary slid over to the edge of the ramp. "I'm being rude. Would you like to sit?"

I wouldn't have wanted to interfere with her kids Christmas present, but was curious about where she could have gotten the money for new clothes, after what Lisa had said about Mary not having money for food.

"If you don't mind."

Jewel patted the space beside her.

A woman with two boys about the girls' ages approached us as they walked down the beach. They were following two German shepherds.

"Mom," Jewel said. "Can we pet the dogs?"

"You don't know them," Mary said. "I don't think—"

Joanie squealed, "Pleeeze."

The woman with the dogs looked over and smiled. "They're friendly."

Mary sighed, shook her head. "Okay, but don't pester the sweet lady, and be sure to thank her when you're done." Jewel and Joanie were halfway to the dogs before

Mary could caution them to be careful. "Great kids," I said.

Mary continued to watch the girls. "I'm blessed to have them."

The kids stood on each side of one of the dogs and hugged it like it was a long-lost relative.

I continued to watch the dog and the kids. "You live here long?"

She glanced over at me. "No. Just since...." She paused and looked at the pier.

"Since what?" I asked, and hoped I wasn't being too nosy.

She looked down at the sand on the step and up at me. "I had a job at a convenient store in Charleston after my husband, umm, was gone, but got laid off because of some tax trouble the owners got in. We didn't have anywhere over there to live, and I got to know some guys here and moved."

"What happened to your husband?" She again looked down at the sand.

I was afraid my Charles-like questioning had gone too far, and I didn't say anything. The German shepherds were sitting in the sand, and the girls were running around them with the boys.

The wind was picking up, and Mary whispered, "He's in prison."

"I'm sorry."

She pointed to her girls. "I'm not. He gave me Joanie, the greatest gift possible."

"She's a doll."

"Yes," Mary hesitated before saying, "My husband was selling drugs, and I didn't know a danged thing about it. I felt so stupid."

"Will he be away long?"

She glanced at the girls, and said, "He was caught in the back of a warehouse selling to an undercover cop. Instead of giving up, the idiot tried to shoot his way out." She shook her head. "He shot a police officer. Thank God it didn't kill him. I don't know when he'll ever get out. I hope he doesn't. I don't want him to see Joanie, and I don't want her to see him again— never again."

She looked back at the sand and a tear rolled down her cheek. I wanted to put my arm around her, but didn't. Laughter from the four kids and a couple of barks from the dogs were the only sounds I heard.

Mary looked up at the kids. "I'm so ashamed. I can't bear to go to a homeless shelter because the people there always want to hear what happened. I can't tell them."

"I'm sure they've heard worse, Mary. It wasn't your fault."

She looked at the girls and yelled, "Jewel, Joanie, come on back now and let the nice lady get on with her walk."

Joanie dropped her head. "Mom."

"It's fine," the lady with the dogs said. "The dogs need a rest anyway. They're okay."

I smiled at Mary. "You're outnumbered."

She wiped the tear from her cheek. "It's nice to see them happy. Doesn't happen too much. Hope her next few years aren't as rough as poor Jewel's."

I wondered how to ask what she'd meant without being pushy and regressed to what I'd learned in college psychology. "Oh."

I was afraid my rusty technique had failed until she said, "I grew up near Chicago and never finished high school." She hesitated. "Don't know why I'm telling you this; don't even know you."

"Sometimes it's easier to tell a stranger than it is to tell someone you know."

"I guess. I was in the tenth grade and started dating." She air quoted, 'the greatest guy in the world.'" She looked down at the sand. "I got pregnant and learned the second I told him he wasn't so great."

"He dumped you?"

She chuckled. "Quick as a hummingbird."

"Sorry."

"If you can believe it, that wasn't the worst of it. My parents wanted me to get rid of the baby, wanted me to get an abortion. They insisted. I wasn't the brightest kid around, after all, I was pregnant and in the tenth grade, but I couldn't see how it was the right thing to do. I told mom I wasn't going to." She stopped and looked back at the sand.

"What happened?"

She looked up and pointed to her children. "Jewel." I patted her arm. "Perfect name."

She nodded. "They didn't kick me out of the house, but I felt unwanted. I took some of my things and the little money I had saved from babysitting and bought a bus ticket to Birmingham, Alabama."

"Why Birmingham?"

She smiled. "Have you ever been in Chicago in January?"

I shook my head.

"I figured I had to go south where it was warmer, and I didn't have enough money to get to Florida, so Birmingham was it. Found a shelter for the homeless that had a special area for kids like me. They helped me get a job at a convenient food store. Jewel was born and was the prettiest baby I'd ever seen."

I smiled. "She still is."

"Thank you. You're mighty easy to talk to."

"Sometimes it helps to talk."

"Wanna know about Joanie?"

"Only if you want to tell me."

"I met her dad in Birmingham. Vernon's his name. It was three years ago, around Christmas, in fact. He came in the store, and I thought he was the cutest guy I'd seen since I was there. He was a charmer. Kept coming in and buying chewing gum and he finally asked me out. Dumb me, I said yes. Well, to make a long story short, he proposed on our third date and we got married at the courthouse two weeks later." She smiled. "I was married when I got pregnant with

Joanie." Her smile faded. "I thought everything was going fine. He had a job and brought in a pretty good amount of money. Honest, Mr. Landrum, I had no idea he was getting it selling drugs."

"I believe you."

"Thank you. And then the drug bust and that's when he shot the policeman. Oh God, I was so ashamed. I had to get away and with Jewel in one hand and a child carrier with Joanie in it in the other hand, I got on another Greyhound and ended up in Charleston." She looked over at me. "So there's mystery. Hope I haven't got you all depressed about it."

I smiled and patted her arm. "All I see is a sweet young lady with two wonderful children who are spending time with their mom, playing with two big dogs, and being thrilled to have the gift of the ocean for Christmas."

She patted my hand. "I am blessed. This may be the best Christmas I've had in forever. You know what happened?"

"What?"

She pointed to her two girls. "All the new clothes, a couple more surprise gifts I'll be giving them Christmas morning, because of a gift from someone I don't know."

"Gift?"

"Two days ago there was an envelope under the door of the house…umm, the house where I'm staying. I still can't believe it, there were six, hundred dollar bills in it. At first, I thought it was a mistake, but since the house was supposed to be, umm, vacant, it had to be for me, didn't it?"

"Seems like it," I said, and thought of the money Bernard and the man in the apartment had received.

"I probably should have turned it over to the police, but what would I say? Besides, Christmas was a few days away and I wanted to take the girls to church Christmas Eve and thought how wonderful it would be if they didn't have to wear tattered clothes. Maybe us having a few days without looking poor would be good. What should I have done?"

"Do you have any idea who left it?"

She looked down at the sand and mumbled, "There was a note."

Bernard all over again, I thought. "Did it say *Merry Christmas from Tabatha*?"

She jerked her head up. "How did you know?"

I started to answer, when she said, "Did you say Tabatha?"

I nodded.

"No, it was from someone named Tiffany."

"Are you sure?"

"Yes," she said and smiled. "It reminded me of that fancy jewelry store."

Could Bernard have gotten the name wrong? Could his note have said Tiffany? If it did, it was far beyond a coincidence some of the jewelry stolen was from Tiffany and now money was being left with a note from Tiffany. Charles was right. There was a connection between the thefts and the gifts.

Mary interrupted my thoughts. "Mr. Landrum, are you okay?"

"Oh, sorry Mary. My mind was wandering. Umm, who knew where you were staying?"

"You're not going to get me in trouble, are you?"

"No."

"A few people know, I guess. People who live nearby see us coming and going. I don't think I've told anyone in town. I wanted to tell the nice folks at Bert's because they help me sometimes, but I didn't."

I remembered a light on next door to Finley's house the night Charles and I were there. Finley had said the house was a rental, and squatters occasionally found their way in. "Mary, are you staying in a house on East Eric?"

She stared at me. "Why did you say that?"

"A few nights ago I was at Finley Livers' house and—"

Mary shook her head and interrupted, "He said he wouldn't tell."

I guess that was yes. "He didn't tell me." I explained about seeing the light on and what he had said about squatters.

"It's us. Finley even gave me a ride to Wal-Mart to buy the clothes for the girls. He said we could stay at his house but he'd already rented out the upstairs. Said if the guys living there ever moved, we could have it, real cheap. He's a nice guy."

"You know you can't stay where you are long. It's a rental, and you never know when it'll be needed."

"Mr. Landrum, I know, but I don't know what to do."

"May I make a suggestion?"

"Sure."

"Preacher Burl is a good friend. He understands the bad situations people can get in, and best of all, he's not judgmental. He cares and has helped many people find housing, find jobs, and find their way through rough times. I'd suggest you talk to him, lay everything out, and trust him. He can help."

She tilted her head. "Do you think so?"

"I know so."

"Funny you say that about him. I haven't been to church for a while, umm, years, but when I heard people talking about the

Christmas Eve service, something told me I should go. It's why I asked him if children were invited. I liked the way he said yes. He didn't even think about it. It's why I was so happy to get new clothes for my girls."

"He'd love to see you there tomorrow night."

The woman was calling the dogs to continue their walk. Jewel and Joanie hugged the dogs bye, and Mary hugged me.

Chapter Twenty-One

On the way home, I kept thinking even though the spirit of Christmas may have been sucked out of the hearts of some because of the missing statue, how Mary, despite what many would consider to be a tragic young life, was making the most of the season. She was sharing the ocean with her children and told them how lucky they were to see it firsthand. She had taken the mysterious gift and bought clothes for her children so they would look their best at church Christmas Eve. Mary was a survivor, a survivor who had valued life enough to stand up to her parents at a huge cost and had given birth to Jewel. Yes, Mary was a survivor who had stood strong when many would have given up.

I walked in the door and felt the blast of heat from the overworked furnace and realized how fortunate I was to have my health, a roof over my head, and enough food to fill, or overfill, my stomach. I moved from room to room staring at the walls and started thinking about the money left for Mary, Bernard, and the man who lived in the apartment near Andy. I was confident the money had come from the sale of the stolen jewelry and the Baby Jesus. Mary was certain her note said the money was from Tiffany, and it wouldn't be a stretch to conclude Bernard's had as well.

Regardless how kind and generous the gifts were, I kept coming back to how they may have been the result of thefts of jewelry, surfboards, and the statue. I prayed I was wrong, although doubted it after hearing Mary. Did the recipients of the anonymous cash know about the crimes I suspect had been committed to get the money? Probably not. Did the recipients need the cash? No doubt.

I grabbed a Diet Pepsi, moved to my comfortable chair in the living room and said out loud, "Mary, Bernard, Andy's neighbor." What do they have in common? Down on their luck was a given. But so were others on Folly, as there were everywhere. Two had received a note, and I'd bet Andy's neighbor got one, but hadn't mentioned it to Andy. Did the three know each other? I wasn't certain.

It struck me that there was something else each had in common other than being needy. Bernard, according to Cal, and by his own admission, because of his quick temper, was not welcomed at the area homeless shelters. Andy's neighbor told him he had too much pride to seek help from anyone. And, Mary had said she was ashamed of what had happened to her husband, so much that she wouldn't seek help. It was tenuous, but still a connection. The phone rang before I could give it more thought.

"I've figured it out," Charles said in response to, "Hello."

I sighed. "Anything in particular?"

"Baby Jesus thief. You home?"

I said yes; he said, "Be there in ten." The line went dead.

Nine minutes later, Charles pounded on the door. He rushed past me into the house. He was rubbing his hands together. His coat was zipped up to his neck. He said, "Burrr," unzipped his coat, and threw it on the ottoman. He wore a navy sweatshirt with *UMaine* in white on the front.

"Get serious," he said and headed to the kitchen.

"I've figured it out."

I followed him as he got a Pepsi and plopped down at the kitchen table.

I sat opposite him. "Okay, who did it?"

He took a sip and leaned back in the chair. "Finley, surfer boy, Livers."

"The Finley who started the group to catch the thief?"

"Yep."

"The Finley who invited us to his house and asked us to help the surfers catch the thief?"

"The same one."

Over the years, we had become involved in murder investigations, which should have been none of our business. Through blind luck, a rare burst of skill, and stumbling on information the police were unaware of, we had solved some of the crimes. Much of our success had been because we had spent hours talking through the situation, bounced ideas, good, bad, and terrible, off each other, and somehow figured things out. It appeared we were heading down that path again.

"How do you figure?"

"Misdirection." He leaned forward. "Of everyone here, who looks the least guilty?"

"Preacher Burl, Chief LaMond, you, me, umm——"

"Finley," Charles said and nodded.

I wouldn't have put him far up on my list, but he would have been on it. "Go on."

"I was up half the night thinking about it. Finley started the surfer group so he'd look as innocent as the pope. To throw us off, he asked us to find the thief. What better way to keep us from suspecting him?"

"Preacher Burl asked me to find the person who stole the statue. By your logic, he would be as likely as Finley."

Charles shook his head. "See, that's where my all- night thinkin' paid off. Burl couldn't have done it because he was with us when the money was stolen from First Light."

"I wasn't saying Burl did it. I was pointing out that because someone asked us to help doesn't mean he's guilty."

He took another sip and tapped his forefinger on the table. "I'll give you that one. How about this: What do Bernard and Andy's neighbor have in common?" Before I could answer, he said, "Hard times," and leaned back in the chair. "Do you remember what Finley talked about two of the times we'd been with him?"

"He hoped the money collected by both Cal and Burl went to people who didn't benefit from the regular groups serving the homeless."

Charles held out both hands. "You do pay attention. And then money shows up at Bernard's sleeping bag and the neighbor's door. Chris, it's Finley. I know it."

I wasn't ready to concede he was right and remembered other surfers had said the same thing about the underserved homeless, but knew the next thing I was going to tell him would have him pulling a muscle trying to pat himself on the back and then reaching for the phone to call the police. I slipped the phone in my pocket and told him about Mary and the note. When I reached the part about her living next to Finley, I thought Charles was going to erupt.

"Wow," he said and jumped up and waved his hands in the air. "We got him. Let's call Cindy and Preacher Burl."

I motioned for him to sit. He returned to the chair and shouted another "Wow!"

"Charles, let's say you're—we're—right. What we don't have is the statue. Let's say Finley is the thief and if he doesn't still have it, he knows who he sold it to. What do you think the chances are he'll tell the police where it is?"

"None."

"I agree. I also think Finley is serious about wanting to help people who aren't served by the traditional agencies, people like Mary, Bernard, and the other guy." I took a deep breath and couldn't believe what I was going to say next.

"We need to talk to him."

Charles stared at me, scratched his head, and stared at me some more. "Chris, if I'd said it, you'd call me a bloomin' idiot, someone with a death wish, and a bunch of other things you college-educated logical thinkers could come up with. Have we died and you came back as me?"

"If Finley took the statue, the only chance we have of getting it back is to talk to him. It's not much of a chance, but it's a chance. And, I don't have a death wish. We could call him and see if he would meet us at a public place. We could tell him we found something about the thefts and wanted him to know before we called the police. I'll offer to buy him supper."

Charles looked at his Pepsi, and at me, and shrugged. "What're you waiting for?"

Finley answered on the second ring. Music blared in the background, and I had to yell for him to hear who it was. The music stopped, and I lowered my voice and made the pitch to share information about the thefts and supper. He hesitated but agreed.

Chapter Twenty-Two

Finley had chosen to meet us at Planet Follywood at six- thirty, and as sure as clockwork—Charles's clockwork—he and I arrived at six. There was one vacant table, the same table Mayor Newman and I had shared a few days earlier. From the jukebox, Bob Marley's distinct voice bopped through "Get Up, Stand Up."

Charles looked at the entry and at me. "Before you ask if I'm going to say, 'Hey, Finley, steal any Baby Jesus statues lately?' what's your plan to get a confession?"

"I've got an idea and still have thirty minutes to figure the rest of it out. I hope he's as concerned about the underdog as I think he is."

"Hi, guys."

I looked up, and Camille was at the table and setting a glass of Cabernet in front of me and a Bud Light beside Charles. She said, "Anything to eat?" I told her we were waiting for someone, and she said to wave when we needed her.

I took a sip and stared at the Christmas tree beside the jukebox. The lights were much brighter and more festive than I felt. Did my plan make sense? Earlier it sounded like a good idea to talk to Finley, but now I was beginning to agree with Charles. I was a bloomin' idiot.

Charles was facing the door and cleared his throat as he nodded toward it. I looked over my shoulder and saw Finley in the entry. He looked around and spotted us. He took a step back, hesitated, appeared to take a deep breath and headed our way. I hoped we didn't look as nervous as he did.

I moved around to Charles's side of the table and pointed to the seat where I had been sitting. Finley gave a slight nod and took the seat.

Charles said, "Bad day for surfin'."

He was trying to put Finley at ease since to Charles every day was a bad day for surfing.

"You bet."

Camille was back at the table and asked if Finley wanted anything. He looked at what we were drinking and said water.

I glanced at Charles who for once was keeping his mouth shut. The ball was in my court. I turned to Finley. "We appreciate how much you've done with your surfer group to make sure nobody takes anything from the Nativity, and the collection you took at the surf shop will help the needy. It took a lot of work to organize the group."

Finley said, "Too bad it didn't work." He looked at the Christmas tree and back at me. "You said you had something about the stealing."

The Beach Boys version of "Little St. Nick" blasted from the juke-box, the savory smell of hamburgers filled the air, and it was my turn to attempt to save the spirit of Christmas for Preacher Burl, First Light Church, and all who had been hurt by the disappearance of the iconic statue.

"Yes, and I think you'll find it interesting. There might still be time to get it back," I said and received a stare from Charles and a shrug from Finley.

"Charles and I decided the only thing we were interested in was finding the statue. We don't care about the jewelry or the surfboards. Insurance will take care of it." Charles looked at me like *we did?* "Remember the money someone left Andy's neighbor?"

Finley said, "Sure."

"I've learned someone had left money for Bernard, a homeless man, and for your friend Mary. They don't know who gave it to them. We're pretty sure we do. Have you heard about it?"

"Umm, don't think so."

Wouldn't yes or a no have been the right answer? I began the story, which sounded much better earlier than it did now.

"Do you know the guy who lives across the street and up a house from you? It's the brick one." I asked, and crossed my fingers the answer was no.

"I don't recall ever seeing anyone there. Don't know who it is."

"That makes sense," I said. "Jimmy Russell's a friend, about my age. He travels with his job; gone weeks at a time. Because he's gone so much, he has a security system that monitors the inside of his house for movement, and he has cameras inside and outside that keep watch on his property."

Thank you, Cindy, for giving me the idea about cameras from you talking the other day about someone capturing the video of someone leaving the porch after stealing the ink cartridges.

Camille returned with Finley's water. Charles and I ordered burgers and fries, and Finley said, "The same."

I took a deep breath and continued, "I don't understand how it works, but through some high-tech gadget, he can monitor the system from anywhere through his telephone. He said it records a couple of weeks of data, and he also can see what the cameras see in real time."

Finley said, "I've heard of that stuff."

Charles looked like he was afraid to break into my story since he didn't know where it was going. All I hoped was he didn't ask who Jimmy Russell was. I didn't know where I was going either, but I continued talking slower than I was thinking.

"Jimmy's been in Oklahoma all month working with a company installing a new computer system. He thought he'd be home for Christmas, but it looks like he'll be stuck there until January."

"That's too bad," Charles added. "I'll miss seeing him at Cal's."

Charles couldn't bear for me to have a friend we didn't share, even an imaginary one.

"Me too," I said to Charles, and returned to Finley. "Jimmy doesn't have family here so it won't be too bad. Anyway, it's way more than you probably want to know. The important thing is he called this morning, and after he told me he wouldn't be here Christmas, he asked what had been going on since he'd been away. I told him about the missing statue, the theft of jewelry and surfboards, and the mysterious cash people had been receiving."

Our food arrived, and another reggae song reverberated off the walls. We each took a bite—Charles and Finley, because they were hungry, and me to stall until I figured out what to say.

I took another breath and said, "Jimmy asked a strange question. He asked if the lady with the two kids who got the money was staying in the house across from his. He said he'd seen a woman with two children coming and going. He knew the house was a rental and was surprised to see three people since there wasn't a car in the drive. Jimmy's a *live and let live* person, and said he didn't care how or why she was there. I told him it was Mary."

Finley fiddled with his fries and stared at his plate. I took a bite of the burger, and impatient Charles said, "So?"

"Here's the interesting part, Finley. Jimmy called me back later and said because of our conversation, he'd reviewed the video that had been recorded and a few days ago one of the cameras caught someone looking like he was sneaking up to Mary's back door and then running back in the direction he'd come from. Jimmy said it seemed strange and wondered if it had anything to do with her getting the money." I paused to let it sink in. "I asked him to describe the person. He said the guy was dressed in black, about your height Finley, and his head was covered with a hoodie."

Finley said, "Are you—"

I waved for him to stop, and continued, "Jimmy said the guy was running back to the house where he had come from. Funny thing Finley, it was your house."

It was my imagination, but it seemed like the world had stopped. If music was playing, I didn't hear it. If people in the crowded room were talking, I couldn't hear them. Was my bluff going to work, or was he going to laugh at me and walk out?

He looked at his burger. Charles was silent, for a change. And, my heart thumped like a bass drum.

Finley picked up his fork and pointed it at me, and started to speak. He shook his head and returned the fork to the table. Silence was deafening until he said, "Mr. Landrum, I'm not a thief. I didn't steal anything. Your friend didn't see me. He couldn't have because I never went over there."

Crap, I thought. I had begun to believe my story. I glanced at Charles, and he looked as dejected as I felt.

Then Finley said, "What if I can get the statue back?"

Charles leaned forward. "How?"

"I don't know for certain if I can, but I think I know what happened to it."

"How?" I asked.

"Are you going to turn me in to the cops?"

"Don't plan to," Charles said.

That's the truth since we didn't know any reason to—yet.

"Dude said I can trust you, so I'm taking him at his word. I honest to God didn't know anything about it until the other day. When I started the surfer group, I hoped we could catch the thief and get the Baby Jesus back to the church. I didn't know about the money for Andy's neighbor." He stopped and caught Camille's attention. "Think I need a beer." He turned back to Charles and me, lowered his voice, and said, "I saw the person take money to Mary's."

Charles interrupted, "Who?"

Finley shook his head. "Sorry, Mr. Fowler. I'm not going to tell you."

I didn't want him to stop talking. "That's okay, Finley. You said you might be able to get the statue back."

"Yeah, maybe. I didn't put two and two together until I saw, umm, the person leaving the money for Mary. I know he, or she, didn't have any to give so he, or she, had to steal the stuff. The next time I saw the person I said what I had seen and asked if he, or she, stole the Baby Jesus, the jewelry, and the other things. Then he or, never mind, I'll say he to make it easier to talk about. It don't mean it was a *he*."

I nodded. "Go on."

"He told me, yes, but if I went to the cops he'd deny it, and there wouldn't be any proof. I asked why he did it, and he said he was tired of seeing so many people in hapless straights who weren't being helped by poverty agencies. He knew agencies were doing a good job, but there were folks who for one reason or another had fallen through the cracks, the invisible ones I had talked about before."

"I remember you mentioning it in one of the meetings," I said, wanting to make him comfortable and to continue talking.

"The person who took the stuff told me he'd heard the statue was valuable. He didn't know why and confessed if he had known the story behind it, he wouldn't have taken it. He said he knew someone in Charleston who would buy it for a bunch of money, something about the person having a buyer he thought would want it. The other stuff was taken to hock. He was going to give every cent of what he got to the people he felt were in greatest need. He said he left bunches of money for people we haven't even heard about." He hesitated, glanced at Charles, and back at me. "Did you know Bernard's a war hero, has all sorts of medals, but came home from Afghanistan with a bad head injury. It knocked some of his memory out and left him with a bad temper."

I had known something was wrong but didn't know why, and it possibly explained his confusing Tiffany for Tabatha. I said, "VA would help him."

Finley shook his head. "Yeah, if he'd let them. He won't. Don't know why, but he's walked away from several VA facilities. They can't make him stay."

I said, "That's too bad."

Charles said, "So how can you get the statue back?"

"You sure you're not going to the cops?"

In twenty-four hours First Light will be holding its Christmas Eve service. Getting the statue back was more important than anything else.

The thefts from the porches were another matter, one I'd deal with later.

I nodded. "Yes."

"How can you get it back?" Charles repeated.

"I'm not certain I can. A person in Charleston bought the statue, paid good money for it. He told the person who took it that the man he was going to sell it to lived out of state and was going to come to Charleston to get it in a few days. I don't know what a few days meant. He might already have it, and it's long gone."

"So it could still be in Charleston," I said. "If it is, how will you get it?"

He took a sip of beer. "I don't know."

Charles said, "Let us help."

Finley looked at the bottle and at Charles. "No. This is on me."

I didn't want to push more than we already had. "Okay, if you need anything or think of anything we can do, call me."

"Sure."

He slid his chair back, stood, and scurried out of the restaurant.

Bruce Springsteen's version of "Santa Claus is Coming to Town" filled the room and I wondered if the Baby Jesus would be coming back to town.

Chapter Twenty-Three

Charles and I stayed in Planet Follywood and debated what to do. We could tell Cindy what we knew, or thought we knew, but we had no proof and if the police got involved, Finley's chances of getting the statue would vanish. Besides, the chief may think the three people we knew who'd received cash had been involved and could get them in trouble. I wasn't going to let that happen. Charles suggested we could follow Finley, and if he got in a tight spot, we could help. The more we talked about that idea, the worse it sounded.

We speculated who the thief was, concluded it was one of the surfers, but that only narrowed it down to a dozen or more people, and those were the people we had seen or met at the meetings. There could be others we didn't know. So, that was little help. It could also be Finley, and he made up the story to get off the hook. As much as it went against Charles's grain, we decided the best course of action was to wait and hope Finley had told us the truth and was able to get the statue back. The only good news was when Camilla told us the temperature tomorrow was going to be warm. It may not have made the children who had hoped for a rare dusting of snow happy, but it was great news for Preacher

Burl who could hold his Christmas Eve service on the beach.

I had a hard time going to sleep. I played Finley's words over in my head. I couldn't remember everything that was said when I was around the surfers and at the meetings, but I kept thinking there were others who were concerned about people who had fallen through the social services safety net. Ryan and Truman rented the second floor from Finley so he had more contact with them than the others. Hadn't Teddye said something? I wondered why Finley had been so concerned about saying he or she. Most people would have said he, regardless of gender. Did it mean anything or was I grasping for answers?

I didn't know about the temperature, but the weather forecasters were right about Christmas Eve being cloudless. Beams of sunshine streamed through the bedroom window, and I realized I had slept a couple of hours later than usual. I also realized I was hungry, so I walked to Bert's, received a cheerful "Merry Christmas Eve," from Eric, grabbed a cup of coffee, and remembered how good the mini donuts looked that Mary's children ate. I bought a pack, and walked to the Tides Hotel where I could sit in a comfortable chair in the lobby and look at the ocean.

"Come to help us?" I turned and saw Jamie, a longtime employee of the hotel and leader of the Folly Beach Bluegrass Society. He was holding a large, clear plastic bag stuffed with ropes.

"Going to hang someone?" I said.

"Not a bad idea, but not on Christmas Eve. We're putting up a tent on the other side of the pier."

The hotel rented tents for special events although I couldn't imagine a wedding reception or any other kind of event today. "What's the event?"

"We heard Preacher Burl was having Christmas Eve service on the beach, and a few of us decided it may get cold and windy, so we pitched in and rented a tent. The hotel helped. We're putting it up now. It's terrible about the Baby Jesus; thought it would be something we could do."

I told him I'd stop by after finishing my healthy breakfast.

Jamie looked at the donuts and the powdered sugar on my shirt. "No hurry. At your age, you couldn't be much help." He chuckled and walked away.

I saw little humor in his comment, but he was right. I continued eating the donuts and wondering when, or if, I would be hearing from Finley. It wasn't ten o'clock, but I was as impatient as Charles.

It turned out to be a beautiful Christmas Eve. Reflections of the sun sparkled off the calm ocean; the temperature was in the low-sixties and several people were walking on the beach and around town in shirt-sleeves. I decided not to go home because if I did, I would stare at the phone and worry about when or if Finley would call. I dropped by a couple of shops and talked with the owners about the weather, and how early they would be closing. At each store, I had to answer if there was anything new about the statue. As much as I wanted to, it was impossible to get it off my mind. I grabbed a quick lunch at the Crab Shack, walked to the small Folly River Park overlooking the river and admired the large, real, Christmas tree covered in colorful lights and ornaments as it watched over the park. It was surrounded by other decorations, which brought joy to young and old. I stared at the river, and headed back to the Folly pier. At the intersection that led to Pewter Hardware and First Light's Nativity, I saw Samuel and Jason sitting on the incline leading to the edge of the park. Their bikes were on the ground beside them, and they stared at the display.

I shook my head and walked the half block to the teens. "Merry Christmas Eve, guys."

They had watched me walking toward them, stood, and wiped the dust off the back of their jeans. Jason looked across the street at the Nativity and at me. "What's merry about it, Mr. Landrum? We failed."

"You didn't fail. You've done everything you could. You found the ink cartridges. You've asked students about the statue. And Jason, to tell you the truth, even though you got me in trouble with your mom, I'm impressed how hard you've worked to help. No, you didn't fail."

Samuel looked at Jason to see if he was going to say anything. He didn't, and Samuel turned to me. "All we wanted was to find Baby Jesus, and all we found was some stupid ink." He pointed to the manger. "Jason's right, we failed."

"You didn't find the statue, but Christmas is more than a carved piece of wood. It's a time to celebrate the birth of the real Jesus. That will happen if the statue is over there or not. It's time to think about all the good in our lives. Jason, you have a great mom," I smiled, "and she has a great son. And Samuel, I don't know your dad as well as I do Jason's mom, but from everything I know, he's a wonderful dad. Think how lucky you are."

"I guess you're sort of right," Samuel said. "But we also know how much the statue means to people."

I looked at the distraught teen. "Many of them will be at church tonight. Why don't you come and look at all the good we have and celebrate instead of the bad stuff that's happened?"

Jason looked at the ground and glanced at Samuel before saying, "Don't worry, Mr. Landrum, we'll be there. Mom'll kill me if I'm not."

Samuel giggled. "Dad will too."

"What's so funny?"

Samuel said, "Dad and Jason's mom are sort of coming to church together."

It surprised me more than him giggling. "A date?"

Samuel patted Jason's arm. "Sort of. He said they are doing it because we're friends. He said they might as well be friends too."

Jason laughed. "Ain't it a crock?"

I looked at Jason. "I think it's nice."

Jason said. "I think it's weird."

To my knowledge, Amber hadn't dated since we'd broken up. To be honest, I didn't know what to think other than I was happy for them and while I hadn't thought of them together, I had a good feeling about it.

"See you tonight," I said as they mounted their bikes and peddled away. If the rest of the teenagers growing up on Folly were half as good as those two, the island's future was in good hands.

I continued to the pier and walked about halfway to the end and looked at the large, white tent at the spot on the beach where First Light met in nice weather. Jamie and a couple of his helpers were carrying folding chairs to the tent from a trailer at the beach access point. I was touched by how the island's residents, regardless of social status, wealth, beliefs, and differences came together to help each other in the time of need. I had seen this level of community support numerous times. I also thought of the misery, demons, and helplessness Bernard must be going through, and how Mary must be having mixed thoughts about how wonderful it was to have her two girls with her, but feeling the weight of such a bleak outlook for their future. I didn't know Andy's neighbor or the other people who had received money but hoped the anonymous gifts had brought cheer and hope.

I had never been a fan of telephones, but I couldn't recall wanting one to ring more than I did at this moment. It was three o'clock, four short hours until First Light's service, and nothing from Finley. Thirty more minutes had passed before I heard the much-awaited ring. The screen showed a number I didn't recognize. I would normally have let it go to voicemail, but not today.

"Mr. Landrum, this is Finley."

I had long championed a more civil and hospitable way of answering the phone. I abandoned my crusade and blurted, "Did you get it?"

There was silence on the other end; I wondered if he had heard my question. I caught myself holding my breath.

"No."

I lowered myself on one of the benches that dotted the pier. "What happened?"

"I tried," Finley said, sounding as depressed as I felt. "Honest, I tried."

"I'm sure you did. What happened?"

"I went to the place that bought it and told the guy I was a friend of, umm, the person who took it. I made up a story and told him my friend had taken it by mistake, and the statue meant a lot to the owner. I told him I'd buy it back." Finley hesitated. "I didn't know where I'd get the money. I figured you and Charles, and maybe the preacher could help. The slimy son of a ... the guy said he'd seen on television where the statue had been stolen, and he didn't think I was telling the truth. He said two old guys had come around asking about buying a wood carved statue from Germany. He said he didn't know how stupid I thought he was, or how stupid the old guys thought he was, but he knew my story was a bunch of sh—umm, crap."

"What did you say?"

"I didn't know what to say, Mr. Landrum. I didn't confess to lying to him but told him how important the Baby Jesus was to the church and even to people who don't go to church over here. I figured he wouldn't call the police after what I knew about him, but I was afraid he was going to throw me out on my ass. Anyway, he calmed down a little and said he was sorry about the missing Jesus, and he was busy and couldn't talk any longer. Busy, huh? I was the only person in his store. I didn't argue with him." Finley sighed. "What else could I have done, Mr. Landrum?"

I assured him there wasn't anything and thanked him for trying.

He said, "Sorry," and hung up.

"Me too," I said to silent air.

Chapter Twenty-Four

T he sun had set an hour and a half before I walked to the beach, head down, and feeling like I'd failed Preacher Burl. Three, duel-headed halogen lights on telescoping stands illuminated the inside of the tent. The heavy-duty work lights were in the rear of the tent, and their power cords snaked across the sand to an electric box under the pier. Solar- powered pathway lights were placed in the sand every six feet to light the way to the service.

Jamie leaned against a post at the beach access point.

He looked exhausted but was smiling. "Where'd all this come from?"

He shrugged. "Called in favors. Got everything donated. It'd take a cold-hearted person to turn down helping a church on Christmas Eve. Besides, I know a thing or two about the builder I got most of the stuff from." He chuckled. "He'd rather I don't share what I know."

Charles had been standing by the tent and came over to Jamie and me. It was a half hour before the service was to begin so we stayed with Jamie as a few other early birds arrived. Charles stared at me. I knew what he wanted, but I wasn't ready to tell him. Jamie said he had a volunteer crew from the hotel who would take everything down after the service, and he'd better check in and make sure they would be around when he needed them. I thanked him for his effort; he grinned and said he didn't do it for me, but would accept thanks anyway.

Charles leaned closer. "Okay, I was trying not to be my nosy, nervous, impatient self, being it's Christmas Eve, but we've been standing here ten minutes."

"Yes," I said.

"And I haven't pestered you about what you learned from Finley. And, you've not thought it was important enough to say anything about it."

I looked at the tent and at Charles. 'Suppose I didn't want to say it. Finley talked to the man who bought the statue and offered to buy it back. He wouldn't sell. He told Finley two *old* men had been to see him, but he had known about the thefts and figured the *old* guys were trying to trick him."

"So it was one of the antique dealers. Damn."

"I heard that." We turned, and Burl was standing five feet away.

Charles took off his Tilley and bowed in Burl's direction. "Sorry, Preacher."

Burl waved the apology off. "What pray tell caused such an utterance, Brother Charles?"

Charles turned to me, and I realized Burl didn't know about Finley. This wasn't the time to get into it.

"Charles was expressing disappointment that Baby Jesus hadn't been found."

Burl frowned. "I echo his sentiment, but perhaps would have chosen another expression. As disheartening as it is, I am focusing on the positive and refuse to let whatever happened to the icon ruin such a glorious night on the eve of celebrating our Savior's birth."

Dude and Pluto were next to join us. In addition to Pluto's rhinestone covered collar and leash, he wore a red and white striped sweater. Dude wore typical Dude. Burl smiled and suggested we move to the "magnificent sanctuary provided by the good folks of Folly." We took it to mean the tent and followed him. Lottie was seated near the front as we stepped under the tent. A steady cool breeze had been coming off the ocean all afternoon, and Jamie had lowered all the sides except the back flap. Before Burl moved inside, he slipped his robe over his jacket. He moved to the portable lectern and placed his Bible and a folder on top of it.

Next to arrive was Dude's snarky employee Stephon, followed closely by Teddye, Deb, Truman, and Finley. The group looked around and mumbled something I couldn't hear. Burl was quick to reach them and gave his best pastoral smile, told them he was thrilled they were here and told them to take seats of their choice.

Others arrived in clumps. Members of other congregations appeared, I assumed to show support for First Light. Another of the surfers, Todd, arrived by himself and quickly attached himself to Truman and Finley. Samuel's dad, Jacob looked around the corner of the tent and stepped inside; Amber was at his side. I was glad their sons had told me about them coming together. They looked around and headed to the back row, left two seats vacant, and sat in the next two.

Bernard arrived next and had on his new jacket and wore a look on his face that looked like a combination of fear and confusion. I rushed to him and said, "It's good to see you."

"Thank you, sir. I almost chickened out. I'm not comfortable in crowds."

I wanted to ask if the name on the note could have been Tiffany, but figured now it didn't matter. I said, "You'll be fine. You can sit with Charles and me if you'd like."

"I might." He nodded and walked over to Finley and said something.

I spoke to George and Shelesa Brew, a couple I recognized from my gallery and knew were regulars at the Catholic Church, and they introduced me to their friends Jim and Dianne Stevens. I told them how much Preacher Burl appreciated their support, and excused myself. I then walked over to Jacob and Amber and said I was glad to see them together. Jacob blinked twice, looked at Amber, and said, "Thank you, Chris. Amber and I've shared a few meals. She's quite a lady." He patted her arm.

I smiled. "Yes she is. Where're the boys?"

Amber looked around. "They're on their way. It's irritating, they're getting more unreliable all the time." She looked at me like it was my fault and then looked at her watch.

"They're teenagers," Jacob said. "Doubt we were any better when we were their age."

Amber grinned. "You're right."

Burl tapped on the lectern—pulpit—with his Bible. "Please take thy comfortable seats provided by the good and generous folks at the Tides."

The harsh halogen lights gave Burl a deer in the headlights look. He blinked a few times before his eyes adjusted to the unflattering lighting. Even with that distraction, his smile was infectious. He began with his traditional *silence thy portable communication devices* opening and looked toward the back of the room, paused, and waved for someone to come in.

I turned and saw Mary and her girls step in the tent, and at the preacher's urging, walked to four empty seats in the next to last row. Mary was wearing her new coat and gingerly stepped through the sand in shiny shoes, which looked to be as new as the coat. She held her shoulders back, her head held high, and motioned for the girls to take the seats beside her.

Burl smiled at the latecomers. "Welcome ladies. Welcome."

At the same time, I caught someone else entering from the back. I was surprised to see Karen looking around the tent. She had called yesterday and said she didn't think she'd make it. A man was sitting beside me, but there was an empty chair on the other side of him. I asked if he would mind moving one chair over. He noticed Karen, grinned at me, and scooted to the next seat.

She took the empty seat and leaned close and whispered, "Sorry for being late. The dead don't keep good track of time."

"Thanks for coming," was all I said before Burl asked us to stand and sing "O Come, All Ye Faithful."

We stood, tried to sing, and if nothing else, sounded spirited. After our enthusiastic, although off-key effort, Burl thanked us for attending, and gave a special thanks to everyone who had helped make the service possible. He opened his folder and glanced down before continuing.

I looked around and wondered if the thief was here, and then focused on Burl.

"Tonight's not about First Light, not about me, it's about everyone. It's about faith. It's about hope. It's not about the past and whatever has been negatively tugging at our minds and bodies. We're gathered to look to the future. I know several of you are members of other congregations on our incredible island. You've been part of the dedicated group who have watched over the Nativity day and night, and have shared with me you are in attendance to show solidarity. Some of you are part of the caring surfer community who has been standing sentry at the symbol of our Lord's birth." He smiled. "Some of you do not attend church on a regular basis but feel compelled to visit a place of worship at Christmas. I say to each of you, regardless of your reason, welcome. I love you, God loves you." He squinted at the bright lights as he looked out at the assembled group. "Please stand and let's join together and blend our melodious voices into singing "The First Noel."

Once again, the group made a valiant effort to not sound like a flock of seagulls fighting over a fish. Perhaps I was in the Christmas spirit, because the singing sounded pleasant.

We finished singing, *Born is the King of Israel!* and Preacher Burl motioned for us to be seated. We did and waited for him to continue. Instead, he stared at the back of the tent, his mouth opened, but no words came out. I turned to see what he was looking at.

Samuel and Jason were at the entry. Their coats were zipped up to their neck, each had a huge smile, and they were holding a dark green blanket wrapped around something. By now, a few of the others had turned to see what had stopped the service. Jason pushed the top of the blanket to the side, and I could see a tiny head peeking through—the head of a hand carved, statue of the Baby Jesus.

Jason and Samuel's smiles were so captivating I barely heard Preacher Burl scream, "Hallelujah!" The next thing I saw was Amber and Jacob rushing to their sons. They beat Burl by a half step.

Samuel cradled the Baby Jesus in his arms and held them out to the preacher. Burl took the statue, which was still wrapped in the blanket and held it close to his chest. He whispered something to the boys; Jason said something, and Burl walked to the front of the church. The boys followed as did Amber and Jacob. There were low mumblings from some of the flock, but most of us stood and stared at the group assembled at the lectern. Burl said something to Amber and Jacob, and they moved behind their sons. The boys glanced at Burl and down at the sand. Burl motioned for us to be seated.

"Brothers and sisters," he said, his voice stronger than ever. "We have witnessed a miracle, the type of miracle that can only come from God. Please join me in silent prayer."

The only sounds that could be heard were a couple of vehicles on Arctic Avenue and the faint sounds of live music from a nearby bar.

Burl broke the silence. "Brothers Jason and Samuel have agreed to share how they came upon the miracle I am now holding to my bosom." He looked at Jason.

Jason turned to Samuel, who gave him a dirty look and said, "Thanks a lot."

Samuel started to speak to the group, hesitated and moved behind the lectern. He was five inches taller than the preacher and visible to everyone.

"Umm, hi folks." He hesitated and glanced at Burl and back at the group before him. "Hi, flock people. Preacher Burl asked us to tell how we found Baby Jesus. Well, some of you know Jason and I have been looking for the missing baby since we heard it'd been snatched." He smiled. "My friend here, Jason, got in trouble from his mom for us nosing around the island—sorry about that, Mrs. Lewis. Anyway, Mr. Landrum told us we better stop nosing around in people's trash, so we sort of did stop. We almost gave up on finding it, and we were on our way over here a little while ago when Jason said we ought to ride by the Nativity one more time. He said you surfers and church people who have been watching it would have stopped and headed to church. Isn't that right, Jason?"

Jason nodded and motioned for Samuel to continue. "Well, we sort of rode by and almost didn't see it. The Baby Jesus, the man from the Methodist Church lent the Nativity, was lying in back in the hay. And holy moly, there was another baby's head sticking out of the manger. I was so excited I nearly ran my bike into a pole before I could stop." He paused and looked at me. "I know, I know, Mr. Landrum. The bad guy could still be there and get us in trouble. We looked around all cautious like and didn't see anyone so we thought it was safe. Jason said we shouldn't be carrying a baby around on our bikes, even if it was made out of wood, so I rushed home and got this blanket while Jason stayed with Jesus." He lifted the corner of the blanket up so everyone could see it. "We came here, and that's the entire story."

Jason leaned toward Samuel and said, "The note."

Samuel reached into his jacket pocket and pulled out a small slip of paper. "Oh yeah, stuck under the baby's head was this." He held the paper in the air. "It says, *Merry Christmas*. He turned the note over and looked at the back of it and turned it back to the front. "That's all it says. Don't it beat all?"

I couldn't have said it better; differently, but not better. I looked around and saw tears in Mary's eyes, and Amber and Jacob were beaming. Preacher Burl wiped a tear from his eye, put his arms around the boys, and then took the statue and its blanket from Jason and placed it on the lectern.

Charles leaned over and said, "I suppose sometime in my many years on this earth, I have been happier, but for the life of me, I can't remember when."

Preacher Burl took a couple of deep breaths, looked at the carved statue, and motioned for us to stand. "How about singing "Away in a Manger"?" He had lost track of where he was in the service, but I doubted anyone cared. I could feel the excitement in the tent as we stood and began:

Away in a manger, no crib for a bed, The little Lord Jesus lay down His sweet head.

The stars in the bright sky looked down where He lay,

The little Lord Jesus asleep on the hay.

Some of us got several of the words right; none of us appeared to care. Pure joy filled the spaces unoccupied by the correct lyrics.

Chapter Twenty-Five

I spent Christmas morning walking around town and enjoying the warm weather. I grabbed coffee from Bert's, received a hardy "Merry Christmas," from Eric, who was way too cheery for someone who had to work Christmas Day. I chuckled at his words, and the red Christmas hat that adorned his well-maned head. I walked to the Folly River Park, looked out at the one small boat meandering downstream, and walked over to the Nativity, the site of the crime, which had nearly stolen the spirit of Christmas from the community. No surfers or church members were looking over the empty manger. The town was silent, not quite *not a creature was stirring* quiet, but close. I smiled as I thought about the look on Preacher Burl's face when Jason and Samuel entered with the statue.

I didn't know who had taken the icon, nor who had stolen the packages or the surfboards off the porches, but I had a strong suspicion. What was I going to do about it? I couldn't prove it. If I was right, the thefts were to get money to help people who needed it the most. Admirable, but stealing was stealing. So, why was I so conflicted about what to do? Maybe it was because I had seen the look in Mary's eyes when she could do something good for her children.

Perhaps it was because I saw the glimmer of hope in Bernard's confused and distressed mind when he could buy groceries and know someone did care about him. I imagined the neighbor who had received the early, and unexpected Christmas gift as he went through a tough time, had also felt gratitude and the strength to get back on his feet. Maybe…maybe I don't know. I did know it was time to get to Cal's party.

The smell of fries met me at the door, the sounds of laughter filled the room, and the festive colors of Christmas lights twinkled from most every surface as well as from the multiple Christmas trees. It was early afternoon, and Cal's Country Christmas Celebration was in full swing. The jukebox, normally full of country classics, had been stuffed with Christmas tunes, and as unbelievable as it may have been to regulars, some of the songs weren't being performed by country artists who were either crooning for their Master or spending eternity in a much warmer climate. Harry Connick, Jr.'s version of "Jingle Bells" could be heard between bursts of laughter. Cal's Christmas day celebration had grown to be one of Folly's most popular events, especially for those who didn't have families to spend the holiday with.

Charles was the first to notice me. I almost didn't recognize him since he had abandoned his college mascot sweatshirts and had on a bright red one with a giant Santa's head on the front.

"About time you got here," he said. "Merry Christmas to you, too."

He put his arm around my shoulders. "I'll let you sugarcoat being late. It's Christmas." He looked behind me. "Where's Karen? She told me last night she'd be coming with you."

"She called this morning. Another death."

Our conversation was interrupted when Cal tapped on a vintage, baseball-sized silver microphone in the center of the tiny stage. "Let this old cowboy interrupt your celebrating for a minute."

Most of the gathered group stopped talking and turned to the stage. One group kept talking and Cal, tapped on the mike. "To paraphrase a preacher I know, please silence thy big mouths."

That got everyone's attention. Cal grinned, the twinkling lights on the crown of his Stetson matched the smile on his face. "I wanted to thank ya'll. This is the fourth year I've had this shindig, and this is the best by a Texas mile. Now some of you have asked if I'd sing a few Christmas ditties so who am I to turn down such nice requests?"

It wouldn't have taken many requests to tempt him. He took his guitar out of the case, strummed a couple of chords, and said, "I'll start with a song my good buddy, Gene Autry, made famous a few years back. Some of you may know it. It's called "Rudolph the Red-Nosed Reindeer."

Cal's *few years back* happened to be before I was born, and from the number of people in the room who started singing along with him, "Some of you may know it," was a Texas-sized understatement. Charles said he was going to spread some Christmas cheer and headed toward the bar. I looked around the room and saw many of the people who had been at the Christmas Eve service. I was surprised to see Dude's employee, Stephon. He was standing at the bar, sipping a beer, and frowning, but at least he was here. I recognized a few of the surfers I had met in the last two weeks. Teddye and Finley were huddled in discussion at one of the tables, and Roscoe, Todd, Slick Surfin' Sal, and Ryan were at the adjoining table watching Cal as he finished singing and placed his guitar back in the case.

Cal said, "Be back a little later with a couple of more of my favorite Christmas songs." He pointed his finger at me, stepped off the stage, and headed my way.

I said, "Merry Christmas. Looks like a full house."

He gave me an awkward hug and said, "Ain't it great news about the Baby Jesus coming home?"

I said it was as he reached in his back pocket. He said, "Was wondering when you'd get here. Got something for you." He pulled out a light-gray envelope and handed it to me. It was addressed *Chris and Charles*.

I shrugged and took it from him. "Where'd it come from?"

"Found it under the door when I opened up this morning."

I looked for Charles. He was talking to Mel Evans and his significant other Caldwell. I caught his eye and he said something to Mel and came over to Cal and me. I showed him the envelope and yanked it back when he tried to grab it out of my hand. I opened it and pulled out a small sheet of paper the same color as the envelope. On the paper was a neatly printed note and I read it to Charles and Cal: *Sorry I stole the stuff. Didn't mean to hurt the city or the church. You see, I had to help my forgotten friends, the invisible ones. Couldn't think of any other way to do it. Please apologize to the preacher for me. He seems like a good person. Also, say I'm sorry to the police.*

Charles glanced at the paper. "Don't suppose it's signed?"

Cal removed his Stetson and pointed it at the note. "Holy horse-radish. We've got a confession right here on Christmas Day."

Nat King Cole's version of "Frosty the Snowman" played from the jukebox and I stood silent and stared at the note.

As if on cue, Preacher Burl stepped in the door. I was surprised and pleased to see Lottie with him. They weren't walking hand in hand, but their body language said they weren't far from it. Burl saw Cal and headed our way.

"Merry Christmas, Brother Cal. Thanks for the invitation." He put his arm behind Lottie and nudged her closer to Cal. "You know my friend, Lottie, don't you?"

Cal tipped his Stetson to her. "I do. Welcome, Miss Lottie."

She smiled, thanked Cal for letting her come, and nodded to Charles and me.

"Preacher," Cal added, "I hear a herd of prayers was answered last night. Baby Jesus came home."

Burl said, "It was a Christmas miracle."

Cal looked at the note in my hand and turned to Burl. "Preacher there's something Chris wants to—"

Before Cal finished the sentence, Bernard stepped between Burl and Cal. "Please accept my apology for interrupting, Preacher Burl, sir. If I didn't say it now, I was afraid I never would."

Burl said, "That's okay. What's on your mind, Brother Bernard."

"Preacher, Mr. Landrum suggested I might be able to unload some, umm, burdens on your ears. He said you might be able to help. Do you think you could spend some time with me in the next few days? I'd appreciate it."

Burl glanced at Bernard and me. "I'd be honored, Brother Bernard. How about tomorrow morning? I'll be in our storefront sanctuary around nine."

"I'll be there, Preacher. Again, I apologize for interrupting. Merry Christmas."

Burl watched Bernard leave and turned to Cal. "You were saying."

Before Cal could mention the note, I said, "I wanted to say how wonderful I thought the service was last night."

Charles gave me a sideways glance and Cal opened his mouth and closed it. Burl thanked me and said the return of the statue made the night the best he's ever had.

Cal said, "Preacher walk up to the stage with me and help me sing a song."

"You know I'm a better preacher than a singer, but it's your party."

Cal and Burl headed to the stage and Charles said, "Why didn't you tell him about the note?'

I watched Cal and Burl on the stage and said, "It's Christmas."

Charles started to say something and I stopped him. Cal, with his duet partner, sang, *Joy to the world! The Lord is Come.*

Mary and her children were the next to arrive. She smiled when she saw me with Charles. I waved her over. "Merry Christmas, Mary," I knelt down. "Merry Christmas, Jewel and Joanie."

The girls smiled and each held up a starfish. "Look what we got for Christmas," Jewel said.

"They're lovely."

The girls smiled; Mary beamed. And Cal and Burl finished with, *And wonders of his Love.*

"Ladies," Charles said, "How about let's go get something to drink? I bet that bartender can rustle up a Coke."

Mary hugged me and followed Charles, Jewel, and Joanie to the bar. I took the opportunity to look around for someone I hadn't seen yet. Still not seeing him, I walked to the group of surfers, nodded, and received lukewarm responses.

I put my hand on Finley's back. "Finley, could I borrow you a minute?"

He looked scared but said yes. I led him to the corner of the room where there were the fewest people.

I said, "Thank you for whatever you did to get the statue back."

"Mr. Landrum, I wish I could take credit. I didn't do anything more than what I told you. It was you who figured most of it out and made me try. All I can figure is the man who bought it felt guilty and brought it back."

"Maybe," I said. "Could the person who stole it in the first place have done something to get it back?"

"Yes."

"Like I told you before, all I cared about was the church getting the statue back, so whatever happened, I'm thankful."

He sighed. "Me too, Mr. Landrum."

I looked at him for a moment and asked, "Where's Truman? He was at church last night but I don't see him here."

Finley looked down at his shoes like he'd never seen them before. I waited, listened to a verse of "Frosty the Snowman" from the jukebox, and Finley said, "Umm, Don't know. I went upstairs to his room this morning to thank…umm…to see if he wanted to come with me." He hesitated again. "He was gone. His stuff was gone."

I wasn't surprised. "That's too bad. I wanted to wish him Merry Christmas."

Finley gave me a knowing glance. "I think he's having a good one, Mr. Landrum."

Cal tapped again on the mike to get our attention. I reached in my pocket and wadded up the note and turned to the stage.

"Ya'll join in," Cal said. And the singing began:

SILENT NIGHT, Holy Night! All is calm, all is bright,
'Round yon Virgin Mother and Child Holy Infant so tender and mild
Sleep in heavenly peace, Sleep in heavenly peace.

Joy

Chapter One

Barb Deanelli was waiting for me in front of her condo building on West Arctic Avenue. It was a little after sunrise on a cold, mid-December morning, and she had on black skinny jeans, a black down jacket with a texture that looked like bubble-wrap packing material, black boots and a black wool beanie cap. She looked like someone planning to break in someone's second-story window.

Barb folded her five-foot-ten-inch trim frame into the front seat of my car and gave me a peck on the cheek. She was sixty-four years old, three years younger than me, yet looked much younger.

"You look more ready to climb Mt. Everest more than hunt shark teeth," I said and leaned closer to receive another kiss.

I was rewarded with an eye roll from the woman I'd been dating for six months. "After last-night's storm, I didn't know what to expect. Besides, the wind's kicking up and from previous trips to the County Park, I knew that there was nothing to block it from chilling my bones."

The Folly Beach County Park anchors the west end of the small South Carolina barrier island and is a mile-and-a-half from Barb's condo. The park doesn't open to vehicles until ten, so I navigated the turnaround in front of the locked gate and moved to the nearest spot where I could pull off the road and park.

Barb was wiser than I was since I didn't have a down coat and had to get by with a lightweight jacket over a long-sleeve denim shirt. I'd never admit that I was cold and on my way to freezing in the brisk wind.

The park consists of more than a hundred acres of mainly flat, sandy terrain, and its beach covers more than four-thousand feet of ocean frontage. There's a picnic area, boardwalks, showers, dressing areas, and restrooms, but we appeared to be the only humans making our way from the deserted parking area to where she hoped to find shark teeth along the receding tideline.

"Tell me again why you decided to drag me out here this morning," I said as I put my arm around her waist to help block the wind. Block it from me, not from her.

"One of my customers, Michelle, makes shark teeth jewelry. I asked where she bought the teeth and she said she found them on the beach, and the best time to find them is after a storm stirs up the surf and extracts them from deeper water. I suppose I've led a sheltered life and didn't know that you could find them here."

"Thinking about making and selling jewelry in the store?"

Barb moved to Folly a year ago from Pennsylvania and opened a used bookstore on the town's main drag.

"No, it takes more patience than I have. I told Michelle I'd carry hers. She did pique my interest enough to ask where she found the teeth. She said anywhere along the beach, and the County Park was a good location, especially before others traipsed along the waterline and grabbed them." She waved her arms toward the ocean. "And, here we are."

Residents and visitors spend hours scouring the beach hunting the teeth that can date to prehistoric times, but in the decade that I'd lived here, I'd never found any. Someone once told me that you don't find shark teeth, they find you. Fortunately, no teeth still attached to a shark have found me, nor have any teeth from their ancestors. I didn't know about shark teeth, but yesterday and last night's tumultuous storm brought some of the largest waves I'd seen in years. Regardless, it was fun spending the morning with Barb.

Then it ceased being fun.

Barb pointed to something at the shoreline a hundred yards in front of us. It looked like a surfboard with someone splayed out on top. My hunch was confirmed as we got closer. The surfboard was barely out of the water and the body of a woman was partially on the board with her arms wrapped around it. Long, black hair either flecked with gray or mixed with sand was spread out and covered part of the white board. She had on tan khaki slacks, a red sweatshirt, and was barefoot. I wasn't optimistic about her being alive since the water temperature was in the low-fifties and prolonged exposure to it could be fatal. The top of her sweatshirt was dry, but the lower half was wet as were her slacks.

I bent down to feel for a pulse when her left hand grabbed my wrist. The sudden movement startled me, and I fell backwards in the damp sand. She let go and pushed up off the board before falling back. Barb moved to the other side of the board, knelt, and whispered something to the woman. The sky was getting lighter, and I noticed the woman's arms shivering.

I removed my jacket and covered her back. Barb laid her heavier jacket over the woman's legs before wrapping her arms around her to provide body heat.

I leaned back and punched 911 on my phone and told the dispatcher where we were and what we found. I suggested that along with medical help, she send the police. I didn't know what had happened but was confident that it wasn't a surfing accident.

Barb was talking to the woman, who'd turned on her side and faced my friend. A good sign.

The screaming siren of a police cruiser could be heard a few blocks away, and the distinct sound of one of the city's fire engines followed the cruiser. Help was on the way. The car's siren shut off, and it took another minute for its occupant to open the park's gate and continue to the parking area near where we were huddled.

"Chris Landrum, is that you?" yelled a Public Safety Officer, the official name of Folly's police officers.

I turned toward the voice and recognized Officer Allen Spencer. I'd met him shortly after he and I arrived on Folly ten years ago. At the time, he was in his mid-twenties, six-foot-tall, and at least thirty pounds lighter. We crossed paths often and had a good relationship.

"Allen," I said and stood to shake his hand.

We shook, and he nodded toward Barb. "Ms. Deanelli."

Barb acknowledged the new arrival and Officer Spencer shifted his attention to the person Barb had her arm around and who was sitting on the surfboard. Spencer saw how much she was shaking and added his heavy jacket to mine and Barb's.

The fire engine pulled beside Spencer's vehicle and two firefighters hurried over. One carried a heavy blanket and wrapped it around the woman. The other firefighter, who on Folly doubled as a certified EMTs, started taking the woman's vitals.

She was in good hands, so I stepped away from the medical team. Spencer followed and looked up and down the shore and then toward the parking area. "Chris, what happened?"

I said I had no idea and this was how Barb and I'd found her. He asked why we were here, and I shared Barb's story about hunting shark teeth. One of the EMTs returned Barb's coat and offered me my jacket.

Spencer watched him go back to his patient and asked me, "Did she say anything?"

"She mumbled something to Barb, but I didn't hear what it was."

Barb was standing back and watching the EMTs work on the woman. Spencer waved her over and asked her the same thing he'd asked me.

"She asked two questions. She said, 'Where am I?' I told her on Folly Beach." Barb looked back at the woman and shook her head.

I said, "The second question?"

Barb looked at Spencer. "She asked, 'Who am I?'"

Chapter Two

The sun had begun warming the air while Barb, Officer Spencer, and I stood back and watched the EMTs load their patient in the ambulance that had arrived from nearby Charleston ten minutes after the first responders from the fire department. The three of us moved to the surfboard to see if it held any clues to what had happened.

Spencer flipped the board over and glanced at its underside. "This isn't a crime scene, so it doesn't matter if I disturb it," he said, more to himself than to Barb and me.

I knew as much about surfboards as I knew about the Harappan civilization. "Learn anything?"

"Not really. It's a Channel Islands New Flyer. Popular and common. Board of the year a few years back."

Officer Spencer spent many off-duty hours sitting on a surfboard waiting for the perfect wave, so I wasn't surprised with his knowledge of the vehicle that transported our mysterious lady to shore. I suspected that's where his knowledge about the event ended.

The first firefighter to the scene had loaded his equipment on his vehicle and came over to the three of us.

Spencer said, "Len, is she going to be okay?"

"I didn't see any signs of physical trauma. She has hypothermia and if you hadn't found her when you did, she might not have made it. Did you notice the red marks around her ankles?"

I said I had.

The firefighter, whom I'd never met before today, said, "It's not uncommon to see something similar caused by a surf leash attached to the ankle. Never around both ankles. She also has marks around her wrists."

"Think she was restrained?" I said.

"That'd be my guess. Don't hold me to it. It's for someone else to determine. Gotta get back to the station."

Spencer said, "Len, before you go, did she say anything about who she is or how she got here?"

"Nothing that made sense. Her speech was slurred, and she didn't appear to know where she was or why. Allen, don't read too much into it. Those are symptoms of hypothermia. She'll probably be fine in a few hours."

"Did you ask her name?"

He nodded. "She couldn't remember."

Len repeated that he had to get back to the station and walked away as a silver Ford F-150 XLT pick-up truck slid to a stop in the sand behind Spencer's cruiser. Cindy LaMond was named Director of Folly Beach's Department of Public Safety two years ago, and I'd known her since she joined the police force six years before that. She was a good friend and married to Larry LaMond, owner of Pewter Hardware, Folly's only hardware store.

The five-foot-three, well built, bundle of energy didn't waste time getting to us. In her endearing style, she said, "Hi Barb, what's that old fart Landrum dragged you into this time?"

I didn't recall dragging Barb into this or similar situations, but I'd inadvertently been ensnared in a few horrific situations since retiring on Folly after a peaceful, a.k.a. boring, life as a bureaucrat in a large insurance company in Kentucky.

Barb didn't know Cindy as well as I did, but knew her enough to ignore her comment. "Hi, Chief. Chris and I were looking for shark teeth and instead found a damsel in distress."

"Crap, Barb, you're beginning to sound like the old fart." The chief turned to me, "Okay, spill it. What in the hell have you stepped in now?"

We shared everything, which wasn't much, about what we'd found.

Cindy gazed out to sea, and said, "My highly trained, police brain tells me that the person who rode in on this board didn't surf from Wales. Any boats out there earlier? Any evidence she was at the park before ending at water's edge?"

"No and no," I said.

Spencer said, "It's possible she came from Kiawah."

Kiawah was another barrier island, and a gated resort fewer than two miles across the Folly River and the Stono Inlet from the County Park.

Cindy sighed. "It's also possible she was dropped out of a space ship and landed on our lovely slice of earth. Officer Spencer, contact the powers that be on Kiawah and see if they have any missing person reports. I'll do the same here."

I said, "Anything I can do, Chief?"

"Yes, you and the lovely lady standing beside you, the one I can't figure a reason in the world why she'd want to hang around with you, continue your search for shark teeth." She snapped her fingers. "Oh yeah, one other thing. Don't, that's do not, get the slightest inkling to butt in police business."

"Cindy—"

She interrupted, "I know, I know." She waved her hand in my face. "There's a better chance of you sprouting wings and flying to the Bahamas than minding your own business. Give it a try, for once."

"Of course, Cindy."

If she noticed my crossed fingers, she didn't let on.

Barb and I made our way to the car and were savoring heat pouring out of the vents. Our jackets were damp from covering the woman and Barb's teeth chattered.

"What do you think happened?" she asked as she rubbed her hands together in front of the vent.

"I don't think she started from the County Park, so Kiawah or from a boat seem like the most logical explanation. Another possibility is that she drifted to the ocean from either the Stono or the Folly River which means she could have gone in the water from several places. I hope someone reports her missing. That'd answer most of the questions."

"Hypothermia can cause temporary memory loss. If the EMT is correct, there's a good chance she could answer questions fairly soon."

"I hope so. One thing I'm certain of is that she didn't decide to go surfing dressed like that. Something happened, something bad."

"I don't disagree." She hesitated, and then in a lower voice said, "Are you going to follow Cindy's advice and leave whatever's happened to the police?"

Barb was aware of my knack of accidentally stepping in piles of problems, occasionally including murder. Less than a year ago, and with the aid of a few friends, I'd helped catch a killer who was seconds away from ending Barb's life.

"I'll try."

She smiled. "Thanks for not lying and saying that you wouldn't get involved. I'll take an *I'll try*."

I returned her smile and said what I wanted to do now was get her home so she could get in warm clothes and so I could do the same. I let her out at the gate to her condo complex and she left me with, "My next search for shark teeth will be at Mr. John's Beach Store."

I thought it was an excellent idea.

MY BEST FRIEND since I arrived on Folly, correction, my best friend ever, is Charles Fowler. We met during my first week here and it didn't take long to learn that he and I were as different as a blue jay was to a blue whale. Charles retired to Folly at the age of thirty-four. Since then and now, as he approached his sixty-fifth birthday, he'd never held a steady job. He picked up enough money to live modestly in a tiny apartment by providing an extra set of hands for local contractors, helping restaurants clean during vacation season, and delivering packages for our friend Dude Slone, owner of the surf shop. I'd spent those same years working in boring jobs while living a boring existence. Charles has quirks too numerous to list. Despite our many differences, we overcame the law of averages, and became closer than brothers. One of his quirks should be mentioned. If I learned something he'd consider interesting, such as discovering a beached lady at the County Park and didn't share it with him in the first seconds after learning it, I would be subjected to a glare, reprimands, and being chastised unmercifully.

I wasn't in the mood to be harassed and called him on my way home.

"Charles, good morning. I just left the County Park with Barb where we found an unconscious woman on—"

"Meet me at the Dog in fifteen minutes."

He'd hung up. It'd been more than a few seconds since we'd found the woman.

Chapter Three

The Lost Dog Cafe was less than a block off Center Street, the figurative center of commerce on the half-mile-wide, six-mile-long island. I and many others consider it the best breakfast spot on Folly. My kitchen was used as often as a wood pencil in the BIC factory, so I'd spent countless mornings enjoying a warm breakfast, the company of my favorite server Amber, and conversations with various friends and acquaintances. It was named the Lost Dog Cafe, although there were approximately a zillion photos of dogs, none of them lost, attached to most every vertical surface in the restaurant. Its two outdoor patios were dog friendly and often occupied by more than one canine. Festive Christmas lights were strung around the railing around the front patio.

"Morning, Chris," Amber said as she met me at the door. "Your regular table?"

Amber was the one person on Folly who I'd known longer than Charles—two days longer. She was on the verge of her fiftieth birthday, five-foot-five inches tall, with long auburn hair, often tied in a ponytail while she was at work. She's funny, insightful, and one of Folly's rumor-collecting-champions. She and I had dated for a while and after that remained good friends. December was one of the few times of the year when the Dog wasn't packed and my favorite table along the back wall was vacant. I told her yes to my seating preference.

She pointed to the table and said, "Go ahead. I'll grab your water."

Two city councilmembers, Marc and Houston, were seated at their preferred table in the center of the room. They had been on the council as long as I'd been on Folly and weren't in danger of losing their elected positions anytime soon. Another position they weren't in danger of losing was as the town's unofficial gossips, especially Marc. To stretch the tree falling in the forest question, if something happened on Folly and Marc didn't know about it, did it really happen?

I said hi to the councilmembers, received pleasant grins, and from Marc, "Hey, Chris, what's new?"

I wasn't ready to throw the events from the County Park into the gossip mill. "Not much, how about you, Marc?"

"Same old, same old."

I smiled and nodded at the phrase I never understood since I wouldn't have a way of knowing what the same was with Marc, much less how the same had happened again. The smile was because I was surprised that he hasn't heard about the woman. I didn't have time to savor that knowledge since Charles barreled through the door and pointed at the table with his handmade wooden cane that he carries for no apparent reason. I nodded again, this time without the smile, and he made a beeline to the table.

At five-foot-eight, Charles was a couple of inches shorter than me and unlike my balding head, his graying hair always appeared to be in search of a comb. He wore a long-sleeve, gray and crimson, Washington State University sweatshirt, jeans that were too large, a canvas Tilley hat, and three-days of unshaven stubble.

He slid in the booth before I could get there, smiled, and said, "What took you so long to get here?"

I didn't take the bait but did take a sip of water from a Ball jar that Amber had slid in front of me.

"Spill it."

I figured he meant the story about the woman and not the water, so in a voice low enough not to reach the gossip-gathering ears of Marc and Houston, began rehashing the trip to the County Park. As with sharing most stories with Charles, I didn't get far before he interrupted.

"Who was she? Did her sweatshirt have a logo on it? Is she going to be okay? Did she have a dog with her?"

"Don't know. No. Don't know. No."

"I'm confused."

I'm usually the one with that feeling. "About what?"

"Which question I asked first?"

Amber returned with water for Charles, one of her endearing smiles, and the question, "What can I get you for breakfast?"

I said, "French toast."

"Lordy, Chris. One of these days you're going to order something different and my little-ole heart won't be able to take the shock."

Charles patted her on the arm. "Don't worry, Miss Amber, your heart's safe. And, if you're interested, I'll have the Loyal Companion."

She ruffled his unruly hair and said that she was always interested in him, pivoted and headed to the kitchen to order my French toast and bacon and eggs for Charles, a.k.a. the Loyal Companion.

"Okay," Charles said, "I'll start over. Are you sure she didn't tell you her name?"

I shook my head.

"I hate calling her *the woman*. Let's go with Jane Doe."

I nodded.

"Could Jane have gone in the water at the Park?"

"It's possible, although unlikely. There was nothing nearby that indicated that she'd been there before she washed up."

"No one goes surfing in khakis and a sweatshirt."

I didn't think that astute observation merited comment. I waited for him to continue.

"If Jane fell off a boat, she wouldn't have landed on a surfboard. Dressed like she was, it's unlikely that she would've willingly stepped in the water off Kiawah or somewhere back in the river. You're sure there was no evidence that someone smacked her in the head and dumped her in the Atlantic?"

"Sure, no. There was nothing obvious."

"She could've been drugged."

"It'll be up to the docs and the police to figure what happened."

"Chris, I was thinking."

Always scary when it came to Charles. I took a deep breath and said, "What?"

"Luck, karma, fate, predestination, whatever led you to Jane. She could've died if you weren't there. You saved her, so it's destined that you must figure out what happened."

"Charles, you know—"

He waved his hand in my face. "Here's the best part. I'll take time out of my busy schedule to help. Great news, right?"

For reasons unknown to anyone, Charles had decided a few years back that he was a private detective. Did he have a law enforcement background? Not unless you count being on weed patrol when he worked for a landscaper fifty years ago in his hometown of Detroit. Did he have private detective training? Absolutely not. Was he a licensed private detective? Nope. he was, however, a voracious reader with an apartment filled with more books than a Barnes & Noble store. He'd claimed to have read every mystery novel written since Gutenberg invented the printing press. That was an exaggeration, although not by much.

"That's a kind offer, considering how busy you are." I hoped he grasped my sarcasm since he didn't work and from what I could tell, had a blank calendar.

"Where do we begin?"

I sighed. "Charles, we don't know anything about her or what happened. I'm sure Chief LaMond will solve it."

He grinned. "See, Chris, Cindy LaMond is your friend. You found Jane. Your involvement is meant to be." He picked my cell phone off the table and handed it to me. "Go ahead, call and see what she's learned and tell her we're on the case."

That wasn't going to happen for more reasons that I could count. "Charles, she hasn't had time to learn anything. I suspect Jane is still at the hospital being evaluated."

"You're right again. Call me this afternoon after you talk to Cindy."

If I wanted to eat in peace, I knew what I had to say. "Sure."

Charles didn't get a chance to pin me down on what time I'd call him. He looked up and saw Burl Iven Costello standing by our table with a smile on his face.

"Good morning Brother Charles and Brother Chris," said the five-foot-six-inch tall, portly man with a milk-chocolate colored mustache who was standing beside the table.

Burl, known to most as Preacher Burl Ives Costello, arrived on Folly two years ago after founding and for several reasons closed churches in Mississippi, Florida, and Indiana. He began First Light, a non-denominational church that met most Sundays on the beach near the Folly Beach Fishing Pier. I'd become better acquainted with him when he became the prime suspect in the murder of two of his followers. Charles and I helped the police catch the killer when he tried to add Preacher Burl to his list of victims.

"Join us Preacher," Charles said, as he slid to the end of the seat to make room for the newcomer.

"If you don't mind."

He slid in beside Charles, not waiting to hear if we minded. He looked around the room and turned to Amber who was quick to the table to see what he needed. Charles told him to order anything he wanted because I was picking up the check. Charles was in the holiday spirit with my wallet. Burl said coffee was all since he'd had breakfast.

"Preacher," Charles said, "any trouble with the nativity this year?"

First Light Church had an impressive nativity scene squeezed on a narrow piece of land between the Folly Beach Post Office and Pewter Hardware Store. Last Christmas someone stole a valuable, hand-carved baby Jesus from the display, nearly sucking the Christmas spirit out of the island. A miracle in the form of two teenagers averted a disaster by finding the missing figurine Christmas Eve.

"Brother Charles, it's been perfect this year. Praise the Lord." He smiled. "Baby Jesus won't be making an appearance until Christmas Day and will be under the watchful eyes of members of our flock."

"Wise move," I said, and since he wasn't here to eat, asked, "What brings you out this morning?"

"Excellent question, Brother Chris. I was looking for Brother Taylor, one of my residents."

The residence Burl referred to was Hope House, which loosely could be described as a halfway house that the preacher had started nine months ago. A wealthy and generous member of First Light donated a six-bedroom house on East Erie Avenue under the condition that Burl would rent to people he felt needed the assist to get back to productive members of the community. Rent was based on ability to pay and ranged from zero to a few hundred dollars a month, with most residents near the zero end of the scale.

Charles looked around the room. "Don't suppose he's here?"

"No, Brother Charles."

"Why are you looking for him?" I asked.

"I learned of an outstanding job that I believe his skills would make him a perfect candidate."

"That's great, Preacher. How's the house doing?"

"Most of my prayers have been answered, although we've had a few challenges," Burl said, and nodded like he was praying. He then turned to me and smiled. "Our benefactor said that the house needed a couple of cosmetic improvements. I didn't realize a new electrical system qualified as cosmetic." Burl chuckled. "At least when the power was off, the residents didn't know that the air conditioner was also, how shall I put it, under the weather."

"What's going to happen?" Charles asked.

Burl looked toward the ceiling like he was checking with God for an answer. "Brother Charles, I'm leaving it in the hands of the Lord."

"Preacher, I don't think—"

"Worry not, Brother Charles, the Lord already sent an electrician and an HVAC specialist to address the issues. The Lord sent them, and Brother Edward sent a check to cover the expenses."

"Brother Edward?" I said.

"Edward Bancroft, the wonderful man who donated the house."

"That's great," Charles said. "How many residents are there?"

"Four, each is blessed with a private room although two of the rooms are so large that we could put two people in each if need be." Burl glanced over my shoulder. "Ah, there's my resident. I would like to stay longer but feel the necessity of sharing with him the good news about the job." He stood, said, "May you have a blessed day," and headed to the door to meet his resident.

Charles watched Burl put his arm around the shoulder of the man as he escorted him to an empty table. He then turned to me and glanced at his wrist where most people wore a watch. His was bare. "Isn't it time for you to call Cindy and find out about Jane Doe?"

I took a sip of coffee, regretted it immediately since it had turned cold, stared at Charles, and said, "No. She hasn't had time to learn more than she would've known fifteen minutes ago when I told you that I'd call her this afternoon."

Charles sighed. "Worth a try. You're going to call me as soon as you hang up with the Chief?"

"Yes, oh patient one."

IT WAS TWO HOURS LATER, and if I didn't call the Chief soon, Charles would be on my doorstep wondering why I hadn't let him know what she said.

"What took you so long to pester me about Joyce?" Cindy LaMond said when she answered the phone.

I would have preferred something along the lines of, "*Hi, Chris. How are you this afternoon? How may I help you?*" I also would have preferred to be twenty pounds lighter, thirty years younger, and have a full head of hair. The odds were equal for any of those events happening.

"Who's Joyce?"

"How quickly you forget, Mr. Senior Citizen. You found her this morning."

"The person we found said she didn't know her name. Is her memory back?"

"Nope."

I sighed. "How do you know her name's Joyce?"

"Superb detective work, an incredibly high level of training and experience, use of all of my Super Chief skills."

"And?"

"And, Joyce was printed with a laundry marker pen on the label in her sweatshirt."

"Wow. No wonder you're Chief."

"True, oh so true, Mr. Senior Citizen."

"Did your superpowers tell you if Joyce was her first or last name?"

"First, I assume. Who ever heard of Joyce as a last name?"

I wasn't a big reader and had seldom paid attention in literature class in school, but it didn't take a scholar to have heard of James Joyce. I shared that tidbit.

"How about anyone with that last name in our lifetime?"

"None I can think of."

"Then I'm sticking with it as her first name."

"Cindy, has she said anything about what happened?"

"Very little. She thinks she remembers being on a boat, a storm, and then in the water clutching the surfboard. Her next memory is of some old geezer staring at her."

"Old geezer?"

She shrugged. "I added that part. Anyway, she claims she doesn't know anything else."

"Had she been injured? I didn't see any sign of physical injury."

"She's at the hospital getting a complete checkup. They're planning on having a head-doc talk with her to see if she understood what happened. They'll hold her overnight and if nothing pops up, release her in the morning."

"Then what?"

"Then I'll see if her memory is back. I'm having my guys check if there's a missing person report matching her description."

"And, then what?"

"Heck if I know."

"Can she have visitors?"

There was an audible sigh. "Chris, is Charles rubbing off on you?"

"What's that mean?" I said, knowing exactly what she meant.

"Are you going to start playing detective like you half-wit friend?"

"Of course not. Barb and I found her and so I wanted to see how she was doing."

"Yeah, right. To answer your innocent sounding question, yes, she can have visitors."

Cindy gave me the room number and a warning that if I started nosing in police business, she'd have me arrested for impersonating an officer, for gross stupidity, and for giving her ulcers. She hung up before I could thank her for being so kind to one of her constituents.

Chapter Four

Barb said she felt a connection to Joyce and offered to accompany me to the hospital. She also hinted that since we'd be in Charleston, it would be a great night to have supper at one of the city's many fine restaurants.

Joyce was barely recognizable as the person from the beach. Her hair that had been mixed with sand and in a state of disarray was now combed and while not styled, was passable. She looked to be in her forties and had healthy color in her cheeks as opposed to the white with a blue tinge they had on the beach. The look of confusion she gave us when we entered the room was replaced by a radiant smile of recognition.

"They tell me that you saved my life," she said, before we could speak. "Thank you."

Barb moved close to the bed and rested her hand on Joyce's shoulder. "We were worried about you. It's wonderful seeing you doing so well. I'm Barb and my friend is Chris."

I moved beside Barb and reached out and shook Joyce's hand. She let go and grabbed the television's remote and muted a game show that had an infuriatingly loud studio audience.

"Nice to meet you. Please have a seat."

There was only one chair, and I motioned for Barb to take it. I stood beside her and leaned on an over-bed table at the side of the room.

"I hope you don't mind us visiting," Barb said. "We were wondering how you were doing."

"Heavens, no. It's great seeing familiar faces. I wasn't at my best the last time I saw you."

"How are you feeling?" I asked.

"Fortunate. I have scrapes and bruises but nothing to complain about. They did an MRI on my brain, so I suppose I have one, although it's a bit scrambled. The main problem was hypothermia, and they had me drinking hot tea and wrapped in warm blankets. I'm fine now and told they're going to kick me out in the morning unless I take a turn for the worse."

I said, "Your name's Joyce?"

She lowered her gaze and in a faint voice said, "That's what they say."

"You don't remember?"

"No."

"It's none of our business," Barb said. "You don't have to tell us anything if you don't want. I was wondering what you remember."

"Like I told that lady police chief and a psychiatrist who visited me right before you got here, all I remember is being on a boat. Don't know where, what kind of boat, or who else was on it. There was a storm and the next thing I remember was being in the water. Freezing water. I was holding on a surfboard for dear life. I remember seeing the words Ocean Pacific on the board. They said that's the brand. It's funny that I remember that. The next thing I knew was you leaning over me." She shook her head. "Barb, Chris, that's all, I mean all, I remember." She closed her eyes and whispered, "I didn't know my name was Joyce."

Barb said, "Was the psychiatrist helpful?"

"She was nice and listened. Helpful, I don't think so. She said I have amnesia, she called it a word I can't remember."

Barb said, "Retrograde."

I glanced at Barb and didn't say anything.

"That's it. Said it was caused by a trauma." She closed her eyes and Barb nodded toward the door.

"Joyce," I said, "we'd better let you get some rest. It's great seeing that you're doing so well."

Her eyes opened. "Thanks for coming. That was kind of you."

Barb and I patted her on the arm.

Joyce smiled up at us, and said, "What now?"

I wish we had an answer.

BARB WAS UNUSUALLY quiet as I maneuvered through downtown Charleston on the way to Fleet Landing Restaurant and Bar, one of many nice restaurants in the city known for fine dining. Barb had never been there, but I'd been twice. The restaurant overlooked the Charleston Harbor and is near the Historic City Market with half of the eatery over water. Christmas lights decorated the entry and from our table we could see other seasonal lights from buildings along the waterfront.

Our server asked if we wanted drinks and an appetizer. We each ordered the house Cabernet while Barb scanned the menu. She added, "An order of Fleet Landing Stuffed Hush Puppies would be good."

Barb had the metabolism of a hummingbird and could out eat people twice her one-hundred-twenty pounds while never gaining a ounce. It was irritating. I had no idea what was stuffed in the hush puppies despite the menu saying it was a veloute of lobster, rock shrimp, and leeks. The server left, and I asked Barb what a veloute was.

"Clueless. Figured anything with hush puppies has to be good."

Her ignorance made me feel better, sort of. It was good hearing her speak after being unusually quiet since we'd left the hospital.

It was dark outside, and Barb nodded toward a row of lights from across the bay as they reflected on the calm water. "That's beautiful. I'm glad we came here."

I agreed, and in a lesson learned from Charles, she changed direction on a dime. "What do you think of her story?"

"I know little about amnesia. After Cal got hit on the head back in the summer he forgot recent events for a few days. The doc called it amnesia, but he could remember things from his past."

Cal Ballew was a friend who owned Cal's Country Bar and Burgers.

Barb said, "That was anterograde amnesia, where the person can't remember current information. His was caused by a brain trauma, the blow to the head. Joyce has retrograde amnesia which is the opposite of anterograde. There are several other kinds of amnesia, but those are the two most common."

I nodded like I understood, which was partially true, and said, "You sure you didn't go to medical school rather than law school?"

She chuckled. "I had a client whose husband suffered from retrograde amnesia resulting from his mother's sudden death. The father died a few years earlier. There was a ton of money involved and my client had been told by her mother-in-law that the bulk of it was to go to her grandchildren and the humane society. The husband with amnesia said he couldn't remember but *knew* that wasn't true and that he was to inherit, and it was up to him to decide what to do with the estate. This is the kind of legal crap you step in when there's no will."

"They didn't have one?"

"No. My client's in-laws were in their fifties and thought they had plenty of time to worry about things like wills. Wrong. Anyway, I researched amnesia to represent her. One of the hardest things I did as an attorney was become an expert on oodles of things in which I had no interest."

"What happened with your client?"

"Other than me using my superior Penn State Law training to win a victory?"

"That goes without saying."

"Perhaps, but I like saying it. The other critical development was when my client's husband regained his memory and found a notarized letter he'd hidden that his mother had given him telling that he would get everything."

Thinking of Joyce, I said, "How long did it take for him to regain his memory?"

"Four months of legal wrestling and delaying depositions."

I smiled and turned serious. "Cal's amnesia was caused by the smack on the head. Joyce didn't have any apparent physical injury other than a few bruises and scrapes. What caused hers?"

"Most likely, a form of retrograde called psychological amnesia, also referred to as dissociative amnesia. It can be caused by a multitude of things, being the victim of a crime, child abuse, witnessing a traumatic event, on-and-on. Basically, any intolerable life situation that causes psychological stress can cause it. It's rare."

"Thank you, Doctor Barb. Any idea how long she could've had it?"

She smiled. "No. I missed that class in law school."

Our drinks arrived along with the appetizer. The server said the bar was backed up or we would've had our drinks sooner. Barb told her it wasn't a problem. Barb ordered shrimp and grits for her entrée. Grits were on my list of least favorite foods and I stuck with the chicken piccata. The server left, and Barb took a bite of the appetizer.

I thought about the causes of psychological amnesia, and said, "The first thing Joyce said she remembered was being on a boat, so wouldn't it make sense that whatever she suffered from occurred around that time?"

Barb held up a finger and pointed to her mouth. Talking with a mouthful of food wasn't unheard of among my friends. Barb had more class than most of my them, so I waited.

She finished chewing, took a sip of water, and said, "Don't know."

I'd waited for that.

"Cal's doctor said that time was the best cure for his amnesia. It was a week before he regained most of his memory. It was scrambled at first, but finally returned to his pre-traumatic head bashing. What treatments are there to help Joyce?"

"Time is the best. If there are underlying physical or mental disorders, psychotherapy could help. Family support is also critical. Orientation aids such as photos, familiar smells, and even music can speed up remembering the past."

"That's if the police find her family."

"That could be awhile unless someone reports her missing. She could be from anywhere." Barb turned to the large windows that overlooked the harbor. "Look how beautiful the flickering Christmas lights look on the surface of the water."

That was her way of saying we'd talked enough about Joyce. We spent the next hour enjoying the scenery, each other's company, and a wonderful meal. She told me about Troy and Nate, two men from Canada, who'd rented the condo next to her for a month and how much they were enjoying the "balmy" December weather on Folly. She crossed her arms and made a shivering motion as she said it.

Several units in Barb's condo complex were vacation rentals, and she never knew from week to week who some of her neighbors would be. That would bother me, but she said it was interesting seeing who was staying there, and besides, the high turnover meant the more books she'd sell in her store.

The ride to Folly was peaceful and quiet, and I couldn't help smiling at the brightly lit crab, dolphin, turtle, and sand dollar decorations that adorned light poles at each intersection along Center Street. I also couldn't stop thinking about the first or last name woman named Joyce. And, that she was going to be released tomorrow. Released to go where?

Chapter Five

I sat up in bed and wondered why I hadn't thought of it earlier. I'd slept later than usual, and the low December sun filtered through the blinds. Was it too early to call Chief LaMond? Over the years, I'd called her several times before eight o'clock and she'd berated me for pestering her before her work day began. I smiled, picked up the phone, and recalled that she'd also berated me for calling during work hours, after her work day, and on weekends and holidays.

"What in the Elf on the Shelf are you pestering me about before I've had time to enjoy a hot brew of hazelnut coffee with my adorable hubby?"

"Elf on the Shelf?"

"You know, Santa's danged scout elf that parents use to trick their kids into being nice rather than naughty before Christmas. Hate that thing, hate ads for it, hate seeing it sneaking around the house."

I was vaguely aware of the Elf, but never considered it a four-letter word. "Did Larry put one in your house?"

I didn't think she was going to answer. She finally said, "If I hear one word about it from anyone other than you, you will not live long enough to get a lump of coal from Santa. Now, in case your feeble mind forgot, you called me. Would it be rude to ask why?"

After the elf talk, I'd almost forgotten the reason. I stifled a chuckle, and said, "Any word on who Joyce is, or what happened to her?"

"Double no."

"That's what I was afraid of. Barb and I stopped by the hospital to see her. She was doing well and said they might release her today. Where will she go?"

"For being such an infuriating pest, you occasionally come up with a good question. That's one of them. My answer is one I give more and more. I don't have a freakin' clue. The hospital has a case worker who'll work with her. Joyce isn't in medical distress, so the options are limited."

"What if I have a possible solution?"

"Hence the reason for this ungodly early call?"

"An astute observation, Chief LaMond."

"Any chance you would share it?"

"Yes." And I did.

She said my idea wasn't horrible, which I took to mean she thought it was great. She asked me to let her know the results. I said I would, and she asked if she could get back to her coffee and peaceful morning. I said yes, and she hung up before I could add anything to spoil it.

My next call was to Preacher Burl Costello who answered in a better mood than had Cindy. I asked if it was too early to call and he laughed and said no that his residents were up and clanking around all hours of day and night. I asked if he was entertaining visitors and he said he was if I was the visitor.

Fifteen minutes later, I pulled in the gravel parking area in front of the large, wood-frame house. A massive live oak butted up to the house on one side and smaller trees and shrubs were grouped on two other sides. The structure was at least fifty years old and its north-facing wall was covered with moss. Despite its unkept appearance, the house had weathered many a storm and was sturdier than most of the houses surrounding it. White, LED Christmas lights were strung around the door frame and along the roofline.

The front door was open and a man in his mid-thirties and cut-off jeans despite the temperature in the forties was on his knees and working on the lock. I asked if the preacher was available and he said for me to go in and yell.

I stepped in the narrow hallway and didn't have to yell. Preacher Burl saw me, shook my hand, said he was waiting for me, and asked if I wanted coffee. Chief LaMond could learn hospitality skills from the preacher. He led me through a long, center hallway. The wallcovering reminded me of a rainforest with its various shades of green and a dark overcast feel. It was ripped in a couple of spots and gave a depressing feel to the house. At the end of the hall, Burl turned left, and I followed him to the large kitchen, the kind in country farmhouses.

A woman was taking something out of the stove and was startled by our entry. "Sorry, Sister Adrienne," Burl said, "Meet my friend, Brother

Chris. Brother Chris, Sister Adrienne was the first person to move in when Hope House opened. She's a great cook and we're fortunate to have her."

Adrienne was probably in her fifties, paper thin and wore her graying black hair in a bun. I told her it was nice meeting her, and she said likewise although I didn't detect a great deal of sincerity. Burl poured two cups of coffee while I was having my awkward conversation with Adrienne, and suggested I follow him to the living room.

"Adrienne's not great with people, especially men," Burl said, as he pointed to the brown vinyl-covered sofa with chrome legs that'd look at home in a doctor's waiting room. He lowered his voice. "Her husband left her for his massage therapist. Poor Adrienne took solace in alcohol before finding the Lord and First Light Church. She now works for a landscaper and by the grace of God, will be moving to an apartment all her own come summer. The move will be wonderful for her, bad for our quality of meals." Burl patted his stomach.

The waiting-room-style sofa was out of place in a residence, but various Christmas decorations warmed the room. A seven-foot-tall pine tree stood in the corner and was wrapped with colorful lights, and adorned with silver and gold ornaments, plus a few homemade, cardboard decorations. A dozen or so colorfully wrapped packages rested on the tree skirt. I smiled at how cheerful the room was. Burl took a sip from his mug and leaned back on the sofa. Adrienne's story was interesting, but time was important, so I wanted to share the reason for my visit.

"Preacher, the other day when you were in the Dog, you said you had four residents and six bedrooms. Has the number of residents increased since then?"

"No. The house was not created to be a permanent home for its residents. Since I've opened, we've had several come and go. In addition to Adrienne, we have Taylor Strong, the gentleman working on the broken lock on the front door, Rebekah Leachmen, she's at work at Black Magic Cafe, been there going on six months and doing well. You just missed her. Then there's Bernard Prine. You're the reason Brother Bernard is here."

I'd met Bernard a year ago. He was homeless, and I learned he'd been a war hero, had received a serious head injury in Afghanistan, and suffered from PTSD, or PTSS as it's now called. He'd been kicked out of several homeless shelters because of his temper and when I told him about Preacher Burl, Bernard sought him out and the two were good for each other. I thanked Burl for all he'd done for Bernard.

"Brother Chris, I don't suppose you're here to take an inventory of my residents."

I told him no, and that I was there to see if he could provide lodging for Joyce.

He said that it would be his Christian duty, and that, "It would be a joy to do so. In fact, if acceptable with her, I will call her Joy." He made an exaggerated nod. "Tis the season of tidings of comfort and joy."

She didn't remember her name was Joyce, so I told him I doubted she'd mind him calling her the shortened version. I also said I didn't know if the hospital would release her to him. He smiled and said one of his flock, which is what he called members of First Light, had been in the hospital, and he got to know someone in the discharge department, and would call her. After he brings Joy to Hope House, he said he'd contact Chief LaMond and tell her, so she would know where to reach Joy if her identity was discovered. I appreciated that he was willing to take-charge of these tasks and asked that he let me know what happens. I also told him how admirable I thought it was for him to have opened the house and asked if it was too much for him to shoulder alone.

He laughed. "I've thought that several times a day. Sister Lottie volunteers when I need extra help, which is often. As I shared with you when we first met, I have carpentry skills and they're being utilized more than I ever imagined. Three of the windows leaked when it rained, and there are more holes in the drywall than I can count. One of my previous residents was a finish carpenter and a tremendous help, a gift from heaven, you might say. I was happy for him and saddened for Hope House when he was offered a high-paying job in Summerville and was able to afford an apartment. It was a sad day indeed when he left. Regardless, Lottie does the best she can, and is especially good with the women."

Lottie was the first member of First Light and after some of us had pestered Burl about it, he realized that she wanted more than a preacher/member relationship. They've dated several months and the rumor among members of the flock was that they might soon be seeking another preacher. More specifically, a preacher to perform their wedding ceremony. I hoped it was true.

"That's good." I looked out the window. "Any static from neighbors about this type of establishment in the neighborhood?"

"Some looked askance at first, but I have strict rules and any violation is cause for immediate removal. Most of the folks who end up here are temporarily, shall I say, disenfranchised, and find their way back to a productive member of society. Or, they have been to this point."

"Preacher, there's one other thing I should mention. All that Joyce, Joy, remembers is being on a boat and then in the ocean clinging to a surfboard, before Barb and I found her."

"I was aware of that, Brother Chris."

"Then you know it's possible something happened on the boat that could've caused her amnesia. Something bad. Whoever was on the boat may not know that she survived. Or, they do, they may try something."

Burl nodded. "In other words, the fewer people who know she's here the better."

"It'd be best if no one knew."

"My guests will know, and I feel I must tell Lottie since she's good with the women."

"That's fine. If we can keep it to those few along with the police, it'd be best."

Our conversation ended with a sales pitch from Preacher Burl for me to attend his Sunday service and his special Christmas Eve service. I told him I'd try. He didn't appear convinced. Neither did I.

Chapter Six

I hadn't told Charles what I'd learned from Cindy, or from the visit to the hospital. I called, and he suggested that our conversation would best take place over an early lunch at the Crab Shack. The popular restaurant was halfway between Charles's apartment on Sandbar Lane and my cottage on East Ashley Avenue. The temperature was still in the forties, yet I decided to walk. The exercise would do me good.

"About time you got here," Charles said, as he grabbed a peanut out of the cardboard container in front of him. He wore a red and blue Walters State long-sleeve sweatshirt, and jeans. My friend has one of the largest collections of college and university logoed sweatshirts this side of Dick's Sporting Goods. I'd tried to find out why he has them and where they came from. The best answer he'd come up with was, "Here and there." I stopped asking years ago, although it never stopped him from sharing trivia about the shirts.

He pointed to his chest. "I know you're wondering, they're the Senators. It's in Morristown, Tennessee."

See?

"Good morning, Charles," I said, ignoring his comment about me being late and the college highlighted on his torso. I picked a nut out of the container and cracked it open.

He sighed. My disinterest annoyed him, but I knew what I was going to share next would hold his attention.

"Barb and I visited Joyce in the hospital. She—"

He grabbed another nut and pointed it at me. "Who's Joyce?"

I realized I hadn't told him about yesterday's conversation with Cindy.

"Chief LaMond found the name in the sweatshirt of the woman Barb and I found on the beach."

His eyes narrowed. "When did you talk to Cindy?"

"Late yesterday," I said, a slight time-shift.

"You didn't call to tell me like you said you would, and then you called Barb and invited her instead of me to visit Jane Doe, umm, Joyce, in the hospital. Oh, and then you got home and instead of calling me, you did whatever you did at home. How am I doing?"

"Time got away."

And, I haven't even mentioned meeting with Preacher Burl and what's going to happen next. Before I could dig a deeper hole, Kaylee, the server, appeared and asked if we were ready to order. She glanced at the container of peanuts and added, "Something other than freebees."

We took the hint and ordered flounder crunch sandwiches and refills on the water she'd added to our table while we were gorging on peanuts.

Kaylee's timely interruption took the steam out of Charles's rant.

He leaned back, slowly shook his head, and said, "You went to the hospital without me?"

I thought that was self-evident but understood where he was going. "Yes. I thought about asking if you wanted to go but figured Joyce wouldn't be comfortable with two strange guys visiting."

"Barb and I could've visited while you stayed in the car. After all, I'm the detective. I could've found out.... Never mind, what'd you learn?"

"Nothing more than I told you the last time we talked. She has retrograde amnesia and doesn't remember anything before being on a boat, and even then, she doesn't remember what happened."

"That's horrible. When will she be well enough to get out of the hospital?"

"Could be today."

Charles leaned his elbows on the table and stared at me. "Where's she going? If she can't remember anything, what'll happen to her?"

I tightened my grip on the plastic water glass and prepared for rant number two. "Preacher Burl said he would see if he could get her released to Hope House. If he can, then—"

Charles leaned across the table and waved his hand in my face. "Whoa. When did this happen? How do you know?"

"That's why I called you as soon as I left Burl," I said, emphasis on *as soon as*.

Food arrived along with more questions. "When's her memory coming back? Will Burl be able to take her to Hope House? Do you think she's still in danger?" He hesitated and took a bite of his sandwich, and then with food in his mouth, said, "How're we going to find out who she is and what happened?"

Instead of saying, "I don't know?" four times, I shrugged and stuck a fry in my mouth.

I was seated facing a colorful mural featuring the Ferris wheel that once towered over Folly and Charles was facing the entry. He jumped up and headed toward the door. I turned to see what'd grabbed his attention and saw Chief LaMond talking to the hostess. Charles joined them and pointed at our table. I imagined that Cindy was thinking she'd chosen the wrong restaurant for lunch. I smiled as Charles put his arm around her shoulder and escorted her to the table and pulled out the chair beside his and motioned for her to join us.

"Hey, Chris, look who wanted to sit with us."

Wanted to turn and run out the door as soon as she saw Charles, would've been my guess. "Glad you could join us."

She glared at me like it was my fault she chose the wrong restaurant for a peaceful meal.

Charles pretended not to see Cindy's glare, and said, "We were talking about the lady Chris and Barb found surfing. He was getting ready to call you and see if you learned who she is and what happened." Charles turned to me.

Cindy glanced at me. "Hmm, is that right?"

"Have you found out who she is?" I asked, skirting Charles's claim that I was going to call.

Kaylee returned to the table and asked Cindy what she wanted for lunch.

"I'd like three bourbons and a liter of gin to put up with these troublemakers. Instead, how about water and whatever they're having."

Cindy shook her head as Kaylee headed to the kitchen. "No, I don't know who she is. There are no missing person reports fitting her description, and her prints aren't in the system. She's still Joyce Doe or Jane Joyce, depending on if Joyce is her first or last name."

I was tempted to tell her that Burl had shortened it to Joy. Instead, I told her of my conversation with Burl and that he was contacting the hospital to see if she could stay at Hope House. Rather than Cindy getting mad at me, and I suppose Burl, for butting in, she said she was glad. She'd be closer when her memory starts returning.

Her food arrived. I'd observed over the years how much quicker a police chief gets served than other mortals. Cindy took a sip of water and a bite of sandwich.

Charles took the break in her talking to ask, "Learn anything else?"

Cindy looked at Charles and rolled her eyes. "Yep, two things."

"Well?" Charles said.

"First, to case the inside of a restaurant before coming in. Peace, quiet, and a relaxing lunch don't go with Chris, Charles, and your pestering."

"Second?" Charles said.

"Do you know Jamison and Renee Caulder?"

I said, "Don't think so."

"I know Renee." Charles said. "Met her walking her dog Bowser. Adorable Pekingese pup, originally from China, Pekingese dogs, not Renee. They're also called lion dogs because they look like the Chinese guardian lions that—"

"Enough," Cindy interrupted.

I silently seconded that.

She continued, "The Caulders are a nice couple. Jamison retired early from a highfalutin, high-paying job, and bought a house out on Tabby Drive that backs up to the river and the marsh. They've got a walking pier that goes from their deck to the river. The last few days they've been up in Asheville visiting relatives and spending some of their oodles of dollars. They got home late yesterday and guess what was missing from their nice little walking pier?"

I didn't know, but knew it was interesting or Cindy wouldn't be telling the story. "What?"

"Their cute little eighteen-foot Tahoe Q4i runabout."

"Do they know when the boat was taken?" I asked.

"Nope, and neither did their neighbors. The people in the nearest house were in Phoenix until yesterday. They're the ones who noticed it missing and told Jamison when he got home."

"Don't suppose anyone's found a lost eighteen-foot-long boat?" Charles said.

Cindy smiled. "Finally, a question I can answer. Yep."

"Someone found it?" I asked.

She nodded. "Not far from where it was taken. It was tied to a pier, a piss-poor knot, I might add. It was behind a deserted house on Seacrest Lane. Some guy a couple of houses away saw it and didn't think anything of it until his wife who likes to stick her nose in every-one's business—like you, Charles—said it didn't belong there and made him call us."

I said, "I don't suppose you found any prints on it."

"Only Jamison and Renee's. Also found an ignition that'd been mangled and hotwired. Want to guess what we didn't find?"

"Not Bowser, I hope," Charles said.

Cindy sighed, and said, "He went with them to Asheville."

"What didn't you find?" I asked.

"Jamison's surfboard."

"Let me guess," I said. "Ocean Pacific?"

Cindy smiled. "You win the opportunity to pay for my lunch."

"Chris always wins the good stuff," Charles said, through smiling teeth.

I ignored him. "So, you think someone hotwired the boat, somehow and somewhere got Joyce on board, and took her out in the ocean to what?"

"A theory is that it was to get her far enough off shore to throw her overboard. Mind you, that's mere speculation. Until her memory returns, we don't know anything other than the boat was stolen."

"What about the surfboard?" Charles asked.

"Charles, did you miss the part where I said, way back thirty seconds ago, that all we know is that the boat was stolen?"

Charles stuffed a fry in his mouth, nodded twice, and said, "So, Chief, what do you want us to do to help figure out what happened out on the deep-blue sea?"

She looked up from her plate, glared at Charles, and said, "In the spirit of the big guy in the red suit coming next week to visit all little chillins, and big chillins like you, Charles, I say Ho, Ho, Ho! In case that's not clear, it means I'm laughing at your suggestion and the best way you can help is to stay out of our way. Leave the coppin' to cops."

Charles took the hint, or decided it wasn't time to argue, and said, "That's a good idea, Chief."

I'd known Charles for a long time, knew his moods, knew his approach to most everything. I also knew he was lying through his teeth.

Chapter Seven

There was a good chance that Joyce had been on the stolen boat, yet several questions remained. Those questions kept me awake most of the night. Who was Joyce, be it her first or last name? What trauma erased her past? Will her memory return? If she's from the area, why hadn't someone reported her missing? And, if she'd been on the stolen boat, why?

I must have fallen asleep at some point. The phone jarred me awake at seven-thirty.

"Brother Chris, did I awaken you?"

I lied and said, no.

"Good. I was excited and wanted you to be first to know. I have been given authorization to collect Joy and bring her here. Praise the Lord."

"That's great news, Preacher. Do you know when she'll be released?"

"They said I could come over now, and they'll discharge her when I get there."

"Great," I repeated.

"Brother Chris, might I ask a huge favor?"

"Sure."

"Would you go with me? You're a familiar face to her. I know she'd appreciate you being there."

"I'd be glad to."

Burl's granite-gray Dodge Grand Caravan pulled in the drive fifteen minutes after I'd agreed to go, and thirty minutes later we were in the hospital visitor's lot.

Burl stepped behind me as I approached Joyce's door, and said, "Since she knows you, why don't you go in first?"

The patient was sitting on the chair. Her hair was pulled in a pony-tail and she wore a long-sleeve, blue T-shirt and the same slacks she had on when we found her. Someone must've given her the shirt and had the slacks cleaned since they were sand free and pressed. She smiled when I entered. The smile lessened when she saw the man behind me.

"You look great," I said. "Ready to get out of here?"

"Yes, but I don't have anywhere—"

"Good morning, Sister Joy, I'm Preacher Burl Costello."

Joyce glanced at Burl and quickly turned to me. "Chris, what's going on?"

I smiled and hoped it put her at ease. "Joyce, Preacher Burl is a friend and the minister of First Light Church on Folly Beach. Part of First Light's ministry is a large house where several people live. Preacher Burl talked to one of the hospital administrators and he agreed to let you stay there until you can get on your feet and your memory returns."

"But, I don't have money. I can't afford—"

Burl took a step closer to Joyce and said, "Sister Joy—"

"Sir, who's Joy, and what's this sister stuff? I'm not your sister... I don't think."

"Joyce," I said, "Preacher Burl calls those who attend First Light either brother or sister. Your name's Joyce, so he thought Joy was a pretty sounding name."

Burl added, "Christmas is right around the corner, so I thought calling you that would be reflective of the joy you will bring to us all."

"Preacher, no offense. I don't know you, crap, pardon my language, I don't even know me. What makes you think I'll bring joy? For all you know, for all I know, I could be a serial killer, or I don't know what."

I wondered the same thing and waited for Burl's response.

He rubbed his hand through his bristle-brush mustache. "Joyce, I hope you don't mind me calling you Joy. As you can tell from looking at this rough-hewn face, I've been around the block a time or two. I've seen evil up close. Regardless, I believe the good in people. Yes, there's a chance that you might not be a saint." He chuckled. "The Good Lord knows I'm not. I see a lady who's suffered a terrible fate. I can't imagine how horrific it must be to not remember the past. I see a lady who needs a break or two to get back on her feet. And, I see someone I, even with my meager resources, can provide a comfortable bed, decent meals, and others who can share with you their hopes and dreams. I would be honored to have you as a part of Hope House for as long as you need, or want, to be there."

She gave a faint smile and said in a faint voice so that Burl and I had to lean closer to hear, "That's kind of you, sir, but I don't have money. I can't afford to pay."

"Ah, Sister Joy, you're in luck. You qualify for the special close-to-Christmas rent of zero dollars a week. And, for no additional charge, Chris and I will provide transportation to your new home."

"Are you certain, Burl, umm, Preacher?"

"Absolutely."

She gave Burl a tentative hug, and whispered, "Thank you."

I gave a sigh of relief.

After what seemed like an eternity getting Joy discharged, the ride to Folly was awkward at best. Burl tried to explain how he founded First Light two years ago and how it met most Sundays on the beach near the Folly Beach Fishing Pier, and during inclement weather, in a store-front on Center Street next to Barb's Books. I shared how I met the preacher when my photo gallery occupied the space where Barb's is now. I didn't get into the deaths that surrounded First Light's first few months in existence.

Joy alternated between listening to Burl patter on about First Light and staring out the window with her mind wandering. Burl didn't notice the difference until he asked if she would be interested in attending his Sunday service in two days.

"I'm sorry, Preacher. What?"

He repeated the question.

"Preacher, are there other churches on Folly?"

"Excellent question, Sister Joy. There are three other wonderful houses of worship on our tiny island. The Baptist, Catholic, and Methodist churches are within sight of each other."

She turned from staring out the window to Burl. "Why start another one?"

"Another excellent question, my dear. First Light is nondenominational and attracts men and women who, for whatever reason, are not attracted to the more traditional denominations." He laughed. "Some of the first to attend were surfers who'd been on the beach waiting to ply their skill in the waves. I'd love to say that my wonderful, spiritual, and inspirational message drew them in. They finally told me that they were bored waiting for, as they said, 'boss' waves, and enjoyed the group singing."

Joy said, "That must've been disheartening."

Burl patted her on the arm. "To the contrary. As I often share from the pulpit, God works in strange and mysterious ways. That day, He provided a flat sea to prevent the young people from surfing and provided members of the flock singing at the top of their lungs to attract those nearby. Several of the surfers have attended religiously, pun intended, since that glorious day."

Burl pulled in my drive and I said it was nice seeing Joy again and that she would find Hope House and Preacher Burl to her liking. I had no idea if that was true, but wanted to reinforce the decision for her to stay there. In a less than convincing tone, she said she hoped so. Our conversation ended with her thanking me for coming with Burl to pick her up and for me to say hi to Barb.

The first thing I did when I got in the house was call Charles to let him know the latest on Joy. I was pleased when he didn't scold me for waiting to tell him. He added that he was planning attend First Light's next service. I said I might see him there, emphasis on might. I was an irregular attender which meant I attended more often than Christmas and Easter, but less, far less, than weekly.

Charles thought he had my commitment to attend, then asked if Joy had regained her memory and shared with what had happened on the boat.

"Charles, don't you think if that happened, I would've led with it?"

"Does that mean she doesn't remember?"

"No more than the last time we talked."

"Doesn't give us much to work with finding out what happened, does it?"

"We're not trying to find out, remember?"

"Good Ole Abe Lincoln said, 'How many legs does a dog have if you call the tail a leg? Calling a tail a leg doesn't make it a leg.'"

Another of Charles's quirks was quoting United States Presidents, or he said they were actual quotes. I had never taken the time to research their origin. As Chris Landrum said, I don't care an atom if they are. That sentiment was shared by others who knew my friend, although it didn't stop him from spewing them.

"Your point is?"

"The point, my friend, is whether you say you are or not, you along with the help of your trusty sidekick are on the case. You can deny it to Cindy, to Burl, to anyone who will listen, and to the Caulders' dog Bowser. That still don't mean you ain't trying."

"Whatever."

He laughed, and the phone went dead.

Chapter Eight

Moving to a strange house, surrounded by strangers, and not knowing who you are, where you came from, or anything about your past, had to be traumatic. I decided to drop by and see how Joy was adjusting. I didn't have anything encouraging to offer except a face that she'd known longer than anyone there. I hoped that would be enough.

It took three knocks before Bernard Prine opened the door. I hardly recognized him. When we'd met a year ago, he had stringy, dark-brown hair, a week-old beard, and wore a faded army jacket and gray dress slacks two sizes too large. Now, his hair was neatly trimmed and combed, he had on a long-sleeve, yellow dress shirt, black jeans, new tennis shoes, and a smile he'd seldom shared a year ago.

"Well if it isn't my friend, Chris Landrum," Bernard said in a Southern drawl. "Welcome, sir."

We'd had little contact since last Christmas, so I was pleased that he'd referred to me as a friend. He shook my hand with a grip powerful enough to open a stubborn food jar.

"It's good to see you, Bernard. How do you like it here?"

He smiled. "One of the best things that ever happened to me was last Christmas when you told me that I could talk to Preacher Burl about my issues. He's a godsend. Crap—whoops, Preacher doesn't like me saying crap—umm, phooey, even if he wasn't a preacher, I'd still say he's a godsend. He's provided room and board, lent me a few dollars when I've needed them, and best of all, he's been there when I sort of threw a couple of temper tantrums, the kind that got me kicked out of homeless shelters. Preacher put his arm around me and took me aside and talked me through whatever inspired me to make an ass, umm, a fool out of myself. I'd do anything for that man."

"I'm glad to hear it. Is your newest resident around?"

"Yes, sir. We were in the kitchen having coffee with Preacher Burl. How about joining us?"

He was leading me to the kitchen before I could answer. We passed one of the female residents, Adrienne, I believe. She was dressed in a light jacket, jeans that were no stranger to manual labor, and calf-high, leather work boots.

Bernard said, "Off to work?"

Adrienne lowered her eyes when she saw me, and mumbled, "Yes."

She headed to the door, and Bernard leaned close and whispered, "If you ask me, she's housing a herd of secrets."

Coming from Bernard, that was something. I remembered how many times Charles and I tried to get him to tell us where he was living when we first met. He never would.

"What kind of secrets?"

He rubbed his chin and stared as Adrienne exited. "If I knew, they wouldn't be secrets. Reckon it's a feeling I get when I'm around her." He shrugged.

Burl was pouring coffee in a mug in front of Joy, and she was laughing.

He saw me in the doorway and without skipping a beat, grabbed another mug, filled it, and handed it to me.

"Brother Chris, if you'd arrived a half hour earlier, you could have joined us for breakfast."

"Yes," Bernard said, "we had crepes, blackberry-mint scones, arugula and pistachio pesto quiche, and, oh yeah, crumpets."

"Really?" I said.

Burl laughed, and said, "Brother Chris, we had a bowl of Raisin Bran and orange juice."

I had forgotten Bernard's sense of humor. "Sounds good."

Bernard glanced at Burl and said, "I must've been thinking about yesterday."

Joy ignored the factual and fictional breakfast menu, and said, "Chris, it's nice to see you again."

"You too, Joy. How do you like it here?"

"It's far better than the room at the hospital. Preacher Burl gave me a choice of two bedrooms and I picked the one with two windows instead of one."

"Brother Taylor moved out and looks like Sister Rebekah will be leaving soon. She's doing well at her job at Black Magic and will be moving to her own apartment after Christmas."

"It's great that your residents find places to live," I said.

"They're blessed, yet I'm always sad to see them go."

Bernard pointed his mug at Burl. "Don't worry, Preacher. I won't leave you."

Burl chuckled. "You have a home here as long as you wish."

Bernard took the last sip and excused himself saying that he thought a walk would do him good. He headed out the back door, and I told him it was good seeing him again.

Joy whispered something I couldn't understand. Apparently, Burl couldn't either and asked her to repeat it.

She stared in her mug and said, "What if I have a house somewhere? What if I have a husband, children? Brothers, sisters, parents? What if..." She held out her hands palms up and repeated, "What if?"

Burl reached out and hugged her. I didn't know what to say and sipped coffee.

A minute later, Joy stepped back from Burl and said, "If you gentlemen don't mind, I'd like to go to my room."

Burl said, "Joy, this is now your home. Feel free to come, go, and do as you please. I lock the doors each night, but I'll give you a key. And, I'm here if you need anything."

She nodded and left the kitchen.

Burl watched her go, and said, "Christmas is a week away and the best gift in the world for Sister Joy would be her memory. I can't give that to her."

"None of us can. What you are giving are some of the greatest gifts possible, a place to call home and a loving environment."

"Yes," Burl said, "I'm afraid that isn't enough when it comes to Sister Joy. My other residents know where they've been yet are uncertain of their future. That's why most end up under this roof. Without knowledge of her past, Sister Joy can't determine whether staying here is a good or a bad thing. She had no perspective on her reality."

"Did she share anything beyond being on the boat?"

He shook his head. "Nothing like a direct memory, but here's something. I was showing her around upstairs and she pointed to a couple of places where I needed to repair the wood trim. She said she could help."

"Perhaps she has construction experience."

"Maybe, although not necessarily," Burl said. "I told her I'd worked construction back in the day. She could've wanted to help and figured I'd show her what to do. She wants to help."

"True. Did she say anything else?"

"No."

"What did you tell the others about her?"

"Nothing other than she's been in the hospital and would be staying here until she got back on her feet."

"Did you say anything about her memory?"

"I told them that she was foggy about the past."

"How does she get along with them?"

"There's been little contact. She stayed in her room most of time. She talked for a while to Bernard, but little to the others."

"Preacher, I'm still worried that there is someone who may want to harm her. Have you told everyone that it's important that they don't talk about her with anyone outside this house?"

"I told Sister Adrienne and Brother Bernard. I haven't had a chance to talk with Rebekah. I will when she returns from work. More coffee?"

I told him I was okay, and he said, "Now, a question. Have the police learned anything about what happened?"

I told him about the stolen boat and surfboard.

"They're certain that the surfboard was the same one you and Sister Barb found with Joy?"

I nodded.

"Have they checked the boat for fingerprints?"

"Chief LaMond said there weren't any except those of the owners."

I told him I'd better be going and asked him to call if Joy said anything that would help the police.

He said he would and ended with, "I look forward to seeing you at tomorrow's worship service."

How could I say no to that?

Chapter Nine

A clear, pollution-free sky greeted me as I left the house to walk to the morning service at First Light. The temperature was flirting with the upper thirties, so I headed three blocks to the church's inclement weather sanctuary. Attendance was lower when the service was indoors, and approximately twenty people were standing around a coffee pot in back of the room. It was easy to spot Preacher Burl. He was wearing a white robe crafted from a bedsheet and pouring coffee in a Styrofoam cup. Lottie was nearby. I was reminded of the first time I'd seen her. She was in this building and helping Burl and a few others refinish discarded church pews to use in the sanctuary. She wore oversized clothes hiding her attractive figure and had a self-cut hairstyle. Today she looked and acted the part of a preacher's wife, something I hoped she'd soon become. She handed coffee to William Hansel, another friend of mine and a regular at First Light.

Joy was in the corner in animated conversation with Bernard. She had on a tan blouse and dress slacks, clothes I assumed donated by one of the other residents. It was good seeing her socializing. Amber and Jason, her nineteen-year-old son, were in the front of the room talking to a woman I didn't know.

Charles was huddled with Mary Ewing and her girls, Jewel, seven, and Joanie, three. Mary had been homeless until Preacher Burl learned of her plight a year ago and worked with her to find a house to share with two women, and to get a job at Bert's Market. Charles saw me, glanced at his bare wrist, and shook his head like he was scolding me for being late.

I was on my way to talk to Charles, Mary, Joanie and Jewel, when Lottie whispered something to Burl and he moved to an old lectern that'd spent its better years in a high school gymnasium. The preacher cleared his throat, and said, "Please repose thyselves." He pointed to the pews.

A couple of older ladies I didn't know moved to the front row and reposed thyselves. They were followed by three more members who heeded his charge. The others either weren't ready to stop socializing or didn't know what the preacher meant. I knew because he announced the beginning of many services with those words, so the regulars who hadn't moved, weren't ready to.

Burl tapped his hand on the lectern and repeated his "call to worship," and gained the attention of the remaining talkers. Dude Sloan, was among that group. He'd seldom attended First Light until earlier this year when one of his employees was killed attempting to save Barb from the hands of a man trying to kill her.

I was going to see if Joy wanted to sit with me, but she was already seated beside Bernard. I slid in the pew next to Dude as Preacher Burl was saying something that began each service. "Please silence thy portable communication devices." Most did, and Burl asked William Hansel to lead the group in singing "Away in a Manger" from the song-book made from sheets of paper stapled together. The songs had been photocopied from a church hymnal.

William had a phenomenal voice and most of us, including me, knew that unless we could improve on the song, he shouldn't try. We mouthed the words as we listened to him sing. Burl's flock was kind, considerate, and many other good things, but except for William, singers we were not.

Burl was in his element, standing in front of *his flock*, sharing a lesson from the Gospel, and reminding us of the historic and spiritual events leading to Christmas, seven days away. Joy was staring at the preacher, and I wondered what was going through her mind.

Burl announced two services for next weekend. He called the first a Christmas Eve midnight service while at the same time saying it'd begin at seven o'clock. He joked—I assume he was joking—that it would be held then instead of midnight because his message would be more meaningful if his flock was sober, and there was a better chance of that at seven. He then said the Christmas morning service would be at the regular eleven o'clock time. Today's service concluded with William singing "O Come All Ye

Faithful" with a few of us humming along and the rest mouthing the words.

Charles was on the sidewalk talking to the two women who'd been on the front pew. I stood aside until he patted each of them on the back and they walked away.

"Who're they? I don't remember seeing them before."

Charles watched the ladies go, and said, "You have to come to the service to see who's here."

Touché. "So, who are they?"

"Dixie and Martha."

"Dixie?"

"Doubt it says that on her birth certificate. That's all I've ever heard her called. She lives in the three hundred block of East Arctic across the street from Martha. Dixie's an ubergardener."

"A what?"

"A super-duper gardener. Her back yard is full of plants, flowers, herbs, and other growing things. Rumor is she has name holders beside each plant with the name, both the common name and the Latin name, printed on them."

"Why?"

Charles rolled his eyes. "Why do you wear boring clothes instead of educational, inspirational, and nifty shirts like *moi*?"

"What's that have to do with Dixie posting names of each of her… plant things?"

"Same answer to each question. Because she wants to."

"That helps."

He rolled his eyes, again. "Can I get back to what I was saying?"

"Please do."

"Martha and Dixie are widows. Kind of quiet, don't think they get out much. I occasionally see Martha walking around carrying a cane." He waved his handmade wooden cane in the air. "Not nice like this, one of those silver ones they sell at Harris Teeter. Enough about them, learn anything new about Joy?"

I told him no, and he was interrupted from asking me why not when Burl approached and said that he, Lottie, Joy, Bernard, and Dude were heading to Loggerhead's for lunch, and wondered if we would like to join them. The invitation was kind, participation by Dude unusual, and the chance for Charles to grill Joy about her past impossible to turn down. He answered yes for both of us.

Loggerhead's was on West Arctic Avenue, four blocks from First Light's foul-weather sanctuary, and across the street from Barb's condo in the Oceanfront Villas. Burl had removed his robe/sheet, so he didn't look like a ghost as we followed him to the restaurant. Charles spent the entire walk talking to Joy, not surprising knowing how curious—nosy— he was. In better weather, the large outside bar and dining area would have been packed. Today we were forced to move inside. Burl must have used his heavenly influence since there was a table available large enough to accommodate our group.

Yvonne, one of the owners, greeted us and said that Joe would be taking care of us. Joe, a long-tenured employee I'd known for a few years, was close behind Yvonne and took our drink orders. Five of us said water would be fine while Burl and Lottie ordered Diet Pepsi.

We were seated at a large, bar-height, rectangular table with Burl at the head and three of us seated on each of its long sides. Various NFL games were on televisions strategically located throughout the room.

"Thank you for breaking bread with me this lovely sabbath," Burl said, sounding more like a prayer than something you would normally hear in a bar.

Lottie was closest to Burl and patted him on the arm. "Preacher, we're delighted to join you."

Joy and Dude were seated next to Lottie and across from Bernard, Charles, and me. Bernard spoke next, but it was so loud in the room that I couldn't hear what he was saying. Joy and Burl laughed, so it must've been humorous. It was good seeing Joy fitting in.

Our drinks arrived, and Dude stood, raised his glass and said, "Toast. Boss preacher."

Dude wore one of his many tie-dyed shirts, was in his mid-sixties and looked like the stereotype of an aging hippie, which he happened to be. He also had a way with words, a way to mangle them.

The rest of us raised our glasses to toast while Joy looked at the life-long surfer like he was speaking Tigrinya. I told Joy that Dude owned the surf shop and had been on Folly many years. I failed to mention that despite his appearance, and extensive vocabulary that may exceed fifty words, that he was one of the island's most successful business-people and well-respected by both its bohemian residents and city fathers.

Joe returned and took our orders, and Bernard leaned across the table and asked Joy how she enjoyed the service. I thought it was an awkward question with the preacher in hearing range.

"Bernard," Joy said, "I thought it was inspiring."

Dude leaned toward Joy. "Be good as other preachin' you been to?"

I realized that Dude didn't know anything about Joy and the reason she was staying at Hope House. I wanted to tell him what'd happened but didn't want her story and whereabouts known outside a limited group of people.

Charles decided that Dude was someone we could trust, and said, "Dude, Joy has amnesia and can't remember much about her past."

Dude tapped Joy on the arm and said, "Cool. You be lucky, bad history gone."

Joy's eyes darted around the table, most likely, hoping someone would comment. No one did, and she said, "Thanks, Dude. I think. I wish it was a cool thing. All it makes me think is that I'm an outcast here."

"Cool," Dude said, repeating one of his favorite words.

I was pleased when Joy said, "Why?"

He pointed to each person at the table. "We all outcasts. You be in good company. Cool."

I wouldn't have put it like that, but the truth was that each of us were either outsiders to Folly, or in the cases of Charles and Dude who'd been here many years, were considered left of quirky, even by Folly standards.

Our commends appeared to put Joy at ease and she asked Lottie what'd brought her to Folly. Lottie hesitated before sharing her story, a story involving physical and emotional abuse, and homelessness. Bernard jumped in the conversation and talked about his experiences in Afghanistan, and how he'd been homeless.

Dude had never been homeless or abused, yet felt he needed to add something and said, "Me have Pluto."

As farfetched as it may seem, Joy didn't understand what he was talking about, and said, "You have a planet?"

Dude shook his head and pointed to the ceiling. "Pluto up there be dwarf planet, not planet."

"Oh," Joy said in response to Dude, as many others had said before her.

He pointed to his chest. "Australian Terrier be my Pluto."

Joy grinned. "Oh, they're so cute."

I wondered how she knew that. Clearly, there was much I could learn about amnesia.

Food arrived, and Burl asked for a moment of silence while he offered a prayer. The noise was getting louder in the crowded restaurant and our table was the only island of silence. The comforting aroma of lunch permeated the area. Burl finished the prayer, and Joy looked at her plate and slowly turned back to Dude, and said, "Dude, what if I have a dog? If I do, who's taking care of it?"

Dude swallowed his first bite of food, and said, "Me be flummoxed."

Charles said, "I'm sure that if you have a dog, it's being taken care of."

I wondered why he was sure.

The conversation turned to what everyone was doing between now and Christmas and Burl shared stories about his younger days growing up on a cattle ranch in southern Illinois. Joy appeared to drift in and out of the conversation and I wondered how difficult it must be for her listening to stories about past Christmases.

Most of us were laughing at something Bernard had said when I noticed Joy staring at the bar along the side of the restaurant. I said, "Joy, what are you thinking?"

She shook her head like she was trying to move back to the present and nodded toward the bar. "Chris, that looks so familiar."

"Like you've been in here before?"

She closed her eyes and said, "Maybe."

Chapter Ten

It turned out to be a pleasant Sunday afternoon. Puffy white clouds dotted the blue sky, and the temperature hovered in the low-fifties. Instead of heading home, I turned on Center Street and started toward Barb's Books, when I noticed Joy hurrying to catch up with me. I made a benign comment about how nice the weather was. She asked where I was going, and I told her the bookstore.

"Would you mind if I tag along? I haven't seen Barb since, umm, you know."

"Sure," I said, not waiting for her to relive the traumatic event in the surf.

"Everyone at the house is so nice. Preacher Burl and Adrienne found me some clothes, and, well, they're kind." We walked a few more steps, and she added, "You know what they can't do?"

"What?"

"Give me my memories. I need to get out and get some fresh air to clear my head, at least the little that's in it."

Two men wearing shorts were leaving the bookstore as we approached. They turned our direction, pivoted, and walked the other way.

Joy shivered and said, "Aren't those guys freezing?"

"I'd be if I had on shorts," I said, and held the door open for Joy.

Barb saw us and smiled. "Hey, Joyce, it's great to see you. Who's that old geezer with you?"

Joy laughed, louder than I thought necessary, and said, "Picked him up on the street. You know him?"

Barb said, "Seen him around. He's not important, how are you?"

"Physically, I'm okay except for a couple of bruises. Can't say the same about my memory."

Barb nodded. "Nothing coming back?"

Joy shook her head.

"Can I offer you something to drink? Coffee, soft drink, water?"

"Coffee would be nice. I'm not as warm blooded as those guys in shorts."

Barb led us to the tiny office behind the showroom. "Oh, did you meet Troy and Nate?"

"No," I said. "They went the other direction."

Barb said, "They're from Canada, Ottawa, I believe. They think it's hot here."

The names sounded familiar. "Are they your next-door renters?"

"Good memory, Chris." Barb turned to Joy. "Joyce, they're staying next to me in my condo building. They're here for a month."

Joy returned the smile and said, "Preacher Burl started calling me Joy instead of Joyce. I sort of like it."

"Then Joy it is."

Joy's smile faded. "Those guys are here for a month. I wonder how long I'll be here?"

Barb inserted a K-cup pod in her Keurig coffeemaker and turned to Joy. "It'll work out."

Joy turned from looking at the coffeemaker to staring at Barb. "What makes you so certain?"

"From what I've heard, you're surrounded by good people at Hope House, and this is a loving community. It may not be quick, but your memory will start returning and everyone will help you with whatever is needed."

"I hope so."

I told Barb who we had lunch with.

She turned to Joy and said Dude was her half brother.

Joy stared at her and said, "You're kidding."

Barb laughed and gave Joy an abridged version of their relationship.

All Joy said was, "Hmm, half brother. Guess that's why he only got half of your vocabulary."

Barb laughed again and said, "Joy, Chris may not have told you, I practiced law for many years before opening the bookstore. I even had a client with the same kind of amnesia you have. I've avoided doing legal work since opening the store, but I'll be glad to help you in any legal entanglements you may encounter."

Barb handed Joy a mug of coffee and inserted another pod in the Keurig.

Joy took a sip, and said, "Barb, I don't have any money. I can't—"

"Joy, we'll deal with that when the time comes. Heck, you may be a billionaire and will want to pay me more than I'm worth."

"Or, I could be broke."

Barb smiled. "Then we'll deal with it later."

My phone rang, I answered and instead of Charles saying anything normal like *hi* or *hello*, he screamed, "Where are you?"

I told him.

"We've gotta go. I'll be out front in five minutes."

"Where?"

The word was wasted. He'd hung up.

I returned the phone to my pocket and Barb said, "What?"

"It was Charles."

"I know that. I heard him yelling."

"He wants me to meet him out front."

Barb shook her head. "Then go?"

"Joy, Charles wants me to go somewhere with him."

Barb answered for her. "Go. Joy and I have some catching up to do. I want to tell her more about Dude and the geezer she came in with. We'll be fine."

I opened the door and Charles's Toyota Venza was already in front of the store and blocking the driving lane. Two cars behind him were patiently waiting for him to move. A third vehicle wasn't as patient and tapped the horn twice. I slid in the passenger seat before road rage commenced, and Charles turned right at the next intersection.

"Would it be too much to ask where we're going and why the hurry?"

"NOPE," he said and kept his eye on the narrow road.

Two blocks later, my question about our destination was answered. Charles pulled in Dude's front yard and parked beside his rusting, green Chevrolet El Camino. The front of the pre-Hugo, elevated, wood-frame house had old-fashioned, multi-colored Christmas lights strung around the front door, up the corners of the house and across the roofline. Straggly shrubs on each side of the steps were covered with more of the near-antique lights.

Before getting out, Charles smacked the steering wheel and said, "Pluto's vamoosed."

Dude must've seen us arrive. He scampered out the front door, down the steps, and was standing at the driver's window motioning for Charles to get out.

"He be gone!" Dude shouted as we exited the car.

Charles put his arm around the distressed, aging hippie. "Let's go in and you can tell us about it."

"What's to tell. He be gone!"

Charles nudged Dude up the steps, and I followed.

This was the second time I'd been in Dude's abode, so I'd gotten over the surprise of seeing wall-to-wall, bright-green shag carpet and the three colorful beanbag chairs arranged in a triangle. Charles helped lower Dude into the green one. Dude slumped down and stared at a lower half of what appeared to be a rubber Santa Claus the size of a large dog bone on the floor beside the red chair.

"Dude, I know Pluto's gone," I said. "What happened."

Dude turned to the back door and said, "Me be at Logger's. Church lunch."

Charles said, "We were with you, remember?"

I wanted to say, "Charles, shut up, and let him finish." Instead, I said. "Let Dude tell us what happened."

"Me skip home from Logger's. See back door cracked open. Pluto gone … gone."

Charles said, "Do you think someone broke in and took him?"

"You be detective. That's why I call you."

With an effort I wouldn't have needed twenty years ago, I pushed out of the beanbag chair, and walked to the back door. The lock didn't appear tampered with and there was no evidence of a break in. I looked at Charles and shook my head.

He nodded, and said, "Dude, did you go out the back door when you left for church?"

"Exit front. Ride be parked in front." He rubbed his unshaven face. "Woe, today backwards. Took trash out back, then boogied to church."

"Is it possible that the door didn't close all the way when you left?"

He again rubbed his face. "Possible, affirmative. Likely, not." He shrugged.

"Has Pluto gotten out before?"

Dude stood and started pacing the living room floor. "Never."

I said, "Don't you think he'll come home when he gets hungry?"

"What me think, don't mean what he do. Australian Terriers be bred to boogie after rodents and snakes. Me never be lettin' him out without leash. Never," Dude said and went through the kitchen, grabbed his jacket off a chair, and exited to the large patio.

Charles and I followed and watched Dude as he stared at the back yard. He turned to Charles and said, "Woe, plum forgot. You be detective. Here be clue." He picked up a red rhinestone-studded collar that usually adorned Pluto's neck and handed it to Charles. "Stuck to branch behind *hacienda*."

The collar was fastened. I said, "Dude, was it loose on his neck?"

"Loose enough that he could have snagged it on a branch and pulled it off?" Charles added.

"Could be. Me no want to hurt cute little neck. Kept it loose."

Charles ran his hands around the collar, and said, "So, Pluto could have escaped if the door wasn't closed tight enough, got his collar caught on the branch, and ran away."

Dude stared at Charles. "You be detective. You tell me."

Dude then said he was going to drive around and look for the missing member of his family. Charles and I said we'd do the same. I wasn't nearly as worried about Pluto. I figured when he got hungry, he'd find his way back.

An hour later, we'd driven every road on Folly, had seen several dogs walked by their masters, and stopped to ask each person if he or she had seen Pluto. All, to no avail. My optimism faded.

Charles dropped me at the house and said he was going to ride around longer. I didn't think his luck would change. I called Barb to see how her time with Joy went. She had three customers and said she'd call later. I settled in the recliner in my living room and alternated between rehashing the busy day and snoozing. Snoozing ruled.

Chapter Eleven

I t wasn't yet six-thirty and the sun had faded behind the marsh. Early sunsets were my least-favorite features of December. I sighed as it departed and realized that I hadn't had anything to eat since lunch at Loggerhead's. I also realized that my cupboard was bare, its normal condition, and I didn't want to eat another meal today at a restaurant. I walked next door to Bert's Market, Folly's iconic, eclectic grocery that prides itself on never closing and was the island's go-to place for everything from beer to Band-Aids. Included in that mix was a deli where I ordered a five-cheese panini and was killing time waiting for the sandwich when Chief Cindy LaMond moved behind me and said, "You're not ordering something healthy, are you?"

I smiled and said, "I plead the fifth."

"That answers my question," she said, and looked around to see if anyone was close enough to hear us. No one was, and she continued, "I'm glad I ran into you. I was going to call after I got home, and despite being pooped from an exhausting day at work, I'm going to fix a fine five-course gourmet meal for hubby."

"Picking up a pizza from Woody's?" I said.

Woody's pizza was an institution on Folly and had been feeding visitors and locals for years.

Cindy smiled.

"You were going to call me?" I said to move her past the dinner menu.

"Two reasons. Our search for anything, I mean anything, about

Joyce Doe, or Jane Joyce, has come up with a big, fat zero. If I hadn't seen her in person, I'd swear she doesn't exist. Her prints aren't on file anywhere. Unless she lost 127 pounds in the last week and changed her skin color, she's not the 215-pound mother of three who's been reported missing in Moncks Corner. The TV stations ran her photo and we've received zero calls from anyone who has an inkling of who she is."

"Cindy, a few of us had lunch at Loggerhead's after church this morning. Joy came with Burl."

"Good," Cindy interrupted. "Burl will be a good influence. Better than some people I know."

I let her comment go. "While we were there, she stopped paying attention to what was being said and looked at the bar. I asked her what was on her mind and she said that it looked familiar."

"Familiar like she'd been there?"

"That's what I asked. She said maybe."

"Or it could be that any bar may look familiar, and it had nothing to do with Loggerhead's."

"Yes," I said.

"So, it doesn't tell us more than she's seen a bar."

"I agree. From what you said about not finding anything about a missing person fitting her description, or anyone calling about her photo on television, do you think she's from outside the area?"

Cindy shook her head. "Either that or she's from another planet. And, speaking of being from another planet, that leads me to the second thing I wanted to talk to you about, your buddy Dude."

The deli clerk handed me my panini, I paid, and followed Cindy outside to her city-owned truck. Charles had often joked that Dude emigrated to earth from another planet, a planet where complete sentences were frowned upon and had a different meaning than they do on earth. This was one of the few times Cindy agreed with Charles.

"What about him?"

"He began calling and pestering me this afternoon about the shorter, more articulate version of him that's missing."

"Dude called you about Pluto?"

"Eventually. Dude first called Mayor Newman, Councilmember Salmon, the preacher at the Baptist Church, Preacher Burl, and then me about his missing canine. Mayor Newman called me and rearranged the priorities of my department from catching bad guys, stopping speeders, and ticketing those law-breaking vacationers who have the audacity to park with a tire or two touching the pavement on our streets. My priority now is finding one lost Australian Terrier. To paraphrase the words of our fine citizen, *Dude be full o clout.*"

I smiled and asked if she's had any luck.

"As much as we've had at learning Joy's identity. Dude told me that you and Charles were the first on the scene of the canine escape. I was going to call to ask if Dude said anything that made you think that Pluto's disappearance was anything other than the critter wanting to get away from Dude to maintain his sanity. Believe it or not, there are times that I don't fully understand what Dude's talking about. You spend more time with him and other oddball characters than I do, so I figured you might understand him better."

I understood Dude better than I understood thermodynamics although not much better.

"Cindy, Dude's upset."

"Duh."

"Pluto means everything to him. Dude doesn't have many close friends and Pluto is probably his best. He was clueless about how Pluto escaped. I didn't see anything that made me think it was anything other than the dog scampering out the back door that was left ajar. Dude had taken the trash out that way before going to church. Most of the time he leaves by the front door since his car's parked in the front yard. He was carrying trash, so it would've been easy for him to not shut the door all the way."

"That's what I thought but wanted your take. When I was there, the poor boy was near tears. My experience with dogs, and with Larry, is that once hunger sets in, they find their way home. Worry not, all my patrol vehicles are out scouring the island for one missing Australian Terrier. If they happen to stumble across a murder in progress, they may stop, unless they're chasing Pluto. And speaking of dogs, Larry, and hunger, I'd better get home with a pizza before he calls the mayor on me."

I wished her luck, headed home, used my one culinary skill, and microwaved the panini that'd turned cold while I was talking to Cindy. I also poured a glass of Cabernet, and wondered who Joy was, and to a lesser extent, where Pluto was.

Chapter Twelve

Christmas was less than a week away although you could hardly tell it from looking at my house, inside or out. I had hooked a ten-year-old, dusty artificial wreath I bought at a yard sale for seventy-five cents on the front door and inside my decorating was a ceramic Dickens Village Victoria Station setting on a table in the living room. Other than the wreath, the Station was the only item I brought from Kentucky that I associated with Christmas. I'd thought of adding more but rationalized that there was no need since I seldom had anyone to the house and considered the party at Cal's Country Bar and Burgers my prime event on Christmas Day. Looking at the Victoria Station reminded me that it'd been a couple of weeks since I'd talked to Cal, besides a burger sounded good. During the off-season, there was less than a fifty-fifty chance that Cal's would be open for lunch or early beer drinking. I had nothing better to do, so I took a chance and drove the short distance since the outside temperature was near freezing.

The front door was locked. If I wanted food my gamble hadn't paid off, but there was still a chance Cal was inside. I went to the side door and had better luck. The jukebox was playing a Hank Williams Sr. classic, and Cal, who could double as an older, much older, version of Hank, was singing along and sliding a table to the center of the room. My friend was seventy-three-years-old, six-foot-three, razor thin with a spine that curved forward from leaning down to a microphone and living for decades out of the back seat of his car. His long, gray hair inched out from around a Stetson that had travelled with him for forty plus years. I smiled when I saw a strand of battery-operated LED lights strung around the crown, his seasonal addition to the hat. Cal wore a black T-shirt instead of his rhinestone covered white coat he wore when performing. *Ho, Ho, Ho!* was in glittery, silver paint on the front of the T-shirt. His holiday-inspired attire also included bright-red slacks and red tennis shoes. The bar, like Cal, was in a marginal state of repair, yet with its beat-up tables and chairs, indoor/outdoor carpet covered floor, and antique Wurlitzer jukebox, the owner swore it was "the perfect country music bar." Cal would know since he travelled the South for more than four decades singing at any venue that would have him.

Cal saw me in the doorway. He tipped his Stetson my direction, and said, "Halleluiah! My Christmas wish is answered. An elf has come to help this old codger."

And, all I wanted was a hamburger.

"Help with what?"

He waved his hand around the room. "I'm running late finishing party decorations. It's getting harder and harder each year for me to get everything done. My energy level ain't what it used to be."

I followed his gaze and saw three—yes, three—seven-foot-tall artificial Christmas trees in the room. Their multiple strands of colorful lights matched the strands Cal had attached to each non-moving vertical surface, and more were hanging from the ceiling. Unless Santa was shoveling snow in front of the room while Mrs. Claus was feeding the reindeer, I couldn't imagine how much more could be done to make the bar Christmas-party ready.

"What can I do?"

He pointed to the corner near the front door. "Look over there. There's a wide-open space begging for a Christmas tree."

The corner's apparent cry for help was lost on the man who had a grand total of zero Christmas trees in his house. What wasn't lost on me was Cal's childlike enthusiasm for the holiday and his desire to make his bar reflect his glee.

"Do you have a tree?"

His smile was as wide as his face. "Sure do, and now I have an elf to help put it up."

Not only did he have a tree, he had a six-foot ladder, and enough strands of lights to humiliate the tree in Times Square. As if on cue, Gene Autry's version of "Frosty the Snowman" began on the jukebox. "Frosty" was one of many Christmas songs Cal added each December.

During the lull between Gene Autry's singing and Burl Ives, the singer, not the preacher, telling us about "Rudolph the Red-Nosed Reindeer," Cal said, "Have you and Charles found Pluto?"

"How do you know about Pluto?"

He handed me the strand of lights to hang around the back of the tree. "Let's see. It could've been when Officer Spencer came in last night and said he'd driven around the island 739 times looking for the dog or could've been when Councilmember Salmon stopped by for a brew and said that his wife made him ride around looking. No, I got it, it was when the Dudester charged in the door whistling and yelling, 'Yo, Pluto, you be here?'"

I laughed, and said, "The word's out."

"A woeful understatement, my friend," Cal said, and pulled a chair to the front of the tree and lowered his body in it.

"What makes you think Charles or I may've found Pluto?"

He pointed to a nearby chair. "Take a load off."

We weren't finished with the tree, but Cal was breathing heavily and needed to rest. I pulled the chair close to his and sat.

"Dude said the police would do their best to find the missing family member, but he had more confidence that you and especially Charles would find him since your buddy was a professional detective."

"He said all that?"

"Not those words, but that's my interpretation of what he was trying to say."

"To my knowledge, neither Charles nor anyone else has found Pluto. I haven't talked to Dude today, so the pup might be safe and cuddled up to his master."

Cal removed his Stetson and set it on the floor beside the chair. "Then let me ask you this," he said. "Figured out who that Joy gal is that you and Miss Barb found surfin' at the County Park?"

"How do you know about Joy?"

"I hope you don't want me to name everyone who told me about her? There've been a dozen or so guys and gals in here talking about it."

"What've you heard?"

"About you finding her? About where she's staying? Or, about what happened to her memory?"

"All of them."

He told me what he knew about Barb and me finding her, and where she was staying. He was one-hundred percent accurate. When it came to what happened to her memory, the percent dropped drastically. The consensus was that she'd been clobbered with a steel pipe and left on the beach. Theories about who clobbered her included her husband, someone robbing her, the jealous wife of someone who was cheating with Joy, and an alien who'd parked his/her/it's spaceship in the County Park because of its wide-open space. Cal said he didn't put much faith in the alien option. Unfortunately, the accuracy of where she was staying was dead on. That shoots the idea that if someone is after her, the fewer people who knew where she was the better.

He exhausted everything he knew about Joy and was rejuvenated and anxious to finish decorating the tree. Frank Sinatra was singing "Jingle Bells," as Cal pushed himself out of the chair and pointed for me to get back on the ladder so he could give me the final strand of lights.

"Chris," he said as I wrapped the lights around the top of the tree, "remember when I told you why my Christmas party was so important?"

"Wasn't it three years ago when you had the first one?"

"Four."

"Time flies. You said it was because you'd spent many Christmases on the road and most of those years you didn't have anywhere to go to celebrate the holiday. You'd met others in the same boat."

"Yeah, I told myself that if I ever had a place where I could throw a party for everyone who wanted to come, regardless if they had a family, were homeless, had any money, whatever, that I'd do it." He smiled and pointed to each tree. "Being able to do this makes me happier than anything I do all year. People are saying this'll be the biggest."

I'd been to most of his Christmas parties and the number attending had increased dramatically.

The sound of Bing Crosby singing "White Christmas" filled the room.

Cal hooked a large ornament on the tree and pointed to the juke-box. "My favorite Christmas song."

He'd told me that last year. I was thinking how strange it was that I'd remembered that bit of trivia when I couldn't remember what I had for lunch two days ago.

He interrupted my thought when he said, "I have three versions on the jukebox: Bing, Eddy Arnold, and Loretta Lynn." He hesitated, glanced at the new tree, and then at the jukebox, and joined Bing singing, "I'm dreaming of a white Christmas, just like the ones I used to know." He turned to me. "Chris, think about how bad it'll be for poor Joy on Sunday. She won't be able to remember anything about the ones she used to know. Christmases with friends, with families, maybe with children. How lonely and sad must that be?"

I'd thought about her lack of memory about family and friends but hadn't thought of it in relation to Christmas. "You're right."

"Chris, ain't nothing I can do about her past and those memories. If you can get her to the party, we'll give her a Christmas she'll remember for a long time."

"I'll see what I can do."

Chapter Thirteen

I left my car at Cal's and walked two blocks to the surf shop to see if Dude's wayward child had returned. The surf shop, with its name in all lower case for reasons known only to Dude, was a goldmine during vacation season. In the winter, its owner spent days in the Lost Dog Cafe drinking tea and bemoaning how bad business was. He seldom got sympathy from the less-successful business owners.

To my chagrin, I was met by Stephon instead of Dude. Stephon was rude and snarky. I'd learned to tolerate his condescending attitude, and he tolerated me to the point that he didn't become hostile when he saw me. Dude kept him on the payroll because he was a surfer and magically meshed with the store's more offbeat customers.

"Good afternoon, Stephon," I said in the most civil tone I could muster. "Is Dude around?"

The clerk was rearranging a rack of wetsuits and wasn't going to let my arrival distract him. "No."

"Is he at the Lost Dog Cafe?"

"No."

"Do you know where he is?"

"No."

This was one of my more civil conversations with Stephon, so I decided to quit while I was ahead.

"Thanks."

I turned to leave, and was surprised to hear, "He's looking for Pluto."

I stopped and looked at the employee who'd turned from the wetsuits and was staring at me. I motioned for him to continue.

"I've never seen boss man so upset. I don't know why, but he likes you. Maybe you can try to find him and help him search. Don't tell him I said this." He looked around and lowered his voice like he was about to tell me the combination to Dude's safe. "You could put your arm around the boss man and say it'll be okay. I would, except you may not know this, but I'm not much at warm and fuzzy. When you asked if I knew where he was, I said no because I don't. Oh yeah, one more thing, when you find him, don't say anything about the Lost Dog Cafe. He might start whimpering if he hears the words lost dog. He's walking the streets. Please help him."

Where was my recorder when I needed it? I said I would and heard two words I didn't know were in Stephon's vocabulary. "Thank you."

The odds on me finding Dude if I walked would be near zero and the temperature felt nearly that cold, so I returned to Cal's and got the car and started my canvas of the island. I was surprised that Pluto hadn't ventured home on his own. I started on Dude's street and drove a grid for fifteen minutes. I saw two couples walking dogs and stopped to ask if they'd seen Dude or a lost Australian Terrier. Each said they hadn't seen Pluto but had talked to Dude who stopped them and asked if they'd seen his missing buddy.

I was about to give up my search when I spotted the surf shop owner in front of Hope House talking with Preacher Burl. I stopped and joined them. Dude wore a stoplight-red unzipped parka revealing his tie-dye T-shirt with a peace symbol on the front, jeans with a rip in each knee, red driving gloves, and hiking boots. He held the leash with the rhinestone-studded collar dangling Pluto-less. He looked more like he was hiking the Appalachian Trail than looking for his pet. He also wore a frown.

"No luck," I said.

Dude shook his head and Burl patted him on the back and said, "We're putting together a search party to help Brother Dude. Brother Bernard and Sister Joy are robing themselves in heavier clothing and Sister Rebekah should arrive any minute. She had to wait for someone to relieve her at Black Magic." Burl held up his phone. "I'm coordinating the search."

"Chrisster, my poor baby could be frozen like a popsicle."

The temperature was well above freezing although it didn't feel it, so I doubted Pluto could have frozen, but it wouldn't do any good to share that observation.

Joy and Bernard joined us, and Burl asked if I was going to help search. Dude looked at me with sad eyes, so I said, "Of course."

Burl said, "Okay, here's the plan. Brother Bernard, you know the island pretty well." Burl pointed east. "Why don't you head off that way? Brother Dude, why don't you go toward town and check behind shops and restaurants? Pluto should be hungry and there are plenty of places where he could root in the trash for food."

Bernard said, "Dude, if you want, I can tell you the best trash cans for food."

Bernard was talking from experience after having been homeless for many months and searching for food and warmth wherever possible.

Dude said, "Okeydokey."

"Sister Joy, you're new here so why don't you go with Brother Chris? That way you'll learn more about the island and will help Chris look while he focuses on driving."

Joy glanced at me, and I said, "Good idea."

"Good," Burl said. "When Sister Rebekah gets here, I'll recommend that she looks west of Center Street."

Joy was quiet the first few minutes or our search. The coat Burl found for her was several sizes too large and she had a challenging time getting comfortable in the seat with the seatbelt and bulky overgarment. She finally took it off and threw it in the backseat. I carried the conversation and tried to point out some sites and homes where I knew the residents.

"Chris," she finally said, "I don't know who my friends were before, well, you know."

"Yes."

She shook her head. "I don't know if I have a family."

"I understand."

"Let me tell you what I do know. Preacher Burl and the others in the house have been fantastic. They're from diverse backgrounds. They've had ups and downs, mostly downs, I'm saddened to learn. Despite that, they've been wonderful. They seem to truly care. I hope that if, no, when, I regain my memory, my past has that many good people in it."

"I do too."

The heater was pumping out hot air full-blast, but she was shivering. I didn't think it was because she was cold since she'd removed the coat.

I said, "Want some coffee?"

She smiled. "That sounds good."

I pulled in a parallel parking space at the side of Bert's Market and asked if she wanted to go in with me. She said sure, grabbed the coat from the back seat, and followed me to the coffee urn. Two men were putting sugar in cups. I didn't recognize them at first, and then it hit me. They were Barb's temporary neighbors. One of them noticed me standing behind them and said, "Oh, sorry. Let us get out of your way."

He stepped aside and pulled the other man with him.

"Hi," I said, "I'm Chris, and this is my friend, Joy. Aren't you Barb Deanelli's new neighbors?"

"Yes," the taller of the two said. "How'd you know?"

I explained that I'd seen them coming out of Barb's Books and she told me who they were.

"Oh. I'm Troy and this is Nate."

Troy shook my hand and nodded to Joy. Nate stood back and didn't seem interested in talking to us.

"You're from Canada," I said, to end the awkward silence.

"Yes," Troy said.

"Troy, we'd better get going," Nate said and took a step toward the door.

Troy shook his head. "Nate's always in a hurry. Nice meeting you Chris. You too, Joy. Pretty name."

She mumbled, "Thank you."

Barb's neighbors were gone, we got our coffee, and I asked Joy if she wanted anything to eat. She said no, and we continued our search. Over the next hour we saw dogs of assorted sizes, breeds, and colors. Not one was named Pluto.

"Joy, Sunday when we were eating at Loggerhead's, you said the bar looked familiar. Did anything else about it come back to you?"

"I thought about it all night. Nothing. You asked if I'd been there before. I still don't know. Sorry."

"That's okay."

I drove out East Ashley Avenue to Thirteenth Street. I didn't think Pluto would have wandered that far but had an idea. I turned on Tabby Drive and past the house with *Caulder* painted in script on a piece of driftwood on the wall beside the front door. The driveway was empty, so I figured no one was home. I asked Joy to follow me to the back yard. She gave me a strange look but followed me to the walking pier that led to the eighteen-foot-long runabout that had been returned to its owners.

"Chris, did you see Pluto?"

I walked to the end of the pier and put my hand on the Tahoe's stern. "No. I was wondering if this boat means anything to you?"

She looked at it and at me. "No, why should ... oh, is this the one that was stolen, the one you think I was on?"

I nodded.

She pulled her coat tighter and returned her gaze to the watercraft. She leaned over and looked in the boat and stepped back and looked at its side.

"I know it would be good if I recognized it, but I don't."

It was worth a try. "Ready to get back on Pluto patrol?"

She nodded, and we headed to the car. Before she stepped off the pier, she looked back at the boat, stopped, slowly shook her head, and whispered, "Sorry."

Forty-five minutes later, we'd covered most every street on the island, some more than once, and decided that if Pluto was wandering around, one of the many searchers would have found him. I was beginning to think that the poor dog had suffered a fate that none of us had imagined, a fate that would devastate Dude. I didn't share that thought with Joy or Burl who was waiting for us. Bernard had already returned and was in the living room sipping on a mug of coffee. Burl offered cups to Joy and me which we quickly accepted. He said that Rebekah was in her room resting after working all morning at Black Magic and traipsing around looking for Pluto. Dude had phoned Burl and said he wasn't stopping until sunset and thanked us for our efforts. Burl went to the kitchen to get more coffee.

"Chris," Joy said during a break in the conversation about Pluto, "who again were those men you talked to in Bart's?"

"Bert's," I corrected, sounding like Charles. "They're Barb's neighbors. She told us about them when we were in the bookstore the other day?"

"I remember. It's just, I wondered if you knew anything else about them."

"No, why?"

"Nothing specific. It's like how the bar in Loggerhead's looking familiar. They're vaguely familiar. I've probably seen them around town, that's all."

Burl returned to the living room and said, "Chris, will you be joining us for our Christmas Eve service?"

"I plan to, why?"

"Curious. What about Christmas Day?"

"Of course."

"Good."

Then I remembered what Cal had said about Joy coming to his

party. "Preacher, will you be at Cal's Christmas party? I remember you had an enjoyable time there last year."

Burl smiled, "Brother Chris, I had a wonderful time until Brother Cal dragged me on stage and made me sing a duet with him. I could've crawled under a table."

"Preacher, you were good. Joy, our friend Cal has a big party each Christmas. I know he'd love for you to come."

"I don't know. Everyone will be a stranger, and——"

Bernard interrupted, "Bologna, Joy. You'll be among friends, lots of them. You'll see. Last year was the first time I went. That's when I talked to Preacher Burl and he helped me, helped me a bunch."

She smiled. "Maybe I'll give it a try."

That would do for now.

Chapter Fourteen

T he weather gurus predicted Tuesday would be the best day of
the week, so I took advantage of the warm, dry morning and
walked two blocks to Rita's Seaside Grille at the corner of
Center Street and East Arctic Avenue. The restaurant was on its third
name since I'd moved to Folly and was conveniently located across the
street from the Folly Pier, catty-corner from the nine-story, oceanfront
Tides Hotel, and across Center Street from the iconic Sand Dollar
Social Club. The lunch-hour was a few minutes away, and I had the
choice of a table or a booth. My preference would have been a table on
the patio, but even though today was to be the pick of the week, it was
too cool to sit outside. I chose a booth along the sidewalk side of the
colorful restaurant and quickly drew the attention of Samantha, a
server who'd waited on me several times over the years. She asked if I
wanted a menu and I told her I knew what I wanted.

She grinned and said, "Cheeseburger, medium rare?"

I smiled and nodded.

"One of these days you're going to order something different and
I'll have to call the *Folly Current*, so they can do a story on the alien who
invaded Chris Landrum's body." She turned and headed toward the
kitchen.

While I waited for my predictable cheeseburger to arrive, I
wondered if Dude had found Pluto. I started to dial his number when
Charles bounded through the entry and headed my way.

"Thought that was your bald head shining in the window." He slid into the seat opposite me. "You already ordered your cheeseburger?"

"Good morning, Charles."

"There you go. Trying to introduce civility. When are you going to give up and start talking like your friends?"

I was beginning to wonder that myself when Samantha reappeared with my lunch and asked Charles if he wanted anything.

"Sam, I'm glad you asked. All morning I've had a hankering for world peace, a cure for the common cold, and a grouper sandwich."

"We can't fry up the first two, Charles, but the grouper sandwich is a no-brainer for the chef."

"I'll settle for that."

"So," Charles said as Samantha went in search of a grouper sandwich, "what's the latest on Pluto?"

"I was going to call Dude when you invited yourself to lunch."

Charles nodded toward my phone on the corner of the table. "What's stopping you?"

You, I wanted to say. Instead, I tapped the speaker icon, so Charles could listen, and then tapped on Dude's number and waited through six rings before his voicemail message said. "Be lookin' for pup Pluto. Unless you know where he be, don't waste time leavin' words."

I didn't know where Pluto was, so I didn't leave a message.

Charles stared at the phone. "Dude says more words on his voice-mail message than he uses in person."

I shared how I, and several others, had spent hours yesterday looking for the lost canine. Charles said he knew because he ran into Dude snooping around Charles's apartment building looking for you know what. Charles then spent an hour walking the streets in his part of the island, to no avail.

Samantha told Charles his food would be out shortly, before she leaned over the table and said, "Any word on Dude's dog?"

"No," Charles said. "How did you hear about Pluto?"

She shook her head. "Do I look deaf and blind?"

"No," Charles said, in an astute observation.

"Everybody knows about Pluto. Dude was in here twice last night asking if anyone had seen an Australian Terrier hanging around. Those weren't his exact words. A couple from New Jersey looked at him funny, but most of us knew what he was talking about and said we hadn't seen the poor creature." She then said she'd better get Charles's lunch and headed to the kitchen.

Charles shared a couple of stories he'd heard about a restaurant closing on Folly Road and about a book he'd been reading about Herbert Hoover. I covered my mouth, so he wouldn't see my yawn of boredom. I said, "Interesting."

He detected my level of disinterest in his choice of books, and said, "Chris, I'm beginning to think something bad happened to Pluto. If he'd hopped, skipped, and jumped away on his own, don't you think he would've found his way home or some of us would have seen him?"

I nodded, and Samantha set Charles's lunch in front of him and moved to the next booth to see if a father and his two young kids were ready to order.

Charles took a bite and mumbled, "Think he's dead?"

"I'm not ready to go there. Someone could've taken him in and planned to keep him. He's cute and friendly."

"Yes, but he's Dude's."

"We know that. He didn't have a collar, so he could've been mistaken for a stray."

Charles took another bite, nodded left and then right, and said, "Think we should start knocking on doors and asking if anyone has a new pet?"

"I don't know."

"We need to do something, if we—"

I interrupted Charles and stood to greet Joy who was headed our way.

"I thought it was you, Chris," she said and smiled.

"You saw his bald head in the window, didn't you?" Charles said and scooted over and offered her a seat.

"No, I recognized him." She looked at the spot Charles had vacated for her, hesitated, and said, "Do you mind if I join you?"

I was pleased that she asked even after Charles moved over. I said, "We'd be honored."

Samantha returned and asking the newcomer if she wanted something to eat or drink.

Joy looked at Charles's plate, then at mine, and said, "I don't have any... I don't think—"

Charles interrupted and said, "Go ahead and get something. It's on Chris."

Thanks, Charles.

She looked at me and I smiled. "Maybe I'll have what Chris has."

Samantha said it was an excellent choice and once again headed to the kitchen.

Charles said, "Out for a walk?"

"Sort of. Still looking for Pluto. Dude came by early this morning and asked if we could help him look. The poor man was near tears. That dog means a lot to him."

"It's his family," Charles said.

I chose not to mention that Pluto wasn't Dude's entire family since Barb was his half sister.

Joy looked out the window and at the bartender pulling a beer out of the cooler behind the bar along the other side of the room. "Wonder if I have pets."

I said, "Do pets sound familiar? Is anything coming back?"

She continued to look at the bar and instead of answering my question, said, "Pets, no." She rubbed her eyes and continued to look at the bar. "Chris, why does that look familiar?"

I looked at the bar. "The bar, the bartender, or what?"

"The bar."

This was the second bar that she'd said looked familiar. "Does it look more familiar than the one in Loggerhead's?"

"I don't know." She shook her head "There's something about it." She exhaled and said. "Don't you think I want to know what it is?"

Charles patted her arm. "It's okay, Joy. We'll figure it out. Won't we, Chris?"

Thanks again, Charles. "We'll do what we can."

She attempted a smile and failed.

Samantha returned with a real smile and Joy's cheeseburger. She asked if we needed anything else. I was tempted to say a memory for Joy. I resisted and thanked her.

Joy took a large bite, and I wondered if it was the first thing she'd had to eat today. Charles asked how she liked staying at Hope House.

"It's okay. Everyone is nice."

"How's your room?" Charles asked, mainly to get her mind off worrying about the past.

"Great. Preacher Burl says I have the best room in the house."

"That's great," Charles said. "The preacher is a great person."

Joy started to put a fry in her mouth, hesitated, and returned it to the plate. "Chris, I don't have a right to, but could I ask a big favor?"

"Sure."

"Would you to take me back to that boat you said I was on?"

"Of course, we will," Charles answered for me.

We, I thought. "Joy, do you remember something about the boat?"

"I might. I woke up in the middle of the night thinking about it. I was half dreaming, half awake, so I'm not sure what was what. If I see it when I'm awake, something might click."

"If you want, we can go after we finish here."

"Good idea," Charles said, answering for Joy.

It could have been my imagination, but Joy finished lunch quicker than she'd started. Charles was waving for Samantha to bring me the check before any of us had finished our sandwiches.

Chapter Fifteen

W e walked to my house with Charles stopping every few steps to holler Pluto and look for the elusive canine behind every structure. It took nearly as long to walk the short distance as it did to eat lunch.

"I like where you live," Joy said, as we approached my car in the drive. "It's cute. Lived here long?"

"Almost as long as I've been on Folly."

"Could use more Christmas decorations," Charles said as he pointed to the lonely wreath on the door.

We piled in the car before Charles, the man who had no Christmas decorations on his apartment, could tell me how to exterior decorate my cottage. The two-mile ride out East Ashley Avenue took longer than man's first flight to the moon. Charles had me pull over at each beach access walkway, so he could get out and yell for Pluto. We also had to stop at each house that had more Christmas decorations than my wreath, so Charles could show me how I could decorate my humble abode. I could tell that Joy was getting inpatient, but since we were doing her a favor, she held her annoyance I wasn't as accommodating and ignored Charles last five requests to stop. Our next stop was in front of the Caulder residence.

Fortunately, the house didn't have as much Christmas decorations as did mine, nor were there any vehicles in the drive. Charles was quick to exit and was nearly to the boat before Joy and I got out. The only witnesses to our trespassing were a dozen pelicans perched on a pier two houses away. Joy was staring at the boat through the window and didn't appear like she wanted to get closer.

"Are you okay, Joy?"

She jerked back from the window.

"Sorry to startle you, you okay?"

She whispered, "I don't know."

"Want to go home?"

She said something I couldn't understand. I leaned closer and asked her to repeat it.

"I think so."

"I'll get Charles."

I walked halfway to the pier and called for Charles who was leaning over the boat looking like he was about to climb aboard. I waved for him to return to the car until I noticed Joy opening the door and walking my way.

She was tiptoeing like she was on broken glass, and said, "You brought me out here and I need to look in the boat. Honest, I do."

Charles shrugged, pointed to the boat, and then at the car.

I put my arm around Joy and led her toward Charles. The temperature was mild, the sun was out in all its glory, and she had on her oversized coat, yet was shivering.

Charles moved away from the craft and let Joy look over the gunwale. She continued to shiver, and I kept my arm around her waist. She stared for just shy of an eternity, before saying, "I was back there."

Charles moved up beside us and looked in the back of the boat. "In the back seat?"

Joy nodded.

I tightened my grip on her, and said, "What do you remember?"

She closed her eyes, and said, "The boat moving fast. Bouncing in the waves. I'm on my stomach on that seat. My head hit the seat every wave. It hurt." She opened her eyes and pointed at the white with blue trim, fold-down back seat. She looked at her left wrist and massaged it with her right hand. "Tied with a rope. Got it loose. Untied my feet. He didn't look back." She continued to look at her wrist.

I waited for her to continue. Charles, who hadn't perfected the art of patience, said, "You were tied up and on the back seat. Then what?"

She looked at him like it was the first time she noticed him standing beside us. "Then nothing." She shook her head. "Nothing."

Charles said, "Are you sure that—"

Joy interrupted, "Can we leave?"

I said yes and moved beside her as she walked off the pier. We got in the car and slowly turned around at the end of the dead-end street and headed to town. Joy remained silent until we were in front of Hope House.

"Thank you for taking me. Sorry I couldn't remember more."

"That's okay. It's coming back."

"Joy," Charles said, "when you were talking about being on the boat, you said, 'He didn't look back.' Do you remember anything about him?"

"No."

I said, "Was there only one person?"

"There could've been more. I only remember the one sitting behind the wheel in front of me."

"And you can't remember anything about him?" Charles said. "What he was wearing. If he had a hat on, or if you could you see the color of his hair. Did he say anything?"

"I don't remember."

"You're doing fine, Joy," I said. "Tell you what, if you remember more about being on the boat or the man, or if there was someone with him, would you give me a call? I can let the police know so they can follow up."

"Okay," she said, and thanked us again for lunch and for taking her to see the boat.

I pulled in Charles's gravel parking lot and waited for him to say something about Joy. He'd been unusually silent since we'd left her.

"Chris," he finally spoke, "I don't know what to make of it. I don't understand amnesia. How could she have been in that boat and then get off the boat and float to shore on a surfboard without remembering anything about it?"

I was no expert on retrograde amnesia but knew it was real. Joy had no reason to fake it. Slices of her memory are coming back, and if Barb was correct, most, if not all, will eventually return.

I shared my limited knowledge with Charles, and added, "I'm more worried about her safety. Whether it be one, two, or more people who took her out on the boat, it was against her will and I can only imagine what he, or they, had intended."

Charles added, "Dump her in the ocean, never to be seen again, alive, that is."

I nodded.

"You're afraid whoever it was will try again?"

"Yes. Despite the best efforts to keep her whereabouts secret, too many people know where she's living."

"That's why we have to figure out who and stop them from causing more harm."

I rolled my eyes. "That's why the *police* need to solve it—emphasis on police."

"Whatever. That's why you're going to pick up your phone and call Chief LaMond and tell her what we heard about Joy and the boat."

I thought about waiting until I got in the comfort of my home before calling and being the recipient of her wrath about me nosing in police business. Why not let Charles suffer with me? I called the Chief's cell phone and hit the speaker icon.

Cindy answered with, "Happy almost Christmas, Mr. Landrum."

Her pleasant comment threw me, and Charles stared at the phone like it was a scorpion.

"You're in a good mood," I said.

"Aren't I always?"

"No."

"Well, aren't you a damn Debbie downer? Get in the Christmas spirit. Take me, for example. I'm standing in this hoity-toity jewelry store in downtown Charleston with my lovey-dovey hubby and trying on an antique gold ring with a beryl stone and a cute little diamond on each side of it."

"Beryl?" I said.

"Light-blue gemstone, my jewelry-challenged friend. Enough about the exquisite ring lovey-dovey is getting me for Christmas. Why have you called to ruin my perfectly wonderful, and I might add, historic, day when hubby takes me jewelry shopping?"

"Charles and I were having lunch with Joy and she asked us to take her to the boat on Tabby Drive."

"Why?" she interrupted.

Charles leaned close to the phone and said, "Because we were hungry."

"Why'd she ask you to take her to the boat, Chris, who now sounds a lot like Charles, that moronic friend of yours?"

Enough foolishness, I thought. "She hoped it would bring back memories."

Cindy sighed. "Did it?"

I shared what Joy had remembered. Cindy asked twice if she said anything about the man in the boat other than he was sitting behind the wheel. Twice, I answered she hadn't.

"What am I supposed to do with that modicum of near-worthless information?"

"Modicum?" Charles said.

"Itsy, teeny-weeny bit," she said.

I was ready to hang up on the chief and throw Charles out of the car, when Cindy added, "Thanks, Chris. It's not much but it confirms that Joy was on the boat, and most likely, in the ocean. The who, what, and why are yet to be determined. Any word on Pluto?"

That kind of abrupt transition was a hallmark of Charles, but not foreign to several of my friends.

"Not that I've heard."

"Me either," Charles added to not be left out.

"Larry has another gem for me to try on. Better go. He only gets in this generous mood every... umm, never."

She ended the call after agreeing to let me know if she learned anything or if Pluto was found. And, at her urging, I agreed to let her know before I got killed playing cop.

Chapter Sixteen

I walked to Bert's to get prepackaged doughnuts for breakfast. It was four days until Christmas and Bert's employees' shirts reflected the holiday. Two guys hard at work behind the deli counter wore red T-shirts, one with a picture of Santa on the front and the other with the head of a smiling reindeer. Mary Ewing was stocking a shelf near the back of the store and smiled when she saw me. She had on a red and white Santa's hat and a green sweatshirt with *Merry Christmas* on the front. When I met Mary a year ago, she was anorexic thin with dirty blond hair. Since then, she'd added twenty pounds to her five-foot-five frame and her hair was clean and pulled in a ponytail. She looked fresh and younger than her mid-twenties.

Her smile lit up the room. "Good morning, Mr. Landrum."

"Mary, you know to call me Chris. Ready for the big day?"

She gave me a hug, stepped back, and continued to smile. "I'd better be. Jewel and Joanie are counting the hours until Santa arrives."

The single mother and high-school dropout was struggling last Christmas to find somewhere warm to spend the nights with her girls. Preacher Burl heard of their situation, found them a place to live, got Mary the job at Bert's, and gave them hope. He also got her enrolled in a GED program where she could work toward her high-school equivalency diploma.

I remembered how excited Joanie and Jewel were last Christmas to get something as simple as new clothes for the holiday. "I bet they're excited."

A customer interrupted our conversation to ask Mary where to find ketchup. Mary smiled and walked the woman to the condiments and returned to where I was looking at the packaged sweets, a.k.a. breakfast.

"They're super excited. This'll be the first Christmas for Jewel in a house where we're actually living."

"That's wonderful."

"I almost forgot," Mary said and tapped the side of her head. "I met someone you know."

"Who?"

"Joy. She said you and your lady friend saved her life."

"Barb and I were in the right place at the right time. Where did you meet her?"

"Yesterday, after work, Joanie, Jewel, and I were walking along the beach. It was windy and cold, but when my gals want to walk on the beach, nothing can stop them. We were bundled up and saw Joy walking toward us. She was wrapped-up in a big coat and looking at the pier. You know Joanie's never met a stranger, so she went over to Joy." Mary laughed and shook her head. "Joanie said, 'I'm excited about Christmas. How about you?'"

That sounded like Joanie. I smiled, and said, "What did Joy say?"

"She knelt and smiled at Joanie. I didn't think there was much happiness behind her smile, anyway, she said she was excited and asked Joanie her name. You know, that's all it took. Joanie not only told the stranger her name but pointed to Jewel and me and shared our names, where we lived, and how much we were looking forward to Christmas. She finally got around to asking the lady who she was. She told us she was Joy." Mary chuckled. "Joanie is obsessed with words, something she's getting from school, I suppose. She pointed to her sister, at Joy, and then at herself, and said, 'That's funny. All our names start with *J*.' That got an honest smile from Joy."

"How'd you learn that Joy knew me?"

"My busybody seven-year-old. After she figured out the *J* names, she asked Joy if she lived on Folly. Joy said she guessed she did. That did it. Joanie asked what Joy meant by guessed she lived here. Joanie said something like, 'Don't you know where you live?' Joy told her it was hard to understand, but that you and Barbara found her, and she was now staying at Hope House. Joanie knows about the house and that it was started by that wonderful man, Preacher Burl. I interrupted Joanie's interrogation of the poor lady who'd been minding her business and walking on the beach. I told Joanie we needed to get going and to let the lady continue her walk."

"That was nice of Joanie to talk to Joy."

"Yes. Joy said it was nice meeting us and that she looked forward to seeing us again. I told her that you and I were friends. I hope that was okay."

I told her it was. Mary said she didn't know anything about Joy but that she was going to stop by to visit her. I said it was a good idea. Another customer asked Mary a question, and I told her that I didn't want to keep her from work.

I grabbed some coffee, paid for breakfast, headed home, and thought how it would be good for both Mary and Joy to get better acquainted, or, knowing as little as I did about Joy, thought it would be good.

I tore open the package of doughnuts and started breakfast when the phone rang.

"I was thinking," Charles said to open the conversation.

"Might I ask what?" I said before stuffing one of the treats in my mouth.

"You might," Charles said, and smiled.

I waited for him to tell me instead of asking again.

"You're no fun. Why don't you come pick me up and I'll not only tell you, I'd do a show-and-tell, and we can see if I'm right."

The logical thing to do would be to ask what he might be right about, or moving past that, suggest that he pick me up. He had a car, and it was his idea. Logical and Charles seldom coexisted. I told him I'd be at his place in fifteen minutes.

"Where are we going?" I asked as he got in the car. I thought it was an appropriate question since all Charles had said was for me to pick him up.

"East Arctic, three-hundred block."

"Why?"

"To visit Martha."

"Martha?"

"Martha Wright. Remember, you asked about her after church?"

"One of the older ladies you were talking to?"

"Ah, ye of declining brain cells, you remember."

I'd turned left on East Arctic Avenue in front of the Tides Hotel.

"Now that we've determined the who, how about why?"

"Martha loves animals. I've never been there but have heard she has bunch of pets. She puts food out every night for hungry, homeless critters. I was told that if you walked by her house around sunset, you could see animals of all sizes, shapes, and kinds. The Ark would've been too small to hold them all."

The purpose of our trip finally dawned on me. "You think Martha has Pluto?"

"It's possible. Martha's house is close to Dude's if you go as the crow flies, or as the Pluto trots. He didn't have a collar and he's adorable. He could've been tempted by the food and as friendly as he is, I can see Martha taking him in. I don't know why I didn't think of it before." He pointed to a large, two-story, new, sky-blue house on our right that backed up to the beach.

I said, "Looks like Martha can afford plenty of pet food."

"I hear she's worth millions. She plops a couple of C-notes in the collection basket each week. Her husband died a few years ago, and she moved here from Atlanta. Rumor is hubby hated the beach and wouldn't leave the Peachtree State. He didn't have to. Now he's planted there, and Martha has her beach. A best-of-both-worlds' marriage."

"What's your plan? Knock on the door and ask if she's stolen any dogs?"

"Doubt that'll work. I'll start with my charming smile, then step aside, and you can ask if she heisted the little fellow."

We climbed what seemed like a hundred steps to the front door, and Charles, good to his word, rang the bell, and moved back. It must've sounded like the dinner bell. There were barks ranging from high-pitched yelps that sounded more like squeaks, to Barry White rumbles. None of the noises sounded like someone answering the door. Charles rang again, again receiving a cacophony of animal utterances.

Charles leaned closer to the door and said, "Hear Pluto in there?"

I looked at him and shook my head.

"I don't either," he said. "Pluto's not a big talker, takes after Dude."

Still no answer.

The garage door was closed so we couldn't tell if a vehicle was inside. Charles suggested we walk around back and see if Martha was in the yard. The back yard consisted of a thirty-foot deep patch of perfectly mani-cured grass, before steps that led to the beach. There must have been two dozen stainless-steel bowls along the rear of the house, with half of them overflowing with dog food. It was no wonder that canines, and I suspected a few cats, racoons, and an occasional opossum chose this restaurant for their evening meal. What wasn't in back was Martha Wright.

"Now what?" I said.

"Other than breaking in?"

"That's not an option."

"You're right," Charles said and looked at the back door. "Some of those dogs sound like they could have us for dessert."

That wasn't my reason for not committing a crime, but if it stopped Charles, I'd agree with him.

"Let's see if the neighbors know anything," he said, and looked to either side of Martha's house.

No one was in the yard, and for as far as we could see, the beach was deserted. We returned to the car and Charles looked across the street.

"Wonder if Dixie's home?" Charles said and started across the street.

Charles had already started up the steps of the house directly across from Martha's, so I assumed it was Dixie's. All I knew about her was that she attended First Light Church, and according to Charles was an uber-gardener and Martha's close friend.

We had better luck at Dixie's door. I recognized the woman who answered from church. She was in her late seventies, tall, at roughly five-foot-nine, thin, with hair so white that I suspected it might glow in the dark. Her face was tanned and leathery. She smiled at Charles and her teeth matched the color of her hair. She had on a white, long-sleeve men's dress shirts and jeans with mud caked on each knee.

"Charles, my oh my, what a pleasant surprise. Who's your friend?"

Charles nodded in my direction. "Dixie, this is my best friend, Chris Landrum. Chris, meet Dixie Thompson."

We exchanged pleasantries and Dixie invited us in, something I'm not sure I'd do if I found two guys who looked like us at the door.

"I wasn't expecting company, so things are a mess. I just came from the garden. Would either of you like a drink?"

"Water would be nice," Charles said.

She winked at me and said, "I've got bourbon."

"Water's fine," I said.

Charles and I sat on a burgundy sofa. Dixie was gone several minutes before returning with water in plastic glasses for Charles and me. She went back to the kitchen and returned carrying what I'd always heard referred to as a rocks glass filled with ice cubes and an amber-colored liquid. The odds on it being tea were slim. Her house wasn't nearly as new as Martha's and the living room furniture had been new in the 1950s. Dixie sat across from us in a white-on-khaki medallion patterned chair. She didn't seem worried that her muddy jeans would hurt it.

"Don't get me wrong, I love company, but what brings you gentlemen out today? Surely it's not to visit an old lady."

"Now Dixie," Charles said, "you're not old."

"Charles, you're a dear. You may not know this, but I pride myself in being able to spot bull dung a block away." She gave Charles a smile incongruous with her words.

Charles smiled. "You caught us, Dixie. We were at Martha's and it doesn't appear she's home. You know everything that goes on around here, so I figured you'd know where she is."

Martha smiled and wiggled her forefinger at Charles. "Did you forget what I said about my bull dung meter. I don't know everything, but I know Martha's whereabouts."

Charles smiled and said, "Where?"

"Dayton, Ohio. She's visiting a cousin who had a stroke."

I asked, "When's she coming back?"

"Christmas Eve, if the danged airlines don't mess up her flights. They're getting worse every day. You wouldn't catch me dead flying anywhere." She hesitated and bit her lower lip. "I do worry about Martha."

Charles asked, "Why?"

She frowned and shook her head. "The dear lady would slap me senseless if she knew I was telling you this. Her memory's slipping. She says she's fine, but she's fibbin'. If you ask me, she's on the road to Alzheimer's."

I said, "I'm sorry to hear it."

Charles jumped in with, "Who's taking care of her pets?"

"I offered to. She said don't be silly that it wasn't safe for me to be crossing the street to her house." She shook her head. "Charles, I've crossed that street for thirty-five years. Haven't been flattened yet. She hired a pet sitter; can you believe that? I'd never heard of such until Martha told me about it. The sitter, a sweet little thing, can't be over twenty, comes twice a day to feed and walk Martha's dogs. Didn't have jobs like that when I was a youngster. They sure didn't."

Charles said, "What time does the pet sitter come?"

"Lordy, young man. Do you think I sit here and keep tabs on what happens across the street? I have no idea when the sweet little thing shows up."

"Dixie," Charles said, "do you know if Martha took in any new pets in the last few days? Maybe an Australian Terrier?"

"Now that's one strange question, Charles. I don't have the vaguest idea." She took a sip, set her glass on the table beside her chair, and said, "You missing one?"

Charles told her about Dude and Pluto

"Oh, dear. I can't imagine Martha stealing someone's pet. No, I can't. Don't get me wrong, my good friend loves, really loves, dogs and cats. I don't understand why she takes so fondly to them, but she does."

Charles leaned forward on the sofa. "Harry Truman once said, 'If you want a friend in Washington, get a dog.'"

Dixie looked at him like he sprouted a second head. "What's that have to do with Martha?"

Excellent question, I thought. "Charles likes to quote US presidents."

Charles glanced at me and back to Dixie. "It means that I understand how your friend can love dogs. Where did she get the ones she has over there?"

"Don't know about all of them. I know she's taken in strays over the years. One look at them and you can tell they were strays. Your friend's dog didn't look like a stray, did it?"

Dude looks like a stray and Pluto takes after his owner, so I wasn't ready to say no.

Charles didn't have my reservation and said, "Absolutely not."

"There you go," Dixie said.

"You're sure you don't know when the pet sitter will be back?" Charles said.

Her hand balled into a fist and she glared at Charles. "I told you I don't know."

She was getting annoyed, and I didn't blame her.

"Dixie, I hear you have one of the nicest gardens on Folly," I said to lower her level if irritation, or so I hoped.

A smile returned to her face. "I like to think so. Would you like to see it?"

Not really, I thought. "I'd love to."

She finished her liquid relaxer and led us through the kitchen to a deck, and down the steps. I knew as much about gardens as I did about the flora and fauna on Iceland but could tell that Dixie's was special. There were fifteen, four-foot-by-six-foot raised cedar rectangular boxes, each a foot high. Three rows of low shrubs and a row of ornamental grasses were behind the beds.

Dixie started telling us what each thing was and pointing out the name holders beside each item. Most of the flowers weren't in bloom, but it didn't stop her from telling us about them. It wasn't long before I zoned out when she was giving us the Latin name of the flowers and described the lasagna method of layering the mulch that works best for each variety of whatever those things were that were planted in each box. Charles, being Charles, was taking in everything the tour guide said. I started paying more attention, particularly where I was walking, when she mentioned having to occasionally "scat" a snake out of the garden. Dixie was in her element and her mood improved with each description, or it could have been heightened by the drink she had before giving us the tour. Charles wisely didn't ask her anything else about Martha or the pet sitter, and I fended interest until I'd reached my limit and said that we needed to be going.

"You can have another drink before you leave."

I said we'd love to, but I had somewhere I had to be. Charles continued to be wise by not asking me where. He wrote his phone number on a piece of paper he found in his back pocket and gave to Dixie and asked her to call if she learned anything about Pluto.

Chapter Seventeen

Confucius said, "A ringing phone after midnight seldom brings glee." Okay, he didn't say it, but should have.

"Brother Chris, this is Preacher Burl. I apologize for waking you."

He knew me enough to know that if I wasn't asleep by ten o'clock, it was a bad night.

"That's okay," I lied. "What is it?"

"Something happened, and I wonder if I could inconvenience you to delay sleep and come over."

The clock read 12:15.

"Now?"

"The police just left and—"

That was all it took. I interrupted and told him I'd be there as soon as I got dressed.

Every light in Hope House was on as I pulled in the parking area. Shadows from the live oak beside the house snaked across the side of the parking lot, giving the house an ominous feel.

Burl was standing at the open front door waiting for me. His eyes were bloodshot and his shirttail untucked. "Please come in."

I followed him to the living room to find Bernard, Adrienne, Rebekah, and Joy seated on the sofa and two of the chairs. The Christmas lights were off and the presents under the tree looked forlorn.

Joy jumped up when she saw me and gave me a hug. She had on a heavy, brown bathrobe and was barefoot. "Thank you for coming. I asked Preacher Burl to call you. I was scared and feel close to you since you saved me."

"I'm glad he called. Is everyone okay? What happened?"

"Brother Chris, would you like something to drink? I have coffee brewing."

"I'm fine, Preacher."

Burl nodded and turned to Joy who'd returned to the sofa. "Sister Joy, would you like to start?"

"I don't know much," she said and pulled her knees up and wrapped her arms around them. "I was falling asleep, maybe already asleep. I heard a noise at my door like someone fiddling with the knob."

Burl added, "The knobs are old and make a lot of noise when they're turning. Sorry, Sister Joy, go on."

"Everyone here respects each other's privacy, so I was surprised that someone was trying to get in without knocking. I sat up and said, 'Who is it?' The noise stopped, and I heard what sounded like someone walking away."

"The old floors squeak a lot," Burl interrupted.

Joy continued, "I rushed to the door to see who was there." She turned to Bernard who was in the chair beside her. "I must've been loud when I asked who it was."

Bernard said, "You weren't that loud, Sister Joy. I was awake."

Burl said, "Bernard's room is beside Joy's."

"Preacher Burl," Bernard interrupted, "may I continue?"

"Of course."

"I heard Sister Joy and opened my door to see what was going on. The hall was dark, but I saw the outline of a guy rushing toward the steps. I started after him, and—"

Adrienne said, "Bernard nearly knocked me down. I stepped out of my room on the other side of Joy's to see what the commotion was about, and Bernard tried to run over me."

"Adrienne, I apologized. You came out so fast I didn't see you."

Adrienne pulled her robe tight and smiled. "Apology accepted."

I said, "Then what happened?"

Bernard looked at his fellow housemates to see who was going to interrupt him next. Everyone remained silent, so he continued, "After Adrienne tried to tackle me, I yelled for the intruder to stop. He didn't. I followed him down the stairs and out the back door. I was barefoot and not quite as fleet as I was in my younger days when I was traipsing around Afghanistan. The troublemaker was out of the yard in a flash. Gone, poof." He held out his hands, palms up. "That's about it."

"Brother Chris," Burl said, "I heard Brother Bernard yell and came out of my room to see what was going on. He told me about the outsider, so I called the police and asked the residents to join me in here."

Rebekah yawned and spoke for the first time. "I slept through the whole thing. Preacher Burl woke me up and asked that I go to the living room. I have to be at work at six and was asleep before everyone else."

"Sister Rebekah, I'm sorry to have disturbed you."

"That's okay, Preacher. I was sharing so Chris would know where I was during it all."

"Did anyone get a clear look at the man?" I asked, again, to get the conversation back on track.

Burl said, "Brother Chris, I don't believe so."

"No, sir," Bernard added.

Joy and Adrienne shook their head.

"I was asleep and didn't see anything," Rebekah said.

"Preacher," I said, "you once mentioned that you lock the exterior doors after everyone is in for the night. How'd he get in?"

"Brother Chris, the doors were locked, but as you can imagine, the locks are old and Officer Spencer, who responded to my call, said the back door looks like it was jimmied allowing access."

I remembered the first time I visited, a broken lock on the front door was being repaired. Burl tried to keep the house as secure as possible, but I could see how someone could get in without much trouble.

"Preacher, why would someone would want to break in?"

"I can only speculate. It should be obvious to everyone that there are no great riches here, no valuable jewelry, little cash. If a burglar sought to steal something of value, he would've been better off breaking in any other house on the island."

Bernard raised his hand.

Burl said, "Yes, Brother Bernard?"

"From my way of thinking, he was after Joy. He was trying to get in her room. Someone took her before. Tied her up, put her on a boat, took her out in the ocean, and probably planned to throw her overboard. Yes sir, he was after her."

Burl said, "Now, Bernard, we don't know that."

"Preacher," Rebekah said, "can I go? I've got to get some sleep before my shift."

"Of course, Rebekah. Bernard, Adrienne, why don't you head upstairs and get some sleep."

The three of them slowly walked upstairs. Joy and Burl remained seated and watched the others go.

"Chris," Joy said, "I'm scared. I don't remember everything, but bits and pieces are coming back. That man was after me."

Burl moved beside Joy on the sofa and put his hand over her hand. "Sister Joy, go ahead and tell Brother Chris what you told me before you went to your room."

"I think I was a bartender, and that's why the bars over here looked familiar. I didn't work in those places, but watching their bartenders struck me as familiar."

"Do you know where you worked?"

"Not exactly. I remember it was smaller than the ones I've been in on Folly. Darker, too. I remember overhearing two guys talking. I wouldn't swear to it, but it seems like they were talking about a robbery."

"Like they were planning one or talking about one that'd already happened?" I asked.

"I'm not certain, I'm really not."

"Sister Joy, you told me that they didn't know you overheard what they were saying."

"Yes, Preacher, that's what I said." She looked at the floor and then at me. "What if I'm wrong?"

I nodded. "And they saw you and figured you were a threat."

"Then caught me, took me out to sea, and wanted to drown me."

I nodded. "Joy, can you remember anything else about where you worked, or about the two men?"

"The bar was dark, really dark. It's small. Most of its customers were dressed like they did physical labor. Muddy boots, yes, I remember several of them wearing muddy boots."

"Anything else?" I said.

"No, sorry. Chris, if that guy who broke in here was one of the men who took me, they know where I live. I'm scared."

"Sister Joy," Burl said, "I'm going to call Larry at Pewter Hardware as soon as it opens and have him install better locks on our doors. I should've done it long ago."

I hoped that would be enough.

Chapter Eighteen

I t was two in the morning before I got home, and another hour before I fell asleep. I don't normally watch the morning news, but it took all my energy to get out of bed after the early morning trip, so sitting in front of the television was all I had energy to do. I wasn't paying attention until the anchor mentioned an overnight break-in at Grogan's Fine Jewelry in Mt. Pleasant and threw the broadcast to a reporter standing in front of the store.

The reporter looked like he was ten-years-old pretending to be an adult dressed in his light-gray suit, red and green Christmas tie, and a white shirt that was loose around his neck. He was standing in front of the strip center that housed Grogan's. Yellow crime-scene tape stretched across the front of the building and provided a visual loved by television cameras. The reporter held the mic in front of an older gentleman with curly white hair, and wearing a black suit, a conservative burgundy and gray rep tie, and an expression that reminded me of an undertaker.

"Mr. Grogan," the reporter said, "how did the burglars get in? Also, can you tell us what was taken?"

"The lock on the back door was picked, and the thief somehow disarmed the alarm. Our most precious items were in the safe and undisturbed. Unfortunately, being three days before Christmas, our inventory was much larger than any other time of the year. Space was tight in the safe and we left several pieces in the display cases that weren't visible from the windows." Mr. Grogan smiled. "Many of our gentlemen customers wait until the last minute to shop for their wives or lady friends, so we're always prepared for the last-minute Christmas rush from procrastinators. As you know, we're known for our high-end jewelry and luxury watches."

"I must confess, I'm one of those procrastinators," the reporter said, and smiled. "One last question, Mr. Grogan. What would you estimate to be the worth of what was taken?"

"We've not had time to do a complete inventory, but I'd guess it was in the one-fifty to two-hundred-thousand-dollar range."

I patiently waited through three commercials to hear the weather. An un-seasonable warm front was pushing thought the area, and the temperatures were projected to soar into the lower seventies. Barb called while a sports reporter was raving about the good season the College of Charleston Cougars were having and his prediction about tonight's game again Coastal Carolina. I answered the phone and missed the prediction.

"Any news about Pluto?" she said, instead of hello. She had become acclimated to Folly phone etiquette.

"None that I've heard."

"Why not? What have you been doing all morning?"

She knew I normally would've been up for a couple of hours and I told her it was a long story and I'd tell her later. She said she was walking to the bookstore and if I wanted, she'd fix me a cup of coffee on the condition that I stop at Bert's and get her something for break-fast. I told her it was the best offer I'd had all day. She suggested that it was the only offer I'd had all day.

"Guilty as charged. I'll be there in a half hour."

Denise, one of the personable clerks, welcomed me with a smile and the question that I hear way too often. "Any word on Pluto?"

I told her no.

She said, "Poor Dude. I hope the pup comes home soon. I can't imagine how sad Christmas will be for him if Pluto's not there."

Denise went to wait on a customer, and I headed to the case where there were two cinnamon rolls begging for me to take them with me. I gave in to their wishes and headed to the cash register.

"It's about time you got here," Barb said, her smile indicating that she was kidding. "I'm starved."

We went to the office in the back of the store where she fixed two cups of coffee and I pulled two paper plates out of the drawer and adorned each with a cinnamon roll.

She looked at her watch. "I can't believe you've gone this long in the day without checking with Dude to see about Pluto. You're slipping."

I told her about my late-night call from Burl and what'd happened at Hope House.

"Do you think someone was there to harm Joy?"

"I don't know. The residents are convinced that's the case."

Barb sipped her coffee and set the mug on the glass-top table. "Speaking of Joy, let me tell you something that happened yesterday after work."

I took a bite of roll and nodded for her to continue.

"You know my vacationing neighbors."

"Troy and Nate," I said and figuratively patted myself on my back for remembering their names.

"Yes. I was in the elevator going to my condo, and before the door closed, Troy came around the corner and asked me to hold it open. He was pushing one of those big luggage carts. It was empty, and I teased him about having such a light load. He chuckled and said that they were checking out."

"Aren't they supposed to be here a couple more weeks?"

"They were. I asked if the weather was too hot for them. He laughed and said no that something came up and they had to leave early."

"That's unusual. All he said was something came up?"

Barb nodded. "I wouldn't have thought much of it until I remembered something, I believe it was Nate who said it the night before. We were in the parking lot talking about the weather, our usual conversation when we couldn't think of anything else to say. Nate asked how Joy was doing. It threw me a little until I remembered that he'd met her. I was vague and said as far as I knew, she's fine. Nate was silent for a few seconds and then asked if her memory was returning."

"Is that all he said?"

"I didn't want to answer yet didn't want to be rude. I said I didn't know. He didn't say anything else."

I watched her take a bite of roll, and said, "Are you thinking that they may be the men who took Joy?"

She swallowed and sipped her coffee before shrugging. "I have no reason to believe that they are. It simply struck me as strange that they were asking about someone they'd only met once, and that they were leaving two weeks early."

"Leaving early because Joy's memory might return, and she'd remember that they took her?"

"You said it, not me."

"You have good instincts about stuff like this. What's your gut tell you?"

Barb smiled. "Good instincts because I spent years defending white-collar crooks?"

I returned her smile. "Could be."

"Okay, here goes. My gut tells me that I don't know. Their actions struck me as strange."

"Strange enough for me to share with Chief LaMond?"

"You know her better than I do. What would she do with the information?"

"First, she'll give me a lecture about nosing in her business. Let's see, second, she'll repeat the lecture adding a few East Tennessee phrases that mean I'm a jackass." I paused and thought about previous times I'd shared none-of-my-business thoughts with Cindy.

Barb said, "Third?"

"She'll hang up on me or say something like, 'Okay, buttinsky, tell me again who these guys are, what they said about Joy, and when they checked out?'"

She took another sip of coffee, looked at my phone I'd set on her desk, and said, "What are you waiting for?"

Two rings later, Chief Cindy LaMond answered with, "This better be important. I have a meeting in five minutes with the mayor and rumor is that he's spittin' nails about how one of my brilliant officers shared his displeasure with a vacationer from Vermont about the speed in which he was traversing East Erie Avenue."

"I wouldn't want you to be late for your pleasant conversation with His Honor. Call me when you get a chance."

I told Barb that by hanging up on me, the chief meant that she'd love to call me.

Neither of us believed it.

Chapter Ninteteen

One thing I've learned over the years is if I'm walking on Center Street, there's a good chance I'll see someone I know. The appropriately named street is only five blocks long, yet most all the island's restaurants and retail establishments are either on it or within a block.

Since the weather was picture-perfect, I left Barb's books and turned right and ran into Cal, more accurately, he ran into me. He was walking with his head down and humming "White Christmas." I put my hand out to keep him from stepping on my foot.

"Oh, sorry. Guess I was daydreaming." He tipped his Stetson in my direction.

"Are you ready for your party?"

"Yes, umm, no, well maybe."

"Glad you clarified that," I said and smiled at the crooner.

"That's where my mind was wandering when I plum near ran you down. Trying to figure out what else I need to do."

"While I'm thinking of it, I talked to Joy, and she's planning on being there."

"How's her memory?"

"A few are coming back."

"She know who she is, other than Joy?"

"Not yet."

"I remember how screwed up I was after getting conked on my

noggin. It's harder for her." He shook his head. "Not even knowing any of the who, what, where, and whys of her life."

"True."

Cal said, "Heard more about Pluto?"

"I haven't talked to Dude today, so I don't know if the pup's still missing."

"That'll be a mighty big Christmas double-downer. No memory and no Pluto."

I agreed and told him that if he needed help to get ready for his party to give me a call.

"Much obliged, pard."

He tipped his Stetson again and moseyed on.

I walked two more blocks to the Folly River Park, the site of several oversized Christmas decorations and the official city Christmas tree. The lights were on, but the cloudless day made it difficult to appreciate the illuminated displays. Regardless, there were two young mothers holding toddlers and pointing to the outline of Santa's sleigh and then at the tree.

At the edge of the park a foot pier crossed a portion of marsh and jutted over the Folly River. Leaning on the wood railing at the far end of the pier was a familiar, bright red University of Arizona Wildcats sweatshirt wrapped around Charles Fowler. He appeared in deep-thought as he stared at the water and didn't notice me walking toward him until I was within a few yards.

"Hi, Chris. Nice day, isn't it?"

I said, "What's wrong?"

"Why think something's wrong?"

I shrugged. "*Hi, Chris. Nice day.* Charles, that's something a normal person would say."

He shook his head and returned to gazing at the water. "Sorry I didn't insult you."

I stood close to him and waited for him to continue.

We watched several cars cross the bridge to the island and Charles finally said, "It seems that this year's been mired in deep manure. Poor Heather was thrown in jail and accused of killing her manager and then tried to kill herself. Now she's gone." He continued to stare at the slow-moving water.

Charles and Heather had dated a few years. She was a country music singer and had convinced Charles to move to Nashville with her at the urging of an unscrupulous manager who took her hard-earned money along with her hopes of a singing career. They returned to Folly six months ago with Heather's dream crushed. She left the island, and left Charles a farewell note, hours before he'd planned to propose marriage.

I was tempted to say that everything would be okay. Not knowing if it would be, I didn't say anything.

Several minutes passed before he said, "Now add to Heather leaving, poor Joy doesn't know who she is, and may be in danger. And, that's not even mentioning Dude missing his best buddy." He looked at me. "Chris, this is a seriously sucky year, and Christmas is almost here."

I remained silent.

He finally said, "Know where I was for two hours this morning?"

"Malibu," I said. An absurd answer to a question I couldn't know the answer to, usually got a smile from my friend. Not this December 22.

"No," he said, expressionless.

"Where?"

"Sitting outside Martha Wright's house."

"Waiting for the dog sitter?"

He nodded.

"Did she show up?"

He shook his head and said, "Guess."

"No."

"No, you're not going to guess? No, you think she didn't show up, or no to Pluto being there?"

I should have stuck with Malibu.

"Did she show up?"

"No."

"Sorry. Want to go back?"

"Thought you'd never ask."

He'd walked to the River Park, so I suggested we go to my house and take my car.

We ran into Bernard in front of Mr. John's Beach Store.

"Y'all looking for Pluto?" he asked to begin the conversation.

I told him we were and asked if that's what he was doing.

"Yes, sir. Dude woke Preacher Burl and me up when he pounded on the door as soon as the sun stuck its head over the ocean. Scared the shi… umm, crap out of me until I saw it was Dude. He said Pluto was still AWOL and wanted to know how long it'd be before we started looking."

Charles said, "What'd you tell him?"

Bernard smiled. "Well, I bit my tongue, so I wouldn't say I hadn't planned on looking. The poor little hippie looked so sad. I told him I'd be out as soon as I got dressed." He pointed to his jacket and slacks. "And, here I am?"

I said, "I know Dude appreciates it."

Bernard started to leave, turned, and said, "Chris, have you talked to Joy this morning?"

"No, why?"

"I was heading out and only saw her a second. She's going to call to tell you she remembered something that could be important."

"Thanks, Bernard. I'll give her a call."

He gave me a quick salute and headed the other direction.

Charles moved to the edge of the sidewalk, leaned against the fence in front of Mr. John's, and pointed to the pocket that held my phone.

Message received. I started to call Hope House.

He grabbed my hand. "Wait. Got a better idea. We need to go see her. That way, both of us can help her remember."

I didn't know if a visit would help her remember better, but the best way to improve Charles's mood was to give him a purpose.

"Good idea."

A block from Hope House, Charles yelled for me to pull over. I pulled between a rusting motorhome and a pile of broken tree limbs. Charles was out of the car before I put it in park. I waited to see where he was going before I opened the door. I didn't have to go far. Charles jogged between two houses and was returning before I saw what had drawn his attention.

He said, "Thought I saw him."

I waited for his findings.

"It was a little dog the same color as Pluto." He pointed between the two houses. "The guy back there was calling Lulu." Charles sighed. "Not Pluto."

I said, "Sorry," and followed my dejected friend to the car.

"Thought for sure it was him," Charles mumbled.

He appeared sadder now than he'd been when I found him on the walking pier. I pulled in Burl's parking area and was afraid Charles was going to stay in the car. I was beginning to agree with him that this year was mired in deep manure.

Chapter Twenty

Preacher Burl waved us in. He said Joy and Adrienne were in the living room watching television. Joy smiled when she saw us, and Adrienne looked like she would have been as well off if we weren't there. Burl asked if we wanted coffee. I told him that would be nice, and Charles showed as much enthusiasm as Adrienne had shown seeing us.

"Joy," I said, "Bernard said you had something to tell me."

Burl returned and handed us mugs of steaming hot coffee. He asked the ladies if they wanted more. They declined, and Burl returned to the kitchen to refill his mug.

Joy watched me take a sip, and said, "Yes, but you didn't have to come over. I was going to call."

I told her we were in the area and thought it would be better to stop.

"Thank you. Don't know if this means anything. I woke up around one remembering being in a little apartment. It had a green blanket on the bed and a kitchen so tiny that the table was up against the wall and there was barely room to walk past it. Funny that I would remember those things."

"Were you there with the man from the boat?" Charles asked, showing more life than he had all morning.

She closed her eyes and turned her head from side to side. "I don't think so. I had the impression it's where I lived."

Charles said, "Remember anything else?"

242

"The whole place was small, not much more than a bedroom, a kitchen, and a bathroom."

I said, "Were there windows?"

Her eyes widened. "I didn't think of it until you asked. I don't remember one in the bedroom, just the ugly green blanket. There was a window over the kitchen sink."

I leaned closer. "Good, you're doing great. Let's say you're standing at the sink. Can you see anything out the window?"

She closed her eyes again. "Not really—no, wait, there's a gravel drive between my building and a long, narrow brick building. There's a *No Parking* sign on the building."

"Is that all?" interrupted Charles, who has the patience of a puppy.

"I think so."

I said, "Joy, let's try one more thing. Is there a door leading outside from the kitchen?"

"Chris, I can't remember." She lowered her head and repeated, "I can't remember."

"That's okay, Sister Joy," Burl said. "You're doing good, isn't she, Chris?"

"Yes, Joy, you are."

Adrienne appeared bored with our conversation and stared at the television. I glanced up to see what was so fascinating and saw a newscaster with a photo of the jewelry store on the monitor behind her. She was talking about the burglary that I'd seen reported on the earlier newscast.

Burl looked at the screen. "Why is it that such a glorious Christian holiday brings out the worst in people?"

"Preacher," Adrienne said, "places get broken in all the time. I don't think it has anything to do with Christmas."

"I suppose you're right, Sister Adrienne. It's just that—"

Joy interrupted, "Turn up the sound."

Joy's tone startled Adrienne. She dropped the remote, uttered a profanity, apologized to Burl, and grabbed the device off the floor.

All of us were now staring at the television. The story concluded with the newscaster telling her viewers to call the police if they knew anything about the burglary. An auto dealership ad promoting it's *gigantic Christmas sale* blared from the screen. Adrienne muted the sound, and Joy continued to stare at the silent screen, and Charles asked who buys someone a car for Christmas?

I waved for him to stop talking and turned to Joy. "What are you thinking, Joy?"

She turned away from the television, glanced at Preacher Burl, and then at me. "Chris," she said, no more than a whisper. "The bar was dark. I had to get a case of beer out of the storeroom. Budweiser. The sound system, actually it wasn't more than a cheap, grease-covered CD player, was blasting a Bob Segar song." She hesitated and looked at the floor. "Two men at the end of the bar were huddled together, and…"

"And what?" Charles asked.

She looked at him, looked back at the floor, and gazed at the television. "I don't know."

"Joy," I said, "why did that jewelry store burglary remind you of being in a bar?"

"I'm not certain. It must've had to do with the men."

"That's good, Joy," I said. "Two men were huddled together. Did you hear something they were saying?"

She glanced back at the television like it would miraculously give her the answer. "Seger's 'Old Time Rock-and-Roll' was playing. Was loud. Then it stopped." She jerked her head in my direction. "I heard one of the guys say the name of that store that was on TV."

"Grogan's Fine Jewelry," Charles said.

Joy continued to look at me, and said, "Yes."

I nodded. "Joy, I know this is hard. Why don't you close your eyes and try to remember back? You were in a bar, a dark bar. You went to get a case of beer, so do you think that's where you worked?"

She didn't answer but nodded.

"Okay, good. The two men were talking but you couldn't hear them because of the loud music."

She nodded again.

"The music stopped, and you heard one of the men say Grogan's Fine Jewelry."

"Said Grogan's, don't think he said the rest of the name."

"Okay, good. Did you get a good look at the men?"

She closed her eyes. Charles started to speak. I put my forefinger to my lips. He remained silent.

"Chris, I'm sorry. No. They faced the other direction. It was dark, so dark."

"You don't remember anything else they said?"

She shook her head.

"Joy," Charles said, "did the men see you listening?"

Good question, I thought.

Burl leaned forward and nearly fell out of the chair. He caught his balance, and said, "Do you think they thought Sister Joy heard them planning to rob the jewelry store?"

Charles tilted his head to the side. "Yes."

"And took her so she couldn't tell anyone?" Burl said.

"There's a good chance that's what happened," I added.

Adrienne finally stopped looking at the television and twisted around on the sofa toward us. "Joy," she said, "do you remember the name of the bar?"

An even better question.

"No," Joy said. She returned to looking at the floor. Her left hand balled in a fist, her right hand trembled.

"Joy," I said. "You've done great. I know this is rough. Why don't we stop pestering you and let you rest?"

Charles glared at me.

Burl stood and said, "Sister Joy, let me get you more coffee."

"Thank you, Preacher," she whispered.

"Brother Chris, Brother Charles, would you like more?"

"No thanks, Preacher Burl, we need to be going."

Charles continued to glare at me. He wasn't ready to leave.

"Brother Burl," Adrienne said, "do you think we, umm, Joy is safe here? What if they come after her again?"

"Sister Adrienne, the man from Pewter Hardware is coming this afternoon to put on the new locks."

"What about the locks to our rooms—to Joy's door?"

Burl smiled. "All the doors will get new locks."

"Thank you, Preacher Burl," Joy said, and made a valiant effort to smile.

"Joy," I said, "Is it okay if I tell the Chief what you shared?"

"If it'll help."

"It will, thanks. Please call if you remember anything else."

Charles and I stood to leave, and Joy jumped up and gave each of us a hug. Adrienne surprised me when she moved behind Joy and when Joy stepped back, she stepped forward and hugged Charles and me, and whispered, "Thank you for caring."

Chapter Twenty-One

"Why'd you want to hightail it out of there?" Charles groused as soon as we were in the car. "Joy was figuring out what happened."

"She was struggling. She couldn't remember anything else. I was afraid it'd hurt more than help if we pushed her, besides, she said she'd call if she remembered more."

He sighed. "She's close to remembering what happened. The quicker she does, the safer she'll be. You don't really think new locks will keep them safe, do you? The burglars broke in a jewelry store. That store's locks had to be better than whatever Larry installs, and the store had a security system."

Charles had a good point. Regardless, Joy will remember when she remembers. We can't push her. I was going to share that morsel of wisdom with him when the phone rang.

"Okay," Cindy LaMond said, "what was so all-fired important for you to call?"

"Hello, Chief, how was the meeting with the mayor?"

Charles was flailing his arm around to get me to put the phone on speaker. I did, and he gave a thumb's up.

"The bad news is despite the best efforts of one of my officers to get me fired, I'm still chief."

I pulled in the drive of a house that appeared vacant, so I could focus on the call instead of driving.

Charles leaned closer to the phone, and said, "What's the good news?"

"Chris, you got a Charles stuck in your throat?"

"Got a Charles stuck in my car," I said.

"Poor boy," Cindy said.

I assumed she meant me instead of Charles.

Not to be deterred, Charles said, "The good news?"

"I'm still getting a paycheck and get to drive around in a nifty vehicle with a siren and I don't have to pay for it."

"Congratulations," Charles said.

"Enough about my wonderful life. Why'd you call?"

I told her what Barb had said about the Canadians checking out of their condo two weeks early.

"Holy moly Chris, you know how many people check out early from rentals, hotels, condos, and tree houses?"

"How many?" Charles butted in.

"First, Charles, I asked Chris, not you. Second, I don't have a flippin' clue. It's got to be several. Things happen that we didn't count on. Plans change."

"True," I said. "There's more. Barb also said the guys were asking if Joy's memory was returning."

"I want to know that myself. So what?"

"So, they're two men from outside the area with no reason to care about Joy or her memory. I know it's a weak link, but don't you find it interesting that they're interested in her memory, and then leave Folly when her memory starts returning?"

"Weak link," Cindy said, "It's a feeble, puny, scrawny link, and that's giving it too much credit."

"I know. Regardless, Barb said she had an uneasy feeling when the guys were talking about Joy."

I heard Cindy sigh. "Suppose it's better than no link. Barb didn't happen to know what the guys drove, their license plate number, or their home addresses, did she?"

"No. She said they rented through Avocet. I suspect a police chief who still has a job and a vehicle with a siren could wrangle that information out of the rental agency."

"Okay, I'll do it for Barb. We chicks need to stick together. Anything else you want to share while you have my less than undivided attention?"

"Yes," Charles said, "we just—"

"Charles, I was talking to Chris."

"In fact, yes," I said. I told her about our visit to Hope House and

Joy's vague memories of an apartment, most likely hers, and seeing two men in the bar and their mention of the jewelry store that was burglarized. She stopped me and said she needed to get something to write on. I heard her rustling papers, and she asked me to repeat everything.

I did, and Charles added, "Larry's going to replace the locks at Hope House this afternoon."

"That I knew," she said. "That's the advantage of sleeping with a hardware store owner."

"Ewe," Charles said.

"Chris, and I mean Chris, did Joy happen to remember the name of the bar or the location of the apartment?"

"Afraid not."

"Anything else, *Chris.*"

"No, sorry."

Charles said, "That's it, Chief."

Charles pointed at the next cross street. "Next stop, Martha Wright's house."

I turned right and back toward town, so I could get on East Arctic Avenue, the one-way street headed toward Martha's. Her drive was empty.

"Crap," Charles said. "How can the danged pet sitter sit if she's never here?"

Add that to the lengthy list of questions to which I had no answer. I pulled in the drive and didn't know if Charles thought the pet sitter walked to the house or someone dropped her off. He bounded up the steps and rang the bell and received the same response that he'd received the last time he tried. Barks in several octaves reverberated through the house, and the door remained closed. We headed to the back yard where we found more of the bowls had food in them then during our last visit. Someone had been here.

Charles shook his head, and said, "Want to wait for the sitter to come back?"

"That could be hours."

"Or minutes," he said, with more optimism than I could muster.

"I don't think it'll do any good to wait. Besides, we don't know that Pluto is still missing."

Charles pulled his phone out his pocket and tapped in a number. "Yo, Dude. This is Charles. Is—" His head bobbed from side to side. "Oh." The head bobbed some more. "I'll keep looking."

He ended the call. "Pluto still 'be bye-bye.'"

"Sorry."

"Me too. Why don't you go on home? I want to stay and wait for the sitter. I'll walk home."

"You sure?"

He said he was, and I left him on Martha's front steps.

I took an extra-long route home in the unlikely event I'd see Pluto hitching a ride, and to think through what Joy had said about an apartment and overhearing two men talking about the jewelry store that happened to be burglarized overnight. I couldn't shake the fear that she was in danger and that I couldn't do anything to lessen that chance.

Chapter Twenty-Two

I awoke early the next morning and realized that I hadn't had anything substantial for supper. I checked the weather on my phone and saw that it was already in the low-fifties; a glance out the window revealed that it was sunny. A walk to the Dog would be good for me even if French toast wouldn't.

I stepped through the entry and was greeted by Amber.

"Merry Christmas Eve, Eve," she said and pointed to my favorite table, which was empty and waiting for me.

I thanked her for holding the table for me.

"You're not that important," she said with a smile. "Nobody else wanted it."

With my ego sufficiently deflated, I slid in the booth and she said coffee and water would arrive shortly. I thanked her and looked around the near-empty restaurant. Marc Salmon was at his usual table near the center of the room. He nodded my direction and said he was waiting for Houston. I smiled and nodded, acknowledging his comment.

Amber returned with my water, a cup of coffee, and a question. "Has Pluto returned?"

I told her I didn't know, but as of yesterday afternoon, he hadn't.

"Nope," Marc said from the center of the room. "I saw Dude on my way here. He was looking for his little buddy."

"That's too bad," Amber said. "Hope the little fellow's okay."

"And, hope Pluto is too," Marc teased.

Amber and I smiled but didn't comment on the councilmember's joke.

Bernard stuck his head in the door and headed my way.

"Would it be possible for me to join you?"

"Sure," I said, like I had a choice with him standing in front of the table eying the seat across from me.

"Thanks, Broth—umm, I mean, Chris. Sorry, sir, Preacher Burl's got me talking like that." He sat and unbuttoning his faded army jacket.

"Chris, do you know what the word mistletoe means?"

That was a question I'd never been asked. "No, what?"

"Get this," he said and smiled. "It's derived from two old-time words that mean poop on a stick. Can you believe that?"

"You made that up."

"No, sir. Saw it on TV this morning. It seems that mistletoe seeds are eaten by birds, and then pooped on tree branches, and the seeds grow into mistletoe. Ain't that a hoot?"

Now there was a Christmas story I hadn't heard before, and doubt Preacher Burl had ever shared from the pulpit.

"Bernard, that's interesting. Do me a favor and don't tell Charles."

"Poop on a stick is safe with me," he said. "Knew you'd be interested."

He didn't know me as well as he thought he did. "What brings you out so early?"

"Thought I'd walk around a while and look for Pluto. Besides, the kitchen was getting a little too uncomfortable for my liking. Joy, Rebekah, and Adrienne were gathered around drinking coffee and complaining about men. I felt like I was the enemy, being of the male species."

I was tempted to laugh, but saw that Bernard was serious. "What were they saying?"

"Not exactly sure. I walked in on the conversation. Joy was saying something about men and escaping off the boat. Adrienne were saying that they knew what Joy was talking about and that she was at the house after being deserted by an abusive husband who left her for his massage therapist. I didn't hear Rebekah's problem with guys, but from the look on her face, it must've been bad."

Burl had shared the information about Adrienne, but I didn't know anything about Rebekah other than she worked at Black Magic. I was curious about Joy and asked Bernard if she'd said anything more about being on the boat since she'd been unclear about what had happened when she talked to me.

Before he answered, Amber was at the table asking what we wanted to eat. I said French toast. Amber acted shocked.

Bernard said, "That sounds mighty good, ma'am. I'll try some."

Amber smiled and said she thought she'd be able to find him French toast.

She left, and Bernard said, "Nice lady."

I agreed, and he asked what my question was again. I asked if he remembered anything new that Joy had said.

"Not that I heard, other than she was on the boat and was tied up by two men."

"She said two men?"

"Yes, sir. I remember because it was the first time I'd heard her talking about being on the boat. It got my attention because there was only one guy who tried to break in her room. Why?"

"She'd only mentioned one man when she talked to me."

Bernard scratched his head. "Wait, there's something else. Some of us were talking last night about how we got around on Folly. Rebekah and I don't have wheels and hoof it. Adrienne has an old Chevy pickup truck. Smokes like a pile of damp logs on a fire. Joy said she didn't have a car or a truck and had to walk from her apartment to work."

That was new, and I asked him if she knew where her apartment was.

"No, sir. All she said was that she had to walk."

"She say anything else?"

"Nothing she hadn't said before."

"How well do you think she's adjusting to Hope House?"

"Better than I'd be doing if I didn't have a memory and didn't know why someone took me on a boat to do whatever they planned to do. I can't see how it could've been anything good. It's fortunate that she managed to slip out of the ropes that were on her ankles and wrists. She said the next thing she remembered was how the storm was flinging water over the bow and how the guys in front were fighting to keep it from overturning. Then she was in the water, clinging to a surfboard."

Some of that was news to me. "Did she tell you that or are you guessing about what happened?"

"She said it last night, sir. I couldn't have thought that up on my own."

Our breakfast arrived, and Bernard stuffed three bites in his mouth like he hadn't eaten in days.

He took another bite and pointed his fork at me. "Got a question for you, Chris. We live in a big place, the biggest house on the street, with lots of bedrooms. How do you think the man trying to break in

Joy's room knew what room was hers? I'm thinking that someone living there must've told him."

"Any idea who?"

"It wasn't me, and I'd wager it wasn't Preacher Burl." He chuckled. "I don't have anything to wager, but you get my drift."

"I understand. What about the others?"

"That only leaves Rebekah and Adrienne. I know Adrienne better than I know Rebekah. She doesn't strike me as someone who would do something bad like that. She's a loner so I don't know who she could tell. Rebekah, come to think of it, has been seeing someone, or that's what she says. None of us have seen him."

"What do you know about him?"

"Near nothing. It's someone she met at Black Magic."

"Customer or employee?"

"Sir, that's more intel than I have access to."

"How do Joy and Rebekah get along?"

"I haven't seen them conversing much. The most I'd ever seen them talking was on Woody's Wednesday."

"Woody's Wednesday?"

"Burl picks up two large pizzas from Woody's each Wednesday. I think he pays for them some weeks and other times they're donated. Other restaurants occasionally kick us a few meals, but Wednesdays are my favorite."

"That's nice of the restaurants."

"Preacher has made a lot of friends since opening First Light. It makes us feel like we're part of the community."

"Back to Joy and Rebekah. Do you remember them saying anything about what happened to Joy?"

"Nah. It was more girly stuff, you know, like makeup, hair, and how stupid men are."

"Nothing else about the men who took Joy?"

"No, more than anything, I think we're all nervous about somebody sneaking around the house and talk to each other to keep our minds off it. We'll rest easier after the hardware store man gets the locks changed. Hope he doesn't charge too much. Money's in short supply. If it wasn't for the donated food, I don't know what Preacher would do."

"I know Larry LaMond, the man who owns the hardware store. He'll give Preacher Burl a good deal."

Bernard nodded. "Good. Money don't grow on trees, you know."

"Bernard, you said you thought it may've been someone living there who told the intruder which room was Joy's."

"Yes."

"What about someone who used to live there?"

"Chris, there've been a bunch of people since I moved in. I don't remember some of them. How could we figure out which one?"

"Most of them wouldn't know which room was Joy's. What about people who recently moved?"

"If they moved before Joy moved in, how would they know which room was hers?"

"Process of elimination."

"Chris, you're going to have to dumb that down for me."

"They'd know which room you, Adrienne, and Rebekah were in, and where Preacher Burl lives. They'd know that Joy was in one of the other rooms."

"Got it. Let's see, there's Al. No, he moved a few weeks before Adrienne moved in. Besides, he moved to California. Scratch him." He took another bite of breakfast and rubbed his chin. "Okay, in the last couple of weeks before Joy arrived, two guys left. There's Alex and Taylor."

"Tell me about them."

"Let's see, Taylor left after Preacher Burl found him a job in North Charleston. Lucky man. And, there's Alex Rockford. Never did trust him and was glad to see him go."

"Where'd he go?"

"Don't know. He was there for supper one evening and gone by the time breakfast was served. I don't like spreading rumors, but I heard he'd been in jail for burglary. Don't know if it's true."

"When did he leave?"

"Give me a minute. Oh yeah, it was the day the faucet in one of the bathrooms broke and water spewed all over the room. Had to get a plumber. I'll tell you, it was a mess."

"Bernard, when?"

"Oh, two days before Joy showed up."

"Would Taylor and Alex have known which rooms would've been vacant when Joy moved in?"

"I would think they'd know that their rooms would be empty."

"Anyone else?"

"Not that I recall."

Bernard took the last bite of breakfast, wiped his mouth with a napkin, and said, "Chris, I sure appreciate you letting me break bread with you." He smiled. "Preacher Burl says break bread a lot. It's rubbing off on me."

I returned his smile and said, "Worse things could rub off on you."

"One more thing. Could I impose on you to lend me a few dollars to cover my breakfast. My inheritance hasn't come through yet, and you wouldn't believe how difficult it is to pull money out of a stock portfolio."

I smiled and told him I'd take care of the breakfast. "Under one condition," I added, "you call me if you hear Joy say anything new about her ordeal."

He saluted, said, "Deal, sir," and left the restaurant with a full stomach and a smile.

I had nowhere else to be, and the Dog had several vacant tables, so I asked Amber for a more coffee. She returned with the coffee and asked if I'd run Bernard off with my boring conversation. I told her no, and that I reserved boring conversations for Charles since he doesn't listen to anything I say.

She patted me on the arm and said, "Don't be too hard on yourself, I'm certain that in the decade you've known him, he must've heard something you said."

I thanked her for the vote of confidence, and she smiled and headed to a table in the center of the room to spread more holiday cheer.

I took a sip of the refreshed mug of coffee and tried to recall everything Bernard said that Joy shared, especially anything new.

Joy seemed more certain that there were two men on the boat instead of only one as she previously mentioned. Also, one of the things that I couldn't previously figure out was how she'd untied herself, grabbed a surfboard, and get off the eighteen-foot-long boat without the men knowing. I hadn't thought about how horrific the storm had been the day before we found her. If the men were struggling to keep the boat from capsizing, it was possible that she could've slipped overboard before they noticed her missing. They probably figured she drowned with the storm so intense, which was probably their intent from the beginning.

Joy also told Bernard and the others that she didn't own a vehicle and that she walked from her apartment to the bar where she worked. It could've been a bar on Folly since they are all within easy walking distance of most buildings with apartments, yet, her description of the bar didn't fit any that I was aware of.

Then, what about Bernard's theory that one of the current residents told the man who was trying to get in Joy's door which one was hers? Even if he was right, how could anyone prove it. Even if you add residents who recently moved, you have the same problem.

I left the Dog with a full stomach, a lighter wallet, and more unanswered questions than I had entered with. At least, I knew the origin of the word mistletoe.

Chapter Twenty-Three

I t was turning out to be one of the warmest late-December days I could remember, so I headed to the far end of the Folly Pier to walk off a few of the hundreds, okay, thousands, of calories I'd devoured with my French toast. The Pier, like much of downtown Folly two days before Christmas, was nearly deserted. A handful of diners were enjoying an early lunch in Pier 101, but there couldn't have been more than ten people strolling along the thousand-plus-foot-long fishing pier. From the end of the structure, I had a view of much of the island's Atlantic shoreline and in the distance a glimpse of the County Park where I first met Joy. With a little imagination, I pictured the area of the ocean where she bailed from the boat. It was a miracle that the surf-board carried her to safety.

The phone rang as I was climbing the steps to the second level of the Pier.

"Mr. Landrum, this is Joyce, I mean Joy."

I asked how she was doing.

"Okay. I just saw Bernard, and he said he had breakfast with you. Are you still at the Lost Dog Cafe?"

I told her no, where I was, and asked why.

"I remembered a few more things overnight, and you told me to let you know so you could tell the police. I could call them but feel more comfortable talking to you."

"Want me to come by the house?"

"I'd like to get out of here. If you're going to be there for a while, I could walk over and meet you."

Thirty minutes later, I saw her heading my way. I waved from the upper deck and she smiled and returned my wave. Her hair was pulled in a neat ponytail and she had on jeans, a white blouse, and a gray jacket.

She said, "Thanks for waiting."

I motioned for her to join me on the bench. I didn't tell her I had nowhere else to be.

She looked toward shore, and said, "This is my second time out here. It's relaxing."

I agreed and waited for her to get to the reason for the visit. If the walk to the end of the pier relaxed her, I'd hate to see her when she wasn't. Her hand moved from her lap to pushing an errant strand of hair behind her ear, back to her lap, and then zipped and unzipped her jacket.

"Joy, are you okay?"

She continued to look at the hotel, and said, "How would I know if I'm okay? I don't know who I am, where I should be, who I should be with, and what'll happen next."

I understood that, yet she appeared more anxious than the last two times I'd been with her. "I don't know how I'd handle it either."

She slowly turned my direction. "Have you heard of a bar called something like Blackbeard's?"

"I don't think so. Why?"

"It came to me during the night. It may be where I worked."

"Have you asked anyone else?"

"No. I'm not sure who I can trust. I know I'm being paranoid, but the guy trying to get in my door freaked me out. I think I can trust you."

I told her she could. I also knew that anyone could say that and saying it didn't make it true.

"Joy, is that all you remembered?"

"I don't think I worked there long."

"Why do you say that?"

"It didn't seem that familiar, like I couldn't find the clean bar towels. I know it sounds silly, and I could've remembered it wrong. It's vague."

I took out my phone and searched for Blackbeard's Bar in the Charleston area. There were numerous references to the notorious pirate called Blackbeard, most of them talked about his terrorizing merchant ships along the coast in the early 1700s. There were nearly as many pirate tales in the Lowcountry as there were ghost stories, and those were in the too-many-to-count range. There was only one bar with Blackbeard in the name.

"Joy, does Blackbeard's Hangout Bar sound familiar?"

"Vaguely. Is that a bar over here?"

I showed her a photo of the front of the bar from its website. "Look familiar?"

"I'd love to say yes. Honestly, I can't tell. Where is it?"

"About seven miles up Folly Road. Would you like to go there?"

She jerked her head in my direction. "When?"

"We could go now."

"Like, right now?"

"Now or later today. It's up to you."

"I don't think … okay. Would you mind?"

"Gosh, Joy, it'll take valuable time away from me sitting here wasting the day away."

She smiled. "I might learn who I am." She closed her eyes and was silent for the longest time. Finally, she said, "Let's go before I chicken out."

We were leaving my drive ten minutes later. I didn't tell Joy, but I started to question what we might face. What if she worked at the bar and someone there was the person who'd abducted her? We pulled off the island, and I wondered if I should've asked Charles to go. What if we're headed into danger?

Joy didn't help when she said, "I'm scared. I want to know who I am, yet, what if I don't like me?" She turned in the seat and faced me. "What if the men who took me are there? I might not know who they are."

I'd driven this stretch of Folly Road numerous times, in fact, one of my favorite restaurants, the Charleston Crab House, was less than a half-mile from Blackbeard's Hangout Bar, yet I couldn't recall ever seeing our destination. When the street numbers indicated we were there, I understood my confusion. There was a deteriorating strip center on the left and at the far end of it was a narrow storefront with a faded-black awning and the words Blackbeard's Hangout Bar in Old English script. If I hadn't been looking for it, I wouldn't have noticed the sign. Several cars were parked at the other end of the shopping center in front of a dollar store and a nail salon. No vehicles were in front of the bar and the plate-glass windows were painted black, so I couldn't tell if anyone was behind them.

"Joy, does anything look familiar?" I said and parked in front of the black awning.

She stared at the door, gripped the center console, and whispered, "That's where I work, where I worked."

Joy's paranoia was rubbing off on me and I thought the smart thing for me to do was to call Cindy LaMond and see if she could "visit" the venue with us. We were out of her jurisdiction, but I would've felt safer visiting with someone carrying a weapon.

"Let's get this over," Joy said before I could make the call.

"Are you sure?"

She nodded and opened the door.

For better or worse, here we go.

Chapter Twenty-Four

Compared to Blackbeard's Hangout Bar, the darkest bar I'd ever been in looked as bright as a polar bear in a snowstorm. We stepped into the darkness to the blaring sounds of "Dark Necessities" by the Red Hot Chili Peppers. There was a dim, red light over the exit door at the rear of the building, and I thought I saw movement from the right side of the room.

The song ended and someone with a deep, gruff voice said, "Well, look what the cat dragged in."

Whoever it was must have been wearing night-vision goggles or was a bat with a bass voice. I couldn't see anyone. Joy walked in the direction of the sound. I followed and hoped I wouldn't trip over a chair, table, or vampire.

"Kevin's going to have a cow when he sees you," said the voice. "You sure you want to be here?"

A refrigerator door opened, and its light illuminated the face of the man who pulled it open, and the person, I assumed, who'd been talking. I wasn't old enough by a couple of hundred years to have seen Blackbeard, but imagined the man standing in front of us shared a striking resemblance. He was at least six-foot-five, weighed two-seventy, with black, stringy hair that reached his shoulders and a beard that reached low on his chest.

My eyes were beginning to adjust to the near darkness, and I glanced around. The room was empty except for Joy, Mr. Blackbeard, and me.

"Do I know you?" Joy said to the unsmiling bartender.

"Crap, kiddo, did you crack your skull and forget the only friend you had here?"

He wasn't far off.

She smiled. "Something like that. What's your name?"

"You're serious, ain't you?"

I stepped closer to the man dressed in black. He could've been one of those creepy creatures in a Halloween haunted house.

"Hi, I'm Chris. My friend Joy's suffering from amnesia. Did she work here?"

"Joy," the man said. "You mean Joyce?"

"Yes, and you are?"

"I'm Darryl. Joyce and I worked two shifts together, and then she disappeared. Thought Kevin was going to blow a gasket when she didn't show her next shift." He turned to Joy. "What happened, sweetie?"

"I don't know. Who's Kevin?"

Darryl waved his hand around the room. "Kevin Beard, owner of this dump."

With no music playing, I heard traffic on Folly Road, and a door slamming in back of the building.

Following closely behind the slamming door, came a higher-pitched voice that said, "Joyce Tolliver, if you think you're going to slink in here and get a check for the two days you worked, you're out of your freakin' gourd."

I stepped between the new voice and Joy. "Hi, I'm Chris Landrum, a friend of Joyce. Are you Kevin Beard?"

The room was still dark, but I thought I saw him nod.

"Is there somewhere the three of us can talk?" I asked and looked around for an office, hopefully with lights.

He headed to the far side of the room, and I followed. Darryl whispered to Joy, "Good luck. He's pissed."

Kevin ushered us into a small office that doubled as a storeroom. I thought Darryl's beard was long until I saw Kevin's. If it didn't reach his belt, it didn't lack much. He wore black slacks, black tennis shoes, and a white T-shirt. Cases of beer were stacked six high on one side, and three cases of liquor were on the floor beside two chairs with rips in their vinyl seats. They'd probably been taken out of service from the bar. Kevin pointed to the chairs, and we sat. He had a chair behind the makeshift desk but sat on the edge of the desk.

"What happened, Joyce? I thought you were going to be reliable. You gave me a song and dance about how you never missed work and had bartending experience. You said you lived in walking distance, so you could be here whenever I needed you."

"Mr. Beard, Joy, umm, Joyce, had a traumatic event that caused amnesia. She—"

"Mister, was I talking to you? I asked Joyce a question. What are you anyway, her doctor?"

"Mister Beard, Chris is a friend who saved my life. He's right about my amnesia so we'd appreciate it if you could tell us what you know about me."

"Joyce, I told you when I hired you to call me Kevin. You serious about losing your memory?"

"Yes. How long did I work here?"

"Two nights. A Friday and Saturday. You were scheduled to be off Sunday and come in Monday. The last I saw you was when you left that Saturday."

"They've shown my photo on television. Didn't you see me there?"

"Joyce, guess you don't remember me telling you this when you hired on. This is probably the only bar in Charleston without televisions. My customers are here to grab a drink and don't want to be caught up in sports and politics, stuff that dominates the danged TV. I don't even have a television in my house, although it wouldn't matter, I'm never there. This place is my life."

"Kevin," I said, and hoped he would allow me in the conversation. "Joyce really has amnesia. What can you tell us about her?"

He glared at me and I was afraid he wasn't going to say anything, at least nothing pleasant. He slid off the desk, moved behind it, opened a drawer, and pulled out a manila folder that had scribbling on the front and a tab that was peeling off the top. I couldn't read what was on the paper he pulled out of the folder, but it looked like a job application.

He looked at the document and up at Joyce. "Your application says that you're Joyce E. Tolliver, age forty-seven. Born in Kansas City, Kansas, and ain't got any living relatives." He looked down at the paper and flipped it over to the other side. "Any of this coming back to you?"

She shook her head.

"You have a management degree from Kansas State University. It's not on the application, but you told me that you'd been married to an eye doctor, an optometrist. Something about him leaving you for one of his patients." Darryl smiled, something I didn't think was in his repertoire. "I remember why you told me someone with a job in management wanted to tend bar. Said you were bored working in an office and took part-time bartending jobs." He glanced at me and turned to Joy. "You remember any of this?"

"Afraid not, Kevin. Did I tell you what brought me to Charleston?"

"Nothing other than you said you moved around a lot. Spent time in Texas, Oklahoma, and I think Georgia. That's all you said."

"Were you here the second night she worked?"

"I'm here every Saturday night. I done told you that's the last time I saw her."

"Do you remember if there was a crowd?"

"Good, but not one of my best. Why?"

I didn't want to tell him too much about what'd happened. For all I knew, he could've been one of the abductors. "Just curious. Something may have happened to Joyce after she left here."

"Like what?"

"We're not certain."

"Joyce, you remember telling me how you walked home after work and I said I'd get you a ride if you wanted? It's not good having an attractive lady like you walking around at two in the morning."

"I don't remember that."

"Sorry," he said. "Of course, you don't."

"Kevin, do you remember Joyce talking to a couple of men more than others that night?"

"Chris, that's your name, right?"

I nodded.

"You saw how dark it was out there. If my hands weren't connected, I'd have trouble knowing where they were most of the time."

I assumed that meant no. "Didn't you wonder what happened to Joyce when she didn't return?"

"Sure. She didn't have a phone, so I couldn't call. Besides, she's not the first person I hired who skipped out after a few days. This isn't the most fun work, and I struggle to get good help. Getting any help. I figured you'd moved on to another job or skipped town."

"Kevin, this may sound like a strange question, where does it say I live?"

He was looking down at the application and slowly raised his head and looked at her. "You really don't remember anything?"

"No."

"Wow," he said and shook his head. He gave her the name of the apartment complex off the application. He told her it was three blocks behind the bar and that it'd been there forever. I asked if an apartment number was listed. He glanced at the application and wrinkled his nose. "Nope. Wonder why I didn't catch that?"

"What about the other paperwork you need on a new employee," I said.

He glanced over at Joy and returned his gaze to me. "I was desperate to fill the bartender's job. The last one walked out on me with the weekend around the corner. Joyce said she had bartending experience. That was enough for me. I told her that we would get all that done the next week when things slowed down." He looked at her again. "You didn't come back to do it."

He was getting either nervous about not filling out the required paperwork, or angry that we were pestering him. We thanked him for the information and stood to leave.

"Joyce, if you get your memory back and want to come back to work, I could find a place for you. Sorry about whatever happened."

Kevin stood in the office's doorway as we weaved our way through the dark room.

I nearly bumped into Darryl who was standing by the front door. He gave Joy a hug and said he was sorry she wasn't still working there. She thanked him, and he glanced back at his boss who was still standing in his office doorway. Joy opened the front door and Darryl slipped me a folded piece of paper, patted me on the back, and said, "Take good care of Joyce. She's a nice lady."

We left on much better terms than when we'd arrived, as Coldplay filled the air with "A Sky Full of Stars."

I didn't know if I should look at the paper in front of Joy, so I slipped it in my pocket and headed to the car.

Joy stopped me. "Can we walk to where I lived, umm, live?"

"Do you remember the way?"

"Not really. Didn't Darryl say it was three blocks that way?" She pointed behind the bar.

We walked three blocks in the direction Darryl had indicated and found two apartment buildings. They were decades from being new and backed up to each other with a gravel alley separating the structures. There were no signs listing the name of the complex or anything indicating there was an office. The apartment numbers were the same style, so I assumed they were part of the same development. *Now what*, I wondered. "Anything look familiar?"

Joy looked at the building on our side of the alley and then at the one on the other side. "Not really."

I jotted the street name and address on a card from my pocket and said that I'd call Chief LaMond and see if she could find out anything about the apartments and the company that managed them, and with luck, which apartment had been rented by Joyce Tolliver. She agreed and said she'd like to get back to people she knew.

Joy was exhausted by the time I pulled in her parking area. She had her hand on the car's door handle. Instead of getting out she said, "The rain was blowing sideways. Ocean water lapped over the side of the boat and my head kept bouncing off the wooden arm rest each time we hit a wave. I was soaked, and I twisted my arms until the rope I was tied with loosened enough for me to pull my hand free." She closed her eyes, gave an abbreviated nod, and continued, "The man in the seat in front of me cussed the weather and kept saying the boat was going to sink. I managed to untie my feet and grabbed the surfboard and slipped over the side. I didn't know where we were but knew the farther away from the boat I could get, the safer I'd be." She stared at the house and then said. "Chris, the next thing I remember was you and Barb looking down at me on the beach."

Chapter Twenty-Five

I returned home, poured a glass of Cabernet, and plopped down in the living room. I would have bet money on Charles's reaction to my trip to Joy's former place of employment and would've won.

"You did what?" he blurted before I got to the part about meeting the Blackbeard lookalike.

"Charles, why don't you let me finish and you'll know what I did."

"You wouldn't have to tell me if you'd let me go," he said, in a voice that would make a sniveling, ten-year-old, with hurt feelings, throwing a tantrum sound like Gandhi.

I continued sharing what we learned at Blackbeard's Hangout Bar, and from the unsuccessful visit to the apartment complex Joy listed on her employment application.

"Joyce Tolliver, Joyce Tolliver. I like Joy Doe better. How did she take it?"

"As well as you can imagine. I was going to call Cindy and tell her but wanted to call you first." I hoped to get a glimmer of appreciation from him.

"You wouldn't have had to call me at all if you'd taken me with you."

"Are you finished reminding me?"

"Not sure. What happens now?"

"I end this cheerful discussion and call Cindy."

"You could've already called her. You wouldn't have had to call me if you'd taken me."

I did what some of my friends had done to me on more than one occasion. I hung up on him.

The next call also went off the tracks before I got it headed the direction I'd desired.

"Glad you called," Cindy said instead of hello, reinforcing my dislike of caller ID. "Let me tell you about our two friends from north of the border."

"The Canadians?"

Cindy made an audible sigh. "No, Santa and Mrs. Claus."

I smiled and asked what she'd learned.

"I got a call this afternoon from Staff Sergeant Major Urton from the Royal Canadian Mounted Police. I'm a lowly ole cop in this humble burg, so I haven't the foggiest how high or low a staff sergeant major is in the RCMP pecking order, but he seemed nice, although a bit stuffy when I asked if her rode a horse to work and wore a red coat and one of those funny wide-brimmed hats."

"Cindy, what'd he say?"

"Patience, Charles in waiting. He was reporting on what he'd learned about Troy Ellis and Nate Cook's early departure from our slice of heaven. It seems that Nate's mother was in an auto accident near Ottawa. A lumber truck driver decided that one of those pesky stop signs wasn't applicable to him and poor Mrs. Cook made the mistake of being in the intersection at the time. She's in critical condition, and Nate's father called and asked him to come home."

"You don't think he had anything to do with Joy's abduction?"

"Unlikely. There goes your number one and number two suspect. Any other brilliant ideas?"

It wasn't brilliant, but I reminded her that I was the one who initiated the call, and shared what Joy and I'd learned from our trip to Joy's former place of employment. Cindy scolded me for not letting her know where we were going. She added that I was too old, or in her words, "Way too fossilized to be gallivanting around where angels fear to tread." I reminded her that Joy and I had simply visited a bar where she may've been employed and not barging in on a gang of thieves, abductors, and other mischief-makers.

"How'd you know that before you got there?"

She was right although I wasn't going to give her the satisfaction of agreeing. I asked if she could use her official resources to learn about the apartment complex where Joy allegedly lived and find the landlord to get a key to her apartment.

"Chris, you know I'm at your beck and call, whatever that means, and live and breathe to seek answers to your countless questions."

She then did what I did moments earlier to Charles. The phone went dead.

It was two more sips of wine before I remembered the note that Darryl had handed me.

It read: *Call me. I know the guys you asked Kevin about.* He added a phone number.

I punched in the numbers and four rings later was afraid no one was going to answer. Finally, I heard a rock song in the background that I didn't recognize, and a voice that I did. "Yeah."

"Darryl, this is Chris, the guy with Joyce earlier today."

"Listen, I can't talk now. Can I call you at this number in about an hour?"

I said he could.

The next hour lasted about a week, or so it seemed, until the phone rang, and Darryl said, "This Chris?"

I said it was.

"Listen, I'm on a break and can't talk long. I overheard you talking to Kevin. It's amazing what you can hear in here when the music's not vibrating the walls. You asked about two guys who Joyce was talking to during her last shift. Kevin's protective of his customers and flat-out lied when he said he didn't know anything about it. He says many customers have been hassled by cops. He wants this to be a, how does he put it? Oh yeah, a hassle-free zone."

That was way more than I wanted to know. "Darryl, the guys?"

"Yeah, them. Listen, I've seen them in here a few times, didn't know them well. I don't know what their deal was, but the last two times they talked all hush-hush like. Looking around like they were planning to overthrow the government and not wanting anyone to hear."

"Did you ever hear what they were talking about?"

"No, but I think Joyce did."

"Why do you say that?"

"The last day she was here, I was getting off shift and grabbing my coat from the back room. Joyce was with me and started to go behind the bar near where the two guys were sitting. She stopped in the doorway for a long time. I couldn't tell what she was doing. I headed out and didn't think anything else of it until I heard you talking to Kevin. I figured it could've been important and had something to do with Joyce losing her memory. Am I right?"

"I think so. Did Joyce say anything to you about it?"

"No. I waved bye when I left and didn't say another word to her until she showed up today."

"Do you know who the guys are?"

"Only their first names. Raymond and Taylor."

"Know anything else about them."

"Raymond's fond of Miller High Life; Taylor's a Bud guy. That's it. Sorry."

"What do they look like?"

"White dudes. Looked like most of our other customers. Jeans, casual clothes. Average height. Raymond's a couple of inches taller than Taylor. Not fat, not thin."

"Age?"

"I'd guess late thirties, could be off several years. I'm not good with ages."

"Have you seen them since that night?"

"I was off a couple of days. They weren't in after that while I was here."

"Anything else?"

"Not that I remember. You really think they had something to do with what happened to Joyce?"

"There's a good chance. I'm going to have the let the police know what you've said, so you might get a visit from someone from Folly Beach or the county Sheriff's Office."

"I'm not a fan of cops. There's a history there." After a long pause, he sighed. "If it can help Joyce, I'll talk to them. She seems like a nice lady."

"She is. I appreciate you telling me about the men."

"No problem," he ended, with one of my least favorite sayings.

Chapter Twenty-Six

I've known a few Raymonds. Taylor was a more unusual and memorable name, and if I'm right, was the name of one of Burl's recent residents. A phone call to the preacher should verify it.

"Ah, Brother Chris, it's good to hear from you," he said, although he hadn't heard anything from me yet, and was responding to my name appearing on his phone.

"Good evening, Preacher. I hope I'm not interrupting anything."

"In fact, you are. We're having a Christmas party. Why don't you hop on your sled and have the reindeer bring you over and join us? Sister Joy was getting ready to tell me about your afternoon adventure. I know she'd love for you to be here."

I remembered how down she was when she got out of the car after our visit to Blackbeard's, but I also knew it was a Hope House party and didn't want to butt in. I thanked Burl for the invitation and shared my reluctance to crash the party.

"Nonsense. You wouldn't be crashing, I invited you. Besides, Sister Joy was saying how much she enjoyed spending time with you, and Brother Bernard was recounting how you and Charles had invited him to last year's party at Cal's. Remember how you encouraged him to speak with me about being homeless and the tough time he'd had finding a homeless shelter? It meant the world to him. He'd like to see you."

I wasn't keen on the idea of going out again. I was more reluctant to turn down a generous offer from a minister this close to Christmas. Besides, I wanted to ask him about Taylor. I said I'd head over.

The seasonal lights around the front door and along the roofline were in full holiday splendor. The house looked in much better repair in the dark than during daylight. Bernard greeted me wearing a stop-light red shirt and black jeans. He also greeted me with a smile, a firm handshake, and, "Welcome to the first annual Hope House Christmas party." He leaned close and whispered. "Alcohol's prohibited. Thought I'd warn you."

I thanked him for the welcome and the warning. He pointed to the living room where from the sounds of multiple voices I assumed everyone was gathered. Burl was standing on a two-step ladder by the tree and fiddling with a strand of lights that weren't working and Rebekah was putting a CD in a portable player on the table in another corner. Adrienne was sitting in the chair farthest from the action and looking either tired or bored.

Joy saw me in the doorway and jumped up from the sofa and rushed over and gave me a robust hug. She looked more refreshed than when I let her off earlier today but wore the same clothes.

"Preacher said you were coming. It's nice of you to join us."

Burl saw me and thanked me for coming while he was holding the unlit lights. He had on a red sweatshirt with a reindeer on the front, gray slacks, red house slippers, and a Santa hat. I asked if there was anything I could do to help, and he said he knew what the problem was and would soon have the lights burning brightly. He asked Bernard if he would take me to the kitchen to get something to eat and drink.

Elvis's version of "Santa Claus is Back in Town" began playing from the CD player and Bernard told me the drink menu included soft drinks and a fruit punch that he whispered was yucky. I selected Diet Coke before Bernard showed me the platter of peanut-butter sandwiches cut in half, and another platter of sliced celery, carrots, and for a reason I wouldn't attempt to guess, dried okra. Apparently, Bernard couldn't guess either. He shrugged.

I filled a paper plate with portions of everything except okra and followed Bernard back to the party.

Elvis was singing "White Christmas," Burl had managed to get the lights working and was sitting on the sofa between Joy and Rebekah, and Adrienne was still in her chair expressionless. Bernard motioned me to sit in the remaining chair and lowered himself to a sitting position on the floor. I felt bad taking his seat, but not bad enough to stand and try to balance my food and drink while eating.

"Here Comes Santa Claus," started playing and Burl said, *"Elvis' Christmas Album.* My favorite."

I knew who it was since at one time I had the same album. Adrienne didn't appear to share Burl's appreciation for the King. She rolled her eyes.

Joy said, "I was getting ready to tell Preacher Burl about our trip to the bar when you called."

"That can wait," Burl said. "Wouldn't want to spoil the party. Chris, this is my first Christmas in here. I've been blessed this year."

Bernard said, "And we're blessed you chose to share the house with us, Preacher."

Rebekah added, "Bernard's right. We are blessed, Preacher."

Adrienne remained silent.

Joy didn't say anything. She was staring at the tree and I couldn't imagine what must be going through her mind. For me, Christmas has always been a time of reflection. It's been a time to look back, think about Christmases past, Christmases with family and friends, and while most people take New Year's Eve and Day to think about the future, I found it more meaningful to focus those thoughts at Christmas. Joy can't see back much more than a week. And, without that perspective, she wouldn't be able to see, predict, or even hope for things to come. I looked over and gave her a smile, hopefully received as one of love, trust, and hope.

She returned the smile, and Burl stood and said, "Brother Chris, we were getting ready to sing some Christmas carols. Now that you're here, we can add another voice to our group. Sister Rebekah, would you ask Elvis to take a break until we get finished caroling?"

Burl knew from listening to me in church that I had a terrible singing voice, so he clearly must be under the influence of Coke, the cola kind.

"That's okay, Preacher. I'd rather listen to your outstanding voices."

I had no idea how outstanding the others would be. All I knew was that compared to me, Alvin and the Chipmunks sounded operatic.

"As you wish, Brother Chris. It's not actually a carol, but let's begin with 'A Holly Jolly Christmas,' a ditty made famous by Burl Ives, a man named after me." The preacher chuckled at his joke; a joke that I was probably the only person in the room to catch. Preacher Burl was named after the singer Burl Ives because his father was a fan of the singing actor.

Burl raised his arms like he was going to direct a choir and began singing, "Have a holly, jolly Christmas; it's the best time of the year."

Few would argue with that sentiment. Many could argue that the sounds of this group singing couldn't make this the best time of the evening. That didn't stop the enthusiastic choir director from smiling and bouncing on the balls of his feet as he led the vocally challenged group through the song. Burl was the only person who knew the words past the first three lines, so he increased his volume to cover up the random words the remainder of the group were spewing. The sounds were sad, the intent uplifting.

The song came to a merciful end and Burl beamed like he'd been conducting the Mormon Tabernacle Choir. "Joyous," he said.

Not the word I would have chosen; regardless, the group was having an enjoyable time. Even Adrienne smiled.

"Great start," Burl continued. "Brother Bernard, what's your favorite Christmas carol?"

Bernard turned and looked behind him like it was another Bernard the preacher was talking to. He then glanced at the Christmas tree and said, "Preacher Burl, I must say I've never given that much thought. I'll go with 'Away in a Manger.'"

"Then let's give it a go. Folks, let's make a joyful noise unto the Lord." He returned to his conducting stance and sang, "Away in a manger, no crib for His bed. The little…"

It may have been my imagination, but the singing sounded nearly on key. I mouthed the words and enjoyed the fellowship. After Bernard's favorite finished, the preacher asked Rebekah the same question, and she didn't hesitate when she said, "O Holy Night." We—they —muddled through it, when Burl turned to Adrienne and repeated his question.

"Preacher Burl, if I had to choose one, it'd be 'Pretty Paper.'"

Burl smiled and didn't tell her that the Willie Nelson penned song wasn't a carol. "Good choice," he said, and the group began singing Adrienne's selection.

It was heartwarming to see how not only the preacher, but everyone, embraced Adrienne's song. I also wondered what he would say to the newcomer who had no memory of the past. Would he ask about her favorite carol, or would he acknowledge her lack of memory?

We finished Willie's "carol," and Burl said, "Wonderful job."

I glanced at Joy who was staring at the floor like she was wishing to be somewhere else. I empathized with her.

Burl moved closer to Joy and said, "Sister Joy, instead of asking you about your favorite carol, let me say that when I look at you, I can't help but think about the beautiful carol 'Joy to the World.' Would you mind if I chose it as your song?"

Joy smiled and nodded.

That level of sensitivity was one more reason Preacher Burl was a godsend to Folly Beach and its residents without traditional church homes.

Burl returned to his role of conductor and led the group in Joy's song. With the final "And wonders of His love," Burl put his arm around Joy and said, "Thank you for being with us."

She mumbled, "You're welcome," and Burl turned to me. "Now Brother Chris, I don't have to ask your favorite. Last Christmas you told me it was 'Silent Night.' Folks, shall we sing the marvelous hymn to the man who's been pretending to sing with us?"

They did, and I was touched.

"I don't know about you," Burl said, "my throat is parched. Shall we take a break and refresh our drinks?"

No one protested and everyone except Burl and I moved to the kitchen.

Burl watched everyone leave, and said, "It wasn't lost on me that you called for a reason. Care to share it was while the others are imbibing?"

"Preacher, didn't you have a resident named Taylor?"

Burl nodded. "That wasn't a question I'd anticipated. Yes. You saw him the day I was in the Lost Dog Cafe. Remember, I told you I was looking for someone about a job."

"I remember, although I didn't catch his name."

"He's Taylor Strong. He moved out the night before we were blessed by the appearance of Joy. Why?"

"Preacher, what can you tell me about him?"

"I assume you will answer my question at the appropriate time."

I nodded.

"Brother Taylor was only here a few weeks. He was quiet, not as quiet as Sister Adrienne, but quieter than the rest. He shared that he was originally from North Carolina, never said what town. Getting him to talk was a challenge. I managed to get that he'd had various jobs over the years. He said he'd been an armored car driver, and a clerk in a convenience store. He also shared that a few years ago he went to school to learn how to be a locksmith. In fact, the day you saw me looking for him, I was there to tell him about a vacant position in a locksmith company in North Charleston."

"Did he get the job?"

"He didn't tell me directly, but I gathered that he did and would be earning enough to move."

"You don't know for certain?"

"No." The preacher smiled. "It was fortunate that he left because that freed up the best room in the house for Joy."

Bernard and Rebekah returned and moved back to their previous locations. Adrienne came back and asked if she could get Burl and me something else to drink. The caroling must have put her in a better, if not more generous, mood. Burl said that another Coke would be great, and I said I'd go with her to get the drinks.

"Brother Chris," Adrienne said as she poured the Preacher's Coke, "this is one of the nicest nights I can remember. I love it here."

I was surprised since she looked bored most of the evening. Once again, I was reminded not to judge others by appearances.

We returned, and Burl led us in a few more Christmas songs, more secular than religious, and I told him I needed to be going. He walked me to the door.

"Preacher, would you do me a favor?"

"If I can."

"Call the locksmith shop and see if Taylor took the job?"

"I'll try, but tomorrow is Christmas Eve. I don't know if it'll be open."

I said I understood and asked him to try.

"You think he was one of the men who abducted Joy?"

I nodded.

"I pray not," he said.

"I'll be calling Chief LaMond in the morning. She'll probably be contacting you to learn everything you know about him. Do you know what kind of car he drives?"

"I'm horrible with stuff like that. I know it's a few years old and black. I doubt that helps."

We shook hands, and he told me to have a pleasant rest of the evening.

Chapter Twenty-Seven

C hristmas Eve began as another beautiful day. The sun rose over the ocean a little after seven and was escorted on its upwards path by wispy cirrus clouds. The temperature was already in the low-forties, ten degrees above average. I decided that this would be a good morning to walk to the Lost Dog Cafe for breakfast. It appeared that I wasn't the only person to have that thought. Amber saw me enter and pointed to the only two empty tables. I chose the smaller of the two, and she had a mug of coffee in front of me before I'd wiggled out of my jacket.

"Merry Christmas Eve," she said and followed up by leaning over and hugging me around the neck.

"And the same to you. What are you and Jason doing tomorrow?"

She glanced around the room to see if her services were needed elsewhere. They weren't, and she turned back to me. "We're going to First Light's service and then to Samuel and Jacob's house for lunch."

Samuel was a good friend of Amber's son, Jason. Jacob, Samuel's dad, and Amber had been dating a year. Their first date was last Christmas at Burl's Christmas Eve service.

"Great. Is Jacob fixing lunch?"

Amber chuckled. "Jacob's a guy; Samuel's a guy. The best they can muster is burning toast. I'll do everything."

Jacob and Samuel's culinary skills had me beat, but I didn't remind Amber of my shortcomings. "It's great you'll get a chance to be together."

"I think so. Changing the subject, have you heard anything about Pluto? Dude was in for lunch yesterday and I thought he was going to cry when I asked him if his pup had turned up."

"I haven't heard anything."

"Don't know what'd happen to Dude if something happened to his short look-alike."

"I agree."

"Any news about Joy?"

Amber had earned her reputation of knowing all the gossip worth repeating.

I told her about going to Burl's party and how well Joy appeared to be adjusting to her new home. I then added, "Do you know Taylor Strong?"

"Name's not familiar. Why?"

I shared what Joy and I'd learned about her job at Blackbeard's and overhearing something that possibly resulted in her abduction.

"Want me to ask around?"

"Yes, if you limit it to people you can trust. I don't want Taylor hearing about it."

"Have you told the police any of this?"

"Some of it. I need to talk to Chief LaMond."

She pointed at me and frowned. "Yes, you do."

She took my order and headed to the kitchen.

My phone rang while I was waiting for food to arrive. I didn't recognize the number and nearly didn't answer. There are only so many "free" vacations I can win, or "opportunities" I must learn about the latest-greatest Medicare supplemental insurance.

"Chris, Chris Landrum," said the voice on the other end. It was familiar, but I couldn't place it.

"Yes."

"Oh good. This is Bernard, you know, the one at Hope House."

"Sure, Bernard. How are you?" I said, although I was more wanting to know why he was calling rather than how he was.

"I'm fine, sir. I was talking to Preacher Burl after you left last night. He told me you were asking about Taylor Strong. The preacher said you asked what Taylor drove, and Preacher didn't know. He's mighty good about knowing the scriptures; he's short on knowledge about some things in this here world. Cars are one of them."

"Do you know what Taylor drives?"

"Yes, sir. A black, 2013 Ford Focus. Got itself a dent in the front bumper. The rear tires have too much mileage on them and are nearly bald."

"Thanks. That may help the police find him."

"There's more, sir. It has South Carolina plates; the first three numbers are 339. I hate to say, I don't recall the last three."

"How do you know that?"

"That's the kind of unimportant stuff I remember."

"Bernard, that'll be helpful. It's not unimportant. Do you know anything else about Taylor, other than he was a locksmith and moved out the night before Joy arrived?"

"I don't know the best way to put it, but he acted like he was in a box and no one could find a way in. Don't get me wrong, he was friendly enough. It's like he had secrets and didn't want anyone to get close enough to figure them out. Does that make sense?"

"Yes. Do you know if he had friends on Folly other than people in Hope House? Anyone ever come to visit him or to pick him up?"

"It wasn't at the house. I saw him on West Ashley talking to a man. They were huddled up against the wall at St. James Gate, near the opening to the outdoor patio. Know where I mean?"

I told him I did.

"I couldn't tell what they were talking about because I was on the sidewalk at the stoplight. It looked sort of sketchy, sir."

"Can you describe the other man?"

"Not really. He looked taller than Taylor and heavier. Sorry, that's the best I can do."

"That's fine, Bernard. Anything else?"

"Nothing about anything I know about Taylor. I know Preacher Burl tried to call the locksmith where Taylor was supposed to go to work. I think the place is closed until after Christmas. He left a message on the machine. I won't take up more of your time. Will I see you at tonight's service?"

I said I'd be there.

"Then, *adios*, sir."

Amber had slid my breakfast in front of me while I was talking to Bernard. I was on my second bite when Chief LaMond came in the restaurant, looked around, and headed to my table.

"Merry Christmas Eve, Cindy. Care to join me?"

"You buying?"

"Wouldn't that be bribing a law-enforcement official?"

"Not unless you plan to ask me to do something illegal, immoral, or considering the season, un-Christian."

"None of the above. Have a seat."

Amber must have figured that the Chief would be joining me. She had a mug of coffee for Cindy before she had time to remove her jacket, and said, "Something to eat, Chief?"

"Anything expensive and put it on his tab." Needless to say, she pointed at me.

Cindy took a sip of coffee, and I said, "Dude find Pluto?"

She shook her head.

"Too bad. You working or taking today off?"

"What do you think? Dear sweet hubby's chained to the cash register at the hardware store and won't get home until every Tom, Dick, and Harriet buy every battery, extension cord, and those cheap, chintzy, *hecho en Mexico* Christmas ornaments that hang on the tree, spin, and play 'Jingle Bells.'"

"Sorry."

"I'm not. That's what makes him enough money to spoil me and allows me to live like a queen."

"A queen?"

"Whoops, I drifted into my fantasy world for a moment. Enough about my phantasmagorias life. Yes, I'm working. In fact, I'm waiting for a call from the landlord at the apartment where Joy lives, or where the owner of that bar thinks she lives. What other trouble have you been sticking your nose in?"

Cindy's expensive breakfast arrived, and I told her what Bernard had shared. She jotted down the vehicle information and said she'd see what she could find out, although she wasn't optimistic since, in her words, without the last three numbers of the license, there were "three billion combinations." I was certain that was a tad high but didn't get in an argument about math. I'd exhausted my latest information, and our conversation drifted to what she was doing Christmas Day—attending Cal's party, going to Planet Follywood's annual Christmas pot-luck dinner later in the day, and acting like a queen. I shared my plans.

I waited for her to finish eating, paid the tab, and walked with her to the door. In a moment totally out of character, she hugged me and said, "Merry Christmas, and thanks for being such a good friend."

She slid back to her normal self when she said, "You tell anyone I did that, and I'll have you arrested for embarrassing a public official."

I told her that the act of kindness was safe with me.

Chapter Twenty-Eight

I was headed home after leaving the Dog when the phone rang again. This time, I knew who it was.

"Merry Christmas Eve, Charles."

"Yeah, yeah. Where are you?"

"In front of City Hall."

"Park your butt on the nearest bench. I'll pick you up in ten minutes."

"Where are we going?" I asked, wasting words since he'd already hung up.

It couldn't have been more than five minutes before Charles' Toyota pulled to the curb and he waved me in.

"Could you tell me where we're going?" I asked, thinking it was not too much to ask.

He turned left on East Arctic Avenue, and said, "Dixie called and said Martha was home."

"Your plan is to barge in on Martha on Christmas Eve?"

"Nope. Figured you'd ring the doorbell and flash your old-man charm. How could she resist inviting us in?"

I could think of several ways and rolled my eyes.

I rang the doorbell and the sounds of her menagerie filled the house. Unlike our earlier visit, the door opened, and Martha said, "Hold on a second, Teri, I'll get your ... Whoa, you're not Teri."

Charles stepped in front of me. "Hi, Martha, I'm Charles from church. This is my friend, Chris."

280

Martha wore gray sweatshirt and sweatpants. She leaned on her cane and looked from Charles to me. "Where's Teri?"

Charles looked down the steps and toward the street. "Who's Teri?"

"The child watching my family while I was away. She's supposed to stop by this morning to get her money." She stepped on the porch, closed the door, probably to keep her herd of family members inside, and looked up and down the street. "If you're not Teri, why are you here?"

"Chris and I stopped by the other day to see you. Your neighbor, Dixie, said you were out of town."

"Yes, I was up in Dayton visiting, poor Tommy. He had a stroke, you know. Got back last night. Flight was three hours late. Can you believe that?"

Charles said that he could.

"Oh, I'm being inconsiderate. Would you like a cup of coffee?" She hesitated and winked at Charles. "Or a hot toddy? I've got some good whiskey to spike it with."

Charles said, "Coffee would be fine."

"Give me a minute to herd my family into another room. Otherwise they'd lick the livin' tar out of you."

She opened the door enough to slip back in the house and Charles turned to me and whispered, "Wonder how long it'll be before we're begging for the hot toddy?"

The animals quietened to a low roar, and Martha opened the door and invited us in and led us to what she referred to as the "sitting room." I would've called it an animal play house. In one corner there was a three-foot-high, triple deck, carpeted cat tower. Beside the tower was a large wicker basket filled with rubber balls, a tennis ball that looked like it'd rolled under a running lawnmower, and a hard-rubber thing shaped like a five-pound weight. Other toys were located on the brown pile carpet.

She told us to sit anywhere we liked while she got the coffee and asked again if we were sure we didn't want a toddy. I declined, although I was getting closer to saying yes. We each chose one of the three wing-back chairs and lowered our bodies in the dog and cat hair infested seats. I noticed an end table beside my chair holding a large aquarium. It wasn't more than a foot away, so I saw there was no water in it. What it was filled with was a boa constructor that was a mile long, or so it seemed. It stared at me and I knew what a mouse must feel like on its way to supper—the boa's supper.

Martha returned to the room carrying two, white china cups of coffee. "Oh," she said, "I see you've met Squeezy. Would you like to hold him?"

Where was the hot toddy when I needed it? "That's okay, Martha. Not today." *Not tomorrow, not ever*, I thought.

"Martha," Charles said, "You have a lovely house."

"Thank you. It's comfortable, and wonderful for my pets."

Charles asked, "How many pets do you have?"

"It varies. Most of the time, there're a dozen of God's wonderful creatures living with me."

That probably meant there were more until Squeezy got hungry. "How many dogs?" I asked, hoping to move the conversation closer to the reason for our visit.

She bit her lower lip, held out her hand and raised her fingers, one at a time. "Let's see, Bruce, Ink Spot, Little Dog, Pooch, Gink, and Lady. That's six today. Now don't neglect asking about my other lovely creatures."

"What're their names?" Mr. Nosy asked.

She pointed her cane at the boa. "You already met Squeezy. There are three cats, Cat One, Cat Two, and Crazy. My poor little parrot, Jolly Roger, must stay upstairs. He doesn't get along with the cats, and his vocabulary is, well let's say, his mouth needs to be washed out with soap more often than I would like. We celebrated his ninth birthday before I went to visit poor Tommy."

Charles wiggled his fingers like he was counting. "Martha, if my ciphering is right, that's only eleven pets. Didn't you say twelve?"

"Oh, you're right. I keep forgetting Davy Crockett." She looked around like Davy was loose in the room. I hoped Mr. Crockett wasn't another snake.

"Davy Crockett?" Charles said.

"A raccoon. He's my indoor/outdoor pet." She put her finger to her lips, and whispered, "It's illegal to have a raccoon as a pet. You won't turn me in to the pet police, will you?"

We assured her we wouldn't although turning her in to a mental institution was becoming a tempting option.

"Martha," I said. "Are any of your dogs Australian Terriers?"

"What a queer question, young man. Gink is."

Charles said, "Gink?"

"The word Gink means 'a peculiar fellow,' in Australian. That's why Vincent and I named our little fellow that. That little bugger, Gink, not Vincent, was as strange as any dog we ever had."

Pot calling a kettle black came to mind.

"Vincent's not here is he?" Charles said.

282

"Heavens no. I dumped him back in Atlanta eons ago. Can you believe he hated the beach?"

"No, ma'am," Charles said.

"Now young men, don't get me wrong. Vincent was a wonderful husband, and we had some great times. I remember back when we got married in '58, and he bought the prettiest blue, 1957 Chevy. For our honeymoon, we drove all the way to the Grand Canyon, soaking in the air from the open windows. Gink would stick his head out the window and gobble up the breeze like he was lapping water. Ah, the good old days."

Now to get back to the not-so-good current days. "Martha, I'm confused. Gink was your Australian Terrier when you were in Atlanta?"

She nodded.

"Yet, when you were naming your dogs, didn't you say Gink?"

"Yes, so?"

"Gink is an Australian Terrier, right?"

She nodded again.

"And he's in the other room with your other dogs?"

Another nod.

"I see," I said, although I didn't. "How long have you had Gink?"

"Let's see. It was a few days before I left to visit poor Tommy. He had a stroke, you know?"

She had my attention. I leaned forward in the chair and motioned for her to continue.

"I was out back filling the food bowls. I put food out for the poor strays. Terrible how some people just throw their pets out to fend for themselves. Terrible. I was filling the bowls when the cutest little Australian Terrier peeked around the corner of the house. He saw the food and zip, he was eating out of the bowl. He was a spittin' image of Gink. Lo-and-behold, the poor thing didn't have a collar and licked my hand just like Gink used to do. Oh, the memories the cute thing brought back. Did I ever tell you about Vincent, Gink, and me going to the Grand Canyon?"

"Yes," I said.

She continued, "I simply had to bring him in, feed him, and give him a warm home to live in." She closed her eyes and slowly shook her head. "I had to."

I didn't know who I felt sorrier for, Martha or Dude. Martha was reliving her past through Gink, umm, Pluto, and we were here to shatter her memories. And, I can't imagine how much anguish Dude has been going though without Pluto. I also realized that Martha hadn't asked why two near strangers appeared at her door.

I was trying to figure out how to broach the subject of her taking Dude's dog. Charles, didn't share my dilemma.

He nodded toward the door separating us from the rest of her family. "Martha, what if I told you that Gink belongs to our friend, Dude Sloan?"

Her hand jerked up to cover her mouth. I would have sworn that Squeezy hissed at Charles. Martha exhaled and said, "Oh my heavens. That's not possible. Gink didn't have a collar. He came to me and begged me to take him in." She lowered her head. "Who's this Dude fellow?"

I explained who he was and how Pluto had escaped, caught his collar on something in the yard, and how Dude and several others had been looking for him for days. She appeared to be shrinking in her chair. It may have been the light, but I thought I saw tears in her eyes. Charles and I remained silent. That was the least we could do after ruining her day.

She pushed herself out of the chair and walked to the door where the dogs had been herded. She opened the door a few inches, bent down, and said, "Here, Gink."

Dude's look-alike inched his way through the door, saw Charles, jumped in his lap, and licked his face. Charles returned Pluto's "kisses" and said something to him in dog-speak.

Martha returned to her chair, and whispered, "What's his name?"

Charles gave his lap mate another kiss, and said, "Dude Sloan."

"No, what's Gink's name?"

"Pluto," I said.

"That's a funny name," said the person who has a snake named Squeezy, and cats named Cat One and Cat Two.

I explained how Dude was an astronomy buff and named his dog after the dwarf planet.

"He must be heartbroken," she said after a long, uncomfortable silence.

I said, "He is."

She stared at Pluto, and said, "You should call him and let him know his pup's safe. He can come get him."

"That's a good idea, Martha," I said.

"Won't you call him now? I feel horrible that I stole someone's family member. Horrible."

I punched in Dude's number in my phone, and was rewarded with, "Unless you know where Pluto is, I don't want to talk to you."

I smiled, told him who I was, and broke the news. Good news for Dude, not so good for Martha.

He screamed so loud that I moved the phone a foot away from my ear. He screamed a second time before I had the nerve to return the phone close enough to tell him where we were.

I heard Dude's 1970 Chevrolet El Camino a block before it pulled in Martha's drive. I opened the front door before he knocked it off the hinges. I'd never seen Dude move so quickly. Pluto ran a close second as he charged out of Charles's lap and met his master in the center of the room.

Watching Dude reunite with Pluto was a sight that would soften the hardest heart. I wouldn't call it a Christmas miracle, but it was close. Even Martha, who'd moments earlier been tearing up about losing Gink, and feeling badly about taking in someone else's dog, broke into a smile.

Charles had tears in his eyes.

I wasn't far behind.

Chapter Twenty-Nine

Charles and I left Martha, Dude, and Pluto/Gink after Martha apologized profusely for taking the surf shop owner's dog, and Dude told her, "Me be giggly gettin' Pluto back." He also told her that he wanted to meet all of Pluto's new four-, two-, and zero-legged friends. We would've stayed longer, but Dude told Martha that it'd "be cool" to wrap Squeezy around his neck. That was our cue to exit.

Charles dropped me at the house after saying he'd had enough excitement for one morning and wanted to take a nap to get ready for First Light's Christmas Eve service. A cold wave was pushing through the area since my early morning walk to the Dog. The sky morphed from chamber of commerce blue to threatening rain. I didn't need a nap yet thought spending several hours inside was becoming a better idea. I knew Dude would be so excited about getting Pluto back that he wouldn't think to let anyone know his dog had been found.

I called the Chief who answered with, "Ho, Ho, Ho! Merry Christmas Eve. If you say anything to stomp on my feelings of great joy, you won't live long enough to wish anyone Merry Christmas tomorrow."

"Cindy, I'm about to make your day of feeling great joy even better."

"You and Charles are moving to Tibet."

"Guess again."

"You and Charles are moving to Tibet and taking my husband with you."

"What if I told you that Pluto has been reunited with Dude?"

"Has he?"

"Yes," I said, through a smile.

"Oh, my God. That's incredible. How, when, where?"

I filled her in on some details, leaving out the names of Martha's animals, my near snake-handling experience, and Martha's honeymoon trip to the Grand Canyon.

"Chris, that's the best news you could've given me. Thanks for letting me know."

"You're the first person I've called. I'll let you get back to whatever police chiefs do on Christmas Eve."

"Don't go so fast, bearer of great news. I have a kernel of news for you although it's not as great as Pluto's return. I talked to the landlord where Joy lives or lived before she moved here. The guy who sounds about as smart as a corkscrew, but not as useful, is on vacation in some town in Maryland I've never heard of. He thought it was a brilliant idea to leave his tenants in a lurch while he's frolicking with some floozy near our nation's capital."

"Did he tell you that's what he's doing?"

"Nah, he sounded like someone who'd be frolicking with a floozy. He remembered Joyce Tolliver, called her a 'hot chick' and said if he was twenty years older, or she was twenty years younger, he'd be camped out on her curb hoping she'd pick him up. Honest to God that's what he said. Yuck. I told him I wasn't a hot chick, but was a police chief and carried a gun, and if he didn't want me camped on his curb, he'd call the second he got back to the complex and let me in her apartment."

"What'd he say?"

"Yes, sir, Chief, ma'am."

"When's he coming back?"

"Day after Christmas."

"You'll call me when he gets back?"

"Nope. I'll be calling the tenant who's paid rent for that apartment. If she wants to let you know that's her business."

"Fair enough. Anything on the whereabouts of Taylor Strong?"

"Chris, you sure know how to drag a girl down after cheering her up about Pluto."

"Sorry."

"Our Mr. Strong has a rap sheet. If Preacher Burl was correct about his former resident attending school to learn locksmithing, either the school specialized in training burglars, or didn't check his background before letting him in."

"Is that what he'd been arrested for?"

"Yep, his career of crime had been given three years off when he was taking advantage of an all-expense paid vacation in Arkansas."

"Any idea where he is?"

"Nary a clue. I'm going to swing by the house this afternoon to see if the driver's license photo that was on record matches the Taylor Strong who stayed there. I'm fairly certain it will, but there's always the chance it's another guy with the same name."

"Anything more on his car?"

"Negative. If I learn anything, you might be one of the first I'll let know."

I knew not to push. "That'd be great, Cindy."

"Of course, it would."

My next call was to Preacher Burl.

"Brother Chris," he said, based on my name appearing on his phone, since I hadn't said anything.

"Yes, Preacher."

"Are you psychic?"

"Preacher, I've been accused of many things. That's not one of them. Why?"

"I was reaching for the phone to call you."

"Why were you going to call?"

"You called first. What do I owe the pleasure of this call?"

I shared the news about Pluto's reappearance, and Burl responded with "Halleluiah," and a prayer. I then told him that he would be receiving a visit from Chief LaMond and the reason for her visit.

"Ah, Brother Chris, perhaps you are psychic after all."

Burl was beginning to sound more and more like some of my other friends with disjointed comments, thoughts, and occasionally, actions. I asked what he meant.

"Brother Lawrence from Holy City Locksmiths returned my call less than an hour ago. That's the company I'd told Brother Taylor about. The store was closed today, but out of habit, Brother Lawrence checks his messages when the store's closed. He said that around Christmas it's not uncommon for people to get locked out of their home or vehicle. Mine happened to be the fifth message left for—"

"That's interesting, Preacher," I interrupted. "What did he say about Taylor?"

"He had little to share. It seems that Brother Taylor never showed for the interview. Can I surmise that Sister Cindy's visit is related to Brother Taylor's past?"

I told him what I knew about his former resident and the reason for Cindy's visit.

It took him a long time to say, "Brother Chris, I have a confession to make, and a dilemma that I face in my profession."

"What?"

"First, the dilemma. Faith is the foundation of my being. I, by personality and profession, seek the good in everyone. Over the years, I have seen firsthand how even the most horrid person can, as we preachers are prone to say, see the light. Men and women of all ilk can turn their lives around. I truly believe that miracles occur." He was silent for a moment, before repeating, "Miracles occur."

"That's wonderful, Preacher."

"There's a downside, which leads to my confession. When I opened Hope House, I did so with much trepidation. It was created as a place where those with little hope could find not only the necessities of a warm bed and a warm meal, but where they could find, as its name says, hope. From hopeless to hope requires change, a change in the residents. It's not up to me, nor is it in me to control the changes. That is up to a much higher power than in this humble, lowly, preacher man. Not everyone is ready or willing to make the necessary changes, hence the reason for my trepidation, and something that has kept me awake many a night with worry." He paused again. I started to ask him to elaborate, when he said, "I have no application for admittance. I have no way to determine where the potential resident is with his or her life; what black holes have existed in the past; and, what evil thoughts may be present. Brother Chris, I continually am in fear of introducing someone to the house who has evil intent. How, pray tell, is it fair to the others if I subject them to such a person?"

"Preacher, I've known you long enough to know that you'd do everything possible to prevent that from happening and look how much good Hope House has done. I know what Bernard was experiencing before you gave him a chance and hope. And look at Joy, she had no hope, nowhere to go. I don't know as much about Adrienne or Rebekah, but from what I see, you've helped them immensely."

"That may be true, Brother Chris. While it's taken me a long time to get to it, my confession is that I never had a good feeling about Brother Taylor."

"What about him?"

"I may not be all-knowing," he laughed. "Heavens, at times I'm not even part-knowing, but what I am decent at is detecting when someone is not being truthful. Brother Taylor often fit in that group. I should never have let him move in. I knew he was lying about previous jobs. That's one reason I was intent on him attending the job interview at Holy City Locksmiths. I figured if they liked him, they would check his background. If there was nothing in it to raise red flags, he'd get the job and be on the road to a productive life. Most everyone lies about something. I told myself that his could be minor and Hope House was giving him the break he needed."

"Preacher, you had no way of knowing. You shouldn't beat yourself up. You do wonderful work."

"Perhaps. I can only pray that by letting Brother Taylor reside here, it didn't contribute to what he did to Sister Joy."

"Preacher, he didn't meet her there. Whatever happened took place before she knew about your ministry."

"I suppose you're right. I must focus on tonight's message and not let this interfere with how I interact with those loyal members of my flock who will be celebrating Christmas Eve with fellow believers. You will be there tonight, won't you?"

"Of course," I said, like there could be any other option.

Chapter Thirty

The weather continued to deteriorate, so First Light's Christmas Eve service will be in the storefront location. Last Christmas, the service was in a tent on the beach, but the tent wasn't available this year.

Joy met me at the door and asked if we could talk after the service. I told her yes, and she joined Mary and her two girls in the second pew. I smiled as I remembered watching Mary, Joanie, and Jewel enter last year's Christmas Eve service. The girls had been wearing new clothes and entered the tent with their heads held high, radiating pride in their appearance.

Charles was in the third pew waving for me to join him. I passed Amber and her son, Jason, seated with Samuel and his dad. Amber nodded to me as I passed. I slid in beside Charles and watched Joy, Joanie and Jewel laughing. Mary hushed them.

Preacher Burl waved his hands for latecomers and those who wanted to continue their conversations to take their seats, and he began with, "Please silence thy portable communication devices." Tonight, it was followed by him encouraging us to make a joyful noise unto the Lord by singing "O Come All Ye Faithful."

We tried to sound joyful, but William Hansel had the lone true singing voice. Burl thanked us for coming and began his traditional Christmas Eve sermon. I had to give him credit, he'd overcome his earlier feelings of trepidation and guilt for allowing Taylor to stay in Hope House. His message was inspirational, heartwarming, and had the rapt attention of everyone present. He followed it with another carol, a reminder of tomorrow morning's regular Sunday service, before asking William to end the service with a solo of "Silent Night."

We slowly wandered out of the sanctuary into a light rain. Joanie asked her mom if the rain was going to turn to snow for Christmas. I didn't hear Mary's answer, but knew it would disappoint her daughter. Joy moved beside Charles and me. I asked if it was okay if Charles joined us. She said sure, and I suggested we make the short walk to the Crab Shack where we could stay dry and talk. Charles was leading the group, followed by Joy and me. As we got to the restaurant, I noticed a black car slowly pass us on Center Street and then turn on East Erie Avenue just past the restaurant. In the glow of the streetlight, it looked like it had a dent in the front bumper. Hadn't Bernard mentioned that Taylor's Ford Focus had a dent? Was the car that passed us a Focus or was I being paranoid? No way to know now.

The restaurant, normally crowded on Saturday nights, was near empty. A couple of others from the church service were seated near the bar, and a half-dozen patrons were scattered throughout the dining room. We were told to sit anywhere, and I suggested a table by the wall and away from others. The server appeared and asked what we wanted to drink. Joy asked what imported beers they had, the server told her, and Joy said Heineken. Charles said Bud, and I ordered the house wine.

"I remembered this morning that I preferred imported beer," Joy said, explaining her order.

"That's great," I said. "Anything else new?"

"That's what I wanted to talk about. Yesterday afternoon, your Police Chief came to talk to Preacher Burl. I didn't know the Chief was there and walked in the kitchen where they were talking. I apologized and Chief LaMond said I wasn't interrupting. She had a driver's license photo and asked if I recognized the person."

"Did you?" Charles blurted, before Joy could finish talking.

She put both palms on the table and leaned forward. "It was him."

Charles said, "Who?"

"The man in the boat."

"You're certain?" I said.

She nodded, and said, "I remember walking home from work and the next thing I remember was laying on the back seat of the boat with my hands and feet tied. My head hurt so much that I figured I must still be alive. There was a dim light by the boat's steering wheel, and I recognized that man Taylor in the front seat. No doubt, it was him. It was dark in the rest of the boat and I never got a good look at the other guy. I already told you what happened next."

Drinks arrived, and the server asked if we wanted something to eat. Charles and I declined, and Joy asked me if she could borrow a few dollars. Charles said that she couldn't borrow anything and that he would pay. A Christmas miracle was in the making. She told the server that she wanted a cup of she crab soup and the house salad.

The server left, and I said, "Joy, do you remember anything else?"

"Not about them taking me out to dump me in the ocean. I remember my apartment in that building that you and I walked around. It came furnished, and I was travelling light. The only thing I had in there was a large suitcase and some hang-up clothes. Nothing more."

"Joy," I said, "did you tell Chief LaMond everything you remembered?"

She smiled for the first time since the service ended. "Everything but liking imported beer."

Charles said, "It sounds like a lot of your memory's back. Had you made friends in your apartment building or from the job at the bar?"

"Not really. I only worked at Blackbeard's two nights, and I hadn't lived much longer than that in the apartment. I nodded at a couple of other ladies who lived at the complex. I already have more friends here than over there or anywhere else I've lived."

Charles patted her on the arm, and said, "Folly folks are addictive."

I added, "You looked like you were enjoying sitting with Mary and her girls."

She smiled and sipped her beer. "The kids are adorable, and Mary actually stopped by yesterday to visit, to visit me. Can you believe that? She could be the daughter I never had." She hesitated, and turned to me, "Chris, Mary tells me that you helped her find a place to live after you discovered that she and her gals were sneaking in vacant rental houses to have somewhere to sleep."

"Several people helped Mary and her children. I didn't do more than anyone else."

Joy smiled. "That's not Mary's version."

I was embarrassed and changed the subject. "Will you be attending Cal's party tomorrow afternoon?"

"Preacher Burl said that it was an event I couldn't miss."

"More than going to church tomorrow morning?" Charles said.

She took another sip, smiled, and said, "Nope, he said the party was the second-best event happening on Folly tomorrow."

We watched Joy enjoying the soup and salad and talked more about what she remembered about the apartment and previously living in Atlanta. Her mood improved the more she recalled and recounted the past. She'd finished her meal and thanked Charles and me for an entertaining and happy evening. From our vantage point, it looked like the rain had stopped, and I suggested that it may be a good time for her to walk home.

Charles's home was the opposite direction, so I told him to head to his apartment and I'd escort Joy home.

Chapter Thirty-One

J oy was euphoric on the way home. She hooked her arm in mine
and kept talking about how much she enjoyed spending time
with the others in Hope House. It was as if an anvil had been
lifted off her shoulders. We were two houses from her place
when a light drizzle filled the air. The house next to Hope had strands
of multi-colored lights on large shrubs beside the drive. If I hadn't been
looking at the Christmas lights, I would've missed a car backed to the
rear of the neighbor's house—the same car that I would've sworn I'd
seen on Center Street when Charles, Joy, and I were entering the Crab
Shack. I was even more certain it was the same vehicle when the red
and green Christmas lights reflected off a dented bumper.

I couldn't tell if anyone was in it without walking up the drive. Joy's
safety was my main concern, so I pretended to not see the vehicle and
continued walking her home. We started up the steps and she asked if I
wanted to come in.

"Preacher Burl always had coffee brewing if you want some."

I opened the door and said, "That's a kind offer, but it's been a long
day and I need to rest up for tomorrow's church service and Cal's
party."

"I should do the same."

I told her to lock the door behind her. She said she would, and good
to her word, I heard the tumbler secure the entry.

The rain had increased, and I wondered what to do. Should I
approach the vehicle? Should I call the police? If the car belonged to

the neighbor and had been there all night, I'd look foolish. I slowed as I crossed the drive where the car was parked. The lights reflected off the vehicle, but the rain-covered windshield, kept me from seeing if it was occupied. I decided to keep walking and regardless how foolish it may make me look, call the police as soon as I was out of sight from the suspicious vehicle.

I was startled to hear the car door slam shut and turned to see what was going on. A man wearing a black, hooded raincoat was heading toward me. My first thought was that it was Taylor Strong although I wasn't certain since the Christmas lights were the only illumination, and I'd only seen him twice. What I did know was that whoever it was gripped a baseball bat, and from his body language, knew how to use it.

Now what? Running wasn't an option. The man was three decades younger than me, and even when I was younger, I wasn't that fast. I probably outweighed him by thirty pounds and would have a chance, although slight, to subdue him in a fair fight. The bat and my age eliminated a fight being fair. It's amazing how much goes through your mind in a split second. My best option was to wait for him to swing at me and try to grab the bat's barrel before it contacted my body. With luck, it would throw him off balance and I might be able to wrestle him down or get the bat. *Might* being the key word.

I didn't have to put my feeble plan into action. I caught a glimpse of someone darting from beside the house and lunge at the bat-wielding assailant. The latest addition to the fray blindsided my attacker and collided with such force that both men were knocked to the concrete driveway. The bat flew in the opposite direction. I grabbed the weapon and stepped back from the men. I then I recognized it was Bernard who'd saved me from being a baseball. The man who was coming after me hadn't moved since he'd smacked into the drive. Bernard slowly pushed himself up and rubbed his elbow that had been under the other man when he struck the drive. The rain intensified, Bernard's hair was plastered to his head, and a wide smile was plastered to his face.

I stared at the assailant. He hadn't moved and must've been knocked out when his head hit the pavement. I reached for my phone to call the police and then heard the siren from a Folly Beach police cruiser less than a block away. The car stopped in front of the drive and Officer Allen Spencer rushed to the three of us.

Spencer glanced at Bernard, felt the unmoving person's neck for a pulse, and called for an ambulance. He then turned to me. "Mr. Landrum, I should have known. What's going on?"

"I walked Joy Tolliver to Hope House after supper." I pointed to the car. "I saw that car and was afraid it belonged to Taylor Strong, the man suspected of abducting Joy. I was going to call the police when a man—"

Bernard interrupted, "It's Taylor Strong, sir."

"Thank you," Spencer said, and turned back to me.

I continued with the story up to when Bernard jumped out of nowhere and collided with Taylor.

The rain continued to fall, and Spencer turned to Bernard. "Why were out in this lousy weather and able to see what was happening?"

A fire engine arrived before Bernard could share his version of the event. One of Folly's EMT firefighters knelt beside Taylor. The other firefighter opened a large umbrella over his colleague and Taylor.

I said, "Officer Spencer, before Bernard answers, could we take this conversation inside? We'd be more comfortable out of the rain."

A second patrol car arrived, and Spencer told the new arrival to keep watch on the unconscious man.

Bernard led us to the door which was opened by Adrienne wearing a long, white robe and house slippers. She waved us in, hugged Bernard, and whispered to him, "Are you okay, hero?"

He told her that other than a sore elbow, he was fine, and followed the rest of us to the living room. Burl met us and asked if we wanted coffee. He acted like it was nothing unusual to entertain three soaked men, including a police officer and a man carrying a baseball bat. I said coffee sounded good, and Bernard and Spencer agreed. Joy had slipped in behind Burl and had a confused look on her face. I didn't blame her.

Spencer took a notebook from his jacket, wiped water off the cover, flipped through a few pages, and said, "Bernard, let's start again, why were you out there?"

"Sir, folks living here are a family, not by blood, but still a family. Families stick together." He pointed to Joy who had taken a seat on the sofa. "Joy is the latest member. I knew you all were looking for Taylor Strong for what you thought he did to Joy."

Burl returned with a tray carrying three coffee mugs and Adrienne handed them to Bernard, Allen, and me.

Allen thanked her and asked Bernard to continue.

"You see, I knew what Taylor drove and thought I saw it cruisin' past the house a couple of times earlier tonight. I wasn't sure it was him, so I didn't say anything. I took a little walk before it started to rain hard and saw the car back in the drive where it is now. It didn't belong to the owner of that house. Sir, that made me more than a mite suspicious. I went around the house and sneaked behind those shrubs out there. The driver was still in the car and not moving. I figured he was waiting to see where Joy was and maybe try to take or kill her." He stopped and caught his breath.

"How long were you there?" Spencer asked.

"I don't have a watch. I'd guess a half hour or so. I also don't have a phone, so I couldn't call for you to come check it out. Sir, I was afraid to leave and not see what the man in the car, umm, Taylor, was going to do. The rain got harder and harder."

"You had to be miserable," Burl added.

"Nah," Bernard said, "I did a lot of recon in Afghanistan, like hours at a time. A half hour in the rain was nothing."

Spencer said, "Then what happened?"

"I saw Mr. Landrum, umm, Chris, walking Joy to the house. I was afraid Taylor was going to try to get her before she got in. He didn't, so I figured he was going to wait until everyone was asleep and do something then. I was surprised when Chris left, and Taylor went after him with a bat."

Spencer smiled for the first time, and said, "So, you took a football tackle to a baseball game."

Laughter, probably fueled by the release of tension more than Spencer's joke, filled the room.

Bernard added to the laughter, and then said, "Couldn't have said it better, sir."

"Allen," I said, "Were you headed here?"

Adrienne answered for the officer. "I called the police. Bernard thought he was hiding, maybe he was from Taylor, but I saw him behind the shrubs from my second-floor window. I remembered what he'd said about Taylor's car so when I saw it parked out there, I called the police. Bernard's right, we're a family, and I didn't want to see Joy, Bernard, or any of us hurt."

I heard the siren from an ambulance approaching and Allen jotted down Adrienne and Bernard's full name and asked Bernard if he wanted the EMTs to check his arm. Bernard said it was fine, and Allen asked if anyone had anything to add. None of us did.

Chapter Thirty-Two

After last night's events, I was tempted to skip First Light's Christmas service. I'd told Preacher Burl and Joy that I'd be there, so I resisted temptation and walked to church. The rain that'd made last night more miserable than it had already been, was gone and nary a cloud could be seen.

I arrived fifteen minutes before I knew Preacher Burl would repeat his "Please silence thy portable communication devices" opening. A familiar group of people were gathered around the coffee urn at the front of the room. Charles was talking with Bernard. Joy, Adrienne, and Rebekah were huddled together in deep conversation, and William was talking with Dixie and Martha.

Charles spotted me at the entry and pointed to his wrist, his way of telling me that I was late. I shook my head, and he mouthed, "Just kidding."

The Christmas spirit had taken hold of my friend. I nodded to Lottie who was helping Burl with his robe. Everyone wore their Christmas best, even Charles, who wore a solid red, long-sleeve sweatshirt instead of one featuring college logos. Burl headed to the lectern and Mary, Joanie, and Jewel entered and looked around. Joy spotted them and asked if they wanted to sit with her. In unison, Joanie and Jewel said, "Yes, oh yes." Mary ceded to their wishes, and the four moved to the second pew.

Barb entered as Burl was beginning his opening. She tiptoed to the back pew where I was sitting with Charles and squeezed my hand as she sat. "Sorry I'm late. I was at the store straightening up after being busy yesterday and lost track of time."

I SAW fatigue in Burl's eyes, but he didn't let it show. His message was uplifting, his enthusiasm for, and telling about, the birth of Jesus was contagious, and miracle of miracles, the congregations singing of traditional Christmas carols, sounded good—okay, passable.

Before the closing song, Charles leaned my way and whispered, "Whenever I have a problem, I sing. Then I realize my singing is a lot worse than my problem."

"Did a President say that?"

"No, I did. Didn't you just hear me?"

William Hansel singing "What Child is This" drowned out more silliness from Charles.

Most of those in attendance appeared to want to linger in the sanctuary after the service. Burl said there was more coffee and a few of us took advantage of it.

Charles took me by the arm and moved to a corner of the room, and in a muffled voice, said, "Why did I hear about last night from Bernard and not from my best friend?"

"Charles, I was exhausted and the only thing I wanted to do was go to sleep. Sorry."

Instead of berating me, he said, "Are you okay?"

The phone rang before I could assure him that I was. The screen read Cindy.

"Merry Christmas, Chief."

"Caller ID strikes again. Can you talk?"

I said for her to give me a second and walked outside where I'd have more privacy. Charles followed me. To keep him for flailing his arms and pointing to the phone, I put it on speaker and told Cindy to go ahead.

"Figured you'd want to know. Your new friend, the baseball batter, ain't what crooks call a stand-up guy. My guys turned him over to the Sheriff's Office when they got to the hospital. The detective called me a little while ago and said that it wasn't fifteen minutes after he started interrogating Taylor before he blamed everything on Raymond Tilford, his partner in crime. According to Taylor, it was Tilford's idea to burglarize the jewelry store, abduct Joy, steal the boat, take her out and dump her in the ocean. He didn't say it, but I suspect if given a chance, he'd blame Raymond for global warming, fighting in the Middle East, and shingles."

"Did he say why he attacked me?"

Cindy chuckled. "It appears that your surveillance skills aren't as good as your detective friend Charles."

Charles smiled, but kept his mouth shut. For once.

"And?" I said.

"Taylor thought he saw you looking at his car when you walked by with Joy, and when you were leaving, he said you slowed down and gazed his way. He figured he had to stop you before you did something stupid like calling the cops. Your reputation for nosing in my business, has spread to the criminal element. Tell Charles he needs to give you some lessons in surveilling."

"Never," I said.

Cindy laughed, and Charles stuck his lower lip out and pouted.

I asked, "Did Taylor tell them where to find Tilford?"

"Yep, and before you ask, they picked him up late last night and found some pretty earrings, necklaces, and watches in his car. Funny how they all were in in boxes with Grogan's Fine Jewelry on the top."

"Cindy, thanks for letting me know. You still plan to go to Cal's party this afternoon?"

"Only if Charles, that idiotic, moronic, weird friend of yours isn't there." She then laughed.

"I'm not those things," Charles said.

Cindy said, "I know, you're not idiotic and moronic. Merry Christmas, Charles."

Charles said, "I'll admit to weird. How'd you know I was listening?"

"Charles, I'm the Chief. I know everything. Besides, do you think I don't know when a phone's on speaker? The only person Chris puts the phone on speaker for is his nosy friend. Merry Christmas to both of you, and bye."

CAL HAD SAID that this party would be bigger and better than ever. From the sounds coming from the room as I opened the door, he was right. Loud conversations mixed with laughter were coming from all corners. Christmas lights twinkled from the bar, the front of the stage, and from four trees.

Cal was in the center of the room standing beside a table holding bowls of salsa, avocado dip, and something with lettuce, tomatoes, and onions in it. Two bowls overflowed with chips. The smiling host wore his much-travelled, rhinestone-covered coat, red jeans, and his Stetson with twinkling lights around the crown. He was talking with Amber and her son while Samuel and his dad were scooping dip on a paper plate full of chips.

Gene Autry's 1950 version of "Frosty the Snowman" was playing on the Wurlitzer.

Charles leaned on the bar and was talking with Joy, Mary and her girls. Joy saw me at the door and waved for me to join her. I did, and Charles said that he was telling the ladies about the police catching the second person responsible for Joy's abduction. Bernard joined us, and Charles started the story over again. He was swinging his arm around. I was afraid he was going to slosh beer on Bernard from the bottle in his hand.

Adrienne and Rebekah had been standing in a corner by themselves, but slowly came our way after they saw that Bernard had joined the group. They each put an arm around Bernard and called him their hero. He turned three shades of red and looked at the floor. That made the ladies squeeze harder. Jim Reeves was singing "Silver Bells" and Adrienne hummed along while she was squeezing their embarrassed housemate.

Speaking of squeezing, Dixie and Martha peeked in the door, and hesitated before getting enough courage to enter. I nodded to Charles and then at the ladies. Charles took the hint and moved to greet them. I saw him get each a beer from the tub next to the appetizer table and they moved to the far side of the room.

Joy watched them go, and leaned close to me and said, "You won't believe this. Preacher Burl talked to Cal about me. Cal told him he had a powerful need for another bartender, that's how he said it, *powerful need*. Cal hired me, and Preacher Burl said I could stay at Hope House as long as I want to. Isn't that wonderful?"

It was, and I told her so.

Dude was next to stick his head in the door. Correction, Pluto stuck his head in and then Dude. Pluto sniffed the air like he knew there must be a hamburger nearby with his name on it. Martha saw Pluto and left Dixie and Charles standing before she scooped up the canine and gave it a series of kisses.

I excused myself from Joy and moved toward Pluto, hopefully to prevent a war over the canine suffering an identity crisis. I hadn't needed to. Dude stood back, smiled, and told Martha that she could visit Pluto any time.

She thanked him, and added, "Can I call him Gink?"

"That be cool. His official name now be Pluto Gink Sloan."

Barb entered wearing a red sweater without any Christmas message adoring it, and came over to me and kissed my cheek and said, "Want to hunt shark teeth in the morning?"

"No," I said, so loud that two people standing nearby stopped talking and stared at me.

Burl was next to arrive. He wore a Santa hat and a sweater that would win any ugly Christmas sweater contest. He made his way around the room patting people on the back, kissing ladies on the cheek, and lifting and hugging Joanie and Jewel.

Cal saw Burl and moved close and whispered something to him. Burl shook his head so hard that the Santa hat nearly fell off. Cal smiled, patted the preacher on the back, and moved to the stage in front of the room. He waited for Brenda Lee to finish "Rockin' Around the Christmas Tree," and unplugged the jukebox.

He clinked two beer bottles together close to the antique mic that he's sung approximately a trillion songs in over the years. "Yo! How about lending me an ear?"

All but Dixie and Martha stopped talking. Cal tried again and this time they stopped and turned to the country singer.

Cal tipped his Stetson to the group. "Merry Christmas. This is our biggest Christmas shindig ever. Thanks for coming and joining this old crooner on his favorite day of the year. Now, I've got a question. How many of you'd like to hear Preacher Burl and me sing a duet?"

All but Burl responded by either clapping or saying, "Yes." Burl stared at the floor and shook his head.

"That's what I thought," Cal said. "If you were here last Christmas, I bet you remember the preacher and me singing, 'Silent Night.' I know I do. Come on up, Preacher."

Burl glanced at the door leading outside. I suspected that's where he'd rather be, but in the spirit of Christmas, he slowly moved to the stage while Cal grabbed his guitar. Burl faked a smile and moved to the mic like he would approach a rattlesnake. Cal whispered something to Burl and Burl responded.

Cal stepped to the mic and pulled Burl closer. "Gals and guys," the singer said, "I can't think of a better song to sing that this one. Here's to you, Joy, my newest bartender, and another fine addition to our community."

They began singing "Joy to the World," and two minutes later ended with,

"He rules the world with truth and grace,
And makes the nations prove
The glories of His righteousness,
And wonders of his love,
And wonders of his love."

Faith

Chapter One

T he Folly Beach Christmas Parade is one of my favorite events of the year. Not only does it pay homage to the celebration that has a magical way of touching most of us on several levels, but it also gives my fellow residents an opportunity to show, no, to shout, their unique, quirky take on the holiday. Marching bagpipers sharing the same street with shiny waste-removal trucks, and golf carts overflowing with colorfully dressed elves. Add a UPS truck driver wearing a giant Santa's hat, city officials and other bigwigs chauffeured in vintage convertibles, riders dressed as reindeer riding yellow mopeds, and since Folly Beach, South Carolina, is not known as the snow capital of the country, a vehicle filling the air with artificial snow. Not a glimmer of beige interrupted the colorful feast for the eyes. Today was festive for children of all ages, for adults who want to relive their days of youth, and for those who simply love to see smiles. Count me among the latter group.

Today was perfect. It was approaching mid-December, yet the temperature was hovering in the tolerable sixties, the sky a crisp blue, with the unfiltered sun reflecting off every shiny surface. My friend Charles Fowler and I were watching the festivities from the ninth-floor walkway of the Tides Hotel, Folly's tallest building. We had a perfect, unobstructed view of the parade as it made its way four short blocks up Center Street, appropriately named since it roughly bisected the small, barrier island plus being its center of commerce. The crowd lining both sides of the street was treated to the festivities. Most of the children were waiting for the arrival of Santa, perched on one of Folly's fire engines instead of riding in a reindeer-propelled sleigh, while their parents reveled in laughing at or laughing with many of the parade participants. Charles and I were in the later stages of our sixties, so we didn't have young children to be sharing the sights and sounds with. We stood along the walkway's railing savoring the enjoyment of others.

The fire apparatus carrying the man most youngsters had come to see turned on Center Street when it stopped. Two firefighters jumped from the rig then moved to the rear of the vehicle while yelling something to Santa's helper. At the same time, the sound of laughter from paradegoers was interspersed with the high-pitched sirens of two police vehicles. A second fire engine pulled out of the combination City Hall and Department of Public Safety, a block from the parade's starting point. Police officers on foot stopped the parade to allow the emergency vehicles to cross the line of the parade. Onlookers scampered out of the way of the emergency vehicles as they crossed Center Street then sped up East Cooper Avenue, perpendicular to the parade route.

Santa was escorted off the fire engine as his handlers commandeered a golf cart holding two colorfully attired elves. The fire apparatus then backed up to turn east on Ashley Avenue, Folly's longest street.

Charles pointed to the police and fire vehicles moving away from the center of town. "Unless they're heading to another parade, something big is going on," he said, sharing one of his rare understatements.

A second parade was a nonstarter, but evicting Santa told me the emergency vehicles weren't responding to a cat stuck in a tree. A glance to the east reinforced my suspicion. Approximately four blocks east of Center Street billowing black smoke invaded the blue sky. From our elevated vantage point, I saw reddish-orange flames under the plume of smoke.

Before I pointed it out to Charles, he grabbed my shoulder, pushed me the direction of the elevator, and said, "Let's go."

I followed without needing convincing. What did take time was the wait for the elevator. It wasn't an eternity but seemed like it before the doors opened. Sure, we could've gone down the stairs, but don't forget our age. We weren't fit enough to traipse to ground level.

Center Street was lined with people enjoying the parade oblivious to what was happening a few blocks away. We weaved through the mass of people clogging the sidewalk along Center Street so we could follow the path Santa's former ride took. The fire was at least three blocks past my cottage on the other side of Bert's Market. Two engines from nearby James Island screamed past us. A few spectators from the parade had made their way the direction we were headed. Fires trump a parade almost every time.

I couldn't see what was burning but didn't doubt it was big. A couple of two-story apartment buildings were on East Ashley. From the number of emergency vehicles plus the amount of smoke filling the sky, I'd wager one of them was the subject of so much attention. The road was blocked two streets in front of us Traffic was backed up from where it was being rerouted off Ashley. I was glad we were walking rather than stuck in the line of stopped vehicles.

We passed the first apartment building realizing the fire was in the other structure. Another fire truck pulled up behind us, siren blaring, with the added sounds of its horn attempting to get the stuck traffic to pull over so it could pass. It was having little success.

Charles tapped the handmade wooden cane he carries for no apparent reason on the pavement like it would give him extra speed. I slowed to catch my breath. The closer we got, the smell of burning wood, ashes floating in the air like leaves from a tree on a windy fall day, combined with shouts from firefighters, indicated little would be left from the burning structure still blocked from our view by two houses.

Allen Spencer, an officer with the Folly Beach Department of Public Safety I'd met when I first moved to Folly more than a decade ago, was in front of his patrol car which was diagonally parked blocking traffic. He was furiously waving his arms to get vehicles to turn off East Ashley. When I met Allen, he was new to the department, young, trim, and moved with the grace of a surfer, which he was. Since then, he'd gained thirty pounds. While still dedicated to work, he'd acquired the cynicism adopted by many law enforcement officials after years on the job. He considered me a friend, so he shared more than he would with most civilians.

We stopped beside Allen's patrol car where we got our first look at what was burning. The fire was, as I'd figured, in the two-story apartment building. The aging, wood-frame, six-unit structure was fully engulfed. Most of the roof had collapsed. Even though several hoses spewed water at the building, flames were still reaching out from the windows on two of the three first-floor apartments. The stairs to the second-floor walkway were barely attached to the building, appearing ready to collapse. It wouldn't have mattered since the walkway across the front of the building leading to the apartment doors had already fallen. Allen nodded in our direction but was too busy to tell us what he knew about the fire. We passed two Ford pickup trucks, a high-end SUV, and a Harley Davidson parked adjacent to the apartment's parking lot. Ashes rained from the sky like large, black, sinister snowflakes dotting the top of the vehicles.

Two ambulances from Charleston, seven miles from Folly, pulled up to Allen's car. He scurried to move it so the emergency vehicles could join the large gathering of first-responder vehicles. My first thought was that if anyone was in the building during the fire, ambulances would probably not be needed.

The building was a total loss, my prayer was that no residents were.

Chapter Two

Yellow police tape was strung fifty yards each direction from the burning structure. The group of bystanders, increasing by the minute, edged close to the barrier. Many of those gathered, Charles and I included, were startled when the remaining section of the roof collapsed. Smoke rolled toward us as fingers of flames darted from around the fallen roof. It may've startled us, but it didn't stop two couples from inching closer to the building, pushing the crime scene tape out of the way as they moved toward the fire.

Trula Bishop, another police officer I'd known since she moved to Folly four years ago, glared at the intruders. She yelled for them to move back as she rushed across the gravel lot to confront the tres- passers. Fortunately, they obeyed. Trula saw Charles and me standing obediently behind the tape, then snarled at the offenders before coming over to us.

"Mr. Chris, Mr. Charles, should've known you'd be here. Something bad happens, you magically appear." She shook her head.

Trula was a double minority in the Folly Beach Department of Public Safety. She was one of the few women wearing a badge and even more in the minority being African American. Like most of Folly's first responders, Trula lived off-island. I knew little about her personal life but knew she was good at her job. Over the years, she'd helped me out of a couple of scrapes I'd gotten in while, along with a few of my friends, helping bring some serious criminals to justice.

That wouldn't have been unusual if my background had been in law enforcement. It was more than unusual since my entire working career was as a human resource professional with a large healthcare company in Kentucky. The closest I'd come to law enforcement or criminals before retiring to Folly was watching TV cop shows. Some cosmic switch was thrown when I crossed the Folly River the first time. My first week here, I stumbled on a murder victim as I was photographing the iconic Morris Island Lighthouse, visible from the east end of Folly. The murderer figured I may've seen him, which I hadn't by the way. His solution for silencing me was to do it permanently. I'm still around, so he clearly failed, but not by much. Oh well, that's a story for another time. In the years since that fateful encounter, I, along with some friends, had helped the police solve a few murders, murders that had either touched me or my close acquaintances. That's how Officer Bishop and I'd become acquainted.

I ignored her comment. "Trula, we were watching the Christmas parade from the Tides when—"

"When the jolly old man was dumped off the fire engine," Charles interrupted. "Chris said we'd better get nosy. So, here we are."

Not exactly how I remembered it, but it'd be a waste of words correcting him.

I said, "Trula, what happened?"

Charles interrupted, "Think someone was roasting chestnuts on an open fire and it got out of control?"

Trula stared at him.

"You know," Charles said, "Like in 'The Christmas Song'?"

The officer shook her head then glanced at the building, or what was left of it. Flames had died down, but black smoke still filled the air. "Chris, I don't know. It was fully engulfed when we arrived. I doubt there was anything we could've done to save it."

I followed her gaze, the one she gave after ignoring Charles's question. "Anyone in there when it started?"

"Our guys got a quick look in the three apartments on the first floor before the roof started falling. They didn't see anyone. The front walkway up there was already about to fall before we could get to the second floor. I hope no one was up there. If they were, well…."

"Any idea what started it?" Charles said.

Trula shook her head. "The building's old, wood, a fire waiting to happen. With that said, it went up fast, too fast."

I said, "Arson?"

"Mr. Chris, I'm no expert, but it wouldn't surprise me. If she hasn't already, The Chief will call in the Charleston Fire Department Fire

Marshall Division. They're the experts. If it was arson, they'll figure it out. Fellas, I need to get back to playing cop."

"One more question," I said. "Do you know if any of the people standing around lived there?"

Trula looked at me with a slight smile. "Giving up your career as a private detective to become a fire investigator?"

I smiled. "Charles is the private detective. I'm the old, retired bureaucrat."

Years earlier, Charles self-proclaimed he was a private detective. He'd never studied to be a detective, nor had he ever worked under a licensed pro, a requirement in South Carolina. What he'd done, or claimed to have done, was read every novel in print featuring private detectives.

Charles beamed, apparently because I'd acknowledged his self-imposed status. Note to self, make sarcastic remarks more apparent.

Charles said, "Don't worry, Officer Bishop, I'll remain a private detective, and my friend Chris will still be old."

Trula sighed. "Over with Chief LaMond. The woman with the boy."

Charles said, "Huh?"

"Mr. Charles, pay attention," Trula said. "Chris asked if anyone hanging around lived in the building."

"The woman with the kid lived there?"

"Mr. Charles, you are a detective after all."

Trula was better at sarcasm than I.

I said, "Who are they?"

Before she answered, the steps to the second floor pulled loose and crumbled to the ground stirring a cloud of dust. The smoke that bellowed moments earlier, was barely visible. A couple of firefighters were moving into the lower apartments, or what was left of them. I doubted they'd find anything usable. One of the ambulances was turning to start its trip back to Charleston. The good news was it would be returning without anyone needing medical attention.

"Yeah, who?" Charles added as if my asking wasn't enough.

Trula grinned. "Mr. Charles, I thought you knew everyone over here."

"Only everyone with pets," he said.

That wasn't much of an exaggeration.

"The woman is Rosalynn Wheeler, goes by Rose. Her son's Luke."

The woman Trula referred to appeared in her mid-forties, about five-foot-five, average weight, with curly brown hair. Luke was nine or ten, although I'm not good at guessing ages. He was chubby and looked at the ground and not at his mother as she talked to Chief Cindy LaMond.

I'd known Chief LaMond since she arrived on Folly a year after I retired to the island. She moved up the ranks quickly, was named Chief three years ago.

"Does her name ring a bell?" Trula added.

"No," Charles said.

I shook my head.

"Wow, Mr. Charles. I know something such an outstanding private detective as yourself doesn't know."

"What would that be, Trula?"

"She's your Police Chief's sister."

Chapter Three

C indy LaMond and I'd been friends going on a decade, but I knew little about her life before she arrived on Folly. She grew up near Knoxville, Tennessee, had worked for a Sheriff's Office before coming here, yet beyond that, not much. I didn't know she had a sibling.

I said, "Sister?"

"Don't feel bad, Cindy is my boss, I've worked closely with her, almost daily, for four years. I didn't know anything about a sister until she brought her by the station two weeks ago to introduce her."

"When did she get here?" I asked.

"Miss Rose arrived a few days before the Chief introduced us."

Charles said, "What else do you know about her?"

"Next to nothing. I'd guess she's recently divorced."

Charles glanced at Cindy, her sister, and Luke, then turned to Trula. "Did she say that?"

"No. Her ring finger has a white band of flesh where a wedding ring would go."

"She have pets?" Charles asked, as only he would.

Trula grinned. "Does a son count as a pet?"

"So, no pets?" Charles said.

Trula sighed. "None I'm aware of."

The fire appeared under control. Two James Island fire vehicles weaved their way out of the lot in front of the cremated building before pulling back on Ashley Avenue. Cindy, her sister, and Luke were moving out of the trucks' way when Cindy spotted us. She rolled her eyes, put her arm around her sister, then escorted her relatives our way.

"Chief," Trula said, "I caught these vagrants hanging around. Figured they were up to no good. Want me to arrest them?"

Cindy smiled. "Good police work, Officer Bishop. Tell you what, why don't you help Officer Spencer herd that line of traffic off Ashley. I'll take care of these troublemakers."

Cindy watched Trula leave, then turned toward Charles and me. "Guys, let me introduce you to Rosalynn Wheeler and her son Luke."

Rosalynn was two inches taller than Cindy. She shared Cindy's endearing smile, when she said, "Please call me Rose. It's nice to meet you. Cindy tells me you're a couple of her friends."

I said, "I'm honored to say that's true."

"We're a couple of her favorite citizens," Charles said, not to be left out.

Cindy tapped his arm. "That's compared to criminals, slimeballs, other assorted deviants I deal with."

Time to move along. "Rosalynn, umm, Rose, Officer Bishop told us you lived there." I nodded toward the smoldering pile of wood.

"Yes, we moved here three weeks ago and found an apartment there until we decide if we want to buy or rent."

Charles asked, "Where'd you move from?"

"Morristown, Tennessee. It's a small town northeast of Knoxville."

"What brings you to Folly?" Charles asked, never fearing to tread on personal ground.

Cindy stepped between Charles and Rose. "Guys, as you can see, no one will be returning to that building anytime soon, correction, anytime at all. They'll stay with Larry and me until they make other arrangements." She pointed to a row of vehicles in the parking lot. "That's Rose's Ford Explorer blocked by our fire apparatus, so it'll probably be a couple of hours before it can leave. Got a favor to ask. Could you walk Rose and Luke to my house so they can start settling in?"

"Cindy," Rose said, "I can find my way. I don't need an escort."

"Rose, I'd feel more comfortable if you'd let them go with you."

"It's no problem," I said. "I'd be glad to walk you and Luke. Cindy, does Larry know they're coming?"

Larry and Cindy had been married eight years and lived in a house on East Indian Avenue. While only six or so blocks from here, it's not a straight shot.

"Chris, you know hubby keeps himself handcuffed to the cash register this time of year. It's his big season. He's the only person I know who gets excited about someone buying a plunger to unclog a toilet. I'll be home long before he gets there and realizes we have boarders."

In addition to being married to Cindy, Larry owns Pewter Hardware, Folly's tiny hardware store.

I turned to Rose, "Ready to go?"

"Let me grab something out of my vehicle."

I nodded.

She walked to the Explorer with Luke matching her step for step.

Cindy watched them step over the firehoses snaked across the parking area, then said, "Chris, she's ten years younger than me, so I missed out on much of her life. I was already out of the house, moved out of our tiny hometown of Kodak, Tennessee, was working at various dead-end jobs in Knoxville during her junior-high and high-school years. The main thing I know is that she's by far the smarter chick of the two of us."

"Cindy, that's going some. You're as smart as most people I know."

"Yeah, maybe, but look who you're comparing me to." She pointed to Charles.

I laughed.

Charles said, "Chief, that makes you a genius."

That got a chuckle out of Cindy before she turned serious. "Don't know all the circumstances why she surprised me by showing up. I know she's fragile. Don't think it'd take much to break her from holding it together. I'd guess the only thing holding her together now is knowing she has to for Luke."

Charles kept an eye on Rose, yet said to Cindy, "You and Larry have a big house. How come they didn't move in with you until they found somewhere to live?"

"Excellent question, Charles. I asked the same thing. She said there was no way she was going to interrupt Larry and my way of life, whatever the hell that meant. Suppose that's going to change now."

Rose and Luke returned. She carried a small box. From the logo on it, I'd guess it held a new cell phone.

I didn't have to guess, when she said, "Got a new phone yesterday. My old one does everything well except make phone calls. The guy at the store said it'd cost more to fix than to replace. Fortunately, I hadn't gotten it out of the SUV. If I had, it'd be, well, you can see what it would've been." She nodded toward the apartment.

Cindy handed Rose a key to her house, then Charles said, "Chris, go on and escort Rose and Luke. I'll stay to talk to some of the folks gawking at the smoldering rubble."

Translating Charles speak, that meant he wanted to nose into whatever happened; nose into things that were none of his business.

Chapter Four

W e were a block from the apartment building before the air stopped smelling like burning wood, but we could still hear firefighters wrapping up.

Luke kept looking back at the frightening scene, before saying, "Mom, everything we have is gone. What're we going to do?"

Rose reached for his hand. He yanked it back. I didn't know if he was being a typical nine-year-old not wanting to show affection in front of a stranger, or something deeper.

She smiled. "Luke, you're right, our stuff is gone. Tell you what, let's look at it like an adventure. We'll get new things. Everything will be okay."

I was impressed with her attitude. I hoped she was sincere, not simply putting on a positive front for Luke.

"Mom, that's the same thing you said when we left home. Maybe we should go back to Tennessee where everything was okay." His voice broke, he hesitated, then said, "We had a house, we had stuff, we had friends. Mom, we had dad."

Rose's hand shook as she put it around Luke's shoulder. This time he didn't pull away. I didn't want to intrude on their personal moment, so I took a couple of strides ahead of them, then continued to Cindy's house.

The festivities on Center Street must've ended. Several groups of people passed us going the other direction, most laughing and enjoying the day with exceptional December weather. Then I saw a familiar face.

Dude Sloan was humming "Rudolph the Red-Nosed Reindeer," while skipping, yes, skipping, down the middle of the street followed by his Australian Terrier Pluto hooked to a rhinestone-studded leash. Dude would've been hard to miss in his white T-shirt with a large DayGlo red and green peace symbol on the front. Dude, real first name James, was a longtime resident of Folly, owner of the surf shop, looked like a five-foot-seven version of a cross between Willie Nelson and Arlo Guthrie, was in his mid-sixties, and comfortable living like an aging hippie stuck in the 1960s. Pluto looked like a shorter version of Dude. I was privileged to count Dude as a friend.

"Yo, Chrisster, Merry Christmas Parade. Got new family?"

Did I fail to mention Dude's vocabulary and speech pattern are challenging to say the least? That's appropriate since Dude's specialty is saying the least.

The first spark of life I'd seen in Luke was when he left his mom's side, then bent to rub Pluto's chin.

"What's his name?" asked the young man who appeared to have gotten over worrying about his future. He'd found a new friend.

"Pluto," Dude said. "Be named for dwarf planet. You be?"

Luke stood, shook Dude's hand, and said in a full, confident voice, "Luke Wheeler, pleased to meet you, Mr. Dude."

"No mister, just Dude."

"Dude," I said, "Luke is Chief LaMond's nephew. This is Rosalynn, Luke's mom."

"Woe, Dude not great at family branches. That make you Chieftress's sis?"

"Yes. Please call me Rose."

"Your sis be great gal. Nephew Luke be polite. Rare in youngins. Be visitin'?"

Rose smiled. "No, we've moved here from Tennessee."

"Cool. Rocky Top state," Dude said as Luke turned all his attention back to Pluto. "Where be livin'?"

Rose shook her head. "We were living in the apartment building that had the fire. Now we're heading to my sister's house until we find somewhere to relocate."

"Woe," Dude said for a second time. "You be in building that be giant weenie roast? You okay?"

"We're fine. Thanks for asking."

"Pluto plus me be at holiday parade, heard sirens like there be convention of fire folks. Someone said, Ashley Avenue apartment building gone. Glad you be okey dokey."

That was a long speech for Dude, so I told him we'd better be heading to Cindy's house.

"Cool. Be needin' anything. Clothes, surfboards, pup to hug, I be at surf shop. Don't be stranger."

Rose thanked him as he continued skipping to wherever.

"Interesting man," Rose said.

That was like calling an octopus an interesting looking creature.

"Mom, do we need a surfboard?"

"Think we need to get to Aunt Cindy's first, then get some clothes, food, then—"

"Got it," Luke said as he rolled his eyes.

"Rose," I said, "were you at the apartment when the fire started?"

"No, I was in Bert's Market yesterday when someone told me about the parade. Thought it'd be fun for Luke. We were standing by Snapper Jack's watching the festivities when I heard sirens. I didn't think much of it. I figured there'd be fire engines and police cars in the parade. They use their sirens when they're in the parades I've attended. Then more sirens, so I looked down Ashley toward our apartment. That's when I saw a fire truck heading toward the building. Luke pointed out the smoke. I didn't know what was burning but could tell it was near our place. We headed home to see for sure. You know the rest."

"That had to be terrifying."

"Not nearly as bad as it would've been if we were in the apartment."

"What floor were you on?"

"First, the unit nearest the street."

"Had you lived there long enough to meet other residents?"

"Not really. The middle unit, the one next to ours, was vacant, had been for five months, I'd heard. A man lived in the far unit, but I never met him. Upstairs there were two women, or that's what the landlord said, and a young man. He introduced himself to me the day I moved in. Think his name was Ty, didn't catch his last name. Sorry, that's all I know."

"Ty Striker?"

"Could be. Who's he?"

"Works at Bert's. He's the only Ty I know. Describe him?"

"Early twenties, tall, maybe six-foot-one, thin, face not yet out of the acne years. He was friendly, smiled a lot. Sorry, I don't know anything else."

"That's okay. I was curious."

"The landlord could give you the names."

"What's his name?"

"Russell O'Leary. I can give you his number. I don't think he lives on Folly."

Luke listened to our conversation, then interrupted. "Mr. Landrum, does that Dude man surf? He looks old for a surfer."

I laughed. "He was a championship-level surfer a while back. He still goes out, mainly to help people wanting to learn."

"Think I'd like to learn. At home, guess that's our old home now, we've got this big, umm…What is it, mom?"

"Cherokee Reservoir."

"Yeah, the Reservoir. It's got a lot of water, but I don't think you can surf it. Maybe he can teach me. Mom, what do you think?"

"I think we need to get settled in your aunt's house, get new clothes, then we can think about surfing lessons. Deal?"

"If you say so." He lowered his head, not showing enthusiasm over her answer. He then raised his head. "Did you know mom is a professor?"

And I thought Charles could change subjects on the head of a pin. "I didn't know that, Luke. What does she teach?"

"English and books, umm…."

"Literature," Rose added. "Actually, I was only an associate professor at Walters State Community College in Morristown."

"How did you get there?" I asked.

"Got my master's in English from East Tennessee State University. After graduate school, I was fortunate to be offered the teaching job."

"That's where she met dad. He's a banker. They got married, had me, then didn't live happily ever after."

"Luke, I'm sure Chris doesn't want to hear all that."

The same couldn't have been said if Charles had been with us.

We'd made it to the front of Cindy's house. It was larger than the typical Folly house, was modern by island standards.

Rose patted my shoulder. "Thanks for walking us over. We could've found it on our own, but my big sis still looks after me like I'm a little kid. Suppose she always will." She glanced at Luke who was paying more attention to a couple of women walking down the street than to us. "Cindy wanted us to move in with her. I didn't want her hovering over us, big sister like, so that's why we rented. We don't have a choice now."

"Rose, I didn't mind walking with you. Sorry about the rude welcome you received. Not every newcomer's house burns."

"Thank you anyway. Could I get your number in case I think of anything else about the others in my building?"

We exchanged numbers. She thanked me again for walking her to Cindy's.

"Mom," Luke said, "can we get a dog like Mr. Dude's?"

"Maybe someday."

I left on that vague promise.

Chapter Five

After depositing Rose and Luke at Cindy's, I called the Chief to let her know her relatives were safely at her house.

"How are they?"

"A little shook, as you can imagine, but overall I think they're fine. We ran into Dude along the way. Pluto distracted Luke, which was good."

Cindy laughed. "I'd also wager Dude distracted my sister, the English professor."

"She said she taught literature, so I imagine she's familiar with the strange versions of the English language throughout history."

"She didn't study anything resembling Dudespeak."

"True. Anyway, they're safe at your place. Know what started the fire?"

"Nothing official until the experts say. I'd put money on arson."

"Why?"

"It went up too fast. The fire spread faster than normal unless it was accelerant fed."

"Any idea who may've set it?"

"Chris, give me a break. I'm standing here looking at what used to be a building. If the arsonist left a written confession, it's part of the smoldering crap."

"Do you know who besides your sister lived there?"

She gave an audible sigh. "Tell me again why I answered the damn phone."

"Cindy, you never told me the first time. I assumed it was to enjoy a conversation with one of your favorite residents."

"Yeah, but then it was you."

"Other residents?"

"Five of the units were rented. Fortunately, we haven't found any bodies. Unfortunately, none of the residents, other than Rose have come to claim their ashes. They're either still milling around the events on Center Street, are on the beach, or off-island. I don't know who they are. We're running plates on the cars in the lot. With luck, that'll give us some names."

"Rose told me she'd only met one resident. The guy in the second-floor center unit is named Ty. She didn't know his last name. The only Ty I know is Ty Striker, a young man who works at Bert's."

"Thank you, detective Chris."

"Just sharing what your sister said. What about the landlord? Rose told me his name is Russell O'Leary. She doesn't think he lives on Folly."

"One of my guys tried to rent an apartment there a year ago. The units were full at the time, but he still had O'Leary's number. I tried it, but with my luck, it's disconnected."

"You can call your house to get the number Rose has. It'd be more recent."

"Thank you again, detective Chris."

I wasn't anxious to go home, so I passed my cottage on my way to Bert's, Folly's iconic grocery that prides itself on never closing. Hurricanes are the only thing that've messed with that tradition. I cook about as often as I skydive, which is never, so having a grocery next door was one of the appealing features when I bought my retirement home. Besides never closing, Bert's carries everything from bungee cords to beer, neither of which I have a need, but between the two, I could find snacks, breakfast items high on calories, an occasional sandwich, plus numerous items to meet my unhealthy penchant for sweets.

Today, I wasn't looking for food. Ty Striker was my focus. He was behind the register waiting on a lady tugging a sad-looking beagle behind her. Ty met the description of the man Rose said lived in her building. He was about six-foot-two-inches tall, thin, in his early twenties, with a narrow face with a long nose. He looked like he could play Ichabod Crane in a prequel to "The Legend of Sleepy Hollow." His long black hair was pulled in a ponytail with a multi-colored scrunchie. A few wayward hairs sprang out the side.

He gave his customer change while wishing her a pleasant day, then noticed me standing off to the side.

"Mr. Landrum, want a dog treat?" he said with a wide smile exposing crooked front teeth.

Bert's kept a supply of treats, normally reserved for canines. For some reason, Ty offers me one most every time he sees me in the store. For the record, I've never accepted one.

"Ty, thanks for the offer, but I'll decline."

"Your loss. What brings you in? Coffee, cinnamon roll, candy bar?"

He knew me well.

"Actually, came to see you."

"That's a first. What about?"

"The fire."

Ty turned to an employee stocking a shelf behind him. "Roger, could you take over a few minutes? I need to find something for Mr. Landrum."

He did and Ty motioned me to follow him to the back of the store near the restroom.

"Mr. Landrum, since you mentioned fire, then said you came to see me, I assume you know I live, lived, in the building that went up in smoke."

"I heard someone named Ty lived there. I hoped it wasn't you, but thought I'd ask. Guess my hoping didn't make it not true."

He nodded. "I've been working since eleven this morning. I wanted to see the Christmas parade, but that wasn't to be. A fire engine and two police cars zoomed past, so I went outside where I saw smoke." He looked toward the door to the office, before whispering, "I sneaked out for fifteen minutes; ran up the street to see what was going on." He shook his head. "My building was one big bonfire. Everything in it had to be burnt to a crisp." He stopped and stared at the floor.

"I'm so sorry. What'd you do then?"

"What else could I do? I hightailed it back here. Figured I'd need every penny I could make. Mr. Landrum, I ain't got clothes other than what you see. Didn't have much furniture, but what I had is gone, gone."

"I hate to hear it."

"Got lucky though."

"How?"

"Lost."

"Lost what?"

"Lost, that's my cat. He's safe."

That led to more questions than I could ask in the limited time Ty had before he needed to get back to work.

"Ty, was Lost outside when the fire started?"

"No, was in my car. On cool days like today, I bring him to work. I leave him in the car. When I get breaks, I go out to talk to him. He doesn't get mad at me, or yell because I'm not checking someone out fast enough."

"I'm glad, umm, Lost is safe. Any idea what started the fire?"

"Not really. I was afraid to ask, but I think the building was probably a fire trap. It was old, sort of run down. The wiring wasn't too good."

"Where are you going to live now that your apartment's gone?"

"For a while, I can live in my car. I've done it before. It's not much, a twenty-year-old Miata. Heck, it's only two years younger than me. It's mighty squinchy to sleep in, but I've managed." He looked toward the front of the store. "I'd better get to work. Can't afford to lose this job since I don't have anywhere to stay that ain't on wheels."

I repeated I was sorry about his apartment.

"Don't worry, me and Lost will be okay."

Chapter Six

The phone jarred me awake. The clock revealed it was seven-fifteen but felt earlier since I had a hard time getting to sleep, having managed to drift off around three. Thoughts about the fire and how lucky the residents had been by not being home dominated those awake hours. Charles's name popped up on the screen.

"Good morning, Charles. Isn't it a little early to—"

"Why aren't you here?" he interrupted.

I wiped the sleep out of my eyes. "Where is here? Why would I be there, wherever it is?"

"The Dog. Duh."

"Now I know where, how about why?"

"Figured you'd want to know what I learned after you sashayed off with Cindy's sis and her youngin'."

After more than a decade of conversations with Charles, talks bordering on Dudespeak, the safest, possibly only response was to say, "I'm on my way."

"Thought so," Charles said before hanging up.

The Lost Dog Cafe was Folly's go-to location for three things: great breakfasts, excellent lunches, and rumors. As I've mentioned, my culinary skills coexist with nonexistent. If I want a meal that's not wrapped in aluminum foil or plastic wrap from Bert's, the Dog is my prime destination. I could almost walk to the colorful restaurant in my sleep. Today, I may be doing that since I was wiping sleep from my eyes as I headed to meet Charles. Fortunately, mild weather was hanging around. Sunday mornings were busy times for the restaurant located less than a block off Center Street. Two couples waited at the door for a table. Another couple leaned on the low railing decorated with a string of Christmas lights. I was glad Charles had commandeered a table. While it was unseasonably mild, it was too cool for dining on the two patios.

"About time you got here," said Amber Lewis, one of the restaurant's longest-term employees. She was one of the first people I met when I arrived on Folly. "Charles has been pestering me so much about when you would arrive, I thought I was going to have to go to your house to drag you out of bed."

The fifty-year-old server and I dated during my early years on Folly, then morphed into a close friendship. Along with her smile and talent for making customers feel at ease, Amber was one of the island's top sharers of rumors.

"Amber, I didn't know I was coming until Charles disturbed my sleep a half-hour ago."

"I know. He said he couldn't fathom why you weren't here when he showed up the second we opened."

Charles was at a table near the back of the restaurant watching my interaction with Amber. He glanced at his wrist where normal people wore a watch. Charles, anything but normal, didn't own one. The wrist glance was his way of saying I was late. He was wearing a navy-blue long-sleeve T-shirt with Wheaton in orange on the front.

"What took you so long?"

"Good morning, Charles. Nice day, isn't it?"

Amber delivered a steaming-hot mug of coffee before Charles could continue chiding me for being late, which, of course, I wasn't. She asked if I wanted yogurt for breakfast, her effort to get me to eat healthier. I said French toast, my effort to resist her healthy suggestion. She smiled, feigned shock at the selection I chose for breakfast ninety percent or more of the time, then left to place my order.

Charles said, "Want to know about my shirt?"

My friend had a larger selection of T-shirts than all the T-shirt stores on Folly combined. I stopped asking about them years ago. That didn't stop him from sharing more than I wanted to know.

"No."

"Wheaton College, it's in Illinois. Know what it's got?"

Don't say you weren't warned.

"No."

"One of the oldest and largest Christmas festivals in the good old US of A."

"Is that why you wanted me to meet you?"

"Nope. That was a bonus, something to brighten your holiday spirit."

Charles took a bite of bacon, one of the few bites left on his plate, reinforcing he'd been here a while, then said, "Ready for the reason I called this meeting?"

I didn't even know it was a meeting. "Absolutely."

"While you were strolling through the streets of Folly with the police chief's lovely sister and her son, I was plying my well-honed detective skills at the site of the former, six-unit apartment building."

"I'm certain the Chief was thrilled with your help."

"Sarcasm doesn't suit you this early in the day."

Neither does trivia about Wheaton College, I thought.

I shrugged. "What'd you learn?"

"That's more like it. The main thing I learned was who lived there." He took another bite, then nodded like he'd discovered Colonel Sanders's fried chicken secret ingredients.

"Plan on sharing who?"

"Sure, once I finish enjoying knowing something you don't know."

Amber arrived with my breakfast allowing Charles to enjoy his knowledge a moment longer.

I poured syrup on my French toast while Charles finished gloating and started naming the residents.

"First, Janice Raque, the lady you accused of killing the bookie."

Charles and I met Janice months earlier when she became a prime suspect in the murder of a bookie whose body Charles and I unfortunately discovered. We also managed to catch the killer letting Janice off the hook. At the time, she was married, then her husband left her for a younger woman. After the divorce, she was forced to move out of her condo, but I didn't know where she'd landed.

"How'd you learn she lived there?"

"Outstanding detective work."

I stared at him.

"Okay, I was standing behind the police line when Janice tapped me on the arm, pointed to where the second floor used to be, and said, 'Oh my God, that was my apartment."

I grinned. "Wow, that's outstanding detective work."

"Sarcasm still doesn't suit you."

I smiled. "Who else?"

"Someone else you know. Would you believe Neil Wilson?"

I'd met Neil about the same time I'd become acquainted with Janice. In fact, he was another suspect in the bookie's murder. Neil's in his late forties, a former college football player, and built like someone I wouldn't want to argue with. He split his work career between being a bouncer in a bar in downtown Charleston, and part-time cook on Folly at Cal's Country Bar and Burgers.

"Neil and Janice in the same building. Weird."

"Neil lived there long before the bookie was killed, Janice moved in because it was the only place she could afford."

"I suppose you used your outstanding detective talents to learn he lived there."

"You're catching on. In fact, I used the age-old detective technique of developing an informant."

"Which means?"

"Listen closely, you can learn something from this. Ready?"

I nodded.

"I said, 'Janice, who else lived in the building?'"

I laughed, skipped the sarcasm, and jumped right to, "Who else?"

"That's where my skills deserted me."

I shared what I'd learned from Ty. I didn't attribute my knowledge to any detective skills.

Charles said, "Then, there was one other apartment, the one on the far side of the second floor. No one I talked to knew who rented it. Janice didn't know her name, but said it was a young, black woman. Janice is nearly sixty, so to her, young could be anyone between twenty and fifty. Janice didn't know much about the mystery woman. She saw her leaving the apartment a few times. Drives a black Dodge Ram pickup truck."

"Good job, Charles."

"You being sarcastic again?"

"Not this time. That's a lot more than Cindy knew when I called to tell her Rose and Luke were at her house."

"What'd she tell you?"

"Not much. She speculated the fire started in the vacant apartment in the middle of the first floor. She was fairly certain it was arson."

"A guy with the Charleston Fire Marshall Division was pulling in as I was leaving."

"Cindy called them."

"Speaking of Cindy, tell me about her sister."

I shared some of what I'd learned about Rose during the walk to Cindy's house. Charles, being Charles, asked me approximately seven thousand questions ranging from what Rose taught, not just what classes but how many students were in each class, why she got a divorce, what her ex-husband did for a living, ending with did she and Luke have pets when they were in Tennessee.

I was never happier to see anyone more than when Amber returned to refill our mugs. She poured coffee, then said, "Guys, where're the residents of the building going to live? Christmas is around the corner. Imagine how horrible it is for them."

I knew the answer for one of the tenants, but only one.

Chapter Seven

I left Charles at the Dog where he stopped to talk with a couple waiting for a table. They had a young border collie making it impossible for Charles to pass without talking to the canine, interrogating the couple about the enthusiastic pup's name, where the couple was from, and I don't know what else, since I told him I'd see him later then left him with the couple who I suspected were there for breakfast rather than an inquisition.

It was still warm for December, so I walked to the apartment building, more accurately, to what was left of the building. The smell of burnt debris assailed my nose a block before I got to the site. Part of the rear of the building and the right side were the only remnants of the structure standing. The roof, front wall, plus most of the left side of the building had collapsed and were barely recognizable in the rubble. Puddles of water from the firefighters' efforts had settled in low-lying sections of the ruins. Few items were identifiable. When the second floor burned through, refrigerators and stoves landed close to the ones in the first-floor units. Burned wood or steel frames were all that was left of the furniture. Glassware was shattered from the heat or from falling from the second floor. One item caught my attention. Inside what had been Rose and Luke's apartment, there was a blackened Christmas tree stand. The tree I pictured decked out with lights and ornaments, had been cremated.

It was hard to comprehend how five households were turned to worthless remnants in minutes. It may've been my imagination, but I thought I smelled gasoline, possibly the accelerant used to spread the fire making it impossible to save much. It was a sad sight to see anytime, but this close to Christmas, it was heartbreaking.

I was so focused on the devastation I didn't notice a black Dodge Ram pickup parked in the far corner of the deserted lot. The windows were tinted, but from the angle of the sun, I saw the outline of someone in the driver's seat. I remembered what Janice Raque told Charles about the building's still-unnamed resident, and what Cindy had said about a Dodge Ram being in the lot during the fire.

As I moved away from the rubble, the truck's door opened. An African-American female stepped out and smiled. She was in her late twenties or early thirties, thin, roughly five-foot-three, with a short afro, and wearing a dark-gray sweatshirt and black jeans. She hesitated before taking a couple of steps in my direction.

"Hi, I'm Chris Landrum." I pointed at the pile of burnt wood. "You lived there?"

Her smile turned to a look of surprise. "How'd you know?"

"I wasn't certain, but someone told me one of the residents drove a truck like yours."

"Oh." She stepped closer and held out her hand. "I'm Noelle Ward. Lived on the second floor."

"I'm terribly sorry about your apartment."

She shook her head. "Not nearly as sorry as I am. Do you live around here?"

"Near Bert's. Live here long?"

"Year next month."

"Did you lose everything?"

She nodded. "What you see is what I have left."

"Again, I'm sorry."

She turned to stare at what was left of the building, slowly shook her head, then barely above a whisper said, "Can't say I wasn't warned."

I wasn't sure I heard her correctly. "Sorry, what?"

"It's not important. Did you hear if everyone is safe?"

Not important wasn't my impression, but I didn't push.

"Yes, no one was in the building when it started. Where were you during the fire?"

"Researching something I'm writing. I was walking along the beach, almost made it to the west end of the island. I didn't know about the fire until late yesterday when I got back. Quite a shock, but glad no one was hurt."

"What are you writing?"

She smiled. "A novel."

No one's ever said that to me. "Your first?"

"Yes."

"What's it about?"

"Really want to know?"

"Sure."

"It's a murder mystery, set on a small imaginary island in Georgia. I picture it a place like Folly. That's why I moved here. I wanted to get my toes wet living and hanging around somewhere like where my novel takes place. You a reader?"

I smiled. "Afraid not. The newspaper is the extent of my reading material. I do have a friend who claims to have read every mystery novel written since Gutenberg."

She laughed. "A man after my own heart."

The more Noelle talked about her book, the more she relaxed, the more her voice, soft-spoken until now, became filled with confidence.

"If you've been around here a year, I'm surprised you haven't met him. His name's Charles Fowler."

She leaned on her truck's fender. "Don't recall the name, but I may have seen him. I'm terrible with names. He works on Folly?"

"He's retired. Occasionally, he helps some of the restaurants clean in the busy season. He also delivers local packages for the surf shop. Delivers them on his bike."

"Sounds like Mr. Fowler could be a character in my book."

"There's no doubt he's a character. If you're still around and he's with me, I'll introduce him. What are your plans now?"

"No idea. I spent last night in my truck."

"Sorry."

She smiled. "Don't be, the space in that big ole' Dodge is larger than the apartment I lived in while attending college. I still want to live over here. It's helping with my plot. You don't know of any little apartments for rent, do you? Don't want it to be too nice. My protagonist lives in a place I describe as a dump. That's the kind of apartment I'm looking for."

"Off the top of my head, I don't. If you don't mind giving me your number, I'll let you know if I hear of something."

"I'd appreciate it."

"Will you be okay until you find a new place?"

"Yes. Got a decent day job so I can buy clothes, food, other stuff. I'll be fine."

"Where do you work?"

I realized I was sounding like Charles with all the questions.

"Ad agency in downtown Charleston."

"Then I suppose writing comes easy."

She chuckled. "Yes and no. I have a degree in English, so I know how to string words together. Trouble is I'm good at writing copy for an ad or a television commercial where the word count can often be counted on my fingers plus toes. For my novel, I'll have to fill three hundred pages with words."

I couldn't imagine even writing enough to fill the television commercial.

"Sounds like a challenge, Noelle."

"You're telling me." She laughed. "Actually, my real name's Imani Marshall. Noelle's my pen name. With my background in advertising, I assure you, fewer people would buy a book written by Imani than Noelle."

Something was bothering me, so I figured that since she was more relaxed than when she got out of the truck, I could ask. "That makes sense. Got one more question. A little while ago when we were talking about when you learned of the fire, you said something like can't say I wasn't warned. What'd you mean?"

Her pleasant expression disappeared. "It's nothing important."

I didn't believe it but didn't know her enough to push for an explanation. "Okay. I'd better let you get on your way. I've enjoyed talking to you. Again, I'm sorry about your apartment."

Her smile returned, but not with the wattage from earlier.

"You too, Mr. Landrum."

She gave me her number. I promised to let her know if I heard about an apartment for rent.

She returned to her truck, slowly pulled out of the lot, then turned toward town. I watched her go, with one large unanswered question nagging me. What did she mean when she said she'd been warned?

Chapter Eight

After talking with two people who lost near everything and were spending nights in their vehicle, I began wondering about the others. Rose and Luke had somewhere to go, but what about Neil and Janice? I called Chief LaMond on the walk home.

"This better be good. This is my day off. Lo and behold, the wonderful, thoughtful, love of my life, brilliant hubby took me to brunch at Poogan's Porch. He—"

I interrupted, "He's listening, right?"

"Duh," Cindy said, answering my question. "He said it'd be a good way for me to get out of Dodge, or Folly, so I could enjoy a peaceful Sunday meal without being distracted by some idiot determined to ruin my day. Did I mention this is my day off—like in day to not work?"

"Sweetie," I heard Larry say in the background, "you may want to let him tell you why he called."

Cindy sighed. "Okay, Mr. Pest, what did I do to deserve a call on my day off?"

I didn't want to tell her after listening to her rant, I'd almost forgotten why I called.

"Chief, a couple of things. First, I was at the site of the fire where I ran into the lady who owned the Dodge pickup that was in the lot during the fire. Did you get a chance to talk to her?"

"Mr. Nosy Citizen, I also have a couple of things. First, why in hell were you at the site of the fire? In addition to nosing in police business and bumbling around catching killers, are you adding catching arsonists to your resume?"

"Chief, of course not. I can't add that to my resume until I catch one."

Cindy made a noise reminding me of a braying horse, then said, "Larry, order me another beer. I'm going to need it. Okay, Chris, the second thing is no, I haven't talked to the owner of the Dodge. What did you learn from her?"

Regardless of how hard a time Cindy gives me, she listens to what I say. I shared my conversation with Imani enlightening Cindy about Imani's pen name. I also gave her Noelle's number in case she wanted to contact her. I didn't share Noelle's comment about being warned since I didn't know what she'd meant. Cindy asked me to repeat Imani's pen name, saying her secretary, aka Larry, was better at running a hardware store than taking notes. I repeated it then added what Noelle said about writing a murder mystery.

"Chris, if you pester me again on my day off, Noelle will have a real murder to write about."

I took the subtle hint, apologized for calling, then said I hoped she enjoyed the rest of her brunch.

"Whoa, Mr. Senior Citizen, you said there were a couple of reasons you called on, in case I haven't mentioned it, my day off. What's number two?"

Told you she listened.

"I know where Rose and Luke are staying, but I was worried about the others. Any idea what's happening to them?"

"I told all of them they could stay at your house. I warned them not to expect a bed and breakfast. A bed, maybe. Breakfast, not a chance."

"Funny. Seriously, know anything about their plans?"

"I called the Red Cross yesterday; talked with a nice man in their disaster relief and recovery program. They'll provide money for food and will put the displaced residents up for two nights in one of three Charleston hotels. I've already told Neil Wilson, Janice Raque, and Ty Striker. Rose and Luke won't need help. Now that some busybody gave me the name of the other person on my day off, I'll contact her."

"Good. While I'm thinking about it, did you ever get in touch with the building's owner?"

"That's three things," she said before hanging up.

Must be her day off.

THE NEXT MORNING, I called Burl Costello, a friend who's pastor of First Light Church, Folly's newest house of worship; or more accurately, place of worship, since most of First Light's services are held on the beach. My call wasn't related to the church, but to Hope House, a halfway house Preacher Burl started two years ago. The large house was donated by a wealthy member of First Light under the condition Burl rents its rooms to people whom he felt needed the assist to get back to being productive members of the community. I asked Burl if he could spare a few minutes. He said he could but only if I shared a cup of coffee with him. He drove a hard bargain, but I relented.

Thirty minutes later, I was standing on the porch of the large, fifty-plus-year-old, wood-frame house on East Erie Avenue. White Christmas lights were strung around the door frame, giving it a holiday feel although the house had seen better days.

"Welcome, Brother Chris," Burl said as he waved me in. "Coffee's brewing."

Burl was in his mid-fifties, no more than five-foot-five, shaped like a football sitting on a kicking tee, topped by a face covered with a milk-chocolate colored mustache and balding head.

I followed him through the long center hallway to the large country-style kitchen.

"It's good to see you again," Burl said, as he poured my coffee and refilled his mug. "I've missed you at church."

At best, I was an irregular attendee at First Light.

"Sorry," I said with little enthusiasm.

"No need to apologize to me, Brother Chris. I'm not the one keeping score."

Time to move along.

"Burl, I'm sure you heard about the apartment building fire on East Ashley."

"It would've been hard to live on Folly without hearing of the conflagration. We had a prayer yesterday and a special offering to give to the survivors most in need. Brother Bernard is taking the love offering to the fire department this morning so they can distribute it to those displaced."

Bernard Prine was one of the Hope House residents I'd known for a couple of years. He's a military veteran suffering from PTSD, more recently called PTSI, post-traumatic stress injury, to lessen the stigma associated with the word disorder. Regardless of its name, Bernard had been kicked out of several homeless shelters for fighting before Burl worked his magic, making him feel like an important part of Hope House.

"Speaking of people in need, Preacher, do you have vacancies? I know two of the residents who're sleeping in their vehicles. There are two others I don't know about."

He took a sip, shook his head, and said, "Brother Chris, I'm saddened to say all six of my rooms are occupied. Two rooms that had been vacant were filled last week. Unless something unexpected occurs, I don't know any residents who've found other accommodations."

"Sorry to hear that, Preacher."

"Sorry to have to convey that news. But, Brother Chris, you know I'm an optimist. I have faith God, possibly working in strange and mysterious ways, will look over them to provide suitable accommodations."

"Preacher, I wish I had that much faith."

Burl smiled. "Ah, Brother Chris, we talk about things like faith on Sunday mornings. Perhaps a refresher would be helpful."

I mimicked his smile. "Subtle, Preacher Burl."

His smile turned to a laugh. "That's why I get paid the big bucks, Brother Chris." He turned serious. "I will keep the displaced residents in my prayers, but if that isn't enough by itself, I will enquire with others to see if there are alternatives we currently are unaware of."

"Thank you, Preacher. And, thanks for the coffee."

"Brother Chris, my coffee pot is always available to you."

Before I reached the car, the phone rang. Cindy's name appeared on the screen.

"Good morning, Chief."

"Did I tell you yesterday was my day off? Larry took me to Poogan's Porch where I had Chicken and Waffles."

I chuckled. "I believe you mentioned it."

"It was fantastic except for an exasperating call from one of Folly's nosiest residents. Can you believe he interrupted my scrumptious brunch to ask if I'd gotten ahold of the owner of the building that disappeared the other day?"

"A Chief's work is never done."

"You can say that again. In case you're interested, the answer is not yet."

"Where is he?"

"Could be swimming in the Mediterranean Sea, skydiving over the Grand Canyon, hell, for all I know he could be floating around in the International Space Station. What I know is he's not answering the number he'd given Rose."

"So, what now?"

"I'll tell you the other bit of trivia I called for, then hang up so I can go to a budget meeting with the Mayor, a dream come true."

"The bit of trivia is?"

"The fire was arson. Don't ask, I don't know who set it."

Chapter Nine

O ne of Charles's numerous quirks was if I learned something he didn't know and didn't tell him in, oh, let's say, three flaps of a hummingbird's wing, a bucket of grief would follow. I'd exceeded that timeframe since meeting Noelle, so a call was overdue.

He was wheezing as he answered the phone.

"Where are you?" I asked.

"Jogging around the island."

I could count on fewer than one finger the number of times Charles had been jogging.

"Jogging?"

"Okay, maybe a brisk walk. Why?"

He took a brisk walk slightly more often than he jogged, but I let it go. "Where are you?"

"Getting ready to plop my rear on the picnic table at the Folly River Park."

Folly River Park is a small park bordered by the Folly River, Center Street, and East Indian Avenue. It's the site of art fairs throughout the year, but shines, figuratively and literally, during the holiday season as the location of Folly's official Christmas tree surrounded by large, colorfully lit seasonal displays.

"Plop down. I'll join you in about fifteen minutes."

Ten minutes later, I spotted him on the picnic table. He would've been hard to overlook wearing a cardinal red, long-sleeve sweatshirt with Arkansas Razorbacks and a fierce-looking hog on the front. He also wore a Tilley hat with nothing written on it, jeans, and tennis shoes that looked like they could've jogged hundreds of miles, although not on Charles's feet.

I nudged him to move over then scooted beside him on the table.

He stared at the Christmas tree, then said, "Why do bad things always happen at Christmas?"

"Bad things happen all the time. They seem worse this time of year."

"That sucks."

"Yes, but look at all the good things happening, especially during the Christmas season."

He glanced at the tree, then turned to me. "I thought I was the half-full kind of guy. You going to tell those folks who lived in the apartment building good things are happening?"

My friend had always been that half-full guy. In the last couple of years, he'd experienced some personal losses that jaded his outlook.

"Charles, I agree. Losing most everything was terrible. On the other hand, no one was injured. Cindy confirmed the fire was set which made it spread faster than would've been normal. They were lucky not to be home."

"When did the Chief tell you that?"

"Right before I called you."

I hoped that would get me off the hook, that is until I tell him about meeting the writer yesterday.

"If it was arson, why?"

I resisted the temptation to tell him to burn the building. Instead, I said, "What do you mean?"

"Whoever set it did it during the day when the odds were great its residents wouldn't be home or would've been awake enough to get out once they knew the building was ablaze. If the arsonist wanted to hurt or kill someone, wouldn't he or she have set it in the middle of the night when the intended victim was asleep?" He glanced at the tree again before turning back to me. "So, why set the fire?"

That reminded me of what Noelle shared about being warned.

"What if the arsonist wanted to scare one of the residents, not hurt him or her?"

"It would've scared the heebie-jeebies out of me if I'd seen everything I owned go up in smoke."

"Cindy also said she couldn't find the building's owner. What—"

"Whoa," he interrupted, "when did she say that?"

Don't say I didn't warn you about his quirk.

"Same time she confirmed it was arson. May I finish?"

343

He harrumphed then motioned me to continue.

I said, "What if the landlord torched his building?"

"Insurance?"

"Yes. It would've been a good time to do it when fewer tenants were at risk."

"How are we going to find out?"

"Charles, the police are looking at all possibilities. They'll figure it out."

"They can't even find the landlord. How do you think they'll prove he started the fire?"

"They'll find him. I didn't say it was the landlord, but it's my best guess."

"What about one of the tenants starting it?"

"Why?"

"Get out of paying rent. One of them may've been behind, figuring he or she wouldn't have to pay if the apartment wasn't there."

"That's a possibility," I said but thought it unlikely since they'd be homeless as a result.

A man walking a boxer passed us on the paved path through the park. Charles, who could never let a dog pass without a brief conversation, hopped off the table then knelt to say a few words to the canine. He apparently ran out of canine-Charles conversation. The man and his dog continued around the park; Charles returned to the table.

"Where were the tenants when the fire started?" he asked as he watched the dog walk away.

"Ty was at Bert's. Rose and her son were watching the parade." I took a deep breath, preparing for an explosion, and said, "Noelle was walking on the beach. We don't—"

Charles's hand flew in front of my face. "Stop! Noelle?"

"I was walking by the site of the fire yesterday afternoon and saw the pickup truck that was there during the fire. The driver was looking at the ruins. Her name is Noelle Ward, actually, her name is Imani Marshall, but she goes by Noelle."

I paused anticipating Charles interrupting.

"Well, go on," he said, hinting he's not always predictable.

I gave him a brief bio on Noelle, including why she was using a pen name. Charles interrupted me twice to make sure she didn't already have published novels. Said if she did, he would've read them. I exhausted everything I knew about Noelle, repeated it twice before Charles felt he had enough information.

"Okay," he said, "what about Neil. Where was he?"

I told him I didn't know, then gave him the same answer when he asked if I knew where Janice was during the fire.

"Wonder how we're going to find out where they were?"

"Suppose we could use one of your well-honed detective skills. We could ask them."

Charles grabbed his phone and punched in a number.

"Yo, Cal, this is Charles, yeah, Charles Fowler. What other Charles do you know? Right. Is Neil there?"

Apparently, he was talking to our friend, Cal Ballew, at his bar where Neil was a part-time cook. Charles tapped his finger on the table while Cal said something. I could tell from the intensity of his tapping it wasn't to Charles's liking.

"Okay, thanks anyway."

He returned the phone to his pocket and shook his head. "Off today. Comes in at three tomorrow. You have Neil's number?"

"Why didn't you ask that before calling Cal's?"

"Well, do you?"

I scrolled through my contacts, tapped on Neil's number, then handed the phone to Charles. He didn't have as much luck as he had with Cal. He handed the phone back to me saying there was no answer.

Charles smiled and asked if I had Janice's number. I told him no before he proclaimed the day a total failure. His half-empty mood was back.

It went more downhill after he asked where the tenants would live.

"Rose and Luke will be fine," I said. "Cindy said the Red Cross was putting the others up for a couple of nights in a Charleston hotel."

"They think the landlord will wiggle his nose and a new building will rise from the ashes before two nights in a motel are used up?"

"That's all they can do."

"What about the others?" He snapped his fingers. "Got it. They could move to Hope House?"

I readied myself for another burst of irritation, then told him about my conversation with Burl.

"Crap. Christmas is around the corner and I doubt any of them could fit in a manger, even if we could find one for rent."

I interpreted that comment to be more out of frustration than my failure to tell him about meeting Burl. He got a far-away look in his eyes, a look I'd learned over the years not to interrupt.

He snapped his fingers a second time. "Got an idea."

I waited for him to share. When he didn't, I said, "What?"

"My apartment's too small for me to live in much less adding someone else."

Charles was right. In addition to being small, he'd added book-shelves to almost every wall, filled them with enough reading material to fill a small-town library. Other than his bed, every horizontal surface was covered with books, including much of the floor.

"I agree."

He smiled. "Your house is another story. Think about that extra bedroom that's only holding a computer with a printer. Acres of empty space. There'd be plenty of room for one of the poor, sad, displaced tenants to hang his hat until better accommodations come available." He nodded. "Great idea, if I say so myself."

I'd come to the same conclusion last night but didn't know if I was ready for a housemate. I'd lived alone for thirty years. Every time I'd considered other options, like adding a spouse, I broke out in cold sweats.

"Charles, there's no bed, besides, who's to say one of them would be interested?"

"You're right. Heck, I'm sure Ty is thrilled to be living like a pretzel in his Miata. Noelle must be feeling like a queen living in her pickup. We don't know anything about Neil or Janice. Think about it. I'll see if I can twist arms to help the others out. Surely I can guilt somebody by playing the Christmas card."

"I'll think about it."

"Good, you can tell me your decision tomorrow when we go to Cal's for a burger, a drink, a powwow with Neil."

Chapter Ten

The next morning began with me heading next door to grab a cinnamon Danish and cup of complimentary coffee. It was at least ten degrees colder than the last two days, so I pulled the collar of my lightweight jacket up around my neck. Over the years, I'd been tempted to buy a heavier coat, but refused telling myself Folly Beach was in the South so I wouldn't need anything warmer. Several times over the years, I'd regretted my stubbornness. This was one of those times.

Ty's Miata was parked in the lot between my house and Bert's. I was tempted to peek in to see if his cat was there. Instead, I rushed to the warmth of the store. Ty was behind the counter where three people waited to check out. He smiled when he saw me then went back to giving a woman change. My feet automatically took me to the case where oversized gooey delights would tempt me. I put a Danish in a paper bag then proceeded to the large coffee urn and filled a cup. By the time I made it to the register, Ty's customers were gone.

"Morning, Ty," I said as I put money on the counter for the Danish.

Ty's smile widened. "Mr. Landrum, it's a wonderful day."

His attitude was better than mine would be under similar circumstances.

"You seem happy this morning. Win the lottery?"

He continued to smile. "Afraid not, Mr. Landrum. I'm thankful Lost and I wasn't hurt in the fire. Things can always be worse, be worse."

"Is Lost in your car?"

"Not today, it's too cold for the little fellow. Left him in the hotel where the good folks from Red Cross are letting me bunk."

I knew the answer, but asked anyway, "How long will you be there?"

"Tonight will be it. It was nice of them to give me two nights."

"What'll happen then?"

"Suppose I'll move back in my car. Not quite luxury digs, but beggars can't be choosers, be choosers. I think that's how the saying goes."

A woman carrying a loaf of bread appeared behind me. I stepped aside so she could pay. Ty took her money, told her to have a wonderful day, then turned to me.

"Mr. Landrum, would you let me know if you hear of any cheap apartments for rent. Lost needs a better place to live than the car."

"What about you?"

He smiled. "Wouldn't mind it myself."

"I'll keep an eye out."

"Lost would appreciate it."

At the risk of sounding like Charles, curiosity got me to ask, "How'd you come up with the name Lost?"

He smiled. "Not the first time I've heard that question. Want the long or short version?"

I looked around and didn't see anyone vying for Ty's attention. "Whichever you have time for."

"I don't suppose you know anything about me other than what you see in here."

"True."

"I moved from Baltimore a little over a year ago. I came to Folly with a couple of friends I worked with at a roofing company. Tell you something, Mr. Landrum, slapping roofs on buildings when it's ninety degrees isn't high on the list of fun jobs, but see, I sort of barely got through high school. They said I was smart enough to go to college, but since I had a better time not being in school than when I was there, I figured I wouldn't be good for college. College wouldn't be good for me. That may not have been one of my better decisions. Anyway, my buds and me were coming here to vacation, surf, drink beer, then, drink more beer. Two days before we were to go back to roofing, we came in here to buy beer." He hesitated, then smiled. "I was standing right where you are when I saw a girl working behind the deli counter. Heard her tell someone her name was Aimee." His smile widened. "Mr. Landrum, she was the cutest girl I'd ever seen. I mean ever."

By now, I assumed, hoped, this was the long version of how Lost got his name. I took a sip of coffee and was tempted to pull some of the Danish out of the bag. I didn't but waited for Ty to continue.

"The next morning, I left my roommates sleeping. I came here, asked if the manager was around. The clerk pointed me his direction, so I asked if he was hiring. Figured it would be the best way to get to know Aimee, Aimee Mason I learned. Suppose you figured out he was hiring."

I nodded.

"Aimee and me got to talking when we were on overlapping shifts, and—"

"Ty!" someone yelled from the back of the store. "Let Caroline take the register. I need your help unloading boxes."

Ty sighed. "The rest of the story will have to wait. Sorry, Mr. Landrum."

"Ty, before you go, do you have a number for your landlord?"

He pulled out his wallet, took out a folded piece of paper, and handed it to me. I unfolded the paper where I found the name Russell O'Leary plus a phone number. I put the number in my phone, returned the paper to Ty, then said we'd talk later.

Sitting at my seldom-used kitchen table, I ate the Danish while thinking about how unaffected Ty was about what was in my mind a horrible situation. I admired his outlook. I also wondered if the number he'd given me was the one the Chief had been using to reach the landlord. Today wasn't her day off, so I figured it'd be safe to call to give her the number.

"Good morning, one of my less-neurotic friends. You calling to apologize for interrupting one of my few days off?"

I smiled. "If it'll make you feel better, yes."

"Apology accepted. You going to say something now that'll need another apology?"

"Never, Chief. I was talking with Ty Striker a little while ago. He gave me a number for Russell O'Leary. I thought if it was different than the one you had; it may help you get in touch with the landlord."

She hesitated before speaking. "Just curious, why in holy hell were you asking Ty for the landlord's number? You want to rent an apartment or buy a bucket of soot?"

"Chief, you were having trouble reaching him. I wanted to help."

"Chris, don't treat me like you're talking to one of my dodo-brain officers. You're nosing in police business. Again."

Nothing would be gained by denying it. She wouldn't believe me. Neither would I. "Want the number?"

"Don't need it. I talked to O'Leary yesterday. Neil Wilson gave me a number I didn't have."

"What'd you learn from O'Leary?"

"Give me one reason I should answer that question?"

"Because—"

"Never mind. The only acceptable answer is because you'll pester me up to my eyeballs if I don't. I need that as much as I need the mayor threatening to fire me unless I start talking and acting like a police chief."

Mayor Newman had been on her case for as long as she'd been Chief. He knew she wasn't about to change, but that hadn't stopped him.

"What'd you learn from O'Leary?"

"Crap on a cucumber, Chris. Do you ever give up?"

See what the mayor meant?

I repeated, "O'Leary?"

"He swore he didn't know anything about the fire until the next day. Claims he was in Atlanta attending a seminar on buying real estate, getting filthy rich, without having to put any money down, or something like that."

"How'd he learn about the fire?"

"Claims he got back from Atlanta, drove by the building, where he perceptively noticed it was no longer there."

"Did you ask if he knew anyone who might've had reason to start the fire?"

"Gee, Chris, why didn't we professional investigators think to ask that."

Got it.

"What'd he say?"

"Claims he didn't know anyone."

"Cindy, why do I have the impression you don't believe his story?"

"What makes you say that?"

"You've used the word claims three times sharing his version."

"Damn, it's annoying you actually listen to me. Annoying and scary."

"Well?"

"I asked him the name of the seminar he allegedly attended. He couldn't remember. I asked when he got to Atlanta. He said a few days before the seminar. If I asked you that kind of question, wouldn't you name a specific day rather than 'a few days'? It's hard to judge someone's behavior over the phone, but my gut tells me he was lying about some of what he was saying."

"What next?"

"I'm going to call him later to schedule a face-to-face."

"Good luck."

"I'll need it if I want him to confess to torching his building."

Chapter Eleven

C al Ballew took ownership of the bar eight years ago after Gregory Brile, the former owner, did what many people only dream of doing. He killed an attorney. Apparently, doing rather than dreaming has serious consequences. Gregory is in prison. The name of the bar switched from GB's to Cal's. The new owner, now in his mid-seventies, had spent most of his adult life traveling around the South, living out of his car, while playing his brand of traditional country music at any venue that would have him. He was performing at GB's when the owner moved from a comfortable house to a less-comfortable prison cell. Cal reluctantly took over even though he knew as much about owning a bar as a gecko knows about playing Chinese checkers.

Because of his decades on the road with nowhere to go on Christmas, when Cal took over, he was determined to hold an annual Christmas party so others who might share experiences similar to his would feel at home; a place where they could enjoy the spirit, fellowship, and calories of the holiday. His party has grown each year. It was now one of the highlights of the year, not only for those who had nowhere to go but for many of us who loved to share the joyous event with Cal. The singer who treated his patrons to a handful of sets during the week wasn't getting wealthy with the business but squirreled away money throughout the year so his Christmas party could provide free food and drinks to all comers.

I'd told Charles I'd meet him at Cal's but hadn't set a time. I was surprised he wasn't there when I arrived so he could tell me I was late. What was there brought a smile to my face. Four, seven-foot-tall artificial Christmas trees anchored the corners of the room. Multiple strands of colorful lights were attached to each non-moving vertical surface, more dangled from the ceiling. The bar spent most of the year looking tired, to put it kindly, but perked up come December. There were a dozen tables, plus a handful of barstools in front of the wooden bar on the side of the room. A twelve-by-twenty-foot laminate dance floor abutted a small stage in front of the room. The rest of the floor was covered with fraying indoor/outdoor carpet.

Seasonal sounds of Bing Crosby's "White Christmas" were coming from the antique Wurlitzer jukebox parked on a corner of the stage. Crosby's mellow voice competed with the country voice of Cal who was standing behind the bar drying a glass with a red, white, and blue bar towel. The owner was six-foot-three, toothpick thin with a spine that curved forward from bending down to a microphone plus living out of the back seat of his car for decades. Long, gray hair poked out from around the Stetson that'd traveled with him for more than forty years. In deference to the season, a strand of battery-operated, colorful lights was strung around the hat's crown. If Santa was anorexic, didn't have a beard, didn't wear a red suit, and didn't ride around the world transported by reindeer, Cal could be his double. I suspect Cal had a better singing voice, although I'd never heard Santa sing.

"Well if it isn't one of Santa's wise men," Cal said, mixing Christmas stories. He waved his hand around the room. "What do you think of this year's decorations?"

I thought they were overboard, but the same as last year. That wouldn't have been the correct answer, so I said, "Incredible, Cal, incredible."

"So you noticed the extra lights I've strung from the ceiling?"

Not really. I repeated, "Incredible."

Cal looked to see if anyone was nearby. No one was. "Truth be told, Neil did all the light stringing. This old broken-down body and ladders don't mix."

"Cal, it doesn't matter who decorated, it looks great. Would Neil happen to be here?"

He moved his head in the direction of the small kitchen. "In back, fixin' burgers for that table of guys by the wall, the ones looking like undertakers dressed in those suits. Must be a convention at the Tides."

Gene Autry began singing one of probably a thousand performers' versions of "Jingle Bells," as Cal handed me a glass of Cabernet, one I hadn't requested. He had my number.

"Chris, know what Charles told me about that song?"

Of course, I didn't, so I shook my head before taking a sip.

"Some cat wrote it back in eighteen-hundred-something as a Thanksgiving song. Can you believe that?"

If there was some archaic bit of trivia involved, I'd believe it. I limited my response to, "Who would've guessed?"

Neil walked out of the kitchen carrying a tray holding three hamburgers, two orders of fries, with an order of onion rings vying for space.

Neil said, "Hey, Chris."

Cal pointed to the table of men who ordered the burgers. Neil took the hint and headed their way.

Cal watched him move around two other tables. "You know about the fire at Neil's place, don't you?"

I nodded.

"Of course, you do, pard. You know everything bad that happens here."

I wouldn't have put it that way.

"How's Neil taking it?"

"Not as good as he wants everyone to think. He comes across as a big ole bruiser, living up to his part-time bouncer job downtown."

Neil could play that role well. He was six-three or four, in his late forties, looks like a former football player whose muscle turned to fat after his playing days ended. I remembered him coming across the way Cal described him earlier this year when he was a suspect in the bookie's murder. In fact, it was Cal who'd told me about a temper tantrum Neil had during a confrontation with the bookie.

I said, "That's the image he portrays."

"Dig deeper, pard, you'll find a big teddy bear. The boy's torn up about the fire, not just because it left him without a bed, but he feels horrible about the others who lost everything." Cal watched Neil as he left the food at the table and headed our way. "Don't tell him I said anything, okay, pard?"

"Deal."

Neil grabbed the colorful bar towel from Cal's shoulder, wiped his hands off, then shook my hand. "Good to see you, Chris."

"You too. I was sorry to hear about your apartment. I was there when firefighters were finishing up."

A new customer arrived and took a seat at the far end of the bar. Cal left to see what the newcomer wanted.

"Everything is gone but my old jalopy, plus some clothes I had in the trunk."

"Where were you when it happened?"

"Working. With the parade going on, it was a big day here. I normally wouldn't have been here for lunch on Saturday, but Cal asked me to come in. I need all the hours I can get."

"I'm glad you weren't in your apartment. Any idea what started it?"

"I hear rumors it was arson. Got a couple of ideas, but nothing to back them up."

"What—"

Charles magically appeared behind me before I could get Neil to share his ideas.

"Hey, Neil, Chris, sorry I'm late."

"Late for what?" Neil said.

Excellent question, I thought.

"Meeting Chris. Figured I'd beat him like I always do."

"Neil," Cal said from behind the bar. "My buddy over there wants a cheeseburger. Let's don't keep him waiting."

"I'd better get cookin'," he said as he smiled at his boss.

"Did I miss anything?" Charles said as Neil headed to the kitchen.

Cal handed Charles a Budweiser, another correct assumption by the bartender. He and I headed to a vacant table. The only other customers were the man at the bar plus the three undertaker look-alikes.

Brenda Lee's version of "Rockin' Around the Christmas Tree" serenaded us as we sat and took a sip of our drinks.

"You didn't say anything to Neil about what we wanted to talk to him about, did you?"

"No," I said. "He was busy, then you interrupted us when he was getting ready to tell me about the fire."

"Good," Charles said as Brenda finished singing. He pivoted toward the bar. "Hey, Cal, old buddy. Chris here wants to talk to Neil when he gets a chance."

"No problem, pard. I'll mosey in the kitchen, tell him to drop everything he's doing. Stop fixing food. Rush out here to take a meeting with two old-timers. Will that work?"

"Good plan, Cal," Charles said, skipping over Cal's sarcasm.

Luckily, Cal laughed as he headed to the kitchen.

Cal delivered the hamburger to the customer at the bar as Neil came our way.

Neil turned a chair around, sat, then put his elbows on the back of the seat. "Cal said two old geezers want to talk to me."

Charles looked around the room, then said, "Don't see any. Since you're here, Chris said you were going to tell him something about the fire."

"I did?"

"Neil, you said you'd heard it was arson, that you had a couple of ideas about who may've started it."

Roger Miller's "King of the Road" proved Cal hadn't replaced all his classic country songs with Christmas music.

Neil looked at the jukebox then at me. "I'm being paranoid. Probably doesn't have anything to do with what I'm thinking. No need to get into it."

"Tell us anyway," Charles said. There was a zero chance he'd let Neil off that easy.

"Remember when Cal hired me?"

"Sure," I said.

"He'd heard I'd been fired from the private security job in Charleston."

Charles interrupted, "Yeah, your boss at that toy factory fired you because you were being questioned by the cops about the bookie's murder."

Neil nodded. "Doing my civic duty and that jackass kicked me out. Pissed me off."

Charles said, "So?"

Charles, let the man talk, I thought. "Neil, go on."

"I'd worked there for four years. You learn a lot about a place when you're a night watchman. Get to snoop when no one's around. Lots of hours with nothing to do. It'd be hard to find a thief who'd want to break in a kid's toy manufacturing company. Anyway, I started piecing together some papers of the owner, Paul Davidson's his name, by the way. Anyway, he was mighty careless about leaving tax papers and P&L statements on his desk. I'm no accountant, hell, I'm just a dumb country boy, but it didn't take a number cruncher to figure there was a bunch of revenue Paul wasn't reporting to the IRS."

"How'd you figure it out?" Charles asked.

Neil smiled. "Didn't have to. All I did after he fired me was make a couple of calls to the IRS office in Charleston. Guys, did you know they have a form you have to fill out to report fraud? They've got a form for everything." He shook his head. "Hell, I wasn't about to fill out a stupid form. I made the two calls, told them where and what, and if they wanted to catch a crook, they'd find him there. I wasn't going to do all the work for them."

"What happened?" Charles asked as if Neil wasn't going to tell us without being asked.

Cal hummed along with Charlie Rich's version of "Behind Closed

Doors" as Neil took a sip of beer he'd brought with him to the table. No one else had entered the bar.

"One of the guys from the factory called a couple of weeks later, told me it was good I got out when I did." Neil laughed. "He didn't know I'd been fired. Said a group of suits swarmed all over the factory hauling out computers and everything from the file cabinets. My buddy wasn't sure what happened next, but Paul spent a lot of time talking to lawyers and storming around the factory looking like his head was going to explode. Best news I got in years."

"Neil," I said, "That's interesting. Sounds like he's getting what he deserves, but how's it related to the fire?"

"Suppose I left out an important part. Last week, my buddy at the factory called bitching about the extra work Paul was laying on him. He was always bitching about something. Anyway, he heard Paul telling one of his VPs he figured out who ratted him out to the Feds. Said he was going to get even with the SOB. Fellas, I'm that SOB."

I asked, "How would he have found out it was you?"

"Don't think he could. That's why I'm being paranoid. I didn't give the IRS my name. I never said anything at work hinting at me knowing about the business end of the company. Hell, I was just a dumb old night watchman."

Two customers arrived, sat at a table on the other side of the room, placed an order with Cal, who whistled for Neil, then pointed at the kitchen.

A subtle hint, it wasn't. Neil said he'd better do what Cal wanted. He didn't want to get fired from another job.

Ernest Tubb's version of "Blue Christmas" was playing, reminding everyone that Christmas was less than two weeks away.

Chapter Twelve

Charles and I went separate ways after leaving Cal's. The temperature had become uncharacteristically warm for this time of year. Adding the bright sunshine made it feel warmer, so I walked a few short blocks to Pewter Hardware to ask Larry how his sister-in-law and nephew were adjusting to their new residence. This was the store's busiest time of year, so I wasn't surprised there were vehicles overflowing the small, crushed-shell parking lot.

The interior of the tiny store was more crowded than the lot. Three customers waited in line at the check-out counter, four were blocking the narrow aisle near the seasonal decorations, while two others were flipping through a battery display.

Larry manned the register. He wore a velvet Santa's hat, but at five-foot-one, weighing a hundred pounds after a Thanksgiving meal, he looked more like one of Santa's elves. He was self-conscious about his diminutive size, so the elf comparison was one he'd not hear from me.

I wasn't surprised by the crowd but was surprised seeing Luke beside Larry bagging purchases. Brandon, Larry's only full-time employee was helping a customer carry three sacks to the door.

The customers who'd been waiting to check out completed their purchases and headed for the exit. Larry saw me standing out of the flow of customers, smiled, then put his arms around Luke. The nine-year-old was only a half-foot shorter than Larry, another observation I'd keep to myself.

"Chris, check out my new employee."

I smiled. "Have the child-labor police been in yet?"

"Hi, Mr. Landrum," Luke said, ignoring my comment. "Uncle Larry says I'm a big help."

"You look like you're doing a great job. You need to ask your uncle for a raise."

Luke chuckled. "Uncle Larry says I'm earning my rent, but I can leave whenever I want."

I started to comment when someone tapped my shoulder. I turned to see Rose standing behind me wearing an orange Pewter Hardware sweatshirt.

"Don't tell me Larry's put both of you to work."

"He's not that cruel. As you know, I'm short on clothes so Larry contributed this to the cause. Cindy and I are going to the mall tomorrow to rectify the situation."

"Rose," Larry said, "why don't you get some fresh air. Luke and I can hold down the fort."

She nodded then turned to me. "Up for a walk?"

"I can cram one in my schedule."

"Mom, don't worry about me. Uncle Larry needs me here."

Another customer was ready to check out, so Rose and I left the store in the good hands of Larry, Luke, and, I suppose, Brandon.

"Which way?" Rose asked as we walked a block to Center Street.

"Have you been on the Folly Pier?"

"Luke and I started there once, but it was so cold we turned around. Today's nicer, I'm up for it if you are."

We walked six blocks to where Center Street dead-ends at the entrance to the Tides Hotel. Our walk was mostly silent, with Rose's only comments being about the illuminated sand dollar, dolphin, crab, and turtle decorations adorning light poles along the way. The Folly Beach Fishing Pier was adjacent to the Tides, so we turned at the hotel, before making our way up the long flight of steps to the pier's deck where a group of women were leaning against the railing watching the surf roll in. A middle-aged man was photographing two children sitting in a red chair big enough to hold someone the size of the Goodyear blimp.

"It's a lot warmer than the last time we were here. This is a great view of the beach."

I pointed to the far end of the thousand-foot-long structure. "It's even a better view from out there."

"What are we waiting for?" Rose said as she put her arm through mine and escorted me to the end of the pier.

When we reached the Atlantic end of the pier, we sat on a wooden picnic table and faced the shore. Rose was silent for a long time, before saying, "It's weird living in the house with Cindy."

"Were you close?"

I asked since Cindy had never mentioned a sister.

"Not really. With ten years between us, we had little in common. We have different fathers, you know."

"I didn't know. Cindy and I are good friends, but she seldom says anything about her life before moving to Folly."

Rose smiled. "That's no surprise. She's self-contained, irritatingly so at times."

I nodded.

"Her dad, Kenneth, was a coal miner near Evarts. That's in Harlan County, Eastern Kentucky. He'd dropped out of high school to work in the mines. Two years later, he married our mom, Ruth, then three years after that, Cindy came along."

"I thought she grew up in East Tennessee."

"Her dad didn't have much formal education, but was smart, or so mom said. She told me he realized if he kept working in the mines, his back would die before he did. He quit when Cindy was three. He'd heard about work in Tennessee from a friend who'd moved there a couple of years earlier. It was with the Sevier County Sheriff's Office. He packed up his family and moved to Kodak."

"Where you were born?"

She looked at the ocean for the longest time. I wasn't sure if she'd heard me. Finally, she said, "Three days shy of Kenneth's first anniversary with the Sheriff's Office, he pulled a man over for speeding. Nothing out of the ordinary. Nothing unusual until the man, later determined to be high on drugs, pulled a gun and shot Kenneth three times. He never had a chance. Cindy was four."

"That's horrible," I said, wondering if that's why Cindy seldom mentions her past.

"It got worse for Cindy. Five years later, Mom married a man named Boyd. He was a traveling shoe salesman, sold to small-town retail stores throughout the region. Mom was pregnant with me when they got married." She chuckled without a hint of humor then stared at the water. "Boyd told mom he could put up with one kid but not two. He left town, never to be heard from again." Cindy was Luke's age when I was born." She turned to me and smiled. "Cindy would kill me if she knew I was telling you."

"She won't hear it from me."

"Good. Not many years after that, Cindy graduated from high school. She had little interest in studying, but to keep mom happy, she moved in a dorm at the University of Tennessee, attended school off and on for three years before quitting. Instead of moving back to Kodak, she stayed in Knoxville. For eight years she bounced around dead-end jobs. She waited tables, tended bar, even sold encyclopedias door-to-door."

"She said she worked in law enforcement before moving here."

"She joined the same sheriff's office her dad was a member of. She never told me this, it's only amateur psychoanalyzing, but I think it was so her dad would've been proud of her following in his footsteps." She sighed. "Sure you won't tell her I told you?"

"You have my word."

She nodded. "Cindy said you were a pain in the ass but could be trusted. Otherwise, I wouldn't have said anything."

I laughed.

"While I'm spilling secrets, there's something else. I haven't told Cindy because I know her well enough to know if I did, she'd go all cop and blow it out of proportion."

"I can see that."

"The day before the apartment fire, my ex called. He was at the Crab Shack, wanted me to meet him."

"What'd you say?"

"Chris, I was shocked. I hadn't heard from him since I moved. He wanted to meet me without Luke. Probably shouldn't have, but I went. Told Luke I had to walk up the street for a few minutes and left him in the apartment. I felt bad about leaving him, but he was watching a monster movie and seemed okay." She turned to watch a large container ship lumber toward the entrance to the Charleston harbor.

I waited for her to continue.

"Lawrence, my ex, was sitting at a table acting smug. It's one of his more-practiced looks. He's a vice president at a Morristown bank, a job he got because his father is on the board. To put it mildly, I didn't greet him with open arms."

"What'd he want?"

"Us to come home—home to Morristown. Can you believe that? Mr. Hot Shot Bank Official got caught having an affair with a twenty-five-year-old teller at another bank. Now I'm supposed to come running back after the chickadee dumped him."

"What'd you tell him?"

She surprised me with a laugh. "With two college degrees in English, I'd learned several ways to tell him to go, umm, have inter-course with himself. I used all of them, then cracked open a peanut and threw the shell at him."

I struggled to hold back a laugh, then said, "How'd he respond?"

"It wasn't the reaction he'd expected. His face turned red, his hands gripped his drink so hard, I was afraid he'd break the glass. He dropped a twenty on the table, stared at me, and whispered, "You'll regret it.""

"Think he started the fire?"

She shook her head. "No. That's why I haven't told Cindy."

"What makes you think he didn't?"

"Oh, I wouldn't have put it past him if it were only me. There's no way he would've endangered Luke, even if there was a minuscule chance his son would've been in the apartment. No way."

It may've been my imagination, but the wind picked up and my skin felt like the temperature dropped twenty degrees. I wish I had her confidence.

Chapter Thirteen

After walking Rose to Larry's store, my growling stomach reminded me I'd skipped two meals, a rare event. Instead of heading home, I stopped at Snapper Jack's, a large, multi-level restaurant on the corner of Ashley Avenue and Center Street. The restaurant is easy to give directions to since it faces the island's only traffic light. A college-age hostess in an aqua Snapper Jack's T-shirt escorted me to a table by a large window overlooking Center Street. In-season it would've been nearly impossible to get a table so quickly.

A server greeted me with a smile, a menu, an introduction, her name is Marcia and an inquiry about my drink choice. She headed to the bar once I said a glass of Cabernet. Since the restaurant had few customers, Marcia had my drink on the table before I could study the menu. She asked if I was ready to order. I begged for additional time, to which she said she'd be near the bar, for me to wave when I was ready.

Instead of studying the menu, I replayed what Rose shared about Cindy's background plus her revelation about her ex-husband's visit. I understood why she was confident he didn't set the fire, but I wasn't as understanding. It struck me as more than a coincidence he was on Folly fewer than twenty-four hours before the fire. Did he return to Tennessee after their meeting or stay in the area?

How could I find out? On a couple of instances when I wanted to know where someone had been staying, Chief LaMond provided invaluable assistance. Her title and charm were more than enough to get hotel desk clerks to check guest registers to see if the people she asked about had stayed in their facility. I'd told Rose I wouldn't share what she'd said with her sister, so asking Cindy was off the table. I knew an employee at the Tides who might be able to remember Rose's ex staying there, but it'd be a long shot.

I nearly dropped my drink, when someone said, "Thought that was you."

I turned to see Janice Raque standing by the table. "Oh, hi, Janice."

Janice is in her late fifties, five-foot-four, with short brown hair with patches of gray sneaking in. She wore an oversized, navy-blue sweat-shirt, and black slacks. She also had a bottle of Lagunitas IPA in her hand.

"You're, umm, now don't tell me, you're Chris, right?" She swung the bottle in rhythm with her words.

"Good memory."

"Remember talking to you a couple of times in Hal's, umm, Cal's."

Janice had been a regular in Cal's when she was married. According to Cal, she and her husband often got in arguments until one of them stormed out.

She looked at the bar-height stool on the other side of the table. I took the hint.

"I'm having an early supper. Want to join me?"

"Supper from a wineglass?" She chuckled. "This is my supper." She held up the beer bottle.

Instead of answering my question, she pulled out the stool.

I handed her the menu. "I was getting ready to order. Want some-thing to eat?"

"This is my third, maybe fourth beer. Suppose I'd better eat some-thing to sop the hops." She laughed.

I began wondering if she'd underestimated the number of beers she'd consumed for supper. I motioned for Marcia. I ordered fish and chips and asked Janice if she knew what she wanted. She ordered a Folly salad. I wasn't sure what it was since I eat salad as often as I eat chocolate-covered oyster shells. Marcia asked if we needed more drinks. I hadn't finished my wine, so I declined. Janice didn't decline. I doubted a Folly salad would sop up enough hops to prevent Janice from falling off the stool.

After Marcia left, I said, "Janice, didn't you live in the apartment building that burned?"

"Damn, Chris, has a secret ever escaped from this island without being caught by a gaggle of people?"

"Someone was talking about the people displaced by the fire. Your name was mentioned. I remembered you from Cal's."

I left out the part about remembering her because she'd been a murder suspect.

"Yes, I'm one of the unlucky people who're now homeless."

"Found somewhere to stay?"

"Why? Want me to shack up with you?"

She definitely underestimated the number of beers she'd consumed. I smiled. "Afraid I don't have room."

"Well crapola."

I was saved when Marcia deposited Janice's beer, then said our food would be out shortly. Janice had the new bottle to her lips before Marcia reached the kitchen. Now to move past Janice's comment about moving in.

"I was asking because I heard the Red Cross provided housing for the fire victims."

She held up two fingers. "Two nights, period. Did they think the apartment building would be rebuilt in two days?"

"Sorry."

"Oh well, that's water under the dam, or over the bridge, or, crap, whatever the saying is. I'm at the Holliday Inn a couple of weeks until I figure something out."

The Holliday Inn, not to be confused with the national hotel chain spelled with one "l," is a fourteen room, locally-owned hotel that's been around since the late 1940s. It's a block from the ocean, has reasonably priced rooms, and is one of only two hotels on the island.

"It's good you have somewhere to go."

"I suppose. Some are living in their cars."

"Did you know many of the others?"

"Not really. I've been there a little over a year. Ever since, umm, never mind. Anyway, I know Neil pretty well. Nice guy. He's been there as long as I have. I only know him from Cal's. He cooks there, you know. Seldom saw him around the apartment." She took another sip. "The young guy, the one with the red sports car, don't know his name for certain. Something like Sly."

"Ty," I interrupted.

"Okay, Ty. Anyway, that's all I know about him. Oh wait, he's got a cat."

"Lost," I said.

"Lost what?"

"His cat's named Lost."

"Damned stupid name for a cat."

I didn't disagree. "What about the African-American lady?"

Janice shook her head. "All I know is she nearly ran me down with her big-ass truck."

"What happened?"

"I got food at Bert's and was carrying it home. I got to our parking area when she whipped out of the lot, not looking where she was going. I was lucky or I wouldn't be here."

"Did she see you?"

"Said she didn't. She stopped, lowered her window, said she was sorry. It's no wonder she almost got me. It was dark, yet she had on these big sunglasses. Did she think she was a celebrity? Anyway, now you know all I know about her."

"What about the lady who moved in recently, the one with the young son?"

"She lived right under me. The kid kept the TV on loud. Thought about complaining. Knew it wouldn't do any good since the building was built cheap. Doubt there was a speck of insulation in it. Everyone could hear everything going on." Our meals arrived. Janice took a bite of salad, another sip of beer, then said, "That building was a fire waiting to happen. The damned landlord didn't fix anything. My bathroom sink leaked from the day I moved in. Suppose it don't leak no more." She laughed and took another drink. "Know what O'Leary, he's the landlord, was good at?"

"What?"

"Collecting rent. I could set my watch by the time he came knocking on the door the first of the month. I spilled the beans to everyone who asked me about renting there."

"Did many people ask?"

"A couple. The apartment on the first floor was vacant several months, so occasionally someone would see me outside and ask. Some guy, looked like a street person to me, asked. Told me he was Jeff, maybe Jerome. Anyway, he was looking for an apartment." She chuckled, took another sip of beer, then said, "Told him the apartment was fine unless the second floor fell on him. Chris, didn't know I was psychic, did you?"

I shook my head.

"Good ole Jeff or Jerome stopped asking me anything after that. Then one time I was telling a woman named Kinsey or Kaycee exactly what I thought. She thanked me."

"Where'd you meet her?"

"Opening my door, in fact, she followed me upstairs. She told me she owned a couple of rental units and had someone looking for a place to rent, but hers were full. She was a fast talker; said a bunch of other stuff I can't remember now. I gave her the full load about how O'Leary doesn't take care of my place. She turned and left, not as fast as Jeff or Jerome, but close. She said something about— Whoops!" Janice slipped off the chair. I grabbed her before she hit the floor.

"You okay?" I said, knowing she wasn't.

She giggled, then finished her beer. "Sure I can't shack up with you?"

"Afraid not," I said and became fascinated with my fish and chips, rather than looking her in the eye.

Marcia returned to ask if the food was okay and if we wanted something else to drink. I said I was fine. Fortunately, Janice said the same—for now.

"Janice, have any idea who may've started the fire?"

She took another sip, played with her napkin, while she looked out the window, then back to me. "Absolutely."

Not the answer I expected.

"Who?"

"My ex."

"Horace?"

"Absolutely."

"Why think it was him?"

"Don't think, know it was."

"How do you know?"

"You know he left me for a floozie in Mt. Pleasant."

"I'd heard you got a divorce. Didn't know the details."

"Left me with nothing except his dirty underwear. I had to move out of our nice condo in Mariner's Cay. I couldn't afford a two-bit ambulance-chasing lawyer to go after Horace for my share of what he had. Finally found one who'd do it on contingency." She chuckled. "He must've graduated last in his class. The poor fella was desperate to get a client. I told him Horace weren't no millionaire, but the shyster said he'd take the case anyway."

Interesting, I thought, but it didn't get me any closer to the reason Horace would've set the fire.

"Janice, why would Horace torch the building?"

"My attorney might not know how to get good-paying clients or have a fancy-schmancy office in downtown Charleston, but I'll tell you what he's good at. He's about driven Horace bananas harassing him for money, telling Horace's employer how much of a deadbeat his employee is."

I'll give it one more chance.

"Janice, why do you think Horace burned the building?"

"Chris, I don't know how many ways I can say it. It's as clear as day. Can't you see, he's pissed at me. Wants me to know it. Clear as day." She nodded like it was, well, clear as day, then took another drink.

It may be clear to her, although, in her current condition, I doubted anything was clear. I hadn't had four, maybe five, maybe no telling how many beers, but nothing she'd said led me to believe Horace had set the fire. Could he have? I suppose. Someone set it.

I made a couple more efforts to see if Janice could clarify how she "knew" her ex started the fire. I would've been more successful if I'd asked her to conjugate the verb imbibe in Hungarian. Then, I asked if she wanted me to walk her to her hotel. She declined and said she was moving to the bar and having one more for the road. Fortunately, her hotel was close, and she wouldn't be driving. As I walked away, she slurred one more effort to ask if she could shack up with me. I hoped she took my ignoring the question as no.

Chapter Fourteen

I had trouble sleeping; must've gone over today's conversations with the two fire victims a dozen times. Rose was certain her ex wouldn't have set the fire, but it still struck me as too great a coincidence that he was on Folly the day before the conflagration. He'd be near or at the top of my list of potential arsonists. On the other hand, Janice was certain her ex set it but provided nothing supporting her proclamation.

I attributed most of my sleeping problems to questions bouncing around in my head. It wasn't necessarily the questions that kept me awake, the lack of answers was my nemesis. Tonight, now this morning was the perfect example.

After three hours sleep, I decided a brisk walk in brisk weather to the Lost Dog Cafe would be good for my health. It would wake me up, provide me with a hearty breakfast, and allow my brain to find answers to the questions that'd kept me awake. Rationalizing was one of my strengths.

The restaurant was nearly full, so I was lucky to get one of the small tables against the front wall. I was even luckier when Amber appeared, set a mug of coffee in front of me, then asked what she could do to make my day better. I told her if she joined me at the table, it would make my day better. She laughed and said she'd have to improve my day by serving, not joining me. I said I'd take what I could get. She must've been in a good mood because she asked if I wanted French toast rather than trying to get me to eat healthier. I said yes, she said she wondered why she wasted time asking.

Before breakfast arrived, Cindy LaMond arrived, saw me, then headed my direction.

"Going to invite me to join you?" she said, as she pulled up a chair, not waiting on an answer.

I said, "You're always welcome to join me, Chief."

"Weren't you getting ready to ask if you could buy me breakfast?"

"Of course, I was," I said, not seeing a wise alternative.

Amber was quick to the table with coffee for Cindy, who smiled at the server, and said, "I'll have what he's having."

Amber returned the smile, and said, "How do you know——"

"French toast?"

Amber chuckled then headed to put in Cindy's order.

Cindy blew across the mug then cautiously took a sip, before saying, "I hear you sauntered to the end of the pier with my younger sister while she deserted her poor son stuck doing manual labor for a slave driver at a local hardware store."

"It's no wonder why you're Chief. You know everything that happens on your six-mile-long, half-mile-wide slice of earth."

"It helps that my confidential informant is a lad of nine who spent two hours last night gushing about how much fun he had at his uncle's store, while his mother gushed, not for two hours, but nevertheless gushed about how great it was talking to an adult without her son hearing every word. The only thing I disagreed with was her calling you an adult. I let her stay in her fantasy world and didn't tell her about the true you."

"Kind of you."

"She was too happy for me to ruin her mood. I wish she could be that happy all the time. Since the divorce, she's been having migraines, bouts of depression, and in general, miserable."

"She was in a good mood yesterday."

"She's coming out of it some. I'm afraid her moods are affecting Luke. Rose tries to shield him from everything bad, but he's perceptive."

"It's been rough on her, plus the fire didn't help. Time will take care of many of the bad moods."

"I hope you're right Psychiatrist Chris." Cindy took another sip as Amber arrived with our matching breakfasts.

We each focused for a moment on food, before I said, "Learn anything new about the fire?"

"Like who set it?"

"That'd be informative."

She rolled her eyes. "If only that easy. I did learn something interesting about the landlord, Russell O'Leary." She took another bite.

I waited for her to continue, hoping I wouldn't have to ask what. I was pleased she was more open to talking about it than she'd been when she accused me of butting into her business the first time I asked about O'Leary.

She finally continued, "Don't you want to know what?"

"Chief, what'd you learn?"

"That's better. For starters, Mr. O'Leary is three months behind on the building's mortgage."

"Was it well-insured?"

"Excellent question, motive-detector Chris. Mr. O'Leary is not only a landlord, he's psychic. Two months ago, he increased coverage on the building."

"Making him a candidate for arsonist of the year."

"If you weren't so old, so very very old, I'd put you on the force."

She could've left out the *very very* part, but I'll let it go. "What else?"

"What else what?"

"When you mentioned he was three months behind on his mortgage, you said, 'For starters,' so what else did you learn?"

"Chris, I wish you'd stop listening to everything I say."

I shrugged.

She took a bite of French toast, then a sip of coffee before continuing, "Remember I told you he said he was in Atlanta at some get-rich seminar the day of the fire?"

"I remember. Did you already forget I listen to everything you say?"

"Smartass."

I smiled.

"He said the seminar was at the Westin Peachtree Plaza in downtown Atlanta. Said he didn't stay there because it cost too much. He claimed to have stayed at a nearby cheaper hotel he—surprise, surprise—can't remember the name of. Before you ask, he said he paid cash so there wouldn't be a record of him staying there even if he could remember the name."

"He would've registered under his name; probably showed ID even if he paid cash."

"Probably, but know how many hotels there are in Atlanta? Besides, his entire story sounds off."

"Sounds fishy, doesn't it?"

"Ya think?"

"I do. Now what?"

"I finish my breakfast, cuss myself all the way back to the office for eating more calories than the total one-day consumption of everyone combined in a small, farming community in Tanzania, then close my office door so I can take a nap."

"I was thinking more about what you're going to do about Russell O'Leary."

"Hell if I know."

"Sounds like a plan."

Chapter Fifteen

W hile Cindy and I didn't solve who set the fire, or for that matter, didn't solve anything other than hunger, she said her plan was to learn more about Russell O'Leary's financial situation. I said my plan was to take a nap. She told me she was jealous.

Charles was parked on my front step when I got home. His 1961 Schwinn bicycle leaned against my screened-in porch. He wore a royal blue and white sweatshirt with Sierra Nevada College under the outline of an eagle on the front, his Tilley, and in a touch of irony, tan khaki work pants, an activity he hadn't participated in for decades.

"You're not home," he said as he pointed over his shoulder at the door.

"Am now. Did you run out of places to hang out?"

"Thought if we're going to catch whoever torched the building, we should talk."

"Who said we were going to catch the arsonist?"

"Me. Didn't you hear me?"

Arguing with Charles is like arguing with a clump of seaweed.

"Want to come in where we can talk in a warm room?"

"Why do you think I'm here?"

I started to open the door, when Charles grabbed my arm, tilted his head toward Bert's Market.

"Isn't that Ty?"

The young man was standing at the corner of the building talking to a man I knew to be homeless. "Yes."

Charles pulled me toward the store. "Look, he wants to talk to us."

I wasn't certain how Ty's talking to a homeless man meant he wanted to talk to us, but I was interested in asking if he'd heard anything new about the fire.

Ty saw us coming, told the man he had to go, then greeted Charles and me with a smile.

"Hey, Charles, you're big into animals. Want to meet Lost?"

"You bet."

Ty grinned like he was going to show Charles the Hope diamond. The Miata was tucked in the back of the small, sandy lot. The car was parked next to a dilapidated sailboat that looked like it hadn't been in the water since the flood that took Noah and his boat for a ride.

The feline's proud papa unlocked the passenger door. It opened to the scraping sound of metal against metal, followed by a meow loud enough to have come from a wildcat. The grey kitten he lifted out of the car didn't look like it could've made such a loud noise, but it was the vehicle's only occupant.

"Meet Lost," Ty said as he handed Charles the kitten.

"Wow," Charles said, "a polydactyl."

That sounded like some sort of a dinosaur.

I said, "A what?"

Charles shook his head like he was having to teach a robin how to catch worms.

"Chris, you never cease to amaze me." He pointed Lost at me then lifted the kitten's leg in my direction. "Polydactyl. A furry little critter with six toes on one or more of its paws. See?"

The front right paw did have six toes. "Oh," I said, indicating I didn't have a future as a veterinarian.

"Ernest Hemingway became a big fan after someone gave him a white one. He named it Snow White. Today there are about fifty descendants of his cats at his former house in Key West."

"Half are polydactyl," Ty added, further reinforcing my ignorance.

Charles had run out of trivia, so he turned to Ty and asked how he got Lost, more importantly, how he'd come up with the name.

Ty proceeded to share the same story he'd told me about coming to Folly on vacation, seeing a girl named Aimee, staying here while his friends returned to Baltimore, getting the job at Bert's. That was as far as he got when he was telling me the first time he'd talked about her, so I began paying closer attention.

Charles suggested we move out of the shadows of the large trees on two sides of the lot and move to where the sun was peeking through so we could stay warm. Ty and I followed him to the side of the dumpster where Charles leaned on the large, industrial-sized waste container, petting Lost the entire time.

"After Aimee and I talked a few times, I wanted to give her something. You know, something to bond our love."

Charles said, "Love?"

Ty lowered his head. "Well, not love exactly. I liked her. A guy I met in the store told me he had three kittens he was trying to find homes. I went to see them. Lo and behold, this little one was the cutest. Just seeing it made me think of Aimee. How could I not take it? Gave it to Aimee a few days later." He stopped, shook his head, then continued, "Fellas, how could I know she was allergic to cats?"

"That's too bad," Charles said.

"That wasn't the baddest part," Ty said. "She was engaged. She didn't have a diamond ring on her finger, so how was I to know?"

Charles repeated, "That's too bad."

"You can say that again. I figured I could overcome the fiancée, but not the cat allergy. That's how I ended up with this little one. Also, how it got its name. I got the cat, lost the girl, so I named it Lost."

Charles said, "Sounds like the right name."

I thought it would've been a much shorter story if he'd named it Six Toes.

I realized we'd been standing outside for a fairly long time. So, I said, "Ty, are we keeping you from work?"

"No, I'm off. I worked most of the night. Going to head to the Walmart parking lot so I can curl up in the car to get some sleep."

Charles handed Lost back to Ty, then said, "Before you go, have any idea who burned your building?"

Unlike many people who talk to Charles, Ty didn't appear thrown by the change of directions

"Wish I knew. If I did, I'd make him sleep in my car a few nights. That's punishment for putting all of us out of our homes."

Charles nodded. "So, no idea?"

"Not for certain, but if I was a betting man, I'd put a few bucks on Nick Matthews."

"Who's he?" I asked.

"Aimee's fiancée."

Charles said, "Why him?"

Lost began meowing so Ty put him back in the car, said he'd be with him in a minute, then scraped his feet on the sandy parking lot surface. "Well, you know how I said I figured I could overcome the fiancée but not Aimee's allergy?"

Charles nodded.

"Well, I didn't give up easily. I think Aimee told Nick how I was showing interest. I heard he had a temper, beat up another guy who'd been sniffing around his gal. Now, he never said anything to me at first, but I saw him in the store a few times after Aimee quit to take a waitressing job at Planet Follywood. He gave me the evil eye. The last time I saw him, he walked close to where I was stocking the bread shelf, and said something like, "You'll get yours.""

Charles said, "You think he torched your building because of that comment?"

"Like I said, I'd put money on it, on it. Not a lot, though."

Ty yawned and Lost made a moaning sound from the car. I figured our conversation was over. I thanked him for telling us about Lost.

Chapter Sixteen

Charles had to deliver a wetsuit from the surf shop to a man from Seattle renting a house on West Ashley Avenue. We walked to my house where he straddled his bike, pedaled off, leaving me standing in the yard realizing I had nowhere to be, nor anything to do. After spending what seemed like a zillion years experiencing the daily grind working in a large healthcare company, it was a good feeling. Something else that made me feel good was spending time with Barbara Deanelli, owner of Barb's Books, a small, used bookstore on Center Street. We've dated for a couple of years. I hadn't seen her in more than a week, so it was time to rectify that situation. While Charles was delivering a wetsuit, I could get some much-needed exercise walking to her store. The bookstore was housed in the same space that had previously been Landrum Gallery, a photo gallery I'd owned until it became clear that losing thousands of dollars a year wasn't the wisest use of my limited retirement savings. Residents and vacationers could live without my photographic prints, so I swallowed my pride and closed the business.

Two customers were browsing rows of books as I entered. Barb had strung multi-colored Christmas lights across the top of the shelves facing the entry. On a small table at the front of one of the aisles, she'd arranged books with colorful dust jackets in a shape intended to resemble a Christmas tree. Three boxes the size that'd hold jewelry were wrapped and set beside the book tree. It looked more like a pyramid-shaped pile of books than a Christmas tree, but I'd keep that observation to myself. The store's decorations fell far short of Cal's display, but the overall impression should put visitors in the spirit of the season.

One of the customers moved to the counter and handed Barb a credit card. Barb was in her mid-sixties, looked younger, stood my height at five-foot-ten, but much thinner. She had short black hair, hazel eyes, and a captivating smile currently being used on her customer.

She didn't notice me standing in the entry until she'd finished bagging the purchase. She used another of her captivating smiles on me. The remaining customer was still flipping through books, so Barb came around to me, gave me a kiss on the cheek, pointed to the door leading to the small office in the back of the store, then asked if I wanted coffee. I nodded. She said for me to fix each of us one, that she'd join me once the customer leaves.

When I'd had a business in the space, the room she called her office served more as a hangout for my friends, where a few of us could goof off, sip on a beverage, and discuss the latest happenings on the island. In other words, share gossip and good company. Barb had transformed the space to look more like a law office rather than a backroom in a retail business. She'd been a successful attorney in Pennsylvania before moving to Folly, so the law office motif was understandable.

I brewed two mugs of coffee in the Keurig, then settled in a comfortable chrome and black leather chair to wait. I began thinking of what Ty shared about who he thought started the fire. I didn't know anything about Aimee's fiancée other than what Ty had said, so I had no way of knowing if he was capable of such a drastic move to, umm, to what? Was the fire intended to harm Ty? If so, wouldn't the boyfriend have been able to see if Ty was working when he started it? If he only wanted to scare Ty away from Aimee, was he evil or reckless enough to burn a building, possibly harming other residents? Did Nick even make the comment Ty thought he'd made, or was Ty's imagination or guilt over trying to steal Nick's fiancée working overtime?

"Chris, are you asleep, or is your head somewhere else?" Barb said.

She was reaching for the coffee.

"Sorry, guess I was daydreaming."

Seasonal sounds from the Trans-Siberian Orchestra flowed from a Bose sound system on the desk.

"Were visions of sugar plums dancing in your head?" she asked, as she rolled her desk chair closer to the door so she could see if anyone entered the store.

I didn't know what a sugar plum was but didn't share my ignorance. "Nothing that jolly. How's business?"

"Excellent. I'm surprised. There aren't many vacationers this time of year, but the locals have been fantastic. Seems there's an uptick in book sales, not only here, but in stores everywhere."

That wasn't something I ever said about photographs when I had the gallery.

"Fantastic. Thought I'd stop to see if you wanted to grab supper this evening."

She smiled. "Thought you'd never ask."

We set a time and location, then she said, "I suppose you heard about the fire out past your house."

"Charles and I walked out there while they were fighting it."

"You chose a fire over the Christmas Parade. I'm shocked." She laughed, then added, "Not."

"We figured it was big when we saw Santa kicked off the fire engine."

"Did you know any of the residents?"

"I knew three before the fire. Didn't know them well but had talked with each a few times."

Barb's eyes narrowed as she stared at me. "Three before the fire. Now how many do you know?"

I told her about meeting Rose Wheeler, her son Luke, and their relationship to Chief LaMond.

"One of my customers told me yesterday the Chief had a sister and her apartment was in the building. Did you know about the sister before meeting her?"

"No, Cindy doesn't share much about her past."

Barb agreed then said, "Do you know Noelle Ward?"

I was surprised she mentioned the name. "Met her in the apartment's parking lot after the fire. Why?"

"She's one of my better customers. Came in a few times when she moved here, but in the last few months, she's been in several times a week. If you've talked to her, you probably know she's writing a novel. She's bought several mysteries, says for research." Barb chuckled. "First time in, she was in the mystery section, then noticed me nearby. She looked at me, or I think she did, I couldn't tell for sure since she had on sunglasses. She looked in my direction and said, I remember it almost verbatim, 'One day my book will be right here, someone will've read it, sold it to you, to be read again.' She seemed both confident and naïve at the same time. I like that gal."

"She told me she was writing a novel but didn't say much about it other than it's set on an island like Folly. The main character is a female private detective."

"I'm surprised she said that much. She's not loquacious. I haven't seen her since the fire."

"She's living out of her truck, so I imagine she has a lot on her mind."

"That's too bad. Have the others found places to live?"

"Rose and her son have temporarily moved in with Cindy and Larry. Janice Raque is staying at the Holliday Inn. I don't think the others have found anything."

Barb took a sip of coffee, then said, "What about Hope House?"

"It's full. I talked to Burl the day after the fire. He's looking for other options."

"That's too bad. I hear it was arson. Does Cindy know who set it?"

"Not that I've heard."

"You mean you're not pestering her daily to find out what she knows?"

"Why would you say that?"

She looked in her coffee mug, then smiled. "Because that's what you do."

"She doesn't know," I said. "It started in a vacant apartment on the first floor, so there's no way of knowing intent."

"I suppose she's taking a hard look at the landlord. That's where I'd start."

"Cindy's checking. Do you know him?"

"What's his name?"

"Russell O'Leary."

"Doesn't ring a bell. What's his financial situation?"

"Three months behind on the mortgage. Spends near nothing on maintenance."

"In my other life, our firm represented a guy accused of torching his five-story office building."

"Did he do it?"

"Jury didn't think so."

"What did you think?"

"My gut said he did, but like a good defense attorney, I never asked. He had more debt than Portugal. Are you and Charles trying to find out?"

"We're more interested in helping the displaced residents find housing."

"Good. Arsonists are dangerous. They can look like anyone, can be part of society like everyone else. In other words, they don't look or act like crooks, don't wave guns around announcing their intentions."

"I'll keep that in mind."

"Any luck finding living arrangements for the displaced residents?"

I shook my head.

Barb jumped up from the chair, said she was needed in front, but before she left, said, "Chris, I have faith you'll be able to help them."

I wish I shared her confidence.

Chapter Seventeen

Ⅰt was four hours before I was to meet Barb. The unseasonably warm weather was still hanging around, so I decided to continue my off and on effort to walk wherever I needed to go around town. One of the New Year resolutions I'd been considering was to eat healthier combined with exercise, which in my dictionary meant walking, not other activities they torture people with in gyms. Why wait until January to begin?

I walked across the bridge heading off Folly then continued past where Center Street morphs into Folly Road. I turned on Mariner's Cay Drive and past the guardhouse with a gate that'd keep out unauthorized vehicles but did nothing to stop foot traffic. Over the years, I had known a few people who lived in Mariner's Cay, including Janice Raque. The large development consisted of a handful of residential buildings plus a marina. Several condos displayed colorful strands of Christmas lights around the perimeter of the screened-in patios, and on three balconies there were popular blow-up cartoon characters wearing Santa hats. I didn't walk through the development often, but it provided a different view than I was used to on my wanders around Folly.

I leaned against the rail on the walkway to the marina to watch several docked mid-size boats gently sway to the movement of the Folly River. I didn't know which building Janice had lived in or if they had a boat but being here gave me a chance to think more about her theory that Horace started the fire. I'd seen Horace a couple of times when they'd been in Cal's but had never spoken to him. From what I'd heard, he and Janice were in a rocky relationship. They'd often argue while at Cal's so I could only imagine how they'd gotten along in the privacy of their condo. Janice had a temper and according to an acquaintance who's a member of the Folly Beach City Council, she attended council meetings and wasn't shy about sharing opinions. What I didn't know was if Horace had built enough resentment to burn her building, nor did any significant revelations come to me as I watched the water flow by.

I crossed the bridge on my return to Folly then detoured on my walk home to stop by the Post Office to pick up what normally consisted of a "once in a lifetime" opportunity to get hearing aids at "unbelievable" low prices, a chance to consolidate all my credit cards into one so I could save thousands of dollars a year, or countless other "fantastic" offers for senior citizens.

I deposited the two "amazing" offers *du jour* in the trash receptacle the Post Office wisely placed near the exit. I thought about walking next door to Pewter Hardware to see Larry but rejected the idea after noticing his lot full and spaces along the road filled with vehicles. Cindy wasn't kidding when she said this was his busiest time of year.

Across the street, on a hill that led to the Folly River Park, Noelle Ward was seated in the shade. She was staring at her phone pointed toward the Post Office. At least, I assumed that's where her eyes were directed since I couldn't tell for sure. She wore her oversized sunglasses, a black sweatshirt, black jeans, and a dark gray jacket. I waved and she gave a tentative return wave as I walked over.

"Planning on robbing the Post Office?" I said, hoping to solicit a smile.

"They don't carry enough cash," she said, then laughed.

"Good point. I'm Chris, by the way. What brings you out here?"

She looked around, stood, and brushed off the back of her jeans. "I remember your name from the other day I'm Noelle. It's getting cool in the shade. Want to move up there in the sun?"

"Lead on," I said.

She moved to the edge of the street. then fifty or so yards toward Center Street, before following the paved footpath into the park. The center of the small park was in full sun, so we sat at one of the picnic tables overlooking the city's Christmas tree.

She stretched her arms over her head, then turned to me. "Bet you're wondering what I was doing back there?"

"It crossed my mind."

"When we met, I told you I was writing a novel. Want to hear what it's about?"

That didn't answer why she was staring at the Post Office, but I was curious about her book. "Sure. You said it was a murder mystery. You were living here for research."

She smiled. "Good memory for someone who doesn't read."

I was surprised she remembered, especially since I told her while we were staring at her burned-out apartment building.

"You're the first author I've met, so I'm intrigued."

"My protagonist is a thirty-year-old, single, African-American female who's a fledgling private detective in a small, predominantly white town in Georgia."

"Sounds a lot like someone I know."

"Except for the private detective and Georgia part."

"Suppose that's why it's a novel and not non-fiction."

She smiled, which I was beginning to see as one of her most attractive and often-used traits.

"Shonda Black, the protagonist, opened a detective agency several months earlier and hasn't attracted any clients. She's depressed, on the verge of giving up, when a fifteen-year-old black teenager walks into her office. He came to her because she's the only black private eye in town." She hesitated, then said, "Let me back up a little. There'd been a bank robbery a week earlier in the next town over. Now to the kid walking in. He tells Shonda he saw the robbers in town when they were in a small grocery. It's a lot like Bert's Market. The boy, I call him Gabriel, tells Shonda he went to the police about seeing the bad guys. They laughed at him, told him he was seeing things, that the robbers had fled the state. That was why he was at her door. As you can probably guess, Gabriel doesn't have money to pay Shonda. She figured if she could catch the robbers the publicity would attract clients, the paying kind. I don't need to tell you more for you to guess Shonda catches the robbers. The end. My dream, only a dream at this point, is to make it the first book in a Shonda Black Mystery Series."

"That's great, Noelle."

"Thank you. Now all I need to do is finish writing it, write the second book in the series, and collect my Nobel Prize in Literature." She laughed and tapped my leg.

I laughed with her, then said, "Is a Post Office in your book?"

"Sorry, I drifted a little from telling you what I was doing."

"It was interesting."

"Interesting enough for you to read it when it comes out?"

"I'll not only read it, I'll write a letter to the Nobel Prize committee telling them they could stop looking. Your book is the winner."

She chuckled. "You make up stuff better than I do."

"The Post Office?"

"Research. Like I told you, the city where Shonda Black works is like Folly Beach. Small town, beach community, full of quirky characters. Most small towns are populated by people who are more similar than different, but I grew up in Missouri, no ocean nearby. Up until I decided to write the next Great American Novel, I wasn't good at observing people, how they dress, how they act, how they talk. I moved into the apartment that's now charcoal because it's like the place Shonda lives. Heck, I even bought the Dodge Ram 1500 pickup because it seemed like the kind Shonda would drive."

"You were researching people leaving the Post Office?"

"Yes. I've spent most every hour I'm not working watching people. Watching how they eat, how close they sit to each other, how some lean over when talking to someone else, how others speak loud not caring if their voice irritates others around them. I'm studying how they shop, how they move over so others can pass them in aisles, or on the sidewalks, all sorts of scenarios." She held up her phone. "I'm also taking videos so I can study people later."

"You're taking this seriously."

"I'm good at my day job, enjoy writing ad copy. If I want to be a good novelist, I have to study all phases of the process. One thing we do in the ad agency is to use focus groups to observe how people react to our various ads. For lack of better terms, Folly Beach is my large focus group."

"I'm not the person to ask about writing a novel, but it appears you know what you need to do."

"Time will tell, Chris."

"Changing the subject, have you found somewhere to live?"

"My Dodge condo."

"I was thinking somewhere without wheels."

"Not yet. I'm making the most of it. Think I'll add that Shonda's apartment gets burned by the bank robbers, so she has to live in her truck."

"That's turning lemons into lemonade."

She laughed, "Hmm, turning lemons into lemonade. I need to put that in an ad someday." She turned serious. "Did I give you my number the other day?"

I patted my phone. "Right here."

"Living in a truck is good for research, not so good for my back. You'll let me know if you hear of any apartments?"

"Absolutely."

She started to rise.

"Noelle, one more thing. When we met and were talking about the fire, you said something about being warned. What'd you mean?"

"Oh, it was nothing."

She'd already used that line on me. Time to press. Charles would be proud of me.

"Noelle, it wasn't nothing or you wouldn't have said it. Please tell me what you meant?"

Her hand gripped the bottom of the picnic table's seat. I was afraid she wasn't going to respond until she said, "Two weeks before the fire, I found a note under the windshield wiper. It was printed on that kind of paper with all the little squares."

"Graph paper?"

"Yeah. It said, this is paraphrasing, if you know what's good for you, you'll pack up and get off Folly."

"Was that all?"

"Yes."

"You have an idea who it may've been from?"

"Wish I did."

"Had you angered anyone?"

"Not that I know of." She removed her sunglasses and squeezed the bridge of her nose. "Not anyone."

"Any ideas?"

"My first thought was someone put it there by mistake. It's not the only black Dodge Ram in town."

"Why did you change your mind?"

"Mine's the only truck like it at the apartment or at nearby houses. How could someone get it confused? I then thought it could've been from someone who saw me nosing around, watching people, shooting video. They could've been doing something wrong and thought I caught them. Something like that. Or it simply could've been someone who doesn't like black folk."

"Do you still have the note?"

She shook her head then shrugged. "It was in the apartment."

"Did you tell the police?"

"No. It'd be like Gabriel in my book going to the police. Nothing could be learned from a note on a piece of scrap paper. Unlike Gabriel, I'm trying to forget it."

"Do you think the person who left it started the fire?"

She stood a second time. "Chris, I don't know what to think," she hesitated, then added, "these are nice Christmas decorations."

That appeared to be her way of ending talk about the note. "They are nice."

"I'd better be going," she said, reached out and shook my hand. "Nice talking to you."

I agreed with her.

She left leaving me with more questions than when I arrived.

Chapter Eighteen

arb and I were to meet at Wiki Wiki Sandbar, one of Folly's newest, and undoubtedly largest restaurants, located a block from my cottage. I was standing outside the multi-level, tiki-themed restaurant ten minutes before our scheduled rendezvous. Barb, unlike Charles who considered thirty-minutes early to be on time, arrived five minutes later. She wore a lightweight tan jacket over a red blouse, black slacks, and a smile that brightened the early-evening darkness.

"Been waiting long?" she said then kissed my cheek.

"A couple of minutes. Hungry?"

She put her arm behind my back and nudged me toward the entry. "Starved. This is my first time here. How about you?"

"Once, but only to the bar. It's interesting."

She pointed to the other side of the L shaped structure. "One of my customers told me the style is mid-century modern, said there are five distinct rooms."

Before I could get a more-detailed architectural description of the building, a bubbly hostess escorted us to what she called the Wave Room where we were seated under a sculpture featuring hundreds of glass balls anchored to the ceiling. We were handed menus and told Karen would be our server.

I looked around the modern-looking room, mid-century or other-wise, while Barb focused on the menu. As promised, Karen appeared at the table before I'd finished gazing around the room. She asked if we wanted something to drink. Barb, who'd already studied the drink choices, said she'd have an Aloha from the Edge, which a quick peek at the menu told me was vodka and passionfruit. I didn't want Barb to have to wait while I agonized over the menu trying to figure out what each drink was, so I said a glass of Cabernet. Karen headed to the bar while Barb continued studying the menu. I envied her metabolism. She could eat like a sumo wrestler yet never gain an ounce. She pointed at my menu and told me to stop looking around and decide what to order.

The server returned with our drinks as I made my decision, thank goodness. Barb ordered a Korean short rib, I went with the pork ribs, mainly because I was more familiar with the ribs than some of the other items.

With the pressure of ordering at a new restaurant out of the way, Barb asked what I'd been doing since I left the store earlier today. She added, what I was doing while she was hard at work.

I told her about my chance meeting with Noelle and what she'd said about the note on her truck.

"Think she was clueless about who put it there or why?"

I nodded. "Sounded convincing. I had to push to get her to tell me about it. I don't know if she was worried about it or thought it was so inconsequential it wasn't important enough to mention."

"Next time she's in, I'll see if I can get her to talk about it. Does she know we're dating?"

"Don't know. Why?"

"If she does, it'd give me a better entrée into the discussion about the note since you could've shared the information with me."

"True."

This was the first time Barb hadn't tried to discourage me from getting involved in something that clearly was none of my business, something best left to the police. I wanted to point out the historic moment but thought it wouldn't be wise, besides, Karen was at the table with our food. Little could keep my companion from grabbing a fork and digging in.

A few bites later, I said, "If you get a chance, check with some of your customers to see if they know of an apartment for Noelle. She's looking for what she calls a dump, something in line with where she was. She wants to stay in character with the protagonist in her novel."

Barb smiled. "So, you want me to ask customers if they know a dump for rent?"

"You could say it more lawyerly, something like a budget-priced rental unit."

Two bites later, she said, "Did Noelle think the fire was set because she didn't take the note's advice?"

"She didn't say. It seems more than a coincidence, although from what I've heard, she's not the only resident who'd upset someone enough to set the fire."

"Chris, remember I told you I defended an arsonist in my previous life?"

"Yes."

"To give him a proper defense, I researched arsonists. The consensus of experts profiled most as young males."

"That narrows it down to a few hundred folks over here."

"Chris, there's more, if you'll let me finish."

"Please do," I said before taking a sip of wine.

"In addition to being young guys, more than seventy-five percent were Caucasian."

I wanted to say that didn't eliminate many of Folly's young males. A dollop of wisdom made me nod instead of speaking.

"They also score relatively low on intelligence tests."

"Did that profile help with your client?"

"Sort of."

"Meaning?"

"He's Caucasian, a graduate of one of the nation's top business schools, plus, is in his late fifties. The profile of an arsonist typically refers to a serial arsonist, someone who's obsessed with starting fires. My client was accused of being a one-off arsonist. He allegedly set the fire for money, not kicks. There was no history of him starting others."

"So how did the profile sort of help in his defense?"

"Reasonable doubt. If I cluttered the defense with other possibilities, regardless of how remote, jurors' minds could be influenced."

"Were they?"

"I told you, he was found not guilty."

I smiled. "Not necessarily innocent."

She returned the smile.

"How does this relate to the apartment fire?"

"Are the police looking for a serial arsonist or someone who set the fire for a reason other than seeing a massive fire? Have there been other unexplained fires on Folly or in the area in recent days, weeks, months?"

"If there've been others, the apartment fire may've had nothing to do with Noelle or other residents. The motivation of the person starting it was to create a fire."

"You're catching on. Want dessert?"

A change of subject, a hint. Barb was motioning for the server before I could say yes.

Dessert was ordered, which led to more pleasant discussions, overall, a pleasant evening. On my way home after escorting Barb to her condo, I decided to call Chief LaMond in the morning to ask if she had any update on the fire. Additionally, I could ask if she was aware of other recent unsolved fires.

Chapter Nineteen

The Chief answered with, "Good morning, Chief LaMond speaking. How may I be of assistance?"

Her salutation couldn't have been clearer than if she'd said, "I can't talk. If you don't hang up, I'll have you arrested for pissing me off."

"Call when you get a chance."

"Of course."

I didn't expect to hear from her soon, so in quest of healthy exercise, I walked next door to Bert's for a heart-unhealthy cinnamon Danish plus coffee. I didn't realize until I was out the door that the weather had tanked overnight. The unseasonably warm December temperatures were gone, replaced by what must've been the mid-forties. To someone from the North, it would've felt mild, but to Lowcountry residents, it felt like the deep freeze. It was easier to keep heading to the store than return home for a jacket. In addition to getting breakfast, I also wanted to see how Ty was doing.

I succeeded in getting the Danish and coffee, but Ty was nowhere to be seen. According to Caroline, another of Bert's helpful employees, Ty had the day off.

I was heading to the register, then home to eat my Danish in peace, when I heard a familiar voice coming from behind the nearby shelf.

"Morning, Mr. Photo Man. I see you're eating healthy as usual."

It's been a while since Charles greeted me with the Mr. Photo Man moniker. On a strange level, it was refreshing to hear. He wore a heavy gold sweatshirt with Wyoming Cowboys in brown letters on the front. No, I wasn't going to ask about the sweatshirt.

"Got to keep my energy level up," I said, "What're you doing on this side of town?"

Charles lived about seven blocks past Bert's but seldom frequented the store.

"Exercise. Teddy Roosevelt said, 'Let us rather run the risk of wearing out than rusting out.'"

Another of Charles's quirks is quoting United States Presidents. He says reading what they said keeps his mind active. I've attributed it to him wanting to be different, something he was without quoting anyone.

"There's little chance of you rusting." His hands were empty, so I added, "You getting something or working on wearing out."

"Out for a walk, but now that I see you, let me tell you about a brilliant idea I had in the middle of the night."

"Tell me, then I'll decide if it's brilliant."

"I'll go with you to your house where you can leave your breakfast, then we can saunter around town while you're listening to my brilliant idea."

I had nothing better to do, besides, I could get a jacket if we were going to saunter around. Charles said he'd get coffee while I paid. Five minutes later, I'd upgraded my wardrobe, took a bite of Danish, then headed toward the Folly Pier with my friend.

I was beginning to question the wisdom of walking on the pier. The stiff ocean breeze made it feel colder than the upper-forties. Why couldn't Charles tell me his brilliant idea in a restaurant or my cottage? We'd walked halfway to the end of the pier, when he said, "Got another idea."

"Is it as brilliant as the one you haven't shared yet?"

"Brilliant, no. Warmer, yes. Why don't we go to the hotel's lobby?"

I didn't know what his other idea was, but to my shivering body, his latest sounded brilliant.

Christmas decorations were scattered throughout the lobby of the oceanfront hotel. Jay, a friend who's worked at the hotel for years, greeted us with, "Merry Christmas, gentlemen. You two spreading tidings of comfort and joy?"

"Always," Charles said.

I wasn't as confident, so I shook Jay's hand and said it was nice seeing him before telling him we were getting out of the cold.

"You're always welcome here. Let me know if there's anything you need," Jay said and left us in the seating area off the lobby.

"Okay, Charles, let's hear your idea."

He warmed his hands by rubbing them together, gazed around the empty area, then said, "Brilliant idea. Ty has a cat, cute little thing." He stopped and nodded.

"Yes."

"Who else do you know with a cat?"

I wasn't ready for a quiz and took too long to answer.

"Well, who?"

"I've got it. Good old Mr. Sarnaw. He used to walk that big black cat with a leash down the sidewalk. First time I'd seen someone walking a cat."

Charles shook his head. "That would've been a good guess, except Mr. Sarnaw died in July. Don't worry, his neighbor took the cat to a friendly shelter where it was adopted. Don't know if the leash was part of the deal."

"Who are you talking about with a cat?"

"I'll give you one more guess. Here's another clue. Who do you know who has a pet snake?"

"Martha Wright," I said, feeling stupid not thinking of her first.

Charles and I met Martha a year ago when Dude Sloan's love of his life Pluto disappeared. After an island-wide search by numerous people, we discovered Martha had taken him in to join her menagerie which included some dozen animals. Martha gladly returned Pluto, apologized for inadvertently thinking he was a stray, and left a lasting impression on me, primarily because of her pet boa constrictor.

"Good guess."

"What about her?"

"She's got cats, Ty has a cat. Martha has a big house, Ty's living in a tiny-tiny four-wheel apartment. Now, the brilliant part. Martha takes in strays. Ty's a stray. Brilliant, right?"

"You think Martha will let Ty move in with her because she takes in strays?"

"How could she not?"

Truth be told, it wasn't a horrible idea. Far from brilliant, but not horrible.

"Why would she?"

"She's an eighty-year-old widow; her poor hubby bit the dust four years ago; she's living in that big house by herself. That lady needs a man around. Ty's almost a man, will do in a pinch. All you have to do is ask her."

"Me?"

"Don't worry, I'll go with you."

Before I could list thirty reasons it'd be a bad idea, the phone rang.

"Okay, troublemaker, what'd you want?" said the less-than-gleeful Cindy LaMond.

"I was talking with Barb at supper about the fire."

Cindy interrupted, "Cheery dinner talk. You sure know how to warm a woman's heart. Get it, fire, warm?"

"Yes, Cindy. Barb was talking about an arson suspect she'd defended. She said there were certain characteristics of most arsonists but was mainly talking about serial arsonists. Her client allegedly set fire to an office building he owned for the insurance."

She interrupted again, "Think you can get to the reason for pestering me before I retire?"

Charles waved for me to put the phone on speaker. Instead of having to repeat everything the Chief said, I hit the speaker icon.

"If the person who set the fire did it because he simply liked to start fires, it may not have anything to do with the residents or the building's owner."

Charles couldn't stand being left out of the conversation. "That makes sense, doesn't it, Chief?"

I heard an audible sigh on the other end of the line. "Chris, did you get a damned talking parrot, or was that your half-wit friend?"

"Cindy, you know the answer."

"That's what I was afraid of. Did I miss the point of your call somewhere in all that?"

"It's a simple question. Have there been other suspicious fires in the Charleston area?"

"I'm sure there were some in the 1800s. Suppose they were caused by the Yanks, or was it Rebels? Civil War history gets me confused. Charles, you were around then, which was it?"

I smiled and turned to Charles, who said, "Chief, I think Chris means something more recent."

She said, "No."

"No what?" Charles said.

She sighed again. "Did you forget the question? No suspicious fires in the last year or so."

I said, "You sure?"

"Yes, that's what the arson investigator told me when I asked the same question the day he told me it was arson. That means you can throw out the profile for the typical serial arsonist. You know, the profile you and that lovely lady discussed. The same lady who, for reasons beyond anything I can understand, enjoys spending time with you."

I was thinking of a humorous retort, although it would've been wasted. She'd hung up.

Chapter Twenty

artha's house was four long blocks from the Tides, so I suggested we drive. Charles said it was a great idea, which, I suppose, wasn't as good as his "brilliant" idea that Martha would take Ty, the stray. Her house was a large, two-story, relatively new structure that backed up to the ocean. Martha met us with a look she probably would've given a Mormon missionary. She was no more than five-foot-two, slightly overweight, with dark black hair pulled in a bun. She opened the door a crack.

"Young men, I don't want any."

It was hard to understand what she'd said for the barking dogs nudging the door.

Charles, who didn't accept the concept of rejection, stepped forward, tipped his Tilley, then said, "Martha, I'm Charles Fowler. We met last year when we came looking for Pluto, Dude Sloan's dog. We've also talked in church a time or two."

I hadn't remembered, but Martha was a member of First Light where Charles was a regular.

Martha leaned on her cane, smiled, then said, "Oh, I remember. Sorry, I thought you were some of those church kids going door-to-door, or worse, traveling salesmen. Give me a second to put my killer dogs in another room." She chuckled as she said it. It was at least two minutes before the door opened all the way. "Come in."

"Martha," Charles said as we followed her in the door. "You remember my friend, Chris Landrum, don't you?"

"Sure," she said, in a tone that failed to sound sincere. "Shall we retire to the sitting room?"

The room looked the same as it had a year ago, resembling an animal playhouse more than a sitting room. A three-foot-high, triple deck, carpeted cat tower occupied one corner. On a small table beside the cat tower, there was an oak cabinet like one I remembered from my childhood that contained a record player, or turntable, as they're called today. Assorted animal toys were scattered around. My eyes immediately went to the large aquarium beside one of the three wingback chairs. I was relieved to see the aquarium occupied, relieved because it held a boa constrictor that had to be a mile long. Okay, that's an exaggeration. On a previous visit, Martha shared she often let Squeezy—no, I'm not making that up—roam around the room. She'd said roam, I translated it to mean slither. I took the chair farthest from the aquarium.

Martha had already taken the second farthest chair from Squeezy, so Charles slowly lowered himself in the dog and cat hair infested remaining seat.

"Charles, want to hold Squeezy?"

"Perhaps another time, Martha. Speaking of pets, how many do you have now?"

Instead of answering, she popped up from the chair. "Fellas, want a hot toddy?"

One of the things I'd remembered about our visits last year, was her fondness for the drink, regardless of the time of day.

"No thank you, Martha," Charles said, and repeated, "Perhaps another time."

She lifted the top of the oak cabinet, fiddled with the record player, then said, "Then you can't say no to music of the season."

Neither Charles nor I had time to say, "Perhaps another time," before Alvin and the Chipmunks began their version of "Here Comes Santa Claus." I prayed the volume control wasn't broken since between the scratches on the record and the less-than-appealing voices of the three animated anthropomorphic chipmunks, a Boeing 757's engine would've been quieter.

Martha screamed, "My animals love the Chipmunks. I've got both of their Christmas albums."

Or, I thought that's what she said. The last part was drowned out by Alvin.

"Martha," I yelled, "don't you think it's a little loud?"

She tilted her head my direction, cupped her hand behind her ear, then reached in the cabinet. The volume lowered to bar-conversation levels.

"Sorry, want to repeat that, Chris? Couldn't hear you."

Now that my ears stopped ringing, I didn't feel the need to repeat what I'd said. Instead, I repeated Charles's question. "How many pets do you have?"

She returned to her chair, rubbed her chin, before saying, "Let's see. It's hard to keep up, you know." She looked toward the door where she'd herded her dogs when we arrived. "Four dogs: Pooch, Lady, Bowser, Ink Spot. No, it's five. I keep forgetting Little Dog. Still have three cats. I'm sure of that. There's Cat One, Cat Two, and Crazy." She shook her head. "Then, got to count Paul."

Charles said, "Your parrot?"

She nodded. "Still got to keep him upstairs, you know. His language would make a sailor blush. Danged hard to teach an old parrot new tricks, or words."

"Know what you mean," Charles said as he glanced my way.

I didn't know, didn't want to know if he wanted reinforcement, or was calling me old. "Martha," I said, "you still have Davy Crockett?"

She lowered her head, glanced around the room like someone was hiding behind one of the chairs, then said, "You know it's illegal to have a pet raccoon?"

I didn't know for certain, but she'd told us that before. I nodded.

"So, I can't count Davy," she said, winked, then whispered, "He's still around."

I nodded a second time.

Charles looked at the aquarium. "Don't forget Squeezy."

"Never, Charles, never." She smiled. "Sure you don't want to hold him?"

"Not this time, Martha."

Alvin and the Chipmunks were now butchering "Silver Bells." Time to move along.

"Martha, we stopped by to—"

She sat up straight in her chair. "I didn't do it."

"Do what?" I asked, figuring it was a reasonable question.

"Whatever you're here to accuse me of, young man."

"Martha, we're not here to accuse you of anything other than being a wonderful lady with some great pets," said Charles the suck-up.

"Oh. The last time you showed up at my door uninvited you accused me of dognapping, stealing that weird hippie's adorable Australian Terrier. Figured you had me on your suspect list if anything bad happens to critters."

"Now Martha," I said, "we know you were doing the right thing with Pluto. He didn't have a collar, he was hungry, you took him in."

"A good deed," Charles added. "Taking in strays is admirable. I've told everyone I know how kind you were to little Pluto."

Told you he was a suck-up. Before Charles pulled out a violin, started singing more praise for Martha, in stark contrast to Alvin trying to sing "Jingle Bells," I'd better refocus the conversation.

"Martha, did you hear about the big, apartment building fire?"

"Lordy, Chris, how could I miss it? It was a block over. Smoke everywhere, sirens blaring. Made my dogs howl nearly as good as Alvin's singing."

"Do you know Ty Striker?"

"Can't say I do."

"He's in his early twenties, thin with long black hair, wears it a ponytail. Works at Bert's."

"Doesn't ring a bell. What about him? Isn't missing, is he?"

Charles piped up, "Not missing, but he's missing a place to live. He was one of the residents of the building that ain't there no more."

The record player groaned, then clanked, dropping another record on the turntable. Different record, same "performers." The Chipmunks started singing "Jingle Bell Rock."

A high-pitched howl came from the other room.

Martha smiled and nodded toward the room holding her dogs. "Bowser loves this song." She turned to Charles. "Where were we?"

"We were telling you about Ty. He has an adorable kitten, it's got six toes on one of its front paws."

Martha beamed. "A Polydactyl. Just like Hemingway's in Key West."

Charles nodded and I wondered if I was the only person in the country who didn't know about the six-pawed felines.

"Exactly," Charles said.

"What's its name?"

"Lost."

"Oh my, Ty's kitten's lost like that weird hippie's pup."

"No, Martha, Ty's cat is named Lost."

"Oh my, that's a ridiculous name for a cat."

That coming from someone who has cats named Cat One, Cat Two, and a dog named Little Dog.

"It's unusual," I said. "Charles, you want to tell Martha what you were thinking about Ty?"

"That's okay, Chris. You go ahead."

Thanks, coward.

"Martha, we were thinking." I generously didn't say Charles was thinking. "You love animals and have this wonderful large house. It had to be hard to lose your husband a few years back. I bet occasionally things need repairing or there are other things that could use a man's touch."

"You can say that again."

This was going better than expected, I thought.

"We were thinking you could let Ty move in one of your spare rooms until he finds somewhere permanently. He's sleeping in his tiny car."

Her hand flew to her mouth. It may've been my imagination, but her face seemed to turn white, snow-white in the vernacular of the season.

"Heavens to Betsy, no way, young man." Her hand left her face and gripped the arm of her chair. "What would Tommy and Dixie think? Me shacking up with a man. Lordy, no."

Tommy was her late husband, Dixie was her friend who lived across the street.

Alvin was singing "Have Yourself a Merry Little Christmas," but it was doing nothing to make my season bright, my heart feel light, or my troubles out of sight.

Charles appeared to wait for me to continue my sales pitch. I didn't.

"Martha," he said, "I'm certain Dixie would understand. She knows how you like to take in strays. You could consider Ty another stray."

"Young man, I've had a wonderful, long life. I'm not going out of it being accused of being a cougar."

From my limited understanding, Martha would be thirty years or so outside the range of cougars, women seeking younger men.

"Martha, I understand." I didn't. "Charles and I wanted to ask because we knew how kind and caring you were. We don't want to take more of your valuable time."

I stood to leave, when she said, "Now if that Ty fellow wants to bring Lost—I still can't believe he named a cat that—by to visit, that'd be fine. Cat One, Cat Two, and Crazy might like a visitor every now and then."

I said I'd share that information with Ty.

Alvin had stopped singing, Bowser had stopped barking harmony, and I felt anything but in the Christmas spirit as we left Martha leaning on her cane waving bye.

Chapter Twenty-One

"I need a hot toddy after that," Charles said as we got in the car.

"How about a beer at Cal's?"

"A close second."

It was early afternoon when we entered Cal's. The tables were vacant, but three men were seated at the bar drinking lunch. Loretta Lynn was singing "Silver Bells" from the jukebox that would've given Martha's record player a run for being the oldest music machine on the island. Cal was delivering a beer to one of the men. He saw us enter, nodded, then pointed around the room, his way of saying sit anywhere.

We chose a table close to the bar so Cal wouldn't have to go far to serve us. He seldom complained, but his knees were on their last legs, pun intended. Instead of asking what we wanted, he arrived at the table with a Budweiser for Charles, a glass of Cabernet for me.

"Hey, Cal," Charles said, "got anything by Alvin and the Chipmunks on the jukebox?"

Cal plopped down in a chair then squinted at Charles. "Pard, you lost your mind?"

"Don't think so, why?"

"Christmas is my favorite time of year. It's plum near here. This room's decorated, all cheery, festive, ready for that wonderful holiday. Then you come in and suck all the cheer out of me."

"Cal," I said, "what're you talking about?"

Cal looked at the bar to see if any customers needed anything, then back to us. "Back in the day when I was a fledgling country star, eighteen years old, with my first hit 'End of the Story,' I was traveling all over the South singing anywhere that'd have me." He looked at the ceiling. "Ah, those were the days. Anyway, was 1962, lord, I played a lot of bars. Not paying gigs, but tips weren't bad. They also let me sell my records. Most had jukeboxes like mine." He pointed to his ears. "Know what I had to subject these here listening devices to?"

It was beginning to make sense. "Alvin and the Chipmunks?"

"Those damned, fake, striped rodents, singing 'The Alvin Twist.' That horrible song, if you can call it a song, came out the same year my hit flew up the charts." He shook his head. "Can still hear '*If you wanna be smart, if you wanna be wise, take up your fun and exercise. Everybody, do the Alvin Twist.*' Know why I can still hear it?"

Charles, of course, had to know. "Why?"

"Because those damned rodents were singing it on every jukebox in every bar I went in. Over and over, over and over. It got worse after that. Those freakin' rodents came out with their first Christmas album the same year. Talk about kicking Christmas in the head. Why in holy vinyl are you asking about those damned rodents?"

Charles smiled. "So, you don't have any of their Christmas songs on the jukebox?"

Elvis, not Alvin, began singing "Blue Christmas," and I was beginning to think we would have a blue one with Cal and his memories.

"It's not important, Cal," I said. "We wanted to stop to see if there's anything we can do to help you get ready for your party?"

Charles looked at me like, "We were?"

"I appreciate it, boys. Think everything's on schedule. My decorations are up. I got some volunteers coming to help with the food and drinks. Don't know how many folks have told me they're going to be here, but it's a bunch. Thanks for offering."

A customer whistled for Cal. The owner said he'd better earn his keep then headed to the bar.

Charles watched him go. "Think I ought to invite Martha to the Christmas party? She could bring her Chipmunks Christmas albums."

That didn't deserve an answer. I took a sip of wine before saying, "Think we need to talk about who might've set the fire."

"Whoa," Charles said, "you an alien that's done invaded Chris's body? I'm the guy who always wants to butt in police business. Chris always tells me it's none of my concern, that I need to leave it to the cops. What'd you do with my friend?"

"You're right. I know—"

"Of course, I'm right. Umm, remind me why?"

"Charles, I know each of the building's residents. Don't know them well, but it seems that I, we, might know more about them than the police know. It's worth discussing."

"Talk on," he said then took a long draw on his beer.

"Janice Raque is convinced her husband set the fire."

"Why would he? They're divorced, he's moved on with some floozy in Mt. Pleasant, Janice ain't around to fight with him every time they're in here, or wherever else they're butting heads."

"She thinks it's because her lawyer is on Horace's case to get her more support."

Charles said, "You buy that?"

"No, mainly because like you said, the fire was set during the day when there was little chance anyone would've been in the building, little chance anyone would've been hurt."

"Could've been to send a message. Leave me alone or I'll get you. A blazing building would be a powerful way to deliver a message."

"That's possible, but I'd put him low on my list."

"Okay, moving along, who would've wanted to burn Rose and Luke's apartment out from under them?"

I hadn't shared what Rose told me about her ex being on Folly the day before the fire. I took another sip knowing I'd need it once Charles started haranguing me for not telling him sooner. I took a deep breath then shared what Rose had told me.

Charles had started to take a drink, instead, he set the bottle on the table, more accurately, pounded the bottle on the table. "You didn't think that was important enough … never mind. Rose's hubby sounds too stupid to be a bank vice president if he thought she'd come crawling back to him if her apartment went up in smoke."

"I agree. I mentioned him because we know he was here the day before the fire. Don't you think that's a big coincidence?"

"Do we know if he was here the day of the fire?"

"No."

Charles pointed in the direction of the ocean. "I'll nose around the Tides. My innocent-looking face makes people tell me stuff they shouldn't."

His countless questions didn't hurt him getting information either. "Good idea, although there are many other places he could've stayed."

"Nick Matthews," Charles said.

"Aimee's fiancée?"

"He could've done it. Didn't Ty tell us he mumbled something like you'll get yours?"

"Yes."

"There you go. Suspect number one."

"How're we going to find out more about him?" I said out loud, although talking more to myself.

Charles picked my phone off the table, pointed it at me. "Call Cindy. Maybe Nick has a record or is known by the local cops for burning buildings."

"I'll call her later."

"Don't worry, I won't let you forget."

Cal returned to the table. "Get you boys anything else to drink?"

Charles looked at his bottle. "Not yet. What if we want something to eat?"

"I'll point you to some good restaurants," Cal said, then pushed his Stetson back on his head. "Neil ain't here, and I'm not in the mood for fixin' food."

"Speaking of Neil," Charles said, "know if he pissed off anyone enough to torch his building?"

"Don't know about him, but if it had a trio of damned chipmunks living there, I would've torched it myself."

Fifty years later, Alvin and his compatriots were still under Cal's skin.

"What about Neil?" I said to bring him back to the twenty-first century.

"I asked him. He said it could've been his old boss. Seems Neil turned the cheatin', thievin' crook's name over to the IRS. The feds came down on him like a pile of manure."

Neil had told Charles and me the same thing.

"That'd be a strong motive," Charles said.

I said, "He also mentioned something about a man he threw out of the bar."

"Don't remember that," Cal said.

"No," Charles said, "the bar in Charleston where he's a bouncer."

Cal said, "I'd stick with the IRS busted boss. Guys get thrown out of bars all the time. They bitch and groan, threaten everyone around, then sober up, before starting all over again. No biggie."

"You're probably right," I said. "Has Neil found a place to live?"

"Far as I know, he's still at the Holliday Inn. Says it costs him nearly everything he makes."

"It'd be nice, Christmaslike, if someone would take him in until he finds a cheaper place, wouldn't it?" Charles said, glancing at me out the corner of his eye.

One of the men at the bar called for another beer. Cal left to meet the need, and Hank Locklin broke the string of Christmas songs from the jukebox with "Please Help Me, I'm Falling."

"That brings us to Noelle," I said to move away from Neil's housing plight. "Let me tell you what she said yesterday."

"Is it like what you learned from Janice and didn't think it was important enough to tell me?"

"Charles, give me a chance, I'll tell you."

Charles held up his empty beer bottle. "Yo, Cal, I need another one of those. Chris is driving me to drink."

I told him about my encounter with Noelle after I saw her casing the Post Office. He was relatively calm until I got to the part about the note on her truck.

"You thought that clue wasn't important enough to lead this discussion with?"

Cal set a second Budweiser on the table then asked if I needed another glass of wine. I declined. Charles said he may need it before I drove him crazy.

Cal added, "Crazier," then headed to the bar.

"I don't know what we can do with that information," I said.

"You can add it to the list of things to talk to Cindy about."

"I'll do that. Let me tell you what Barb said about arsonists."

"Is it something else you should've told me before today?"

"No," I said, more defensively than I had intended. "Learned it last night."

I proceeded to tell him about Barb's research about arsonists, how it appeared whoever burned the apartment building probably wouldn't be considered a serial arsonist, but someone who burned it for a specific purpose. The most likely suspect would be the building's owner Russell O'Leary."

"Insurance?"

"Probably."

"He has money trouble?" Charles asked.

"Three months behind on the mortgage."

"Does Cindy know?"

"That's who told me. She's already looking into it. He also told her he was at a meeting in Atlanta, but the story was weak. He didn't remember where he stayed, paid cash, lots of wiggle room in his alibi."

Charles took a sip of the second beer, started peeling the label off the bottle, then said, "What do we do now?"

"Enjoy looking at Cal's Christmas decorations, his beautiful trees, then think how lucky we are to have a place to live."

Merle Haggard sang "If We Make It Through December."

Chapter Twenty-Two

I called Cindy after Charles and I had gone our separate ways.

"What now?" she said then sighed.

As strange as it seems, I was happier to hear that rude response than her trying to be friendly. Cindy was being Cindy.

"Have you talked to Noelle Ward about the fire?"

"You mean Imani Marshall?"

"Yes."

"She want to confess starting it?"

"Don't believe so, but if you say pretty please, she'll tell you about a note slipped under her windshield wiper a week before the fire."

"Did the person who wrote it say he or she was going to incinerate the building, then sign the note?"

"Noelle didn't mention it. It told her to get off the island or something like that."

"Was your new buddy Noelle ever going to share this with the police?"

"I asked. She said it wouldn't do any good." I didn't tell Cindy that Noelle wasn't going to law enforcement because her novel's protagonist wouldn't.

"I'd like her to tell me that. Do you know where she's staying?"

"In her truck. I bet your crack police force could find one big Dodge Ram pickup without much trouble."

"You have more faith in them then I have. Would you happen to have Ms. Ward/Marshall's phone number?"

I not only told her I did but gave it to her.

"Cindy, now that you're on the phone, I have another question."

"Of course, you do, Charles in waiting."

"Do you know Nick Matthews?"

"No. Who's he?"

"How about Aimee Mason?"

"Chris, there are two thousand residents on Folly Beach. Are you planning on asking about each of them until I admit knowing someone?"

I chuckled. "No."

"So, who are Nick and Aimee?"

I shared what little I knew about them, omitting any mention of Lost, Ty's cat.

"Let me see if I have this straight. Ty was hitting on Aimee who happens to be Nick's fiancée. Nick didn't take kindly to it and maybe-kind-of-sort-of threatened Ty. How am I doing?"

"Perfect. No wonder you're Chief."

"Your theory is Nick thought Ty failed to grasp the importance of his maybe-kind-of-sort-of threat and burned an entire apartment building to communicate more strongly his objection to Ty's advances on his gal?"

"You've got it."

"That sounds like a stretch."

"Yes, but—"

Cindy interrupted, "Hold the but, the one with one T. Because you're such a friend, a pain in the butt with two Ts friend, I'll see if I can find Nick and have a pleasant talk. You don't happen to have his number, do you?"

"Sorry, no. By the way, how are Rose and Luke doing?"

"Luke's pestering Larry for a raise. Says he wants the extra money to buy his mom a nice Christmas present. Rose is trying to use some of her highfalutin education on me. Can you imagine her learnin' me proper grammar? I told her I'm dumber than a pretzel compared to her college students. I think she's figurin' that out."

Cindy is one of the smartest people I know. Her grammar may not always live up to textbook standards, but she's an effective communicator. She's also one of the most stubborn people I've run across. Rose will have her hands full. I wanted to ask if Rose told her about her ex's visit the day before the fire, but honored Rose's request that I not share it.

"Has she said much about the fire?"

"More about how rough it's been losing everything except the clothes on her back. She knows how lucky she and Luke were. The arson investigator figured the fire started in the apartment next to theirs, so they would've been close to the origination point if they'd been home."

"Does she think it had anything to do with them?"

"Why would it? She just moved here. They didn't know anybody, didn't even know others who lived in the building."

Which means Rose hadn't said anything about her ex's visit.

"Just curious."

Cindy laughed. "More than anything, Rose and Luke are putting their energy into decorating the house. Larry and I've never done anything more than put a wreath on the front door. No tree, no wrapped presents, no stockings hung by the chimney with care. Crap, we don't even have a chimney. By the time Christmas rolls around, Larry is shuffling around like an elf zombie. Tell him I said that, and you'll be hung by a rope by somebody's chimney."

I chuckled. "Your term of endearment is safe."

"Rose said our house shouldn't be decorated for Christmas the same way it is for Groundhog Day. She found an artificial tree in the attic, must've come with the place. They cleared a century of dust off it, plopped it down in the family room. Then Luke convinced Larry to give him strands of lights from the store so he and his mom could string them around the tree. Then Santa's little helpers went to Harris Teeter, bought wrapping paper, and candy canes. Now they're hanging on nearly everything you can hook a cane on."

"That's great, Cindy."

"I'll admit, it looks good. I put my foot down when she suggested I bake Christmas cookies. Luke said not to worry, he and his mom will bake them. I hope Larry will have enough energy left in his petite body to enjoy everything. Hell, I may even buy him a Christmas present. What man doesn't want a snow globe?"

"That's what we live for, Cindy."

"Perfect. I'll be sure to tell Larry you said that."

I hoped she was kidding. "Ho, Ho, Ho! Anything I can do to help?"

"Come to the house after Christmas to take down all the stuff Rose and Luke used to transform our humble abode into a Christmas village."

"Anything else?"

"Yeah, I'd love to spend more time talking about Christmas but I have to see if I can find Noelle, or whatever her name is, living in a pickup truck; Nick, the jealous fiancée; plus any other person who may've been on Folly in the last week who might've started the fire."

"That should keep you busy for a few minutes."

"I wish."

"One more thing before you go to solve the mystery. Don't forget Cal's annual Christmas bash."

"Gee, Chris, how could I forget, he only does it every Christmas. I'm not old like you. I don't have to be reminded to get up every morning."

"I was thinking you and Larry might want to bring Rose and Luke by to meet some others on Folly."

"Good thought. I'll talk to them about it. Larry, of course, will sleep all day after he drags his tiny butt in from working ninety-four hours a day at the store."

"In addition to Rose teaching you proper grammar, you may see if she can refresh your knowledge of math."

I'm certain she was going to thank me for the suggestion, but the phone went dead before she had a chance.

Chapter Twenty-Three

The most likely person with a reason to burn the apartment building was its owner, Russell O'Leary. He was three months behind on his mortgage, one of the apartment units had been vacant for several months which would've made it more difficult to cover the mortgage. He claimed to have been in Atlanta at a meeting on the day of the fire but told Cindy he didn't stay at the hotel where the event was held. He said he'd rented a room at a nearby hotel whose name he couldn't remember. A feeble alibi at best. So, how do I prove it?

I didn't know Russell but knew someone who might. Bob Howard, a friend, and former Realtor who'd handled countless sales in the Charleston area.

"Good afternoon, Bob," I said after he answered on the third ring.

"Well if it isn't my worthless acquaintance who thinks he's too good to spend time with his good buddy."

Despite having had a successful career in real estate, Bob had the personality of a hippopotamus and nearly the same weight, yet, for reason's unknown, we'd become friends after he helped me find my cottage on Folly, the space I'd rented for Landrum Gallery, plus sharing information over the years allowing me to catch a couple of bad guys.

I ignored his comment, a wise decision when spending time around Bob. "Do you know Russell O'Leary?"

"Yes."

I waited for more. It was a waste of time.

"What do you know about him?"

"Chris, I figure the CIA, KGB, NCAA, or one of those other evil agencies has this phone bugged. Suppose you'll need to come over to hear it in person. Oh yeah, while you're here, you can buy a cheese-burger, double order of fries to share with me, plus some of that nasty red wine you sip in the winter."

"Will you be there in an hour?"

"Hell yes, damned slave-driver Al won't let me leave."

I hung up on him. It felt good.

When Bob retired from selling real estate, he bought Al's Bar near downtown Charleston. While it's too long a story to relay here, suffice to say Bob knew as much about running a bar as a jumbo shrimp knows about needlepoint. He bought it because his long-time friend Al Washington, the previous owner, was suffering serious health issues after running the bar for decades while raising nine adopted kids, much of that time as a single dad. Bob couldn't stand seeing Al suffer.

Forty-five minutes later, I was pulling in a rare empty parking space a half-block from Al's in an area of town near two hospital complexes. Other than the often-expanding health care facilities, much of the resi-dential area would be considered pre-gentrification. If you'd called Al's Bar a hole in the wall, you'd be giving it too much credit. It was in a concrete-block building it shared with a Laundromat. The building hadn't been clothed in fresh paint since the Vietnam War. Regardless of its physical condition, I was certain Al's cheeseburgers were the best in the state. Bob claimed they were the best in the country. He could be right.

I stepped from late-afternoon daylight into cave-like darkness to be greeted by Al, who since Bob purchased the bar, served as the business's Walmart greeter.

"Praise the Lord, you're here," he said, gave me a warm, extended hug, then whispered, "Blubber Bob's been asking every two minutes if you were here yet."

The only illumination in the room came from a Budweiser and Budweiser Light neon signs behind the aging bar, but Bob was seated close enough to see each time the door opened. In other words, he had no reason to pester Al about my arrival.

Al was eighty-two-years-old, with short, gray hair, coffee-stained teeth, with skin the color somewhere between dark brown and light black. He looked as well-worn as the room's yard-sale tables and chairs.

"Old man," came a bellowing voice from the rear of the room, "stop hugging on the damned scrawny honkie so he can get over here and spend money. How in the hell am I going to pay your astronomical salary if you don't let customers blow their cash in here?"

That was Bob at his best. Al had the good sense not to remind Bob he was working free. Two men were seated at a table near the large plate-glass window, the lower-half painted black to provide privacy for the diners. They were sipping beer and playing cards. A pile of wooden matches was in front of each of them which I suspected had value other than for starting fires.

Other than the cardplayers, the bar was empty except for Al, Bob, and me. Al said he'd throw my cheeseburger on the grill if I promised to keep Bob quiet. I told him I'd do my best. During busy times, which were fewer and fewer, a part-time cook fixed the food. I hated that Al had to move around that much but knew that the chance of Bob manning the grill was about the same as him being named Pope.

"About time you got here," Bob said as I squeezed in my side of the booth, a space barely wide enough for me since Bob had taken up twice the normal space on the other side of the table. "Nosing in police business again?"

"Why do you say that?"

"Oh, could be because you called to ask if I knew Russell O'Leary who happens to own the building someone turned black and flat a couple of blocks from your house. Or, could be because you stick your pasty white nose in everything bad happening on Folly. How am I doing?"

Before I could answer, one of the cardplayers raised his hand and hollered to Al, "How about a couple more beers?"

Bob, being the customer-friendly, service-oriented bar owner, said, "Marvin, can't your Afro eyes see the man's busy fixing food for my young friend here?"

Bob was white; ninety-five percent of his customers African American. After Bob bought the bar, Al told me the main reason he wanted to stay on was to prevent a race riot in the place where he'd spent most of his work life. The more the regulars learned that Bob didn't like black people, they realized he didn't like brown, yellow, white, or any other color people. He was a textbook example of an equal-opportunity offender. He didn't like anyone, or so it appeared.

Marvin mumbled something under his breath, then went to the cooler and got the drinks. Bob mumbled something that sounded like, "Thanks, Marvin," but I had a hard time believing he could've said the word thanks.

Marvin returned to the card game, riot averted, for now. Bob turned back to me.

"Where was I," he said. "Oh yeah, you were going to tell me I was right about you nosing in police business."

I agreed but wasn't about to give him the satisfaction of hearing it.

"What do you know about O'Leary?"

"He's a heavy-truck mechanic at a shop over here. Decent income, but hard work, long hours. When his dad died a few years back, he inherited the building where you're snooping where you shouldn't."

Al made his way to the table, set a cheeseburger with a double order of fries in front of me. Before I'd arrived, Bob told him what I'd want, and what he'd want with the extra order of fries. Al also set a glass of wine beside my plate.

"Set your bony ass down while I tell my good-buddy Chris how brilliant I am."

Al lowered himself beside me. "Don't need to hear it. You say it every day."

"Old man, the truth will set you free."

Al rolled his eyes, as the sounds of the Four Tops' hit "Reach Out, I'll Be There," reverberated off the walls.

Bob yelled, "Marvin, you do that?"

Marvin smiled "Yes, Master Bob. You needed some good music."

"Next time you punch those numbers in the jukebox I'm getting a restraining order to keep you from entering this fine dining, drinking establishment ever again."

Marvin's smile turned to a laugh. "Yes, Master Bob."

Bob turned back to Al and me. "Damned radicals."

"Bob, how do you know so much about O'Leary?"

"He walked into my office soon after inheriting the building. Said he knew everything there was to know about fixing a Peterbilt but nothing about owning an apartment building. Wanted to talk about selling. I worked up comps and met to talk to him about the details of selling a multi-unit structure. He pondered it for a couple of weeks before calling to say he and his wife talked it over. They have two teenagers, college-age by now, I guess. Much to my thinning wallet's dismay, they decided to hold on to the building. Said they wanted it to be a legacy they could leave to their kids, which meant no money for me to leave to my kids."

"Bob," Al said, "you ain't got no kids."

"Hell, Al, get with the program. I was being figurative-speaking-like, making the point that his gain was my loss."

"Sounded stupid-like to me," Al said.

I agreed with Al. "Bob, is that all you know about O'Leary?"

"That's more than you knew when you walked in."

"True. So, that's all?"

"Nope."

"Heavens, Bob. Tell the man what you know. Use plain English while you're doing it."

"Hush, old man. Let me tell the story the way I want."

Instead of smacking the fry out of Bob's mouth, Al smiled, then leaned back in the chair.

Despite tremendous differences ranging from skin color to socioeconomic background, to kindness to others, Bob and Al had been friends for decades; they'd do anything for each other.

"After you called to tell me you'd love to come over and buy a cheeseburger, I called a realtor I know over your way to see if he knew anything about Russell. He said rumors were flying that the mechanic turned landlord was in deep financial straits. Late paying bills, months behind on his mortgage, one kid in college, one in trouble with the law."

"Is that all?"

"What more do you want, his social security number and cholesterol level? I suppose you think he torched the building for the insurance."

"Maybe."

Bob stuffed another fry in his mouth, then said, "Hell, I know I would've."

Chapter Twenty-Four

Another below-average temperature the week before Christmas greeted me as I stepped outside for the walk next door for coffee, something to eat, and with luck, a chance to check on Ty. Three construction workers were standing around the large coffee urn—one pouring coffee, two adding sugar and milk to their caffeinated drink. I drew a cup after the workers headed to the exit, then moved to the cabinet holding three large Cinnamon rolls, where Preacher Burl Costello was holding two boxes of prepackaged donuts.

"Morning Burl, didn't your chef show up to fix breakfast?"

As he smiled, his milk-chocolate colored mustache wiggled like a caterpillar inching its way along his upper lip. "And a good morning to you as well, Brother Chris. One of my fantasy dreams is for a chef to take up residence at Hope House. Until then, the bakery in, umm," he looked at the bottom of the donut package. "Cleveland, Ohio, will have to prepare our morning meals. My skills are limited to burning toast and offering a prayer."

I pointed to the shelf where I was eying my breakfast. "Burning toast would be an upgrade in my culinary skills. Don't suppose you have vacancies since we talked the other day?"

Burl's smile transitioned to a frown plus a slow head shake. "Still full. Are some of the residents of the burned building still without somewhere to hang their hats?"

I glanced around looking for Ty, not seeing him, I said, "Unfortunately yes. Rose Wheeler and her son are the only ones who've found accommodations."

"Are they the relatives of our outstanding Chief?"

"She's Cindy's sister, Luke, Cindy's nephew. The others are living in their vehicles or staying at the Holliday Inn."

"Brother Chris, I have faith our community will come together to aid the displaced."

"I wish I had that much faith."

He smiled and patted my arm. "Tis the season of faith, Brother Chris. The season of faith."

As if on cue, Ty appeared at my side. He asked if he could help us find something. He had on what looked like the same shirt he'd been wearing the last time I'd seen him. His ponytail shined like it was covered with a layer of oil.

I introduced Ty to Preacher Burl.

"Preacher, Ty is one of the displaced residents I was talking about."

Burl set the donuts on the table, then put one arm around Ty. "Brother Ty, I'm terribly sorry about your loss of residence."

Ty took a step back from Burl. "No biggie, Preacher. I've lived in worse places than in my car. Besides, Lost is safe."

Burl looked at the young man like he'd look at three-legged deer. "Brother Ty, don't believe I understand."

I wouldn't have either if I hadn't known about Lost. "Preacher Burl, Ty is living in his Miata. Lost is the name of his adorable kitten that was in his car during the fire."

"Oh," Burl said, still looking confused. "It's nice meeting you, Brother Ty. I have faith you'll find somewhere to live, perhaps with more living space than your car. Gentlemen, I hate to run but need to get back to the house with breakfast or I'll have several residents ready to move me to my vehicle."

"Preacher," I said, "will you be at Cal's Christmas party?"

"I wouldn't miss Brother Cal's event, although I'd be more inclined to be there if that old country singer didn't feel the need to drag me on stage to join him in a Christmas song."

The last two Christmas parties, Cal thought singing a duet with Burl was something the group would enjoy. The bar's owner said it combined the spirit of the holiday with the religious significance of the sacred event. Burl thought there must be better ways to communicate the message, but went along with Cal.

"Preacher, that's the highlight of the event."

"Not to me, Brother Chris. Not to me,"

Burl headed to the register.

Ty watched him go, then said, "He talks funny, doesn't he? Several customers told me they go to his church. I should give it a try. He has more faith than I have about me finding somewhere to live."

I shared more information about First Light, Hope House, then added, "Ty, another reason I came in was to see how you're doing."

"That's kind of you, Mr. Landrum. I'm doing peachy." He snapped his fingers. "There was one thing I wanted to mention when I saw you." He stared at me like he wanted me to say something.

"Now would be a good time."

He nodded. "Remember I told you about Aimee's fiancée?"

"Nick something."

"Nick Matthews. He came in yesterday. I didn't see him at first. He was over by the beer cooler. I was stocking the book rack, know where I mean?"

"Yes."

"He got a six-pack, then walked close to me. He had this big look on his face. Looked like one of those Cheshire cat grins."

"Did he say anything?"

"Not a word, but figured the look was like him telling me he burnt the building, a smirk because he did it."

"Ty, you're certain he didn't say anything?"

"Certain."

I wasn't aware of laws against smirking but thought he should tell the police his suspicions.

"Ty, I doubt it'll do any good but I suggest you tell Chief Lamond the next time she's in."

"I will if you think it's a good idea but if I was the Chief and some kid told me he was reporting a smirk, I'd nod and forget it."

"Ty, she might do that but she's trying to figure out who set the fire. Anything related, regardless of how small or inconsequential, may help."

"If you say so," he said, sounding as convincing as I had suggesting it. "Better get back to work. Don't know what I'd do if I lost this job." He laughed. "I'd hate to have to give up my luxurious living quarters."

I was impressed by how well he was taking his uncomfortable situation. I couldn't handle it as well.

Chapter Twenty-Five

I called Neil after I got home. He'd told me a lot about the man he'd sicked the IRS on, but little about the person who'd threatened him after being bounced from the Charleston bar.

"Neil, are you at Cal's?"

"I go in at four. Why?"

"I was wondering about something you'd said. Thought I'd drop in if you were working."

"You can come tonight, or I could meet you somewhere now. The less time I spend in this room the better."

We agreed to meet at St. James Gate, a restaurant on the corner of Center Street and Ashley Avenue that prides itself on being a "proper Irish pub." From its distinct green and tan exterior to the dark wood and stone interior, the restaurant has the feel of how I pictured an Irish pub.

I would've preferred to sit on the back patio, but the temperature made that impractical, so I chose a table in front of the window facing Center Street. A half-dozen customers were at the bar. Four men sat at a table in the center of the room with two of them staring at laptop computers, most likely salespersons discussing whatever salespersons discuss. A server wearing a green and white T-shirt with a three-leaf clover over his heart was quick to the table. If I drank beer, I would've automatically ordered Guinness, the beer of choice in the pub. The server appeared disappointed when I stuck with water. He cheered slightly when I told him I was waiting on someone and might order more when my guest arrives.

I didn't wait long. Neil came in the door and headed my way. The server arrived with my water at the same time. Neil did what was expected in the Irish pub when he ordered Guinness and a menu. The server looked at me with an expression that said, "See, that's what you're supposed to do," then went to get Neil's drink.

"What's on your mind, Chris?"

Nothing like getting to the point, I thought. I told him I was wondering how he was doing, the same thing I'd said to Ty.

"Okay, I guess. Cal has been kind to give me extra hours, so I have enough money to replace some of the stuff lost in the fire. My car's a gas guzzler, so I cut back on my job in Charleston. Walking to Cal's helps save some."

"Still living in the Holliday Inn?"

"Yes, but I'd love to get out of there. They gave me a good rate, but I still can't afford it. Also, I can't stand being pent up in the small room. This time of year, it's even worse. It … never mind."

"Worse because of the holidays?"

"Sort of."

That's the kind of comment Charles would be all over. I liked to think I wasn't quite as pushy.

"Neil, when we were talking the other day, you said one of your customers in Charleston threatened you after you, umm, evicted him."

"Nothing unusual. It happens more than you might think. Alcohol does strange things to folks."

The gods of irony arrived the same time the server arrived with Neil's alcoholic drink. The server asked if we were ready to order. Neil said the beer was all he needed for now, so I ordered a soft drink instead of food. I didn't know if Neil wasn't hungry or didn't have money for lunch.

"Neil, didn't you say the man you threw out threatened you?"

"Yeah." He chuckled. "They all do."

"Could he have started the fire for revenge?"

"I suppose so, but he didn't know where I lived."

"Could he have followed you home?"

Neil smiled. "Not that night. I don't think he was in any condition to find his nose, much less my apartment."

"Seen him since then?"

"Once or twice. He's a regular."

"He give you more trouble?"

"He made a couple of smart-ass comments, nothing more."

"No more threats?"

"Not really. I don't think he started the fire. If anyone did because of me, it was the guy who owns the plant where I worked."

"Do you have a reason to think that anything other than because he'd be angry?"

"He's got a temper. I remember several times where he yelled at an employee, or when he pounded his fist on a wall."

"Have you seen him since you turned him in?"

Neil took a sip of beer, looked out the window, then said, "No."

"He never directly threatened you?"

"No."

Other than two people who may have a beef with him, Neil didn't know anything to tie them to the fire, which brings me back to something he'd said, or more accurately, hadn't said about this time of year being worse than other times.

"Neil, what did you mean when you said this time of year was bad?"

He took another sip as he resumed staring out the window. I was afraid I'd irritated him.

He finally turned to me. "My dad died three days before Christmas. I was seventeen."

"Neil, I'm sorry. What happened?"

"Cancer. He'd been sick for months. We knew his time was short, but he told mom and me he wanted to be here one more Christmas. He didn't make it."

"That would be a good reason to be depressed this time of year. Again, I'm sorry."

He slowly shook his head. "There's more."

The server returned and asked if Neil wanted another beer. He nodded but didn't say anything. I told the server I was fine.

Neil watched him leave, then said, "I was married once."

"Oh," I said.

"She was the most wonderful person I ever knew. Married five years, five wonderful years."

Do I ask what happened? The server was back before I decided.

Neil took a long draw on the beer, then said, "Three years ago, Lisa, that was her name, went to visit her parents. They lived thirty miles from our house. Her car was T-boned by a drunk driver. Killed her instantly."

"Neil, I'm terribly sorry."

"Was Christmas Eve. Know what happened to the damned drunk?"

I shook my head.

"Airbag broke his little finger. Lisa dies and he gets his damned pinkie broke."

Not knowing what to say, I shook my head.

He took a sip, looked out the window, hopped out of the chair, and headed to the restroom. It was becoming clear why this time of the year was rough on Neil. It was also clear I was running out of ways to say sorry.

Neil returned, gave me a feeble smile, then said, "Know what I did the next Christmas?"

I was afraid to guess. "What?"

"Got arrested. Aggravated assault."

"What happened?"

"Sitting in a bar, feeling sorry for myself. Christmas Eve, a year to the day I lost Lisa." He held up his beer. "Drinking way too many of these. A guy sitting next to me started ragging on the gal bartender. Bitching about her being slow. I blew a gasket. Before I knew it, we were exchanging blows, then I was being hauled away by what must've been a dozen cops. Chris, ain't nothing good about spending Christmas in jail."

"Neil, no wonder this is a bad time of year."

"I'd be lying if I said it wasn't." He hesitated, then added, "You're the only person I've told all this to. I'd appreciate it if you didn't share it with anyone."

"It won't leave this table."

He smiled. "Thank you. Know what's picked me up more than anything?"

"What?"

"Cal. Watching that old crooner get so excited about Christmas. Helping him put up the trees, decorating the bar. Being part of something positive about the holiday has kept me from thinking too much about the bad ones. He's a lifesaver."

Before I left St. James Gate, Neil had put most of his negative thoughts behind him. I encouraged him to talk about working at Cal's. He shared a few humorous things he'd witnessed, how interesting it was to spend time with Cal reliving his experiences with many of the country legends from fifty years ago, and a few quirky regulars who frequented the bar. Neil said he wasn't a country music fan, but hanging around Cal, he had a new appreciation for the genre. He especially had a growing appreciation for Cal, his outlook on life, his tolerance of all people. I didn't know how long Neil's good mood would last since we were only a handful of days before Christmas, but when we went our separate ways, he was laughing.

I WAS CROSSING Center Street when I heard a horn, turned, and saw it was coming from a black Dodge Ram pickup. The truck, driven by Noelle, I assumed, pulled off the road in front of me. I moved to the driver's side and was greeted by a smiling Noelle Ward.

"Good to see you, Chris. Where you headed?"

"Nowhere in particular."

"Want to hop in? I could use some company."

I walked around to the passenger door, opened it, slid in, then looked at the back seat that held a sleeping bag, a small suitcase, and three Walmart bags.

"Still driving your apartment?"

Noelle, dressed in a black sweatshirt, black jeans, and red tennis shoes, laughed, then said, "Got some new duds at Walmart. All I have to do now is figure out how to get cable TV in here."

"Gets a little tight back there, doesn't it?"

She laughed. "One big advantage of being short and scrawny is I fit almost anywhere."

She waved at Ty standing in front of Bert's, drove past my house, then proceeded to her former residence.

She shook her head, then said, "Sad looking mess. It wasn't Shangri-La, but provided decent, almost decent housing."

The rubble looked exactly like it had the day after the fire.

"Sad, especially for those who were displaced."

"I have faith something will work out for all of us. After all, it's Christmas. Time for miracles, they say."

A blue Toyota Prius slowed, started to turn into the lot, then continued out Ashley Avenue.

Noelle watched the car slow and then leave. "That's the landlord."

"Have you talked to him since the fire?"

"No."

"Hear anything else about who started it?"

"Not really, or not really anything credible. I told you before that I'm spending time walking around observing people. Vacationers act different than locals, youngsters act way different than, umm, old-timers."

"Like me?"

She grinned. "No, not you, I mean old people."

"Ever thought about becoming a diplomat?"

"Too much work."

"For me, it'd be easier than writing a book."

"Anyway, in addition to observing folks, I've talked to several, mainly to see how they react to a stranger. A few want to talk about the fire." She chuckled. "It was hard getting some to stop talking about it. Besides the Christmas parade, the fire was the biggest thing that's happened around here in a while."

"It doesn't take much to get folks gossiping."

She stepped out of the truck and leaned against the hood. I joined her in front of the vehicle.

Noelle stared at the ruins then said, "One old man in the Crab Shack said he was certain the fire was started by a pyromaniac traveling from New York to Miami. The old guy said the man stopped here on his way to practice starting fires. He also said President Kennedy is living in a beach house on Kiawah."

"He lost credibility on that one, didn't he?"

"Did with me. Did you hear the fire started in the middle unit, first floor?"

"Yes, it was vacant, I believe."

"Vacant several months. Another guy at the Crab Shack told me he heard the fire was started by a kid sneaking in the empty apartment to smoke. The man couldn't explain how the kid spread gasoline around to make the fire accelerate."

"Noelle, that probably scratches the surface of rumors going around about the fire."

"Chris, there's one other thing. It could be my imagination." She smiled. "Novelists have big imaginations you know. Anyway, a couple of days before the fire, I noticed a guy standing back there." She pointed to the back of the lot. "Seems he was staring at my apartment. The reason he got my attention was that I'd swear I saw him three other times in recent weeks. I noticed because he was always looking around like he thought he was being followed."

"What'd he look like?"

"White dude, little older than me, long shaggy black hair."

"What about clothes?"

"Had them on every time I saw him," she said, then laughed.

"Cute."

"Sorry. He looked like every other dude. Jeans, sweatshirt, backward ball cap, think it was red."

"Anything else?"

"Not really. If I was putting him in my book, he'd be someone on the run, because of the way he kept looking around like he was worried about someone seeing him."

"Seen him since the fire?"

She looked toward the sky, then back at me, "Don't think so. Now you know everything I know about the guy."

"If you would, call me if you see him again. The police chief and I are friends. I can have her check him out."

"Deal. By the way, I was in the bookstore yesterday. The lady who owns it said you two are an item."

"We've been seeing each other a while."

"She's really nice."

I agreed.

Chapter Twenty-Six

I was to meet Barb for supper at Loggerhead's Beach Grill located across the street from her condo in the Charleston Oceanfront Villas. I was there fifteen minutes before the time we were to meet. The restaurant has one of the nicest outdoor decks on the island, but tonight was too cool to enjoy it. As I was walking across the parking lot, I noticed a man getting out of a blue Prius. He was middle-aged, six-foot-tall, average weight with a slight limp. I followed him up the steps and into the building where he took a stool at the bar. Most of the indoor tables were taken, so I was fortunate to get one along the wall. I wasn't certain, but the Prius was the color of the one Noelle said belonged to Russell O'Leary.

I didn't give the man another thought and ordered a Diet Coke while I waited for Barb. She was seldom late, but unlike Charles, she assumed on-time meant on-time, so I wasn't surprised she wasn't here yet. I was beginning to wonder when it was ten minutes after the time she was to arrive. I didn't wonder long. The phone rang with her name on the screen.

"On your way?"

"Not yet. Two groups came in as I was closing. It was as if they just realized Christmas was four days away. They're rummaging through the books trying to do all their Christmas shopping. It'll be a little while before I can get there. Want to postpone, or am I worth waiting for?"

I'm far from the smartest person in my orbit but knew there was only one acceptable answer. "Of course you're worth waiting for. Take your time."

"I appreciate it."

Three couples were at the door waiting for a table. Rather than hogging the real estate for no telling how long, I told the server I'd be at the bar. Besides, it'd give me a chance to introduce myself to the man I suspected to be the apartment building's owner. I took the bar-height seat next to him, then realized I had no logical way of identifying myself or asking about the fire. It didn't help that he was gripping his beer glass with both hands and staring at the liquid it contained like his mind was a thousand miles away.

I did my Charles imitation. "Hi, I'm Chris. You live around here?"

His hands never left the glass, but his head tilted slightly in my direction. "No."

Charles does Charles way better than I do.

"Then you probably didn't hear about the big fire on Folly a week ago."

This time he took one hand off the glass, then turned toward me. "Who'd you say you are again?"

"Chris Landrum."

He reached out in a motion I assumed meant to shake my hand. I shook his wet hand as he said, "I'm Russell O'Leary. You won't believe this, but it was my building that burned."

"You're kidding, that's terrible. I hear it's a total loss."

He sighed. "Unfortunately."

"What caused it?"

"They said arson."

"I'm sorry, Russell. Who would've done that?"

I thought that was better than asking if he'd torched it.

He shrugged.

"Own it long?"

"Been in the family twenty-three years. Dad had it until he passed a few years ago. I got the building. Inherited it and all its problems."

"Problems?"

He hesitated long enough for me to think my question had gone too far.

Finally, he said, "I'm a mechanic, big trucks. I didn't know anything about maintaining a building like that. Dad got the best years out of it, I got the leaky pipes, busted air-conditioners, wiring problems, outside constantly needing paint, that's not even counting deadbeat tenants who'd rather pay for cigarettes and cell phones than rent."

I remembered what Bob Howard had said about Russell considering selling the building.

"Ever think about selling?"

"Only every day, and twice in the middle of the night when I'd get
a call about something wrong. What'd you say your name was again?"

His glass was empty. "Chris. Let me buy you another beer."

He glanced at his watch, then smiled, finally. "I never turn down a
drink."

I waved for the bartender, ordered a beer for Russell, said I was
okay with my drink.

"If it was such a headache, how come you didn't sell? From what I
hear, the market's strong."

"Don't think I didn't come close a time or two. I've got two kids,
guess they're not really kids anymore. They're eighteen and nineteen,
almost grown men. Every time I said something about selling, they went
bananas. Say they're going to take over, help do all the work, want it for
their inheritance. My wife is on their side."

His second beer arrived, and he didn't waste time taking a long pull.

"How much help are the boys?"

"Chris, you got kids?"

I shook my head.

"Then I'll forgive you for that question. They're worthless. I was
holding it to keep peace in the family."

"Going to rebuild?"

"Excellent question, my friend. Don't know."

"Were you at the fire?"

"I wasn't even in South Carolina, was at, umm, a meeting in
Atlanta. I didn't know anything about it until the next day."

"That had to be a shock."

Another sip later, he said, "I probably shouldn't say it, but I'm glad
it's gone. The insurance money will help clear some debts. With that
said, I feel bad for my tenants."

"Have they found places to live?"

"The only one I've seen since the fire is a kid who works at Bert's.
He said he's living in his car."

"That's rough."

"He's young, will be okay."

I remembered how Cindy said he'd been vague about the meeting
he allegedly was attending and where he stayed in Atlanta.

"I haven't been to Atlanta in years. All I remember is construction
downtown. Traffic was always disrupted. Is it still that way?"

"Don't know. I was a few miles from downtown."

Hadn't Cindy said the meeting was at a downtown hotel? I also couldn't figure a way to ask if he torched the building. Even if I had, I didn't get a chance. He looked at his watch for the third time since I sat down.

"Better get home. My wife will be calling out the police if I don't show up soon. Thanks for the beer, Chris. Nice meeting you."

He slid off the chair and was out the door before I paid his tab. I not only bought his second beer, but the first was also on me.

Barb probably passed Russell on the way down the stairs. She arrived with a smile and proclaiming that she was starved, a common occurrence, or so it seems. The crowd had thinned so we had a choice of three tables. We ordered then Barb told me about her day, the closing-time rush, then a story about a customer who wanted Barb to gift wrap a dozen books he was giving to his three children. He eventually bought the books but was disappointed she didn't gift wrap.

I started to tell about meeting Russell O'Leary, but her body language told me she didn't want to talk about the fire. We found much more pleasant topics to enjoy with our meal. After supper, I walked her across the street to her condo, where our pleasant topics continued.

Chapter Twenty-Seven

Barb had kept my mind off the fire for several hours, but the next morning, I couldn't shake what Russell had said about being glad the building burned, and his comment about not being in downtown Atlanta. Had I misunderstood what Cindy shared about his meeting? A phone call would be a simple way to find out.

"Morning, Chief."

"Are you on your way to the Dog?"

"No, but I can be. Why?"

"Because if you're not here, how can you buy me breakfast."

"See you in a few minutes."

"Don't you love it when a plan comes together?" she said, then hung up.

The temperature was beginning to feel like Christmas, so I drove rather than walked. My half-hearted exercise plan would have to wait. There was a rare empty parking space in front of the restaurant, reducing my exercise by more steps.

Cindy was at a table in the center of the room. As I made my way over, she motioned for a server to bring a second cup of coffee.

"I thought you'd be home fixing bacon, eggs, hash browns, and toast for Rose, Luke, and Larry," I said, knowing that'd be the last thing she'd be doing.

"You've been hanging around Noelle Ward too long. She's the fiction writer."

I was surprised she knew Noelle. "Why did you mention Noelle?"

"She said she knew you."

"Where'd you meet her?"

"Did you forget there was a big-ass fire at her building?"

"No, but—"

"She stopped by the office yesterday. Said something about telling you about seeing someone nosing around the apartment. You said if she saw the guy again to call you, so you could tell me, or something like that."

My coffee arrived. Cindy interrupted her story to tell the server what she wanted for breakfast. I exhibited as much originality as I usually do when I ordered French toast.

"Your new writer friend said instead of dragging you in the middle of something that was none of your business, she told me directly about the guy who'd creeped her out."

I took a sip of coffee, then said, "Is that how Noelle said it?"

Cindy smiled. "I added none of your business."

"I figured. Did she give you anything that'd help find the guy?"

"Nothing that wouldn't describe a third of the population. I told her to call me—I repeat, call me—if she sees him again."

"Good plan."

"Chris, if memory serves me correct, you called me. Any particular reason other than to raise my blood pressure?"

"Didn't you tell me Russell O'Leary was in Atlanta the day of the fire?"

She took a small notebook out of her coat pocket, flipped through a few pages, then said, "The owner of a pile of charcoal said he was attending a get-rich-quick rip-off seminar in downtown Atlanta. He didn't say rip-off, that's my astute analysis of the hotel-meeting-room con-artist seminar."

"Are you sure he said downtown Atlanta?"

She flipped another page. "Said the seminar was at the Westin Peachtree Plaza, downtown Atlanta. Why did someone see him here?"

"I met him last night at Loggerhead's."

She shook her head. "Let me guess, you were minding your own business nibbling on a fry when low-and-behold Russell popped up out of nowhere and introduced himself."

"Close. I thought it was him, so I introduced myself."

"While minding your own business, I'm sure. Moving right along, why ask about Atlanta?"

Breakfast arrived. I poured syrup on the French toast, then said, "He told me he'd stayed a few miles outside downtown Atlanta."

"Pray tell, how did that come up in the conversation?" Cindy asked, then took a bite of toast.

"You'd told me he was in downtown Atlanta, so I said how bad construction had been the last time I was there. Asked if it was still bad."

Cindy rolled her eyes. "Chris, have you been to Atlanta since Sherman burned it?"

"Not quite that long ago."

"Charles must be learnin' you private detective techniques for tricking suspects. Did he say anything else about his trip?"

"Not about the trip, but said he was glad the building burned. Insurance would let him pay off debts."

"Suppose you would've already mentioned it if he told you he set the fire?"

"Chief, you would've been the first to know."

"Do you think he did?"

I shrugged. "Told me he wasn't good at maintaining the building; he hated getting called at all hours about problems; he threw out he wasn't fond of dealing with tenants. He didn't say it, but as you shared, he was behind on the mortgage."

"Does that mean you think he did it?"

"Cindy, I talked to the man for fifteen minutes. He seemed like a nice guy, but who knows. It bothers me he'd either lie to you or to me about where he was in Georgia, especially when it didn't matter one way or the other to me."

"And, he said he was glad the building burned."

I smiled. "That too."

"I suppose I'd better have another talk with the confused, former landlord."

"Sounds like the chiefly thing to do."

The server returned with refills on our drinks. Cindy took a sip of the refreshed coffee, then said, "Ho, Ho, Ho!"

"How are you and Larry adjusting to houseguests?"

"Larry hasn't been home enough to know they're there. When he gets home, he's so exhausted he flops in bed not acknowledging any of us. Sort of pleasant. Luke is still spending several hours a day at the store. He told me last night, Larry made him, how did he put it, umm, vice president of Christmas sales. It thrilled the heck out of the kid. I figure it was Larry's way of not giving Luke more money."

"How about Rose?"

"Fine most of the time."

"Most of the time?"

"Her a-hole ex keeps calling. It screws up her mood every time."

"What's he want?"

"What do you think? Wants her to come crawling back to Morristown."

"She thinking about it?"

"The first Thursday after hell freezes over."

"Good."

Cindy stuffed a bite of egg in her mouth, then mumbled, "Yep."

Chapter Twenty-Eight

An hour after breakfast with Cindy the phone rang. Her name appeared on the screen.

"Didn't get enough of me at breakfast?" I said.

"I'm beginning to see why you detest caller ID. How many favors have you asked me for since we've met?"

"The exact number?"

"Never mind. It's a zillion, give or take."

"Sounds right," I said, wondering where the conversation was headed.

"How many have I asked you for?"

"Way fewer than a zillion."

"How about fewer than three?"

"Close."

"I figure you owe me a few, quite a few."

"Cindy, you have a favor to ask?"

"Wow, you're smarter than the average bonehead I deal with."

"Flattery is not one of your strengths," I said, then chuckled. "What do you need?"

"Since Rose has been at the house, I've spent less time with her than I've spent with the town drunk. Luke has been at the hardware store every day, but I know how tired of Larry someone can become. Plus, how many AA batteries can a nine-year-old put in bags before his battery runs down?"

"Your point?"

"Rose told me Luke has been wanting to eat at Planet Follywood, so today she's taking him there for lunch. Think you could miraculously happen in about the time they're arriving? I think conversation with someone other than the television would be good for Rose. Luke seems to like you. Heck if I know why."

"There you go with flattery again. When are they going?"

"I'm guessing noon, but Rose didn't say."

"I'll be there."

"Great. I would say I owe you one, but since you're a zillion favors behind, I'll leave it at thanks."

Planet Follywood was at the intersection of East Erie Avenue and Center Street and was one of Folly's most-established restaurants. It's also known for a large mural painted on the side of the building featuring larger-than-life paintings of Hollywood icons including John Wayne, Marilyn Monroe, Sammy Davis Jr, Elvis, plus a few others.

I arrived ten minutes before noon and stood across the street where I could see diners entering the restaurant. I wasn't there long; my intended targets arrived before noon. Luke pulled his mom past the entry where he pointed at the mural. Rose smiled then escorted her son to the door. I gave them a couple of minutes to settle before I "miraculously" entered.

The interior looked like what I imagine beach restaurants and bars looked like in days gone by. Luke and the food were probably the newest things in there. It was apparent why Planet Follywood was popular with residents and vacationers who wanted to relive their past. Neon beer signs were attached to most walls; another mural was painted on the concrete block wall to the left; wood paneling covered another wall and the ceiling. Overall, a warm, welcoming feel permeated the room. Luke and his mom were seated at a bar-height table in front of the mural and across from a Christmas tree. Luke wore a red sweatshirt that looked like it'd just come out of the package. It probably had. Rose had on a starched, white blouse and a tan lightweight jacket.

Luke spotted me standing in the entry. He waved then said something to his mom. She turned and waved me over.

"Hi, Chris, having lunch?"

I told her I was, then Luke said, "Want to sit with us?"

"I don't want to intrude," although, of course, I did.

"Nonsense," Rose said, "have a seat."

Luke watched me sit. "Been in here before?"

"Many times," I said. "How about you?"

"Our first," Rose answered for her son. "Luke's been talking about it since he saw the mural on the wall outside."

"Cool," he said. "Mom said all those people were in movies, like old movies."

"It was painted by a man from Charleston named James Christopher Hill."

"Think it was okay for him to paint all over that wall? I'd get in trouble if I did something like that."

"I'm sure he had permission."

A server arrived and took our drink orders.

The server left. Luke pointed at the Christmas tree. "Cool tree."

Guess we'd talked enough about the mural.

I said, "It is neat."

"Mom and me put up a tree in Aunt Cindy and Uncle Larry's living room."

Rose touched Luke's arm. "Mom and I."

Luke rolled his eyes, and said, "Mr. Landrum, never marry an English professor."

I smiled. "I'll keep that in mind."

The server returned with our drinks, saving Luke from more English lessons. She asked if we were ready to order. Rose said we needed a few more minutes. Luke took over the conversation from that point, telling me about working at the hardware store, about how cool his bedroom was, how he could see the Folly River and the marsh out his window, and several other things that were important to him but which I forgot as soon as he finished mentioning them. Rose sat back and watched her son share his day to day, almost moment to moment experiences.

The server tried again to see if we were ready to order. Rose asked Luke if he was. He turned to the server and asked if they had hot dogs. They did, so he ordered one, Rose stuck with a cheeseburger, and I ordered a chicken finger basket. Rose excused herself and headed to the restroom.

Luke watched her go, leaned close to me, then said, "Mr. Landrum, think you could do something for me?"

"Suppose it depends on what?"

"I want to get Mom something nice for Christmas. I heard you could find teeth from old, dead sharks on the beach. Can you believe that?"

I nodded.

Luke looked toward the restrooms, turned to me, and said, "Someone who came in the store said people make jewelry from the teeth. Do they sell them somewhere here?"

"In fact, they do. Barb's Books has several pieces of shark tooth jewelry made by Michelle, a local artist."

"Could you buy a necklace with a shark tooth on it for me to give Mom? If it's not too expensive. I have money Uncle Larry paid me for working, so I can pay you back."

"I'll be glad to."

He again glanced toward the restroom. "I'd also like to get one for Aunt Cindy. She's been nice to us."

"I'll do that, Luke."

"Make Aunt Cindy's a little cheaper than the one for Mom. I want Mom to know she's number one."

I smiled and said I would. "What about Uncle Larry?"

"All he wants for Christmas is to sleep for two days without being interrupted or hearing his cash register ding. I'm going to give him a quiet house. No TV, no playing loud."

"That's a great gift."

"What are you two men plotting out here?" Rose said as she returned to the table.

"Nothing, Mom. Guy talk."

"Luke, why don't you go wash your hands before our food arrives?"

He sighed, then slid off the chair.

"Rose, you have a great kid."

"Most of the time."

"Have you told Cindy about Kenneth's visit?"

"No."

"It's none of my business, but I think you should. I know you disagree, but he'd be a prime suspect in starting the fire. Cindy would have a good chance of learning if he was here the day of the fire. Don't you want to know?"

"Yes, but I don't want her going ballistic."

"Rose, I've known your sister a long time. She's at her best when faced with difficult situations. I'd trust her with my life. You can trust her with the truth."

Luke returned wiping his hands together. He smiled, then said, "What are you two grownups plotting out here?"

Touché.

Our conspiring ended when the food arrived. We spent the next hour enjoying the food, the eclectic restaurant, and each other. Cindy was right. Rose and Luke left the restaurant in better spirits and more relaxed than when they arrived. So did I.

Chapter Twenty-Nine

I headed to Barb's Books after leaving Rose and Luke full of food and smiles. A woman I didn't recognize was perusing the romance section while Barb was behind the counter thumbing through a book. She was wearing one of her signature red blouses and black slacks. She saw me at the door, closed the book, and smiled.

"What brings you in? I know it's not to buy a book."

"Right again," I said, then moved to a small table near the checkout counter that was covered with a white velour cloth. "I'm not looking for a book but a couple of these." On the velour, there were several silver necklaces, a couple of bracelets, plus five sets of earrings, all featuring black, shark teeth.

"Christopher, if I may be so bold, I suggest if you're looking to buy jewelry for a woman, you may not want to shop in a store owned by the lady you're dating."

I laughed. "I'll file that wise advice. Actually, I'm Christmas shopping for a gentleman I know." I then shared my assignment.

"In that case," Barb said, "I think these earrings would be perfect for our Chief." Barb held one up to her ear. It had a half-inch long shark tooth dangling from the short chain. "First, they're pretty. Second, they could visually communicate to local miscreants not to mess with the Chief."

"Perfect. How about Rose?"

She modeled three necklaces before we agreed on one that not only had a shark tooth but a small, silver heart. She asked if I wanted her to gift-wrap the gifts.

"Didn't think you gift-wrapped."

She looked at the customer browsing in the romance section, then said, "I don't unless it's for someone special, someone like Luke."

"Or for me?"

"Nope. I'll also give your young friend the family discount."

I thanked her for the discount, to which she said she wasn't doing it for me, but for Luke. I told her about having lunch at Cindy's suggestion with Rose and Luke. She said she was glad Rose was getting out, hoping it'd keep her from thinking about the fire or losing most everything. I told her how I'd suggested, again, that she tell her sister about her ex-husband's visit to Folly the day before the fire.

"Speaking of fire victims," Barb said as she reached under the counter to pull out a roll of red and gold wrapping paper, "Noelle was in an hour ago. She's off work this week. Said without having an apartment to hang out in, she didn't know what to do with her time. She was heading to the library to work on her book."

"How's she doing?"

"She's young, adapts fairly well to adversity. Better than I would."

I shared what Noelle told me about thinking someone was watching her.

"She told me."

"Think she's right?"

Barb shrugged. "No way to know."

The browser carried a stack of books to the counter. Barb rang them up, then thanked the shopper, who left the store heavier than when she arrived.

Barb finished wrapping the gifts, waved off my attempt to pay, then said, "Let me bounce an idea off you. Noelle seems like a nice woman. She's funny, has a responsible job in Charleston, shows a huge amount of initiative with the book she's writing."

"I agree."

"I hate seeing her living out of her truck. I've got a spare bedroom going to waste. What do you think about me offering to let her stay in my condo until she finds the kind of apartment she's looking for?" Barb laughed. "The perfect dump she calls her dream apartment."

"Are you comfortable with it?"

"I'm leaning that way."

"I think it's a great idea, as long as you're comfortable."

THAT NIGHT BEGAN with me alternating between wondering if Rose would finally tell her sister about her ex-husband's visit, and my thoughts about Barb asking Noelle to move in with her.

My mind shifted to wondering who'd started the fire. Regardless of what Rose thought, I could see it being her ex. He could be eliminated if he was in Tennessee on the day of the fire. Ty could also have made Aimee's fiancée angry enough to start the fire. Most likely, he would've or could've known Ty was at work, so the fire was set to make a point rather than to harm Ty. That brought me to Horace, Janice's ex-husband. She was convinced he's the culprit, but it seems like a stretch. He'd moved on, although Janice's attorney was still after him for money. Was that reason enough to burn her building?

Neil's former boss had more than enough reason to want revenge for being turned in to the IRS. It'd been some time since Neil did that, so would he still be angry enough to set the fire? Then what about the customer Neil had unceremoniously thrown out of the bar? Granted, the man threatened Neil, but, as Cal said, that wasn't uncommon, and seldom led to anything. Could this be the exception?

Noelle was convinced someone was following her, or at least, keeping an eye on her, plus someone left her the note. Without knowing why there was no way to determine if she bothered someone enough to torch the building.

The most logical arsonist was Russell O'Leary. He was behind in his mortgage, appeared to have little means to catch up. His alibi for the time of the fire was suspect at best. Finally, he'd told me he didn't want the building in the first place.

From my limited time with Russell, he appeared to be a nice man, yet was in over his head maintaining the building. The fire was set when the building most likely would've been vacant. That seemed like something Russell would've taken into consideration.

Cindy knew everything I did about Russell, so I was confident she was following up. So, with all of that cleared up, I should be able to get a good night's sleep.

So, why didn't I?

Chapter Thirty

Despite little sleep, I was awake at six o'clock. I closed my eyes attempting to catch a few more minutes sleep. I failed. The next thing I knew, it was eight-thirty, far more than a few minutes later. While well-rested, I was hungry. The unseasonably warm weather from a few days ago had returned, so I walked next door. Ty was at the register adjusting a string of Christmas lights attached around the check-out stand.

"Hey, Mr. Landrum, want a treat?"

"No thanks, Ty. I wanted to stop by to see how you were doing."

"I'm doing better than these lights, Mr. Landrum."

"You're brighter than they are," I said. He could take it any way he wanted. "How's Lost?"

"Great. That little critter loves the warmer weather. She isn't a fan of staying in the car but handles it good when the temperature ain't too cold."

I nodded, thinking that'd apply to all of us.

Ty continued, "Anything I can help you with?"

"No. Grabbing coffee and something for breakfast."

"You know where it is. Merry Christmas."

"You going to Cal's Christmas party?"

"I don't know. I'll be working Bert's free community breakfast. It's over at ten, so I don't know if I'll be here longer than that. Besides, ain't most of the people at Cal's party old, umm, older than me?"

"All ages will be there," I said, although on average age he was right. "I'd love to see you."

"I'll ponder it," he said, then started waiting on a man who'd arrived at the counter.

I grabbed a cinnamon Danish, drew a cup of coffee, then returned to the register.

Ty took my money and said, "Done pondered it, Mr. Landrum. If I get out of here early enough, I'll be there."

"Fantastic."

I started home, smiled when I saw Ty's Miata in the back of the small parking lot, then jumped out of the way when an older-model white Chevrolet Malibu with a dent in the driver's door pulled in, nearly hitting me.

Janice Raque stepped out, gave me a dirty look like I had some nerve getting in the way of her car, hesitated, then smiled.

"Sorry, Chris. Didn't recognize you."

I wondered if that meant she wouldn't be sorry if she'd run down anyone else.

"Hi, Janice."

"Glad I ran into you." She smiled. "Didn't mean literally. Got something to tell you. Got a minute?"

I told her I did.

Her arms were wrapped around her torso like she was cold. "Let's get in the car? It's warmer."

I wasn't cold but agreed. Since she had something to say, I remained quiet and took a sip of coffee.

"Remember the other day when we were talking? I told you I was certain Horace was the one who set the fire."

That wasn't something I could easily forget. "Yes."

"Wasn't him."

"How do you know?"

"We had, guess still have, a mutual friend. Name's Sally. She called yesterday to see if I'd heard about Horace. I'd heard a bunch of things about the no-good, two-timing, goat herder. I wasn't sure what she was talking about, so I asked. You'll never guess what she told me."

She hesitated. I wondered if she wanted me to guess. Instead, I said, "What?"

"He had a stroke. happened two days before the fire. The two-timer was in the hospital in Mt. Pleasant. Nearly kicked the bucket."

"That's too bad."

She sighed. "Not bad enough. He didn't die. Got released yesterday.

That's what Sally called to tell me. Like she thought I cared. No sir, I didn't."

"He couldn't have started the fire."

"I figured the stroke was caused by the old man pretending he was a youngster fiddlin' with that floozy he ran off with if you know what I mean." She offered a sly grin.

I did. Scratch one suspect. Which reminded me of something that'd bothered me since I had lunch with her in Snapper Jack's, something that contributed to me getting little sleep last night. It was something she said before nearly falling off the chair. Instead of following up at the time, I thought it better to catch her before she hit the floor.

"Janice, remember when we met the other day in Snapper Jack's?"

She smiled. "Not much. I was a bit under the weather if you know what I mean."

Drunk would have been the word I would've chosen.

"We were talking about the apartment building and you said people had asked you about living there. You mentioned two people, a man, I believe his name was Jeff, and a woman named something like Kaycee. Remember?"

"I remember them, but don't remember telling you. Sure it was me?"

Her not remembering didn't surprise me considering her condition at the time.

"What do you remember about them?"

"The guy, Jeff, or something like that, looked like a street person if you ask me. He stopped me in the parking lot one afternoon, said he was looking for somewhere to live and wanted to know what I thought about the apartment building. I told him I didn't think much of it, but that's about all."

"What about the woman? You started to tell me something, but, umm, we were interrupted." I didn't add, "by you falling off the chair."

"Let's see. I believe she said her name was Kaycee Ericson. She came knocking on my door, suppose a week or so before the fire." Janice closed her eyes, then tapped her fingers on the steering wheel. "Told me she owned some apartments. They were full and she had someone she was looking for a place to live. Think I told her about the vacant unit on the first floor. She then asked how long I lived there. If I liked living in the building. Then she asked how many people lived in my apartment. That got my dander up. I asked if she was a census taker or what. I wanted to find out if she was something official before I told her it was none of her damned business who lived in my apartment. Nearly slammed the door in her face." She could tell I was getting pissed." Janice looked out the side window, scratched the side of her face, then said, "She then told me she was looking at buying the place. That got my attention, so I let her in, offered her a beer, told her everything she wanted to know. Even told her about the leaky faucet, although I didn't have to since she could hear it drip, drip, drip all the way in the living room. Figured if she bought it, she couldn't be as bad a landlord as O'Leary. Our conversation then headed a direction I didn't like."

"How?"

"She started whispering like there were other people in the room nosing into what she was saying. Said she was trying to figure if she could fix the building up enough so she could increase rents enough to make the deal work." She looked at me and shrugged. "Didn't think it was too wise telling a tenant all that. I'm no math wizard, but it sounded like it would've had me digging deeper in my pocketbook to live there. Hell, Chris, if I could afford a higher rent, I wouldn't have been living in that dump."

"Janice, did she give you a card or her contact information?"

"Sure did."

"Do you have it?"

She frowned and looked at her hand on the steering wheel. "It was in the apartment." She clapped her hands together like she was wiping something off. "It's ashes."

"Janice, I appreciate you sharing. I don't want to keep you any longer."

"Chris, you ain't keeping me. All I have to do is go back to the damned hotel room."

"I'd better be going anyway. Are you going to be at Cal's Christmas party?"

She nodded. "Anything to get out of the hotel room."

Chapter Thirty-One

I finally made it home and to the cinnamon Danish I'd been carrying for a half hour. I microwaved the cold coffee then sat at the kitchen table. It was good eliminating Horace from the suspect list, although I never had him near the top.

Janice did say something that struck me as significant, more than anything about Horace. That was Kaycee Ericson's visit to Janice's apartment a week before the fire. She apparently was someone who wanted to buy the building. Was Russell O'Leary going to sell to her? I'd never heard of Kaycee Ericson until Janice shared her name. Was she local?

A call to Chief LaMond might provide answers.

"What do you want now?" she said.

I'd given up long ago trying to get my friends to answer with anything resembling a civil response.

"What do you know about Kaycee Ericson?"

"Chris, you've been around Charles way too much. What's Kaycee have to do with anything?"

I shared what Janice Raque had told me about the visit.

"Interesting. Are you trying to screw up my theory that O'Leary torched his building?"

"Cindy, you're Chief. I'm simply a lowly citizen sharing a story. I have no business sticking my nose in your investigation."

"Chris, I say this lovingly, you're as full of crap as Dumbo the elephant."

"Glad you said it lovingly."

"Want to pout or learn about Kaycee?"

"What do you think?"

"She lives in a condo across from Harris Teeter. Been here two years at the most. Someone said she moved from New Jersey, is connected to money. She's built a couple of new oceanfront McMansions, sold them for a tidy profit."

"How do you know all that?"

"I'm Chief. I know everything."

I waited, knowing once she got past the bluster, she'd elaborate.

"She's been all the talk around City Hall. With the two McMansions and now a condo building she wants to develop out West Ashley near the County Park, she's good at pushing the zoning regulation boundaries. So far, she hasn't crossed the line, but according to folks who know more about zoning than this lowly public servant, she's within millimeters of violating the regs."

"Cindy, is this enough for you to talk with Kaycee?"

"To be determined."

"Meaning?"

"Meaning, in fifteen minutes after I get a pesky citizen off the phone, Russell O'Leary will be in this big impressive office of Director of Public Safety. It's time for me to ram sharpened bamboo sticks under his fingernails to get the truth about his alleged visit to the metropolis of Atlanta. Truth like where he stayed, how long he was actually there, and if he's fortunate, proof he was there instead of here incinerating his building."

"Cindy, other than bamboo under his nails, that sounds like a good plan. Will you add questions about him selling the building?"

"Wasn't until three minutes ago. Bye."

Progress, she said bye before hanging up.

Thirty minutes later, the phone rang. At first, I thought it was Cindy, then realized she'd be talking to Russell. The screen read *Barb*.

"Good morning, my favorite bookstore owner."

"Only bookstore owner."

"You're my favorite, regardless how many bookstores there are. What did I do to deserve a call?"

"Nothing. I wanted to tell you something I did last night."

That got my attention. "What?"

"Invited Noelle to move in with me until she finds the kind of apartment she's looking for."

"That's wonderful. What did she say?"

"Short version, yes. Slightly longer version, she was thrilled. She said if she had to spend many more nights in her truck, she'd either have to find a chiropractor or a witch doctor to work on her back. Before she told me that, she kept saying she didn't want to inconvenience me. I told her she wouldn't. She kept offering to pay rent. I told her no. I couldn't tell for certain because of her sunglasses, but I think I saw tears."

"You're a kind person. She's lucky to have you as a friend."

"Don't know about that, but it made me feel good being able to help."

"The Christmas spirit in action."

"'Tis the season. I met her at Loggerhead's. Before she left, know what she said?"

"I hope it was thank you."

Barb laughed. "She got serious, touched me on the arm, looked across the street at my condo building, and said something like, 'Don't take offense, Barb. Your condo is way too nice for what I'm looking for.' I told her I wasn't offended. She's moving in tonight."

I was touched by Barb's generosity. After her call, I got up from the table, carried my coffee cup to my office. Charles was right, all that was in the room was a small table holding my computer and printer, a chair, and a filing cabinet holding years of tax papers, plus other items I probably didn't need to save.

I sat, took a sip of coffee getting cold again, and punched in Neil Wilson's number. I didn't think he was going to answer, but he finally did. He sounded like the phone awakened him. It may have. I told him who was calling then asked if he was available for lunch. He said he was due at Cal's at three but could meet me at the Lost Dog Cafe in an hour.

Good to his word, he was standing in front of the restaurant when I arrived. He looked like he'd just climbed out of bed, although I knew he'd been awake an hour earlier. He wore a royal blue sweatshirt with The Griffon Pub in large block letters on the front, tan slacks with fraying cuffs. His hair was sticking out from a Charleston RiverDogs cap. He looked like he'd slept in his clothes.

We were escorted to a table in the center of the room. There were only four other tables occupied. Neil put his hat on the edge of the table, yawned, and ran his hand through his hair. It did little to get hairs going the same direction.

"Did you work last night?"

"Until two this morning. Can't you tell?"

I smiled. "Yes."

A server, who said her name was Anna, appeared with pen in hand.

"Coffee," Neil said. "That'll get my eyes open enough to read the menu."

I told her the same.

I filled the time until Anna returned by talking about the near-countless photos of dogs adorning the walls. Neil observed how different the decorations and colors were from those in Cal's. Anna returned with mugs of steaming hot coffee. She said she'd be back to take our order. Neil took three sips before speaking.

"I appreciate you calling," he said, then hesitated, "although it made me wonder why."

Good to her word, Anna returned asking if we were ready to order. While I'd told Neil the invitation was for lunch, he had breakfast on his mind. He started to order a bagel until I said I was buying. He switched to bacon and eggs; I went with French toast, surprise, surprise. Anna said, "Excellent choices," and headed to the kitchen. I wondered if she ever said, "Terrible choice."

"Chris, I appreciate you picking up the tab. Staying at the hotel is breaking me."

"That's what I wanted to talk to you about. I have an extra room at my place. If you want, you could move in until you find somewhere of your own."

He stared at me. "You're kidding."

"It's nothing luxurious. The room's small. Has a blowup mattress, no real bed."

Okay, it doesn't have a blowup mattress, but with luck, it will before he gets there.

"Not to be unappreciative," he said, "how much?"

"Nothing. It's yours until you find a place to stay."

He repeated, "You're kidding."

"I'm serious."

He stood, walked around the table, and shook my hand. "Thank you. I can't believe something good is happening to me at Christmas."

Anna arrived with our food, so Neil returned to his chair.

He took a bite of eggs, then said, "I won't be able to move in until tomorrow. Besides, I've already paid the hotel for tonight. Wouldn't want that money to go to waste."

Good. That'll give me time to find a blowup mattress.

"That's fine, Neil."

Two more bites and he said, "Chris, you're really not kidding?"

Chapter Thirty-Two

Before leaving the Dog, Neil told me he needed to get to the hotel to take a shower before heading to work. He wanted to use as much of the hotel's water as he could to get his money's worth. I remained at the table to call Charles.

"Ready to go?" I said.

"Sure," he said, not asking where.

"I'll be there in ten minutes." I hung up on him, a move he'd perfected. It felt good being on this end of the line for a change.

Ten minutes later, I pulled in his crushed shell and gravel parking lot to see him standing in front of his apartment. He was wearing a maroon Texas A&M sweatshirt under a lightweight jacket, well-worn jeans, and his Tilley.

"We going to buy my Christmas present?" he said as he slid in the passenger seat.

"No," I said, then pulled out of the lot.

He snapped his fingers. "Done figured it out. We're going to catch a flight to Bora Bora for the holidays?"

"No," I repeated. This was nearly as much fun as hanging up on him.

We'd pulled off the island and past Harris Teeter.

"I see we're not grocery shopping. You can fill in our destination at any time."

Five minutes later, I pulled in Walmart's parking lot.

"Let me guess," he said, "we're going to Walmart."

"I see why you think you're a detective."

Before he could respond with one of his many smart-aleck remarks, the phone rang.

"Good afternoon, Cindy."

I parked and Charles motioned for me to put the phone on speaker. Rather than having to repeat everything she said, I tapped the speaker icon. Charles smiled.

"It's getting better by the minute," Cindy said. "Don't be surprised the next few days if you hear Russell O'Leary has been arrested for torching his apartment building."

"He confess?"

"It's not what he told me but what he didn't."

Charles leaned toward the phone. "What's that mean, Chief?"

"Chris, you done gone and got a talking disease. You sound like your worthless friend."

Charles said, "Chief, he doesn't sound anything like Bob Howard."

I heard her chuckle before saying, "His other worthless friend."

Enough! "Chief, what did Russell tell you?"

"He stuck to his story that sounds like a fairytale. Still claims he was in Atlanta, as in downtown Atlanta, attending a get-rich-quick seminar, sleeping in a nearby cheap hotel, paying cash, and not able to remember the name of where he stayed. His body language and failure to look me in the eyes made me not believe a word of it."

Charles said, "Who wouldn't want to look in such a lovely lady's eyes? He's definitely lying."

"Charles, your BS is appreciated, but it doesn't prove guilt."

"Cindy," I said, "if that's the case, why do you think he'll be arrested?"

"The only thing he appeared certain of in his far-fetched version of a trip to Atlanta, was where the seminar was held. After he left, I called the Westin Peachtree Plaza, the hotel he could remember. I had a pleasant talk with a nice lady with a cute southern accent. Seems she's in charge of meetings and seminars."

"Let me guess," I said, "there wasn't a get-rich-quick seminar the day of the apartment fire."

"Not that day, not the day before, not the day after, in fact, not the week before or after. The closest thing they hosted was a two-day meeting on financing options for large office buildings held two days after Russell returned to South Carolina."

Charles said, "So why isn't he sitting in a jail cell?"

"Charged with what, fibbing to the fuzz? We need more. I told him to bring proof, anything, gas receipts, restaurant receipts, hell, I'd even take a receipt written on toilet paper from a panhandler if Russell donated to the bum's liquor fund. Otherwise, my hands are tied until I have something more than a hunch to arrest him on."

"Cindy," I said, "you're convinced he did it?"

"Plum near a thousand percent."

"Have you talked to Kaycee Ericson?"

"I'm calling her as soon as I get off the phone with Folly's nosiest troublemakers."

It didn't take Charles's detective skills to know who she was talking about. I wished her luck.

"Did you drive me out here to sit in the parking lot?" Charles said after Cindy ended her call with the troublemakers.

Instead of telling him where we were going, I took the show him approach. It took several unsuccessful trips up aisles before I found the blowup mattresses in the sports and outdoors section. I savored the walk by not telling him what I was trying to find. Cruel, but sweet revenge for him doing similar things over the years.

I finally gave in and shared why I was looking at blowup mattresses.

"Wonderful. You took my advice about taking in Neil."

He'd suggested it, but I hated giving him the satisfaction of knowing he was right. Oh well, why not? After all, it's Christmas.

"Yes, it was your idea, a good one."

He beamed and curtsied. It was worth telling him the truth to see him happy. We studied our options when he came up with another good idea. I should buy an electric pump to inflate the mattress. It was a good idea, but he didn't have to add I'd need the pump because I was too old to blow it up with my fossilizing lungs.

On the way home, I called Bob Howard and hit the speaker button for Charles. While I had confidence Cindy was on the right trail with Russell, and that she'd contact Kaycee Ericson like she told me she would, I wasn't ready to convict the landlord. He seemed sincere with everything he'd told me. It also seemed counterproductive when he told me he was glad the building had been reduced to ashes. If anyone had dirt on or would know someone who would know anything bad about Kaycee, it'd be Bob.

Willie Nelson was singing "On the Road Again" in the background, when Bob answered with, "On your way to get a cheeseburger?"

"No."

"Then why are you wasting my valuable time?"

"Bob, I appreciate you taking time out of your busy day to talk to me," I said, exuding sarcasm.

"Damned right, I'm busy. You know how much energy it takes to sit, drink a beer, and watch the overpaid cook fixing burgers? What do you need?"

See why we're such good friends?

"What do you know about Kaycee Ericson?"

"You nosin' in something that's none of your business?"

"Yes."

"Figures. Don't know much. She's bought a few buildings over here, hear she's itching to be a big-time developer. Heard she either is or was married to Alan, who actually is a big-time developer. That's it, my well of information's dry."

"Thanks."

"Does this have something to do with the apartment building fire?"

"Yes."

"Think she set it?"

"Maybe."

"Let me make some calls to guys who'll know more about her than what I said."

"Bob, I'd appreciate it."

"Don't appreciate it enough to frequent this fine-dining establishment." He hung up.

I was impressed, first because Bob gave me some information without me having to buy food, and second, Charles hadn't interrupted.

Chapter Thirty-Three

After dropping Charles at his apartment, I went home to repurpose my office into a bedroom. I was glad Charles encouraged me to buy the pump, otherwise, it would've taken me five years and probably a heart attack to inflate the mattress with lung power. Using the pump, I had the bed inflated, covered with sheets that were too large, and added a pillow I'd forgotten I had. All Neil's bedroom lacked was a piece of chocolate on the pillow and a Gideon's Bible.

With my hotelier duties completed, I moved to the living room to review what, if anything, I'd learned during the extraordinarily busy day. Since I'd innocently walked to Bert's for breakfast and coffee, I'd talked with Ty, Janice, and Neil, residents of sixty percent of the five occupied apartments in the ill-fated building. Janice eliminated Horace as a suspect, while adding Kaycee. Two of the displaced residents, Noelle and Neil, had found somewhere to live. And, it appeared another suspect, Russell, was on the verge of being arrested.

While a lot had transpired, I wasn't closer to figuring out who set the fire than I'd been on my walk to Bert's. My phone rang as I came to that realization.

Charles said, "I'll pick you up at nine in the morning."

"Going to buy my Christmas present, or taking a flight to Bora Bora?"

Silence was the response to what I thought was a humorous comment. He'd hung up.

Charles's definition of nine o'clock was eight-thirty, so I was waiting for him on my screened-in porch when he pulled in the drive.

"On time, good," he said as I slipped in the car.

He wore a navy-blue sweatshirt with Auburn University in orange on the front.

"Morning, Charles," I said, and resisted asking where we were going.

He drove two blocks then turned on East Arctic Avenue, before saying, "Know why I wore this sweatshirt?"

"To keep you warm?" I said, knowing it wasn't the answer he wanted.

"Guess again."

Then it struck me.

"Auburn has a well-known college of veterinarian medicine, so we're going to Martha Wright's zoo."

His head jerked my direction. "Wow! I may give you a promotion in my private detective agency."

"Charles, now that I know where we're going, how about why?"

"Martha called last night. Asked if I could stop by this morning."

"Why?"

"Suppose because of my charm, good looks, way with women."

I rolled my eyes. "Again, why?"

"Clueless. I'm bringing you in case she got a stray mountain lion."

I didn't waste time saying the mountain lion theory was as remote as her wanting him to visit because of his good looks, charm, and way with women.

Martha greeted us at the door. I was surprised no barking dogs were surrounding her.

"Glad you could make it," she said. "I see you brought Chris."

She was smiling so I couldn't tell what she thought about Charles's plus one.

"Chris loves hearing about your animals, so I thought he'd enjoy visiting."

I did?

"Great," she said, with little enthusiasm. "Come in. We're gathered in the sitting room."

Other than Squeezy, I didn't know who "we" could include. Seconds later, that mystery was answered when I saw Martha's neighbor, Dixie Thompson, seated in one of the wingback chairs. I'd met Dixie before meeting Martha. She lived across the street from Martha and had been her friend for years. She was in her late-seventies, five-foot-eight, thin, with white hair that would put the whitest paint color to shame. Her hair looked even whiter compared to her tanned, leathery face.

Dixie stood, held up a tumbler holding an amber-colored liquid, and said, "Moscow."

Charles was the invited guest, so I let him respond, besides, I had no idea what to say.

"Huh?" he articulately said.

Dixie held the tumbler higher. "It's five o'clock somewhere."

Martha laughed. "In Moscow."

"Oh," Charles said.

Watching Dixie sway as she chuckled at Martha's remark, I wondered where it'd been five o'clock an hour or two earlier.

"Fellas," Martha said, "how about a hot toddy?"

"Or bourbon," Dixie added.

"No thanks," Charles said. "Wouldn't happen to have any coffee brewed?"

"Heaven's no," Martha said. "That stuff's not good for you. Let me grab a chair from the kitchen. Wouldn't want you to sit on the floor."

Charles said, "Martha, I'll get it."

She pointed her cane in the direction of the kitchen like Charles wouldn't know how to find it. Fortunately, Dixie was in the chair closest to Squeezy's occupied aquarium, so I sat on the only vacant seat. Charles returned and pulled the kitchen chair up beside Martha.

Martha waited for Charles to get comfortable, then said, "Gentlemen, I appreciate you coming over. I wanted to—"

Dixie interrupted, "Martha, God love her, wanted to be an unvarnished jackass. I told her so in no uncertain terms."

Martha pointed her cane at Dixie. "Dear, why don't you let me explain?"

Yes, Martha, please, I thought.

"It's your house," Dixie said, then took another sip.

"As you recall, when you visited the other day, you asked if I'd let the young man from Bert's stay here until he found satisfactory housing."

"Ty Striker," Charles said.

"Yes, anyway, I reacted strongly."

"Like a jackass," Dixie added, only to receive a dirty look from her friend.

"I was concerned about how my good friend Dixie and my dearly beloved deceased husband would react to a man moving in with me."

"Cut to the chase, Martha," Dixie said. "You thought we'd think it was for sex."

Martha's face turned red. "Dixie, I don't think that's appropriate talk—"

Again, Dixie interrupted, apparently one of her strengths, "Martha, you know that's what you thought. What did I tell you?"

"Dixie, I don't think—"

"I told you the man from Bert's was young enough to be your grandson, heavens, possibly great-grandson. The last time you had sex that peanut farmer from Georgia was President. I promise sex won't be popping in Ty's head when he sees you. I think it'd be great for you having someone who walks on two legs living in here not slithering around like Squeezy or walking on all fours like most of your family members."

"But, what about—"

"I know, I know. What would Tommy think? I told you he ain't doing a bit of thinking down in that hole in the ground. Not a bit."

Martha leaned forward in her chair, glared at her friend, then said, "Dixie, enough." She turned to Charles, then to me. "Guys, Dixie has some good points. Crudely put, but good. If you think the young man would be interested, I'd be honored for him to move in. As I think you said the last time you were here, this place is too large for me to keep up by myself."

Charles glanced at me. I said, "Martha, I think Ty would be thrilled."

"So would his kitten, Lost," Charles added.

"Martha," I said, "You'll make Ty's Christmas."

"Ladies," Charles said, "will you be at Cal's Christmas party?"

Dixie said, "Can't speak for Martha, but I'll be there. We always go to the potluck supper at Planet Follywood, but that's later."

"Don't know why you can't speak for me, you always do."

"Okay," Dixie said, "Martha will be there. She may even bring her new boy toy." She slapped her knee and laughed. "Then after we get home, he can come-a-courtin' over my way if Martha don't wear him out."

On that, it was time to leave. I told Martha I'd talk to Ty and get back with her.

In the car, I said, "At least we didn't have to put up with any of Martha's animals."

"You got enough dog hair on your butt from the chair to build a dog. I think I would've hugged Squeezy before listening more to Dixie."

"Good point," I said, "as long as it was you holding the boa."

Instead of turning in my drive, Charles drove a hundred feet farther and pulled in Bert's lot.

"Let's tell Ty," Charles said.

Ty was behind the register talking to Shawn, another friend of mine, holding his tiny dog Bruiser. He was paying for a loaf of bread while Ty was breaking a treat in half and giving it to Bruiser. Shawn left so Charles asked Ty if he had a few minutes. I was no expert, but it appeared Ty was working. I wondered how he'd have time for us. Charles added, "It's important."

A woman stepped behind us with a bag of chips. Ty looked around and asked a man working behind the deli counter if he could cover the register. The man nodded.

Ty said, "Let's go outside. I need to check on Lost."

On the way to his car, I asked if he knew Martha Wright.

"By reputation. Isn't she the woman who feeds strays, has a hundred pets?"

I smiled. "She does feed strays, but her pet count is closer to a dozen."

"Don't think I've talked to her, or if I have, I didn't know who she was. Why?"

I shared that we'd come from her house where she said she'd love for Ty to stay there until he found somewhere more suitable. I explained that Martha's house was on the ocean and had about two-thousand times more living space than his Miata.

"Why would a stranger want to take me in, me in?"

I resisted saying it was because she took in strays. "She knew about the fire, heard you were living in your car, and had Lost. She's an animal lover, so she thought her house would be perfect, that is, if you had any interest."

Yes, some of that was reimagining history, but I wanted it to sound like Martha's idea.

"I'd be thrilled for the opportunity," he said. "When can I meet her?"

I asked when he got off work. He told me six. I told him I'd let her know he'd accept her kind offer, and if okay with her, he could go to her house after work.

"How's that sound?"

"Wonderful."

I gave him Martha's address and Charles gave him her phone number in case he couldn't get there today.

"Oh, one more thing, Mr. Landrum. You were asking me if I knew of anyone who might know about the fire, anyone other than us who lived there."

I vaguely remembered saying something about it. "Yes."

"Did you see that lady behind you in line before we came out here?"

I noticed someone, but that was all. "Yes, why?"

"Today was the first time I've seen her since the fire. It reminded me she talked to me two, maybe three, weeks before the building burned. I was heading to my apartment and she was in the parking lot."

Charles said, "What'd she want?"

"Nothing important. Stuff like how I liked living there, how long I'd been there, if the landlord kept up the building good."

He was right, I didn't see how any of that was important. "Why'd you mention it?"

"I could be wrong, but I think I saw her near the building a time or two after that. Sort of thought it was a little strange, that's all."

"You saw her two or three times before the fire?" I said.

"Think so."

Charles said, "Did she give you her name?"

"Yeah. It was something like Kelsey."

I said, "Could it be Kaycee?"

Ty nodded. "Kaycee, umm. Could be."

I looked back toward the store. A blue SUV was pulling out of the lot, but the windows were tinted. I couldn't see the driver. "Ty, is that her in the blue SUV?"

He looked at the vehicle heading east on Ashley Avenue. "That's her car."

She was driving a Maserati SUV, a blue Maserati like the one parked adjacent to the apartment building's parking lot during the Christmas parade. Of course, there could be more than one blue Maserati SUV on Folly, but what were the odds?

"Ty," I said, "other than asking about the stuff you already mentioned, do you recall her saying anything else?"

He tapped on the Miata's window. Lost jumped from the seat to the headrest then gave Ty a *where's my food* look. Ty opened the door enough to get his hand in and wrapped it around Lost's stomach. The kitten purred as Ty lifted him out of the car, cradling him in the crook of his elbow. Charles being Charles stepped closer to Ty and rubbed Lost under his chin, then told the feline he was getting a new home, a home with animals to play with.

Ty handed Lost to Charles, then turned back to me. "Sorry, Mr. Landrum, what was the question?"

"Do you recall Kaycee saying anything else?"

"Not really. I think she must've been interested in renting an apartment."

Charles continued to rub the underside of his feline friend's chin, but said, "Why think that?"

"She wanted to know if there were vacant units."

He hadn't mentioned that earlier.

I said, "You sure?"

"Yeah. I told her the one on the first floor was empty. I offered to give her the landlord's name and number. Said she already had it."

Charles handed Lost back to Ty, and said, "Guess that's why she was asking how well he maintained the building."

"That's what I figured."

It could be as simple as that, I thought. Or not.

Charles said, "Did she say anything else?"

"Don't recall anything." He looked at his watch, then slipped Lost back in his car. "Guys, I'd better get back in there. I really need to keep this job."

I thanked him for talking with us and said I'd let Martha know he'd be stopping by after work.

He headed to the store. Charles headed to his car, until I said, "Charles, remember when we were on our way to the fire?"

"Duh, how could I forget? We were on—"

"Let me finish."

He shrugged. "So?"

"Do you remember seeing vehicles in the lot near the apartment building's parking area?"

"Chris, I remember black smoke, red flames, red fire trucks, and two ambulances that nearly ran us down. I don't remember what was parked nearby. Why?"

"One of the vehicles was a blue Maserati SUV."

Charles looked toward Bert's. "Like the one what's her name was driving?"

"Exactly."

"Coincidence?"

"What do you think?"

He continued looking at Bert's like the SUV would return. "Could she live in the building beside the apartment building?"

"No. Cindy told me she lives in a condo near Harris Teeter."

"Think you need to tell Cindy."

I said, "I will."

"I mean now."

I reached for my phone, when Charles added, "Don't forget to push that little speaker icon."

Instead of getting a live voice, Cindy's message informed me she was unable to take the call, for the caller to leave a message. I asked her to call when she got a chance. Charles harrumphed, then mumbled something about where were the police when you needed them.

I told him I'd let him know after I talked to the Chief. He asked if he needed to drive me home so I wouldn't have to walk thirty yards. I said I could manage the voyage. He left me standing in Bert's side parking area.

I was still in the lot when the phone rang. I figured Charles missed hearing Cindy by seconds, but I was wrong. Close, but wrong.

"Chris, this is Rose, Cindy's sister. Did I catch you at a bad time?"

I said no and resisted asking her if she could teach my friends phone etiquette.

"I'm calling as Luke's social secretary," she said then chuckled. "We're heading to Planet Follywood in a few minutes for lunch. Luke said how much you liked the restaurant. He wanted me to call to see if you'd join us."

I said I'd be honored. I also realized this was the first time in my adult life a pre-teen had his social secretary call to invite me to share a meal.

Chapter Thirty-Four

I approached Luke and Rose's table.

"Mr. Landrum," Luke said, "You said you loved eating here, so I asked mom to call you."

I thanked him for the invitation as a server arrived and put a glass of what appeared to be iced tea in front of Rose, a soft drink beside Luke. He asked if I wanted anything. I said water was fine.

"Luke," I said, "did Uncle Larry give you the day off?"

"No, he said with Christmas two days away, he needed all the help he could get. I told him even a little boy has to eat. He said I could bring mom here for lunch."

"You're a tough negotiator," I said.

He smiled like I'd called him king of the world.

"This is part of my Christmas gift," Rose said. "Luke is using his own money to buy lunch."

"Mr. Landrum, because you've been so nice to me, I want to buy yours too."

The phone rang before I told him that wasn't necessary. Bob Howard's name appeared on the screen.

"Hi, Bob."

"Aren't you going to insult me like you usually do?"

"It's Christmas, besides, you have that backward."

"Whatever. I have el scoopo on that woman you asked about."

"Hang on a second," I said, then told my lunch mates I needed to take the call then headed to the back of the restaurant.

"Okay," I said.

"If that was a second, you need a better watch. Ready for el scoopo?"

"Ready."

"Kaycee Ericson. Late-forties, good looking according to the old coots I talked to. She divorced Alan Ericson a while back. Alan is a big-time developer in Charleston, but he's done projects as far away as Asheville. Mostly large apartment complexes. Anyway, his ex took a bunch of money in the divorce. She built a small office building a half-block off Center Street in your town, and either two or three ocean-front McMansions. My source was vague on the number. As even you, as ignorant as you are about anything building wise, know, your zoning regulators are doing everything they can to limit new construction, especially super-sized buildings on property that originally held small beach houses. In other words, Kaycee has been running into brick walls instead of open arms from those in control."

I'd heard something similar from Cindy and shared that with Bob.

"Okay, know it all, did you hear she's trying to find properties, mostly multi-unit properties where the owners are, let's say, having financial difficulties?"

"That's new."

"Like all good storytellers, I saved the best for last."

I waited for him to continue, he didn't, so I assumed he wanted me to beg for the best. "What's that, Mr. Fount of Information?"

"That's better. One of my sources said several years ago, one of Alan Ericson's apartment buildings had a horrible fire. Was it caused by lightning? No. Electrical problem? No. How about by Aunt Sally leaving something on the stove? Nope, again. Now that I've given you all the clues, think you can guess the cause?"

"Arson?"

"You're smarter than the average cucumber. There was a ton of speculation that Alan set the fire, but not an ounce of proof."

"You're saying that Kaycee is guilty by marriage?"

"Nope. I'm telling you what happened. You figure out the rest."

"Anything else?"

"Hell, do I have to get you a signed, notarized confession?"

"If you don't mind."

He must've minded. He hung up.

That didn't prove Kaycee started the fire but was information Cindy needed. Seeing Luke staring in my direction, it'd have to wait.

I returned to the table and Luke's broad smile.

"Mr. Landrum, I made an executive decision, although mom said I shouldn't."

"What was that, Luke?"

"I ordered your lunch. I got you the same thing you had when we were here the last time. I figured you liked it, or you wouldn't have got it then."

"Excellent decision, Luke."

His smile increased. "See Mom, told you so."

"Everything okay?" Rose said, then nodded her head in the direction where I'd been.

"Yes. Is your sister working today? I left her a message earlier but haven't heard from her."

"As far as I know. She said she had several meetings."

Luke interrupted, "Aunt Cindy said yucky meetings."

"Luke, you know not to interrupt," Rose said.

He bowed his head.

Rose turned to me. "You haven't heard from her today?"

"No, why?"

"Last night, she told me she had news about the fire. She was going to call you."

Lunch arrived. I wasn't the only one to order the same meal as last time. A hot dog was placed in front of Luke, a cheeseburger for Rose, and my chicken fingers. As much as I wanted to fight it, most of us are creatures of habit. We ate silently for a couple of minutes, but I kept going back to what Ty and Bob had said.

"Rose, this may be a strange question, but do you remember seeing a blue Maserati SUV parked near the apartment complex?"

"I don't pay much attention to cars, never have."

Luke said, "I do."

Rose said, "Luke's best friend's dad owns a Chevy dealership in Morristown."

"Len's dad is cool," Luke said. "He lets us roam around the lot. When the repair shop is closed, we can go in there. His dad says insurance wouldn't let us go in when mechanics are working."

That got my attention, about paying attention, not about his friend Len. "Do you mean you pay attention to cars, or do you remember seeing a blue SUV?"

Rose patted her son on the arm. "See, Luke, how you say things is important."

He sighed, "I know, mom. You tell me all the time."

I can't imagine how it would be growing up with an English teacher mom.

I said. "Luke, help me understand what you mean."

He glanced at Rose then turned to me. "It's sort of both, Mr. Landrum. I like looking at cars, especially new ones. And, I remember seeing a blue Maserati."

"Do you remember when you saw it?"

"Day after we moved in. I thought it was cool looking. I hadn't seen one."

"Was that the only time you saw it?"

"Umm, two more times, I think."

"When?"

"Suppose the next time was the day before the fire. It was close to our lot. Then I saw it the morning we were walking to watch the Christmas parade."

"Where was it?"

"Parked at the road. I figured the lady in it was going to move in our building."

"Why?"

"Mom and me were walking up our street when—"

"Mom and I, Luke," Rose said.

Luke made a noise that sounded like a braying horse. I bit the inside of my lip to keep from laughing.

"Yes, mom." He continued, "Mom and I were headed toward the street where the parade was going to be. I looked back and saw the lady carrying a large box, sort of like those boxes we packed stuff in to move here. I figured she was moving in."

"Luke, are you sure she came out of the blue SUV?"

Rose looked at Luke, then at me with narrowed eyes.

"Yes, sir. Know it was her. She didn't move in, did she? Someone said the next-door apartment was still empty when the fire started."

I ate the chicken fingers, but they could easily have been glued sawdust for all the attention I paid to them. I held my need to talk to Cindy in check and tried to make Luke's lunch for his mom and me as positive as possible.

I must not have shown as much anxiety as I felt. We finished and Luke said it'd been a wonderful Christmas lunch, that we ought to do it again.

All I wanted to do again was talk to Chief LaMond. She may be convinced that Russell O'Leary torched his building. I thought I had a persuasive argument she was wrong.

Chapter Thirty-Five

I nstead of going home after lunch, I crossed Center Street and headed toward the combination City Hall and Department of Public Safety building. Cindy's pickup wasn't in the lot behind the building, so I changed direction to head home.

Patience may be a virtue, but with me, it's often in short supply. I was tempted to leave the Chief another message but knew she'd call when she got a chance. By five-thirty, my head was about to explode from waiting.

Fortunately, it didn't, so I was able to answer the phone. It was Cindy.

"Thank goodness you called," I said. "I've learned—"

"Hold that thought. Meet me at the Surf Bar in fifteen minutes. A day of meetings, boring meetings, and a trip downtown with the mayor, have me needing a cold beer more than anything you have to say."

The Surf Bar was across the street from the entrance to the Public Safety building, making it convenient for Cindy when she needed to escape her office. I got there in ten minutes to find her at a table near the door, gripping a beer in a Terrapin Beer Company glass. The turtle in the logo looked happier than the Chief.

"Rough day?" I said as I sat across from her at the small table.

"Spent most of it battling two councilmembers who think I'm spending too much money on overtime, one councilmember who thinks I need to increase police presence near his house, of course, then two hours in the car with our mayor listening to three million things he thinks the police need to do better. How do you think my day was?"

"You've had better."

"I've had better days at the dentist when she forgot to give me enough numbing juice before jackhammering on a molar. With griping out of the way, there is a bright side and a bad side."

"I suppose you're going to tell me both."

Cindy looked at the ceiling where dollar bills were attached to most non-moving surfaces. White Christmas lights were strung from the columns and roof trusses. I call them Christmas lights because that was their original purpose, but they're year-round fixtures in the Surf Bar.

"Chris, that's the least I can do since you're buying me this, and another, and another."

"It's my pleasure," I said with a tinge of sarcasm.

"Russell O'Leary," she said like that explained everything. "I had a nice long conversation with him this morning before every elected official in our fair city tried to take a chunk of my hide."

I've known the bartender for a few years, so he had a server bring me a glass of red wine without me having to say anything. That's one good thing about living in a small town. I took a sip, while Cindy stared at me.

I said, "What?"

"I'm waiting for your full attention. This is a fun-filled story."

"Proceed."

"Landlord Russell lied about where he was and why?"

"Is that the bright side?"

"Is for him. Seems he has a heart condition, some long Latin word I couldn't define, pronounce, or spell. Suffice to say, it's serious. His Charleston cardiologist referred him to some world-renowned specialist at the Emory University Hospital near Atlanta, the keyword being near, as opposed to being in downtown Atlanta. Russell didn't want his employer to know about the condition. He especially didn't want his wife and kids to know. Didn't want them to worry, he claimed." She took a sip of beer, shook her head, then continued. "He made up the whole story about being at a get-rich-quick seminar."

"Why'd he lie to you? Did he think you'd tell his employer or his wife?"

"Chris, in my entire life, I've never been a man. Most of the time, I don't know how you dudes think. Hell, I know how you act, but not think. Assuming you think. I don't know why he decided to stick me with the feeble story. He's still above ground, so I assume it worked with his wife."

"What did the Emery doctor say?"

"Said he has a heart. Whatever is wrong with it can be fixed with some expensive meds, or that's what Russell said. Since he's a proven liar, I don't know if I believe it. What I am certain is he was in Georgia when his building went up in smoke. He showed me a hotel bill, two gas receipts, and a food receipt from a Waffle House." She shook her head. "Who in the hell keeps Waffle House receipts?"

"You're a female, you wouldn't understand," I joked, or thought it was a joke.

Cindy didn't laugh, didn't smile, didn't say anything. Women often don't appreciate how witty men are.

"Chief, if that's the good side, what's the bad side?"

"I'm sitting here, feeling sorry for myself, without anyone to nominate for arsonist of the year."

I took a sip, smiled, then said, "Let me see if I can help. Did you get a chance to talk to Kaycee Ericson?"

"Not yet. Been wasting my time trying to prove Russell did something far worse than lie to his wife and me. Why? No, don't answer that. Did she start the fire? Do you have proof?"

"Proof, no, but let me tell you what I've learned."

She finished the beer and raised her glass for the server to bring a refill. "I'm all ears."

"I was talking with Ty who told me Kaycee approached him at the apartment building days before the fire. Started asking questions like how long he'd lived there, was the building well maintained, etc."

"What got Ty talking about that?"

"Charles and I went to Bert's to tell him that Martha Wright said he could stay at her place until he found somewhere else to live."

"Whoa, how'd that come about?"

I told her the story about approaching Martha a few days ago, her rejection of the idea, and why.

"Cindy almost choked on her beer, cleared her throat, then said, "Martha, the woman who's about two hundred years old, thought her neighbor would think she was a cougar? Crapola, I thought I'd heard it all."

I didn't add what Martha said her deceased husband would think. Instead, I told her about Martha's change of heart.

"That's great, but what does it have to do with Kaycee?"

"Nothing other than it's the reason Charles and I were talking to Ty."

"Charles was with you?"

I nodded.

"Figures. Okay, go ahead with something I'd be interested in."

"Kaycee asked Ty about vacant units. He thought she may want to rent one."

"More interesting. Like the vacant unit where the fire started?"

"That's the one. Ty also told us she was driving a blue Maserati SUV. He pointed it out in Bert's lot."

"That's important, how?"

"When Charles and I were walking up Ashley Avenue on our way to see what was burning, I saw a blue Maserati SUV in that small lot beside the apartment's parking area. Didn't you tell me Kaycee lives out by Harris Teeter?"

Cindy nodded.

"So, I wondered why her car, okay maybe not hers, but isn't it unlikely there're two blue Maserati SUVs over here?"

"I've never seen one. So, it's rare but not impossible. Go on."

I told her what Bob Howard's research uncovered, with emphasis on how Kaycee's ex-husband had been a suspect in an arson. I took a sip of wine, then added, "Do you know who I had lunch with today?"

"Dolly Parton?"

"Guess again."

"I'm guessed out. Who?"

"Your sister and nephew. Luke said he had so much fun eating with me last week, he had his mom invite me today."

"That boy needs to get out more and meet some fun people. How did Larry let him escape from the store?"

I laughed. "Luke said he told Larry that employees need to eat."

"Smart kid. I suppose there's a reason you're telling me this."

"Yes, a good one." I then bullet-pointed the highlights of our discussion.

"Are you telling me Luke saw Kaycee carrying a box to the apartment building less than an hour before the fire?"

"That's what I'm telling you."

"Let me wrap this around my undersized brain. I had the most significant clue to who started the fire living under my roof."

I nodded.

"Crap, I should kick myself in the butt and turn in my badge."

I didn't ask how she planned to do the first part of that. Instead, I said, "Cindy, you couldn't have known. It only came up because I asked Luke about the blue SUV."

She lowered her head and stared in her beer. "Yet an old geezer with no law enforcement training figures it out."

I smiled. "Yeah, but Charles is teaching me all the tricks of being a detective."

She let out a string of profanities, none of which bear repeating.

I waited for her blood pressure to lower to non-stroke levels, then said, "It's a lot of circumstantial evidence, but what are the chances of getting a conviction on what you now know?"

"Slim, but it gives me a lot more to talk about tomorrow when I pay a Christmas Eve visit to Ms. Ericson."

"Excellent plan," I said, then told her I had to get home to wait for Neil Wilson, my new housemate, to arrive.

"You letting someone stay at your place. Will Christmas miracles never cease?"

Chapter Thirty-Six

Christmas Eve began with me sleeping late combined with rumbles of snores coming from my former office, current guest bedroom. It took a minute to remember why the snoring wasn't in my dreams but from my new houseguest. Neil had arrived last night, thanked me just under five hundred times for letting him stay, then adjusted to his new environment. He knew from working at Cal's I wasn't a beer drinker, so he brought a six-pack with him. Three cans were in the refrigerator this morning. He'd shared he often worked late, so I shouldn't expect to see him much in the mornings. I thought that was great since I'm a morning person who enjoys peace and quiet. I hadn't contemplated snoring.

I turned on the Mr. Coffee machine, then headed to Bert's for a box of donuts, and a chance to ask Ty about his move to Martha's. Ty wasn't at his usual hangout behind the register, so I asked if he was working. Denise, another of Bert's uber-helpful employees said he wasn't coming in until noon.

When I got home, Neil was at the kitchen table, wearing orange and green flannel pajamas, and staring in one of my red I Love Folly Beach mugs. He continued staring in the mug, and said, "Did you know there's nothing to eat in your kitchen?"

I dropped the box of donuts on the table. "Bon Appetit."

I think he smiled, although it looked more like a frown.

"Sleep well?" I asked instead of telling him there was never food in the kitchen.

He opened the donuts, took a bite, then mumbled, "Think so."

Fifteen minutes later, with food in his stomach, caffeine in his veins, Neil reentered the world of the living with full sentences and stories about some of last night's more memorable customers. I suspected much of his conversation was from nervous energy rather than wanting me to know what each customer ordered, or what they were doing Christmas.

Ten o'clock rolled around quicker than it does with me here alone. I was wondering if Cindy had caught up with Kaycee Ericson. By eleven, I was tempted to call the Chief. Remember, patience isn't one of my virtues.

I didn't have to show the Chief my lack of patience. My phone rang at eleven fifteen revealing her name on the screen.

She began with, "Is this the Chris Landrum homeless shelter?"

"What'd you learn, Cindy?"

Okay, she was reminded of my lack of patience.

"Chill, it's Christmas Eve. Tis the season to be jolly."

I said, "Ho, Ho, Ho. What'd you learn?"

"You're no fun. Okay, at oh-nine-hundred this morning, I knocked on Kaycee's condo door. At nine-hundred one, nine-hundred two, nine-hundred three I knocked, all to no avail. Additionally, there wasn't a Maserati SUV in the lot. I used all my chiefly skills to deduce she wasn't home."

"What now?"

"Glad you asked. This is where it gets interesting. I returned to my majestic office and used my chiefly skills to access my secret, super-duper databases to check on Kaycee's said condo. Want to guess what I found?"

"It's too early for guessing."

"You wouldn't get it anyway. It seems the condo isn't owned by Kaycee but belongs to one Anthony Craft, a resident of Coral Gables, Florida. I called Mr. Craft, a call answered by his wife Madeline, who, once I assured her I wasn't Anthony's mistress, handed the phone to her hubby. I identified myself. then after explaining there wasn't anything wrong with his rental unit, he calmed down."

There was a long pause, so I said, "You still there?"

"Cool your jets. I'm looking for the rest of my notes. Got them. Okay, Anthony rented his condo to Kaycee two years ago. She occasionally was late on rent, but always paid, didn't complain about anything, and according to Anthony, was perfect for his condo, whatever that meant."

"I don't suppose he mentioned that she was an arsonist?"

"No, but know what he did share?"

"What?"

"His tenant called two days ago saying she was moving. Her lease expires the end of the month and she wouldn't be renewing. Anthony was saddened since she'd been such a good tenant, in other words, all he had to do was sit in beautiful Florida and cash rent checks."

"Did he say where she was going?"

"Nope. That would've been too easy. She said something about going back up north, which could be New England, Canada, the North Pole."

"What now?"

"I'm going to pick you up in ten minutes and we're going to make another visit to Anthony's condo."

"I thought you determined no one was there?"

"There isn't, but helpful Anthony gave me the keypad lock combination, plus the lawyerly super-important authorization to inspect the unit."

Cindy was out front blowing her horn five minutes later. Five minutes after that, we were standing in front of Kaycee's condo, with Cindy punching numbers on the keypad. She asked me to stand back as she entered. Not seeing anything amiss, or Kaycee pointing a gun at her, Cindy invited me in, reminding me not to touch anything.

The large, open floor plan unit was painted a cheery off-yellow with typical condo-package furniture. I didn't see anything indicating it'd been inhabited. There were no knickknacks or photos on the tables, no newspapers, magazines, or brochures setting around. Cindy took a quick scan around the room then went into the kitchen. I followed her and noticed a dirty plate, a butter knife, and three glasses in the sink. The Chief pulled out a tall trash container from under the counter. A used coffee filter, coffee grounds, and three pieces of paper torn in half were all the container held.

I followed Cindy down a narrow hall to the first bedroom. It looked like it'd never been used. A colorful bedspread was untouched, the pillow looked like it'd just come from the store. The closet was empty. The second bedroom didn't look any more used than the first.

The master bedroom was another story. The bedspread lay on the floor, the sheets mussed, the pillow dented where a head would've rested. Several hangers were strewn across the bed, two more on the floor, the closet door stood open, with more hangers on the rod. All were empty.

I was searching the corners of the closet, then looking under the bed, hoping to find anything indicating Kaycee was the arsonist. Cindy had begun pulling out dresser drawers.

She said, "Huh?"

"What?"

She pointed at two books she'd found in the bottom drawer. One was about buying real estate in both good and bad markets, the other on creative financing options. She was flipping through a copy-paper sized Office Depot wire-bound notebook.

"Where was that?"

"Under the books."

I moved closer to see what Cindy was seeing. Part of the first page had been ripped out. There were sketches on the next three pages. They looked like draft floor plans. What really got my attention was the paper, more accurately, graph paper.

"Cindy, remember I told you about the note under Noelle's windshield?"

"Politely telling her to get off Folly or no telling what?"

"That's the one."

"So what?"

"It was on graph paper."

"You didn't tell me that."

"Didn't think it was important."

"Bet you do now."

She didn't give me a chance to answer. She continued, "You said the note burned in the fire?"

I nodded.

She sighed. "More circumstantial evidence."

I took my phone out of my pocket and tapped in Noelle's number. She answered on the second ring.

"Noelle, this is Chris. Where are you?"

"Barb's Books, why?"

"If you're going to be there a few minutes, I'd like talk to you."

She said she'd wait. I hung up and turned to Cindy. "Let's visit Noelle."

"Why? The note's gone."

"I have an idea."

Cindy was kind not to push. "Okay."

"Take the notepad."

"Don't suppose you're going to tell me why?"

"Not yet."

Barb was behind the counter running a credit card through the machine then bagging three books.

She saw Cindy and me, pointed to the backroom, and said Noelle was waiting for us.

Noelle was pacing the small room. She wore a gray sweatshirt, jeans, and of course, sunglasses. She smiled when she saw me, the look turned inquisitive when she noticed the Chief behind me.

"Thanks for waiting. Have a seat."

She slowly lowered herself in the chair behind Barb's chrome and glass desk. "Is everything okay?"

"Yes," I said then pulled a chair up to the side of the desk. Cindy remained standing as I removed a sheet of copy paper from the printer.

"Noelle, didn't you tell me the note you found under your windshield was on paper that looked like it'd been torn from a larger sheet?"

She looked at Cindy, then her gaze turned to me. "Umm, yes. Why?"

"Noelle, this may seem silly, but bear with me." I handed her the piece of copy paper off Barb's printer. "Tear this about the size of the note you found."

"Chris, I don't remember exactly how big it was."

"I understand, give it your best shot."

She took the paper, began to rip it in half, stopped, then tore it about an inch lower than where she first started. She handed me the piece that was about one-third of the paper I'd handed her.

Cindy must've figured out what I was doing. She flipped open the pad she'd brought with her and set it on the desk. I took the piece Noelle had given me and laid it on the open pad. It wasn't a perfect match for what had been torn out of the pad, but close.

Noelle who hadn't said anything since she handed me the torn sheet, touched the pad, looked at Cindy, at me, then said, "Graph paper."

"Like the note you got," I added.

"Exactly."

Chapter Thirty-Seven

Christmas began with a call from Cindy wishing me Merry Christmas, then telling me there was an APB out on Kaycee Ericson's SUV. She hadn't been found, but she'd used her credit card to buy gas at an Interstate station in Lumberton, North Carolina, and later near Richmond, Virginia. She may not have been caught, but was heading away, far away, from Folly Beach, South Carolina. For that I was thankful.

I was then surprised when Neil stepped in the kitchen and handed me a bottle of Cabernet with a red ribbon tied around it.

My housemate said, "Merry Christmas."

I was touched. "Neil, you didn't have to do that. I didn't get you anything."

"Chris, hush. You gave me the best gift I could ever get. You gave me a place to stay and knowing someone cared enough to make it available."

I thanked him then asked what he was doing up so early.

"Cal's so excited about his party, he wants me to come early to help get everything ready. I've never seen that old boy so amped."

"Christmas is his biggest day of the year." I told Neil about why having the party meant so much to the country crooner.

"I'll do whatever I can to make sure it's a success. Saying that, I'd better get dressed and over there. I'll grab something at Bert's community Christmas breakfast, so you won't have to fix anything fancy." He laughed at his joke, patted me on the back, then said he'd see me at the party.

Cal's Christmas gala was scheduled to begin at one o'clock, but the allure of free food and drink always brought attendees before the official opening. I wanted to be there early in case I could help.

I walked through the door surrounded by colorful lights at twelve-thirty. The room was already half full. Brenda Lee's "Rockin' Around the Christmas Tree" was playing, along with laughter coming from people at a table in the center of the room holding three bowls of salsa, avocado dip, and a basket of chips large enough to hold a beachball. Always early Charles was talking with Dude Sloan cradling Pluto in his arms. Dogs aren't allowed in Cal's, but it was Christmas. Besides, a good argument could be made Dude needed a service animal. I don't know what was said, but Charles was laughing louder than I'd heard in months.

All four trees were glowing brightly as were the countless strands of Christmas lights throughout the room. Cal was standing behind the bar pulling a beer out of the cooler. The LED lights on his Stetson blinked, his red polo shirt was so bright I suspected it'd glow in the dark. His smile was priceless. Neil was at the other end of the bar fiddling with a stack of red napkins.

Two men I didn't know arrived next. They waved at Cal who returned the wave then pointed toward the chips. They filled a paper plate with chips and headed to the bar where Cal shook their hands and offered each a drink. They didn't hesitate taking the drinks. Kristin, a part-time server who'd worked at Cal's for several years, and Joy, another server who'd joined Cal's a year ago, were moving a couple of tables around so there was more room for people to stand.

Burl arrived wearing a Santa hat and the sweater he wore to last year's party. It was easy to remember since it could win any ugly Christmas sweater contest.

"Merry Christmas, Brother Chris."

"The same to you, Preacher. Glad to see you. I know Cal will be happy you're here."

"Hope he's not happy enough to drag me on stage."

"Preacher, it's a Christmas tradition."

"Like grandpa getting drunk on eggnog," Burl said, then smiled.

Charles left Dude and Pluto talking with someone I didn't know and headed to the bar, where he said something to Neil, then grabbed a couple of drinks from the cooler. He handed the drinks to two men who were leaning against the bar. I smiled, knowing how much Charles loves helping others. He was in his element.

Gene Autry's version of "Here Comes Santa Claus" interrupted Burl's bemoaning the Christmas tradition. He said he'd better say hi to the host and left me standing near the front door enjoying the festive environment. I didn't see Martha Wright until she tapped me with her cane. She had a gleam in her eyes, either for being able to celebrate Christmas at Cal's or from Christmas morning hot toddies. Dixie was behind her. Each wore red Christmas sweaters; neither sweater could compete with Burl's for tackiness.

Dixie stepped in front of her neighbor. "Martha tells me this is one whale of a party."

Martha had attended for the first-time last year.

"She's right," I said. "Is Ty with you?"

"That boy's a gem," Martha said. "He was up at the crack of dawn. Fed my kids, fixed toast to go with my oatmeal, and," she chuckled. "Fixed me a hot toddy. Then he went to work for a few hours. Did I mention he was a gem?"

Yes, but didn't remind her. I didn't catch the answer to my question, so I repeated, "Is he here?"

"He's parking my car. I let him chauffeur us in the Lincoln. Told him he didn't even have to wear one of those chauffeur hats." She looked over my shoulder. "Heavens, here he is."

"Merry Christmas, Mr. Landrum," Ty said as we shook hands.

"Martha," Dixie said, "are we going to stand here and yak all day or we going to the bar?"

I had the impression she'd already found one. Martha put her arm around her neighbor and pulled her toward the drinks. Ty shrugged and followed the women. Three more people, two women and a man, I knew to be regulars entered and headed to the food.

Noelle, closely followed by Barb, stepped through the entry and looked around. Barb saw me and motioned for Noelle to join her as she gave me a hug and a kiss. I looked up to see if there was mistletoe. There wasn't. Noelle gave me a tentative hug. Both ladies wore red blouses and black slacks. I suspected Noelle's blouse came from Barb's closet.

We weaved our way through a group of people on our way to the salsa table, as Barb said, "Noelle told me about what you wanted with her in the store yesterday. Has Cindy found Kaycee?"

We got plates of food, Noelle went to thank Cal for hosting the party, and Barb and I moved to a corner of the room.

I told her Kaycee hadn't been caught, but she was several states away and traveling away from Folly.

"Good, Noelle was so worried, thinking she should have done something different when she got the note."

"I doubt it would've helped, besides what she told Cindy about the paper will be a big help."

"That's what I told her. Any idea why Kaycee set the fire?"

"The theory is so she could buy the lot from Russell O'Leary. He'd originally said he'd sell to her, then his kids and wife convinced him to keep it for their future. Kaycee probably figured he'd have no need for it if it was reduced to ashes."

"Putting on my lawyer's hat, they could probably get a conviction based on a decent amount of circumstantial evidence, especially the note. I'm still confused about why Kaycee wrote the note only to Noelle. If she was going to burn the building, and not harm anyone, why not warn everyone?"

"I suspect it had to do with Noelle spying on everyone around town while getting ideas for her novel. She could've seen Kaycee near the building. Kaycee could also have seen her and figured she was a loose end she needed to scare off before starting the fire."

"Makes sense."

"Know what makes more sense?"

"What?"

"Getting a drink, some food, and enjoying Cal's party."

We were on our way to the bar when I saw Rose, Luke, and Cindy at the door. Rose and Cindy were in red sweatshirts, Luke had on a white and red T-shirt. All wore huge smiles. With their entry, there was more red in here than at a University of Georgia football game.

Luke ran over, motioned me to lean down, and whispered, "Mom and Aunt Cindy love the shark jewelry. Thank you for helping me with it."

I told him it was my pleasure, took his hand, and walked him to the bar.

"Cal, you have a special drink back there for my young friend?"

"How about a root beer, partner?" Cal said and tipped his Stetson to Luke.

Luke laughed. "You're funny."

Cal fixed him his drink then he headed back to Rose.

Cindy had her phone to her ear, nodded, then headed out the door. I started to follow, but figured it was none of my business. She returned with a big smile on her face and motioned me over.

"Chris, guess who's spending Christmas day in the hoosegow in Hartford, Connecticut?"

"Our favorite arsonist?"

Her smile widened. "Yep."

"Sorry she's missing Cal's party, aren't you?"

"Nope."

"Me either."

"I'd better go tell my baby sister."

She headed toward Rose, and I moved closer to Noelle who was still standing beside Cal. She said, "Cal, this is my first time in here. I think I need to add a bar like this in my novel. Add a character like you."

Cal tipped his hat, this time at Noelle. "Darlin', I'm a whole novel all by myself."

Noelle laughed. No truer words had ever been spoken.

Cal excused himself, saying he had to say a word or two to the group that now was filling the room, with more arriving.

Fifteen minutes later, Cal tapped on the antique silver microphone in the center of the low stage, then said, "How about lending me an ear?" It took a second tap on the mic before Cal had everyone's attention. "Guys and gals, Merry Christmas. This here's our biggest Christmas shindig ever. Now let me tell from the get-go, I'm not going to be happy unless all of you are. We've all got a bunch to be thankful for, so let's celebrate it. After you eat and drink a bunch more, me and Preacher Burl will be entertaining you with a Christmas duet."

I saw Luke tug on his mom's shirt and whisper something to her, probably, "Cal should've said, Preacher and I, not me and Preacher." Rose smiled and fluffed his hair.

Janice Raque was standing in the doorway, looking around. I left the bar to meet her. Before I could make it through the crowd, Preacher Burl was talking with her. She looked toward the ceiling, then hugged Burl before I could reach the two.

Janice turned to me. "Chris, you'll never guess what Preacher Burl told me."

"What?"

"Someone moved out of Hope House yesterday afternoon. The preacher said I could have the room if I wanted it. You bet your as— umm, you bet I do."

Burl smiled. "Brother Chris, I told you I had faith it'd work out."

"That you did, Preacher."

Hank Williams Sr was finishing his classic version of "I Saw the Light" when Cal pulled the plug on the jukebox, stepped behind the silver mic, and said, "Y'all ready for it?" He cupped his hand behind his ear.

A few celebrators took the hint. "Yes."

"Preacher, get your holy body up here."

Burl was standing beside me and I was afraid he was going to bolt for the door. In the spirit of Christmas, he didn't. He sighed as he slowly made his way to the stage. Cal slung his guitar over his head, whispered something to Burl, then pushed the preacher close to the mic. Cal played two chords, nudged Burl's head closer to the mic, then sang:

"O Come, all ye faithful,
Joyful and triumphant,
O come ye, O come ye, to Bethlehem...."

About the Author

Bill Noel is the best-selling author of eighteen novels in the popular Folly Beach Mystery series. Besides being an award-winning novelist, Noel is a fine arts photographer and lives in Louisville, Kentucky, with his wife, Susan, and his off-kilter imagination. Learn more about the series, and the author by visiting www.billnoel.com.

www.ingramcontent.com/pod-product-compliance
Lightning Source LLC
Chambersburg PA
CBHW061035030726
47504CB00002B/384